Praise for *New York Ti...*
Jillia...

"Jillian Hart's *Every Kind of...*
story in the McKaslin Clan miniseries."

—*RT Book Reviews*

"Jillian Hart's compassionate story will most certainly please readers."

—*RT Book Reviews* on *Everyday Blessings*

"It's a pleasure to read this achingly tender story."

—*RT Book Reviews* on *Her Wedding Wish*

"Jillian Hart conveys heart-tugging emotional struggles."

—*RT Book Reviews* on *Sweet Blessings*

Praise for Ruth Axtell Morren

"Morren's latest historical is a must-read. [Her] flair for the unexpected will keep readers turning the pages. The ending is classic romance at its best."

—*RT Book Reviews* on *The Making of a Gentleman*

"A delightful read; Morren's characters are full of life."

—*RT Book Reviews* on *A Gentleman's Homecoming*

"Morren does an extraordinary job of putting two unlikely people together and showing us how love and romance can flourish despite difficulties. This exciting story has a wonderful climax, fast-paced story line and just the right amount of spiritual truth that leaves the reader feeling wonderfully satisfied."

—*RT Book Reviews* on *A Bride of Honor*

New York Times Bestselling Author

Jillian Hart
and
Ruth Axtell Morren

High Country Bride
&
A Man Most Worthy

⟨H⟩ HARLEQUIN® LOVE INSPIRED® CLASSICS

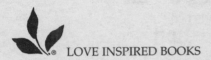 LOVE INSPIRED BOOKS

Recycling programs
for this product may
not exist in your area.

ISBN-13: 978-1-335-00756-8

High Country Bride & A Man Most Worthy

Copyright © 2018 by Harlequin Books S.A.

The publisher acknowledges the copyright holders
of the individual works as follows:

High Country Bride
Copyright © 2008 by Jill Strickler

A Man Most Worthy
Copyright © 2008 by Ruth Axtell

www.Harlequin.com

Printed in U.S.A.

CONTENTS

New York Times bestselling author **Jillian Hart** grew up on her family's homestead, where she helped raise cattle, rode horses and scribbled stories in her spare time. After earning her English degree from Whitman College, she worked in travel and advertising before selling her first novel. When Jillian isn't working on her next story, she can be found puttering in her rose garden, curled up with a good book or spending quiet evenings at home with her family.

HIGH COUNTRY BRIDE

Jillian Hart

I wait quietly before God, for my hope is in Him.
He alone is my rock and my salvation,
my fortress where I will not be shaken.
—*Psalms* 62:5–6

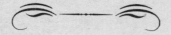

Chapter One

It was a hot day for a wake. Joanna Nelson swiped the dampness from her forehead, closed the oven door with her foot and slid the sheet of biscuits onto the wooden cutting board. The kitchen window was open wide to let in the sweltering wind. It gave her a clear view of the horse and buggy lumbering along the road, kicking up chalky dust.

Few mourners had shown up for her pa's brief funeral in the graveyard behind the church. None had yet made their way to the house. Just this lone horse and buggy ambling tiredly through the heat waves on the dirt road. When the vehicle was near enough, she recognized the driver. Not a mourner, but one of the bankers from town, dressed up in his fancy work suit.

This was not a social call, she suspected. No, Edwin Wessox had been a regular visitor over the last year, because of the bank's worry over Pa's debt. With her father gone, this visit did not necessarily mean good news. Without a doubt, it concerned the mortgage on the farm. She knew, because this had happened to her once before—after her husband died, one year and three months ago. The banker had paid a visit to her not three hours after she'd laid her husband to rest.

Would they be allowed to continue on with the payments? Her stomach twisted in a nervous knot. Don't expect the worst, she told herself. She slid the biscuits from the baking sheet into a cloth-lined bowl. Her half brother had come to stay when the doctor had given Pa the diagnosis. Lee said he wanted to keep farming the land, although he didn't like farming.

It will be all right, Joanna. She took a deep breath and poked her head into the parlor. Lee sat by the open window with a hand to his forehead, looking as shocked as she felt. He didn't so much as blink an eye, much less look in her direction. He clearly had a lot on his mind.

"The banker's coming," she said, then went back to her kitchen work.

She didn't know if that news would make her brother stir. They were not close; he'd only come after she'd telegraphed him. As she hefted the pot of beans from the oven, she tried to keep hopeful. Heaven knew, hard times had rained down on her before like the worst kind of storm. Things had started to get a little easier, finally, while she'd been staying here with her pa.

Please, Lord, she prayed, *don't let things get worse for us.* Praying these days was more habit than belief. She set the bean pot down on the battered wooden table and feared the Lord and all his angels had forgotten her.

Upstairs, she heard the patter of her young son's bare feet, as if to remind her of all she had to protect. Her little girl trailed after him. The two of them sounded like a stampeding herd barreling down the steps.

"Ma! Ma!" James burst into the kitchen and ran straight to her skirts, burying his face in her waist.

Daisy raced after him. She was too young to remember the consequences of her father's death, but was upset because her older brother was. She fisted her hands in the extra material of Joanna's skirt and held on tight.

Since she was as good as hobbled, Joanna left the potatoes to their boiling and scooped her little girl into her arms. Poor baby. Joanna kissed her daughter's brow and snuggled her close. "Why are you crying, little one?"

"I don't wanna live in the wagon. James said."

"Is that true? Did you say that to your sister?"

James held on tighter and didn't answer.

Too many losses, too many upheavals, too much uncertainty. Joanna hated how it had marked her children. "I have dinner on the table. Let me take a look at you. However did you two get so dirty?"

"In the attic, Ma." James tipped his head back to look at her, his sweaty brown hair sticking straight up.

She smoothed it down, wishing she could smooth away bigger troubles as easily. "It will be all right. Now, go wash your hands and faces while I see to our company."

The worry did not leave James's features when he released his hold on her, or when he took his sister's hand and led her to the washbasin by the back door. Joanna straightened, her skirts sticking to her as she left the hot kitchen for the front door.

Mr. Wessox was tipping his hat to her on the other side of the screen. "Ma'am, I'm sorry for your loss."

"Thank you." Dread quickened her heartbeat and made her hand tremble as she unlatched the door. "Please, come in. Can I get you something to drink?"

"No, I've come to speak with Lee."

Of course. It was a man's world, and Lee was to inherit the ranch. She knew that. But the nerves jumped in her stomach like oil on a hot pan as she hurried back to the kitchen. Her gaze went first to her little ones in the sunny corner. James was holding the towel for his sister as she splashed her hands in the basin.

What is going to happen to us, Lord? To them? She tried to believe—she had to believe—that Lee would be able to stall the banker as handily as their father always had. She and her children would keep this solid roof over their heads. The garden was flourishing, the cow was giving good milk and the chickens were laying so well there would be plenty of food on their table.

Harvest season was coming up, and although Lee hadn't wanted to talk about it, he would clearly need her help when it came to threshing time. Joanna knew there would be harvest workers to feed—that was a large task he could not do without help—and then they had the canning and preserves to do and the garden to put up. Come winter, perhaps she could get some kind of job in town, cooking or cleaning for part of the day to bring in a wage.

All this had kept her up the last few nights, and it all—her future and her children's—depended on Lee and the banker. She couldn't help peering through the doorway, but the men were sitting in the corner, out of her sight. She heard the drone of their voices, too low for her to make out a single word.

"Ma, we're all washed up." James held the towel while Daisy dried her little hands.

"We're real clean, Ma." Daisy's flyaway blond hair stood out at all angles in the dry air. She looked like the precious blessing she was in the little calico frock and white apron Joanna had finished sewing last week, cut down from one of her own dresses. She wished they had money enough for a new piece of fabric, but Daisy looked dear, anyway.

"I'll dish up your supper for you, and you two can eat on the back porch in the shade." At their enthusiastic response, she took a couple of clean plates from the drainer and filled them from the stove.

When she carried the full plates to the back door, she noticed a team pulling a wagon down their driveway. Well, good, at least someone had come. She couldn't make out the driver through the blistering glare of the sun. The big dark draft horses looked familiar, however. Then she recognized the man on the seat. It was their neighbor to the north, Aiden McKaslin. The dour, disagreeable man had come to pay his respects? That surprised her. He and Pa had not gotten along at all, even though they attended the same church.

"Sit down right here, you two." She set both plates on the small wooden table she'd brought out from the kitchen earlier. The chairs scraped as the little ones climbed up and settled in. "James, say the blessing, please."

"Yes, Ma." The little boy scooched forward in his seat and gave his sister a serious look. "Are your hands folded, Daisy?"

"Yes." She blew out a sigh of frustration, stirring

the long platinum-blond strands of her hair. "He's bein' bossy again, Ma."

Joanna pressed a kiss to the crown of her daughter's head. It was hard being little. She remembered it well. "I need to go greet Mr. McKaslin, so you two mind your manners, all right?"

"Yes, Ma," they both said gravely.

She left them to the sound of James's serious prayer, trying to keep them in her sight through the window as she headed through the house toward the front door. She was surprised to see the banker and Lee in the front yard already, shaking hands. They were both smiling, and her brother seemed relieved.

Apparently their business was over. Their smiles had to be a good sign—the bank must be willing to let her brother continue on with the payments. The burden of worry slid right off her shoulders like rain from a tin roof. Her children would have a solid, good home. It was a lot to be thankful for.

Aiden McKaslin pulled his draft horses to a stop and stared straight at her. "I've come to take back the cow I didn't receive full payment for."

"What? You're not here for the wake?"

"I'm busy, ma'am. I've only got time to take the cow."

"The milk cow?" Her children needed the milk. She looked to Lee, but he stopped chatting with the banker to shrug in a careless way.

"Let him take the cow, Joanna. We can't keep her."

"We c-can't?" She hadn't considered they might be that bad off. Her brother turned his back and continued walking the banker to his horse and buggy, which were parked in the shade.

Well, they could get along without a cow. Heaven knew they had been much worse off before and managed well enough. What mattered was that they could keep the house and land. This thought bolstered her as she hurried across the crackling dried lawn.

Aiden McKaslin stopped to face her. "I'll return the payments your father already made."

He tugged some folded twenty dollar bills from his muslin shirt pocket and held them out with a steady, sun-brown hand. A capable hand, she noticed, not quite able to meet his gaze. Shyness seized her, for he was a big man, tall and physically intimidating. She felt very small as she took the bills.

"Thank you, that's awful decent of you. I—" She blushed, realizing how sorry she must look. She smoothed the grease spackles on her patched apron. "The cow is picketed out in the field. You can't see her from here, but she's just behind the barn in the shade by the creek."

"I brought my own rope, so I'll leave you her halter, picket rope and pin. You may be able to get another cow later on, and those will come in handy."

It felt as if a rock had settled in her throat, and she couldn't seem to answer him. She could only nod as she slipped the two twenty dollar bills into her pocket.

"I'm sorry for your loss, ma'am." He tipped his hat. She could see his shadow on the ground at her feet before he whipped around and strode away toward the barn.

"Ma?" Little Daisy stared at her through the slatted porch rails, clutching the weathered wood with her small hands. Tears stood in her eyes. "My plate slid off the t-table. It's all in the d-dirt."

From around the corner, just out of sight, James called out, "Weren't my fault, Ma!"

One tear trickled down Daisy's cheek. "I real s-sorry."

Joanna remembered to count to ten and then took a deep breath of the hot, dusty air. She reached between the boards and caught the wetness on her fingertip. "It's all right. Go help your brother clean up, then come around to the kitchen door and meet me."

"Y-yes, Ma." Her daughter hiccuped once, spun in a swirl of pink calico and padded off on bare feet.

Poor baby. Joanna watched to make sure no more tears fell as Daisy hopped down the step to kneel beside her brother. Their hands worked quickly. The mess couldn't have been very much. After she filled a second plate for Daisy, Joanna would see to the rest of the cleaning up.

She felt an odd tingling at the back of her neck. It wasn't a good feeling. She peered around, but Mr. Aiden McKaslin had already cut behind the barn and was out of sight and earshot—and quickly, too. A staid bachelor like him, close to thirty years old, probably had an unpleasant opinion of children and their messes. She'd married a man just like that.

The last thing she intended to do was pay him any mind. The banker was driving away, kicking up more chalky dust into the heavy air. Lee headed off to the barn. Most likely to talk with Mr. McKaslin, who was likely tying the cow to the back of his wagon now.

If only they had enough money in hand. Joanna wistfully glanced into the blinding shafts of June sunlight.

She would have liked to have milk for the children. But beggars could not be choosers, and she was glad for what they did have. As she hurried around to the door, she spied the garden beginning to crisp beneath the harsh sun. She'd have to remember to give the vegetables an extra watering after she was through in the kitchen.

While she dished up another plate, she caught sight of Mr. McKaslin returning from behind the barn with their Jersey cow on a lead rope. Something about the man caught her eye. She'd seen him in church, of course, but he was the type of worshipper who arrived at the last moment, kept to the back and slipped out before the final hymn. There was a sadness to him that hung over him like a storm cloud. It was that melancholy that kept him from being truly frightening.

Had she offered him a meal? She couldn't remember. Her mind was a muddle and she felt frayed to the last thread. She put more fuel in the stove and more water to heat. She went to the back door, but Mr. McKaslin was already in his wagon and driving off, the cow trailing behind. Before she'd blinked twice, there was only a dust cloud where he had been.

Daisy stood leaning at the rail with those wide blue eyes of hers even wider. "Why's Uncle Lee all packed up on the horse?"

"Packed up? No, he's probably out back in the fields, gone to chat with Mr. McKaslin. Don't you worry about it, honey." She set the plate on the table. "Here, sit down and eat your dinner."

"*Okay...*" Daisy said in one long, drawn-out sigh.

As Joanna brushed a comforting hand over her

daughter's head, a movement caught her eye. There, against the background of the growing wheat fields and the fading patches of red on the barn, was Lee astride Pa's horse. Daisy was right. There were two bulging packs behind his saddle and a satchel hung over the saddle horn. Lee had his black hat drawn low and didn't look her way.

James glanced nervously over his shoulder. "Ma, where's he goin'?"

"I'm sure to settle a few business matters in town, is all." A punch of apprehension hit her square in the stomach. Something was very wrong. She forced a smile into her voice for the children's sake. "Stay right here on the porch, eat your dinner, and I'll get you a surprise for dessert."

"There's dessert?" James swiveled toward her, his uncle forgotten. "Honest?"

"Is it cake?" Daisy asked with a fork halfway to her mouth.

"You'll have to wait and see."

Lee rode out of sight behind the house, and it was hard to keep her step natural as she headed straight to the kitchen. The moment the door slapped shut behind her she rushed through to the front yard. Lee didn't look behind him, but his back stiffened, so he had to know she was hurrying after him.

"Lee?" She had to keep her voice low so the children would not be able to overhear this. "Lee? Where are you going?"

"Away." He bit out the word, then appeared annoyed as he reined in the horse. "Truth is, I sold the place."

"You *what?*" She couldn't be hearing him right.

Maybe it was the lack of sleep last night and the emotional upset over the funeral. It was all the hard kitchen work in this stifling heat. Yes, that's what it was. "For a moment there, I thought you said you'd sold out, but there's still the crop in the fields."

"I sold it, too. The banker said you've got until nightfall to get out."

"Get out?" There was something wrong with her mind. She could hear Lee's words, but her brain was not making sense of them. Surely he didn't say— "You want me to get out of the house?"

"You can't live in it if it belongs to someone else. The banker bought the place for his sister. She'd like to get settled tonight."

"Tonight?" The earth began to spin. "Lee, what about the children? You aren't putting us out, are you?"

"You aren't my lookout. They're your ragamuffins, not mine. I'm not beholden to them or to you. Pa left me this place fair and square. It's mine to sell."

"But before Pa died, you said…" Not only was the earth spinning, but it was tilting, too.

No, this can't be happening. This cannot be right. She had to be ill from the heat, that was it. Her mind was fuddled from too little sleep and too much worry. "Y-you said we could live here."

"I know what I said." Lee glared down at her. "I came to help you take care of the old man. The crops are still doing well in the fields because of me. The banker met my price and I took it. Leave the pigs and the chickens when you go. They're part of the sale, too."

"But—" Her brain seemed stuck on that word like her feet to the dirt. "It's not right. You just can't—"

"Sure I can. I only came back here for the money. You know I never held much regard for our old man. He was a louse."

"But you said—"

"In this world, you've got to look out for yourself and no one else. It's the only way to survive." Lee gazed down on her with pity. He pulled his billfold from his shirt pocket. "Here."

She stared at the twenty dollar bill he held out, the end flapping in the brisk scorching wind. The truth hit her like dry lightning. "You really sold the land and you're keeping all the money."

"It's legal. Pa left everything to me. You know that."

"But you said you would stay to farm. You promised. You gave your word."

"Yeah, well, I hardly expected you to help me out if you knew." Since she didn't take the money, Lee tossed it at her. The wind snatched it and blew it away like a dry leaf. It stuck to the wall of sticker bushes growing along the road and flapped there, helplessly trapped.

Joanna gulped hard. She fisted her hands, fighting to stay calm. Getting upset would not make this easier. "You lied to me. Lee, you're my brother."

"Half brother. Take my advice and start packing. That banker's not a nice man. He'll put you and your young ones out by force. Do you want that?"

A bead of sweat rolled down her spine. She shook her head once, but the horse was already trotting away, kicking up bits of earth and small rocks. In the matter of a few heartbeats, all that she could see of her brother was a thick cloud of dust.

He'll put you and your young ones out by force. The

image of that tore through her and, without thought, she moved forward. She snatched the twenty dollar bill from the bush, ignoring the bite of scratches across her knuckles. She added the bill to the money Mr. McKaslin had given her. The sun was already sinking in the sky, the day more than half over. She had a lot to do if she wanted to spare her children any unpleasantness.

Woodenly, she stumbled into the kitchen, checking through the open window to see them seated at the little battered wooden table, comfortably finishing their meals. The wind puffed James's dark hair straight up like one big cowlick. Daisy sat as dainty and as dear as a princess.

Lord, please help me to manage this well. For their sake. She might have prayed further for shelter and work and somewhere to go, but she'd learned from experience that the good Lord did not hear many of her prayers. So she kept them simple.

"What's for dessert, Ma?" James had hopped off his chair and stood at the window, happily watching her through the mesh screen.

"You sit down and watch your sister, handsome, and I'll bring you both big pieces of cake."

"Cake! I knew it." Delight rounded his sweet face and he dashed the short distance back to his chair.

That's my answer, she realized as she found a knife and went to work on the cake hidden in the cellar to keep cool and fresh. This will be an adventure, a special trip. Not a scary life living out of the wagon. They would be explorers, like in the book she was reading to them, a few pages at a time, at night.

She swallowed all her fears and worries, put a smile

on her face and cut two huge slices of cake. Her mind was busy making plans of how to pack and what they would take as she pushed her way through the screen door.

Two darling faces turned toward her in sheer delight. "Cake!"

She knew from sad experience that the Lord might not provide for them, but she would find a way.

Chapter Two

If it wasn't one problem to deal with, it was another. Aiden McKaslin drew his horse to a halt and squinted into the long rays of the setting sun.

Sure enough, there at the edge of his property, just inside the boundary fence, was a squatter. A covered wagon huddled in the shelter of an old maple. Judging by the fraying cover, it had seen better days. The smoke from a newly lit fire rose thick and unsteady from a tidy circle of stones.

What with the glare of the sun, and the shadows the tree made on the ground, he couldn't see a living soul. Just two horses nipping at the growing grass.

He yanked his Winchester from the saddle holster by its barrel and cocked it with one hand. Aiden carried the weapon mostly for the wild predators that got to eyeing his livestock for dinner now and again. But when he ran into trouble of the human sort, he was doubly glad he always rode armed. He'd had trouble like this before, and experience taught him that squatters were mostly criminals.

He hated trouble, but the law was a good five miles away, so he approached the camp with caution, studying the lay of things with a careful eye. There was wearing of the earth around the stubborn tufts of grass at the creek bank. The careful sweeping of footprints out of the dirt seemed to be a clue that whoever was staying here might not want to leave a sign of how many of them there were. The trampled grass around the wagon was another hint—still fresh, but with significant usage.

What if the men were dangerous? Aiden drew his horse to a stop and considered. He was out in the open now. Too late to retreat. Trouble like this had occurred early last year, and a ranch hand had been shot and left for dead by squatters. They'd never been caught. Thankfully, the hired man had survived.

Aiden would rather deal with dangerous wildlife anyday than a pack of armed criminals.

Then he saw something in the dust by the right rear wagon wheel. He leaned forward in the saddle, squinted a bit and realized it was a small, crudely carved wooden horse—a child's toy. A child's toy? Not what he'd figured on finding here in a squatter's camp. Then he heard a rustle, and a puff of dust rose from beneath the wagon.

He lowered the hammer and the rifle. "Is your pa around?"

A round face peered between the spokes of the wheel. "Nah. He rode away to heaven."

Aiden studied the wide brown eyes and dark hair sticking straight up, recognizing the child. The widow's kid who had lived on the neighboring ranch for a spell. Probably another sad story, he figured as he dismounted. He was learning that life was full of sad stories. Even though he'd lost his heart long ago, and there was nothing but an empty hole where it had been, he steeled himself. He didn't want to feel a thing, and he knew this situation was going to be full of sadness. "Your ma then?"

"She said not to talk to nobody. Shh, Daisy." There was more rustling and the boy drew back.

To his surprise, a little girl with white-blond hair held back with a bright pink ribbon crawled out from beneath the wagon bed. She brushed the dust off her skirt primly. "Ma didn't say *I* couldn't talk to nobody."

Aiden couldn't rightly say that he wasn't affected by that cute little girl. Such a wee thing, not much to her at all, and living out of a covered wagon. The little boy crawled out, too, looking annoyed with his younger sister. He drew himself up tall—he couldn't be more than seven or eight years old—and scolded his sister for not minding.

They hadn't been living here long, Aiden decided as he glanced around. Everything was neat and tidy, and a woman's presence might explain the swept dirt. While he didn't have the best opinion of most women, he'd learned even the worst of them liked to dust and sweep with a vengeance.

The little boy was shaking his finger at his sister. "Ma said to stay hid. You oughtn't to be talking to strangers."

"Are you a stranger?" The little girl gazed past her brother and straight into Aiden's eyes.

He choked a little, feeling a gnawing of something

in his chest. He didn't like it. He didn't like feelings.
Life was too hard for them. A smart man didn't give
in to them. He set his jaw tight and answered between
clenched teeth. "Your brother is right. You ought to
mind him."

"Oh." The little girl wilted like a new seedling in a
late freeze. "Do you know where Ma is?"

"No. She's not here? Did she go off and leave you?"
There it was. Fury. It roared through him unbidden and
with a power that he hadn't felt since—

"Excuse me." A woman's voice carried like a gunshot
on the wind. "Step away from my children."

He did as she asked, so as not to startle her. But as he
pivoted on his boot heel to face her, he steeled himself
a tad more. He still wasn't prepared for what he saw.
Exhaustion was a mask obscuring her young face. Her
dress was clean and proper and pressed, and her soft
blond hair braided casually in one long tail that fell over
her shoulder. The air of her, the feel that hung over her
like a cloud, was pure hardship.

His emotions weren't ironclad enough, because he
felt the tug of pity. And more. The fury remained, digging deep. "This is my land, ma'am. You can't go leaving your children alone here."

"I didn't leave them alone. I was down at the creek."

As she strode to the crest of the rise, he could clearly
see the two five-gallon buckets she carried, one in each
hand. She was a tiny thing, and water was heavy. He
was striding toward her before he realized he was moving at all.

There was fear in her eyes—fear of him, he realized,

as he yanked the first bucket out of her hand. She drew back fiercely, sloshing water over the rim and onto her faded skirts, clutching the remaining bucket's handle with a death grip.

"Give me the water." He tucked his rifle against his forearm and held out his free hand.

Her eyes widened at the sight of his rifle, pointed downward at an angle toward the grass.

Women. He ought to have remembered what they were like, having once been married. He did his best to keep his annoyance out of his voice: "I use my rifle for defense, nothing more, ma'am. Now, give me the bucket."

She swallowed visibly, as if she were about to hand over a potful of money. He had frightened her more than he'd realized.

Shame filled him and he took care when he lifted the heavy bucket from her small hand. He cleared his throat, not at all sure how to say what he had meant to say. Talking had never been his strong suit. He hefted the heavy water buckets and lugged them toward the camp, where both little children watched him wide-eyed. Anyone could see they were well-behaved, that their ma was doing a good job raising them up.

"Where you want these?" He glanced over his shoulder, but the woman seemed frozen in place on the rise. Mrs. Nelson looked like a sensible sort. Her pink calico dress might be faded, but it was simple and clean, void of frippery.

She came across as a decent lady down on her luck. And she was staring at him with fear on her face. Not the terrified sort of run-and-hide fear. No, the fear he saw on her delicate features was the kind that made him even angrier. The kind that spoke of ill-treatment.

"Where do you want me to put the water?" he repeated in as clear of a voice as he could manage.

Mrs. Nelson visibly swallowed. "Under the tailgate."

Without a word he turned and marched angrily on, his boots clumping against the hard-packed earth. He hauled the buckets to the back of the wagon and dropped them with a small puff of dust. When he straightened, he realized both children had followed him, single file, and were staring up at him with dust-smudged faces. Mrs. Nelson's skirts snapped as she hurried to stand between him and the young ones.

That only made him madder. "What are you doing here?"

"I'll not have you using that tone in front of my children." Her dainty chin came up, and she was all protective fire, though the old, worn fear was still there.

He hated that fear. It was all he could do to keep his tone low and his voice calm. "This being my land, ma'am, I'll use whatever tone suits me. Now, answer my question."

That chin lifted another notch before she turned to speak to her little ones. "You two go on and wash up for supper, while I speak to Mr. McKaslin."

They nodded and politely went straight to it. The little boy fetched a bar of lye soap and a worn but clean towel from the back of the wagon, and took charge of seeing to the hands and face washing of his little sister.

With the children busy, Aiden followed Mrs. Nelson

out into the grass. She turned to face him with her arms crossed over her chest and her spine straight. "We had no place to go, Mr. McKaslin."

"You have family."

"Family? I have no one and you know it." She held herself very still. "If you'll excuse me, I'll get my children into the wagon and we'll be off your property by sundown. That is what you want, isn't it?"

"You just said you have no place to go."

"And a man like you cares?" She heard the heartlessness in her own voice and stopped, took a breath and a moment to compose herself. She might be homeless, but she had her dignity. "I cannot reimburse you for our stay on your land. I am sorry for that."

"Sorry?" A muscle worked in his granite jaw. He repeated the word as if he'd bitten into something sour. "Sorry?"

"There's no need to be so angry." She took a step back and drew in a gulp of air. "We hardly did any harm."

"Any harm?"

"We wore away some of your grass, and the horses grazed on the bunchgrass, but it wasn't as if you were using—"

"This is unacceptable." A vein throbbed out at his temple. *"You've been living here for how long?"*

"Since Mr. Wessox found us camped out at the edge of his farm on the other side of the creek." She curled her hands into fists, keeping her chin set and her tone even. This was not the first irate man she'd ever had to manage.

"How long?" Tendons stood out in his muscled, sun-browned neck.

"We were only there a few weeks." She felt very small. "We've been on your land for a little longer."

"And you have no family?" A tick started in the corded muscles of his jaw.

"You already know the answer." She took a few slow steps in retreat. She could not get to her wagon—or her children—without going past Mr. McKaslin. "My half brother has no interest in helping us. There is no one else."

"What of your husband's side of the family?"

"As he's passed away, and his family did not approve of me, they want nothing to do with us. Not even for the children's sake." She didn't know how it could possibly be, but her words seemed to make the man towering over her even angrier. He appeared to be restraining his fury, but it was a terrible sight. He was more than twice her size and strength, and as he began to breathe heavily with his anger, he seemed invincible.

A thin thread of fear shivered through her, but she firmly clutched her skirts, lifting them so she would not trip. Her first wobbly step took her closer to him. Closer to his rage. "Excuse me."

To her surprise, he let her walk by. She did her best to ignore the stone pillar he seemed as she hurried past him, adrenaline kicking up with every step she took. Her children were waiting, sweet and good, with their faces and hands washed. They were carefully wiping up their water splashes. Her heart warmed toward them as it always did, and she hoped she could keep them safe.

"Ma?" James leaned close, all brightness gone from his face. "That man's gonna make us leave again, ain't he?"

Before she could answer, Daisy fisted her little hands in the folds of Joanna's skirts and looked up with frightened eyes. "I don't wanna go."

"Why ever not?" She did her best to put a smile on her face and soothing love in her voice. She knelt down so they could look into her eyes and clearly see they should not be worried. "We always knew this was just a stopping off place. Why, we're ready to go and start our next adventure. Doesn't that sound fun?"

"No." James would not be fooled, her poor little boy. "Do we gotta go now? Before supper?"

Aware of Daisy's lower lip trembling and how intently the little girl watched her, Joanna tried to weigh her next words carefully. She did not want to make promises she could not keep. But neither did she want to be so truthful it shattered her children. She was out of options, and her prayers had simply gone unanswered for so long, they might never be again.

All she could do was the best she knew how. "All right, you two, start rounding up your toys. Be sure to get them all. We don't want to leave any behind."

"Okay, Ma." James sighed with sadness, his shoulders weighed down as he went to bring in his wooden horses.

"Yes, Ma." Daisy sniffed, her head down, and trudged away.

The wild grasses crunched beneath Mr. McKaslin's boots. She dreaded facing him again. He strode toward her through the waving stalks, his work clothes rippling slightly in the strong westerly breeze and hinting at his steely strength. Vulnerable, she braced herself for whatever wrath he'd come to inflict on her.

He had some right, she admitted, for they *were* squatters. They *were* illegally using the land he worked hard to pay for and to maintain. She was, essentially, stealing from him. That shamed her.

Silence stretched between them, and she felt the rake of his gaze, taking her in from the top of her windblown hair, where escaped tendrils snapped in the wind, to the toes of her scuffed, patched shoes. She watched him fist his big, work-roughened hands, and expected the worst.

"You never told me, Mrs. Nelson. Where are you going to go?" His tone was flat, his jaw tensed, as if he was still fighting his temper. His blue eyes glanced past her to where the children were going about their chore.

"I don't know." Her throat went dry. Her tongue felt thick as she answered. "When I find employment, I could wire a payment to you. Rent. Y-you aren't thinking of—of bringing the sheriff in?"

"You think I want *payment?*" Aiden's voice boomed like winter thunder. "You think I want *rent money?*"

"Frankly, I don't know what you want."

"I'll tell you what I *don't* want. I don't want…" His words echoed like cannon fire as he paused, and a passing pair of geese overhead honked in flat-noted tones. He grimaced, and it was impossible to guess what he would say or do.

She trembled not from fear of him—she truly didn't believe he would strike her—but from the unknown.

Of being forced to take the frightening step off the only safe spot she'd found since she'd lost Pa's house.

When you were homeless, everything seemed so fragile, so easily off balance. It was a big, unkind world for a woman alone with her children. She had no one to protect her. No one to care. The truth was, Joanna had never had those things in her husband. How could she expect them from any stranger? Especially this man she hardly knew, who seemed harsh, cold and hard-hearted?

And, worse, what if he brought in the law?

"You can't keep living out of a wagon," he said, still angry, the cords straining in his neck. "Animals have enough sense to keep their young cared for and safe."

Yes, it was as she'd thought. He intended to be as cruel as he could be. She spun on her heels, pulling up all her defenses, determined to let his hurtful words roll off her. She grabbed the towel the children had neatly folded and tossed it into the laundry box in the back of the wagon.

"Mrs. Nelson. I'm talking to you."

"Yes, I know. If you expect me to stand there while you tongue-lash me, you're mistaken. I have packing to get to." Her fingers were clumsy as she hefted the bucket of water she'd brought for washing—she wouldn't need that now—and heaved.

His hand clasped the handle beside hers, and she could feel the life and power of him vibrate along the thin metal. "Give it to me."

Her fingers let go. She felt stunned as he walked away, easily carrying the bucket, which had been so heavy for her. Quietly, methodically, he put out the small cooking fire. He did not seem as ominous or as intimidating—somehow—as he stood in the shadows, bent to his task, although she couldn't say why. Perhaps it was because he wasn't acting the way she was used to men acting. She was quite accustomed to doing all the work.

James scurried over, clutching his wooden horse, to watch. Daisy hung back, eyes wide and still, taking in the mysterious goings-on.

He was different when he was near to them, she realized. He didn't seem harsh, and there was no hint of anger—or, come to think of it, any other emotion—as he shook out the empty bucket, nodded once to the children and then retraced his path to her.

"Let me guess." He dropped the bucket onto the tailgate, and his anger appeared to be back. Cords strained in his neck and jaw again as he growled at her. "If you leave here, you don't know where you're going and you have no money to get there with?"

She nodded. "Yes, sir."

"Then get you and your kids into the wagon. I'll hitch up your horses for you." His eyes were cold and yet not unfeeling as he fastened his gaze on hers. "I have a shanty out back of my house that no one's living in. You can stay there for the night."

"What?" She stumbled back, and the solid wood of the tailgate bit into the small of her back. "But—"

"There will be no argument," he snapped, interrupting her. "None at all. I buried a wife and son years ago, what was most precious to me, and to see you and them neglected like this—with no one to care..." His jaw clenched again, and his eyes were no longer cold.

Joanna didn't think she'd ever seen anything sadder

than Aiden McKaslin standing there in the slanting rays of the setting sun.

Without another word, he turned on his heels and walked away, melting into the thick shadows of the summer evening.

Chapter Three

As he led the way across his land, it was all Aiden could do not to look behind him. He knew the covered wagon was following him across the rolling prairie, but he steeled his resolve. He would not turn around and see that woman alone, thin from hunger and pale with strain. He could not take any more, so he contented himself with listening to the plod of the tired horses' hooves on the sun-baked earth, and the rhythmic squeak of the wagon's rear axel.

Yep, he didn't like this one bit, but he hated even worse the notion of sitting home tonight, comfortable and safe and fed, knowing that a nice woman and her children were unprotected and uncherished and alone.

No, it just wasn't right. Emotion clogged his throat, making it hard to swallow, making it hard to breathe. He refused to let his gaze wander to the east, where the family cemetery lay in shadow, the headstones tall enough to see from his saddle. That's what got him all stirred up. Seeing this woman alone, and her small children homeless, rubbed at the break in his soul that had never healed properly.

He didn't see how it ever could. A loss like that was too much for a man to take.

It was a long ride home through the low rays of the sun. A cooling breeze kicked up, and he drew in the fresh air until it settled in his lungs. He let his chest empty of all the feelings in there. By the time he spotted the sun winking on the windows of home, he was safe from his wounds again.

The young boy's voice rose above the call of a quail and the rustling wind in the grass. "Ma! Ma! Is that where we're gonna live?"

Aiden tried not to be affected by the young'un's excitement, nor by his mother's gentle response.

"No, sweetheart, that's where Mr. McKaslin lives."

"But it's so *big,* Ma. Are you sure?"

"Yes. We're going to live in his shanty."

"Oh."

Aiden steeled himself to the sound of the small boy's disappointment, too. He told himself the shanty was snug and would do just fine for them all, but the truth was, he couldn't stomach the notion of having another woman in the house he'd built for Kate.

He followed the fork in the road that skirted the barn and led south from the main house to the small dark structure of wood and plaster. He heard the children's quiet questions to their mother and tried not to hear the soothing lull of her answers as he dismounted.

Opening the door and finding the nearest lantern kept his mind off the ragged family climbing down from their wagon in the front yard. By the time he'd lit the second lantern, the boy stood in the open door-way, looking smaller for the darkness and shadows cast over him.

The child's serious eyes were unblinking as he watched Aiden cross the one-room house to the cook-stove in the corner. If his guess was right about Mrs. Nelson, she would want tea with supper and wash water for cleaning up. He knelt down and began to build a fire with the bucket of kindling and sticks of wood left over from when his middle brother had been living here.

The boy said nothing, just watched with wide eyes. Aiden tried not to think much about the child. Not out of heartlessness—no, never that.

By the time he got the fire lit and flames licked greedily at the tinder-dry wood, the woman arrived at the door with her littlest on her hip. Without a word she glanced around the shanty. Her face was gaunt in the half darkness, her feelings masked. He couldn't tell if she was disappointed in the shelter or relieved.

After closing the stove door, he rose to his feet. "I'll bring in some water for you, ma'am. I'll send my brother out with supper."

"No. Thank you, but no." She looked stricken. "I've already been so much trouble to you. I can't be—I won't be—more beholden to you. I—"

"You shoulda thought of that when you decided to live on a piece of my property." He watched her rear back—just a step, just a small movement, but somehow it felt like a larger motion. As if he'd truly insulted her. It was not what he'd meant.

Tread softly, man. He checked his voice, gentling it

as much as he was able. "Just put aside your worries for tonight. I'll sleep easier knowing you and your young ones are safe instead of sleeping out there alone on the prairie. Do you understand?"

"Fine. Then we'll speak again tomorrow. I am grateful." Tension still tightened her face, and the flickering light seemed to emphasize the hollows and lines there, in those lovely features that ought to be soft with happiness and contentment.

It was not a fair world, and he knew it as much as anyone. He jammed the match tin onto the shelf with a little too much force. Watching the way Mrs. Nelson's gaze moved with relief and pleasure around the shanty shamed him. The place wasn't much. He wasn't sure what his Christian duty was, but he hoped he was doing his share. He touched his hat brim. "'Scuse me, ma'am, I'll say good night, then."

"Thank you for your kindness." She moved from the doorway with a rustle of petticoats and a hush of skirts, careful to keep her distance from him. "Good night, Mr. McKaslin."

When he crossed the threshold, he could feel her sigh of relief. He made her uneasy, and it troubled him as he hiked through the growing grasses, for he was uneasy, too. He'd never thought there would be another woman on his land—even for just the night and even in the shanty.

He kept going until the shanty was nothing more than a faint black outline against the shadowed sky. Kindness, Mrs. Nelson had called it, but it was nothing of the sort. He was only doing the right thing, and that did not come without cost.

* * *

"Ma, that was a mighty fine supper!" James's grin was so wide it was likely to split his face. "I cleaned my whole plate."

"Yes, you did." Joanna lifted the kettle of water steaming on the back of the stove. "You be sure and thank Mr. McKaslin the next time you see him."

"Yes'm. I'm puttin' him in my prayers tonight. I was gettin' mighty tired of creek fish." The little boy slid his plate and steel fork next to the washbasin on the table. "Are you sure we can't stay here forever?"

"Yes, I'm sure. This is only for tonight." Holding her heart still, Joanna carefully poured the steaming water into the basin and returned the half-full kettle to the stove. Mr. McKaslin. Now, there was a puzzle. She could not figure that man out. In the field, when she'd come up with water from the creek, she'd been afraid of him. He'd been so angry. Now she realized it wasn't anger at all. No, not if he'd brought them here.

She reached for the bar of lye soap she'd brought in from the wagon earlier, and began to pare off shavings, which fell into the hot water to curl and melt. She felt a little like those shavings, wilting a bit. She wasn't used to taking charity, but as she watched her children move about contentedly, she was grateful to Mr. McKaslin. Somehow she would find a way to repay him for his kindness.

Daisy sidled close with her plate and yawned hugely.

"Is it time for bed already?" Joanna glanced at the shelf clock, which sat mute, the motionless hands frozen at ten minutes after one, clearly the wrong time. "Go on, you two, wash up and get changed."

"Ma." Daisy tugged on a fold of Joanna's skirt, looking up with big blue eyes full of worry. "What about the angels?"

Joanna's heart twisted hard. The first night they'd slept in the wagon, she had told them that the wagon cover was better than a roof because it made it easier for the angels to watch over them. "The angels will be able to keep an eye on you just fine, baby. Now, you wash up and we'll read more from our book. How's that?"

Daisy's smile showed the perfect dimples in her cheeks.

"That'd be mighty fine!" James, listening in, looked as if he could not believe his luck.

As they scampered to finish their washing up, Joanna left the dishes to soak in the water and plucked a sheet from the small box she'd brought in earlier. There, in the small mirror above the washbasin, her face was staring back at her.

That's me? She froze, gazing at the strange woman in the mirror. She'd never been pretty, and she knew it. Her husband had always taken pains to point out her plainness. But she could never remember looking this poorly. Her hair—her only vanity—was dry and flyaway instead of glossy and sleek. Her face was ashen and the hollows beneath her eyes were as dark as day-old bruises. Her cheeks were gaunt and her eyes too big. Sadness had dug lines that had not been there before.

That was not her, she thought, ashamed. That was not the face of a twenty-eight-year-old woman. No wonder Aiden McKaslin had barely glanced at her, and, when he did, it was with that shuttered look of annoyance. What must he see? What must he think of her? And why was she remembering how kind and strong he'd seemed, too? And how changed he'd been around the children?

It didn't matter. After tomorrow she would never see him again.

Tomorrow. That was one thought she wanted to avoid. As hard as she tried not to admit it, she and her children were now covered-wagon people—the homeless people of the West—and she could no longer deny it.

Should they stay in the area? Find another forgotten piece of prairie to park their wagon on? It was too early for harvest work in the fields. And where would she leave her children while she was working?

Should they leave Angel Falls? The horses were in no condition, as old as they were, to pull the wagon a long distance. She did not have the money to stay—particularly come morning, after she squared up what she owed to Aiden McKaslin.

"Ma!" Daisy's sweet voice broke into her thoughts. "I can't reach."

She blinked, realizing her daughter was waiting for her to unbutton her little dress. Joanna banished her worries with a shake of her head—there would be enough time to dwell on them later, when she was unable to fall to sleep—and tackled the tiny buttons marching down the back of Daisy's pink calico dress. "There, now. Go get your nightgown and I'll have your bed nice and ready."

"Yes, Ma." Daisy scampered off to where their satchel of clothes sat on the floor. She knelt, all sweetness, to peer inside the bag and search for her nightie.

Yes, Joanna had some decisions to make. She shook

out the worn muslin over the straw tick with a snap. The fabric fluttered into place, and she bent to smooth and tuck quickly. Her troubled thoughts turned to Aiden McKaslin. Funny, her pa had lived next door to the McKaslins for the last five years, and he'd never said much about Aiden except that he was highly disagreeable. Then again, Pa had been highly disagreeable himself.

Joanna had seen Mr. McKaslin in church since she'd come to stay with her father, but didn't know anything about him at all. Certainly not what he'd said. His words came back to her. *I buried a wife and son years ago, what was most precious to me, and to see you and them neglected like this—with no one to care—*

Not only was she sad for this man who had lost so much, but she admired him, too. He was a good man—rare, in her opinion—or at least good enough to care about someone not his concern. There were men who would have thrown her off the land without blinking. Some would have threatened her with the sheriff.

But Aiden McKaslin had brought her here. She looked around the structure, so solidly built, and clean, except for a little dust here and there. There was a stout roof overhead and not a single crack in a wall. Real glass windows stared out at the gathering darkness and showed a round moon hanging low over the valley. Yes, she would remember Aiden McKaslin in her prayers tonight.

By the time she'd added a top sheet to the straw tick and the quilts from the wagon, the children had said their prayers and were ready for bed. She tucked them in, kissed their brows and told them what a good job they'd done today. When she turned out the lantern by the bedside, after reading to them as she'd promised, she left them sound asleep. She finished the dishes in the meager light of a single lantern, listening to the sounds of the night. Thinking of her problems and her limited choices to solve them overwhelmed her.

When the dishes were done and put away into the crate, she sat down with her mending. She worked while the fire burned down and moonlight moved across the floor of the shanty. Midnight came and she was still sitting with a needle in her hand, wondering what the morning would bring.

She hoped she would be strong enough to face it.

Aiden looked up from his newspaper when he heard Finn's boot steps pounding into the kitchen. Sure enough, there was his little brother—twenty years old—worked up into a fever. No surprise there. Aiden took a sip of his tea, assessing the boy's mood over the rim of his cup. Finn could surprise you, but it was best to try to at least figure out his state before attempting to deal with him. As much as Aiden loved his youngest brother, he had to be honest about his flaws and weaknesses—there were many of those. Judging by the disgruntled frown, the crease of annoyance in Finn's forehead and the angry way he tossed the harness strap across the back of one of the chairs, Aiden figured his brother was working himself up into a temper.

Best not to react to it or encourage it. "I see you had trouble fixing that harness. Why don't you get a cup of tea? We'll tackle it tomorrow."

"Trouble? I didn't have any trouble." Finn took off

his battered work hat and plucked his newer, going-to-town hat from the wall peg. "What I have is a problem sewing that up for her."

"It's what I asked you to do. Technically, you would be doing it for me."

Finn cursed. "Do you think having a woman live out there is a good idea?"

"No, but what else would you have me do with her?"

"I could name a few things, all of which would involve her moving on to take advantage of someone else. She's trouble, Aiden."

"Oh? Do you know the Widow Nelson?"

"I know her type. Whatever she's offering you, beware. She's just trying to get her hooks into you."

"I'll keep that in mind." Wryly, Aiden finished the dregs of tea in his cup, trying to imagine quiet, proper Joanna Nelson as Finn was attempting to paint her.

It was impossible. When he thought of her, he recalled how gentle she was, how diligent and kind to her children, and of all the work she must have been forced to do for her father. That old man was the type who wouldn't give shelter to his daughter and grandchildren without expecting a good amount of profit from it.

No, when Aiden thought of Joanna Nelson, he thought of hard work and that simple beauty of hers. The good kind of beauty that was more than appearances. She was the brand of woman who would face down a man twice her size if she thought her children needed protection.

That was the type of woman he could understand. He folded the newspaper in half, then in half again, watching Finn exchange his work shirt for one of the clean ones folded in the basket near the door, where the laundry lady had left it. It appeared that Finn was heading to town. Would it do any good to forbid him to go?

Finn had that belligerent look to him, the one he got when he was in no mind to be told what to do. "Fine, don't mind what I'm saying. You'll see I'm right when she's got you standing up in church wearing your wedding ring."

An arrow to the heart, that's what Finn's words were to Aiden. Finn was thinking he was so smart, as he always did when he got up a full head of steam. He was just talking to impress himself. What did he know about real life? Not one thing. He spent most of his time dreaming about the bottom of a whiskey bottle.

Finn had never loved so hard that his breath and heartbeat were nothing, nothing at all, compared to a woman's breath and heartbeat. He had never sat the night through, bargaining with God every second of every minute of every long, long hour to take his life—to just take it—and to please let her live.

A wife? That was far more than a wedding ring and a minister's words. A marriage was more than something a woman hoodwinked a man into. Anything short of that was a falsehood and an affront to God, whose love was a great gift. Pressure gathered at Aiden's temples, and he dropped the paper. He was in no mood to read now.

Finn grabbed his Sunday coat from the wall peg.

Yep, Aiden could see exactly what his brother was up to. "I don't want you going out."

"You're not my lord and master, are you?" Finn had

the audacity to wink. "C'mon. I worked hard today. I deserve a little fun."

"No you don't. What you deserve is to work harder tomorrow." Yep, he knew exactly what Finn meant by fun. He meant trouble. "We're getting up an hour earlier tomorrow and hitting the fields."

"Aw, Aiden. It's all we do around here."

"If I find out you went to town and drank even a drop of whiskey, you're off this property. Out of this house. There'll be no more roof over your head. No food in your belly. You'll leave with exactly what you came with, which was the clothes on your back."

Aiden braced himself for the coming wrath. He regretted his current headache because it would only pound more when Finn slammed the door on his way out.

"Whoa there." His brother's chin shot up. For the briefest moment there was the hint of the good boy he'd been—honest and sensitive and a little afraid—but in a flash it was gone. Replaced by the easier emotions of anger and bluster. "We agreed before I got out of prison and stepped foot on this land—*our* land—"

My land, Aiden thought, but he let it pass. He wasn't a greedy man, but he figured more than twenty years of blood and sweat and backbreaking work made the place his. He'd worked harder than their drunkard of a father to clear and build this place from a wild quarter section of prairie. And it was his name on the deed. His name on the mortgage.

"—that I just had to stay out of trouble and do my work around here. No one said I couldn't have a little fun on my own time."

"No one's debating that, Finn. What I am saying is that you show up half-drunk or hungover for repairing the north field fencing, and your free ride is over."

"What free ride?"

That did it; he'd pushed too hard. Aiden shrugged. His head throbbed. His burden was heavy. Seeing Widow Nelson's troubles today had cinched it for him. He was heartsick thinking of the way some men could be. He didn't need to look at it in his own house, in the house where he'd once been happy. He squeezed out the memories that hurt too much. He blotted out the images of her here, of the feminine scent of her lotions and soaps, of her cinnamon rolls baking in the oven just for him, where her laughter and sweetness had made life—his life—better for a time.

"No man tells me what to do." Finn's tirade broke into his thoughts. "Yes, even you, Aiden. You might be my brother, but you are not my keeper."

Aiden waited for the door to slam, and Finn didn't disappoint. On his way out, he slammed it so hard the sound echoed in the kitchen like summer thunder. The windowpanes rattled. The cups swung on their hooks beneath the cupboard. Pain sliced through Aiden's skull. Great. Exactly what he needed on his plate right now: more worries about Finn. The boy was going to make a terrible mistake sooner or later; Aiden knew it. He didn't like that sad fact, but there was nothing he or their other brother, Thad, could do about it. Finn would either pull himself up by the bootstraps and make a man of himself, or he'd keep going on their father's sad path. Only he could make that choice. No one could do it for him.

I sure wish I could. Aiden rubbed his temples, but that didn't stop the pain. No, the real pain was deeper than worries, broader than a physical hurt. His spirit felt heavy with troubles that could not be healed. He pushed himself from the chair and put out the light on his way to the window. He didn't want Finn to see him standing there, filled with regret, watching him stalk to the barn.

The round moon hung over the prairie valley like a watchful guardian, a platinum glow over the growing fields. The night looked mysterious, as if touched by grace, as if solemn with possibility. Aiden leaned his aching head against the window frame and wished he could feel hope again. Wished he could feel even the faintest hint of it.

What he could see was the shanty's faint roofline, as dark and as quiet as the night.

She's just trying to get her hooks into you. Finn's words came back to him. Hooks? Joanna Nelson didn't have any hooks. Not a woman who wore her heart and her love for her children on her sleeve. Not a woman who was so thin, the hard lines of her bones were visible through her summer dress. She'd gone without eating in order to give more to her children, so their bellies would be full while she went hungry.

The void where his heart had been was suddenly filled with an unbearable pain. *That* was love.

Chapter Four

The cow grazing in the yard lowed quietly, the only sound in the entire world. The serenity of the morning seemed to swell as the first trails of gold flared above the deep blue mountains. She squeezed her eyes shut and let the soft warmth wash over her, willing the pure first light to cleanse away her fears and her doubts. She prayed that it would give her courage and insight for the hard morning ahead.

The cow mooed again, impatient this time. Joanna opened her eyes to see the animal Aiden had taken back from Pa's farm gazing at her with pleading eyes. The cow must have scented the small portion of grain in the bottom of the feed bucket, and was straining against her picket rope to get at it.

"I'm sorry, Rosebud. Here you are." She set the bucket down at the cow's front hooves. Instantly, the animal dived into her breakfast, tail swishing with contentment.

At least she looked better fed here on the lush grasses of Aiden's land. Pa had always been stingy with the livestock's feed, although Joanna had always sneaked grain and treats to Rosebud. She set the three-legged stool on the cow's left side and placed the milk pail between her feet. Holding it steady in case Rosebud lurched suddenly, Joanna stroked the cow's flank, talking to her for a few moments before starting to milk.

She could no longer see the rising sun breaking over the mountains, but the light was changing, the darkness turning to long blue shadows. A golden hue crept across the land to crown Aiden's two-story house. Painted yellow, it seemed to absorb the slanted gold rays and glow.

I buried a wife and son years ago, what was most precious to me. Again, his words came back to her like a haunting refrain. His wife had chosen that soft buttery color. Joanna didn't need to know anything about Aiden or his past to know that. No Montana rancher would choose that feminine, comforting color for his house. Just like the carved wooden curlicues decorating the top pillars of the porch fronts. Or the carefully carved rail posts. Such workmanship must have been done out of love for his wife.

Joanna felt in awe of such devotion. What a deep bond Aiden must have known. Respect for him filled her like the rising sun, and suddenly, there he was, as if her thoughts had brought him to life, striding down the porch steps with a milk pail in hand. She didn't know if it was just her lofty opinion of the man, but he looked wholly masculine. With light outlining the impressive width of his shoulders, he strode through the long shadows.

Not even those shadows were enough to hide the

set of his frown and the tension straining his jaw as he marched toward her. "Who said you could milk my cow?"

"Sorry, I guess I've helped myself to your morning chores. I wanted to make your load easier, for doing the same for me last night." She spoke over the hissing stream of milk into the pail. "It's a fair turn. Surely you're not angry with me for that?"

Was it her imagination, or was there a weakening of that grimace in the corners of his mouth? "You are a surprising woman, Mrs. Nelson."

"You can call me Joanna." She could not resist saying it, even though she knew he would refuse to. "I gathered the eggs in the henhouse, too."

"There was no need to do my chores."

"How else am I to pay you what I owe?"

Aiden came closer, casting her in his long shadow. "Who said you owe me anything?"

"Please don't try that tact, Mr. McKaslin."

"What tact?" He knelt beside her, bringing with him the fresh scent of soap. "And you can call me Aiden."

"You're a decent man, Aiden. I'll not take advantage of that."

His hand, so very large, reached out and covered her wrist, stopping her. His fingers, so very warm, squeezed gently. "I'll finish up here. You had best go see to your little ones."

"They'll be fine enough until I finish."

"Please." It was the plea in his eyes that moved her, that revealed a man of great heart. "I'm not comfortable letting a woman do my work. I'll bring you some of the milk after I strain it."

How could she say no to the man who had given her one night of safe harbor? One night of peaceful sleep? He was like a reminder of hope on this perfect, golden morning, even with the shadows that seemed to cling to him.

"Go on." It was softly said, and surprising, coming from such a hard-looking man. "You have done enough for now."

She swallowed, lost in his midnight-blue eyes. They were shielded from her, and as guarded as the peaks of the Rocky Mountains towering over the long stretch of prairie. Curiosity filled her, but he wasn't hers to wonder about, so she pulled away and rose from the stool. With the first step she took, she felt a pang of lonesomeness. Her hand, warm from his touch, was cold in the temperate morning.

He watched her with his penetrating gaze, unmoving. Behind him on the porch, another man came to a sudden halt, yanked down the wide brim of his hat to shield his eyes from the sun without bothering to disguise his disdainful frown in her direction.

Last night Aiden had mentioned a brother. A brother who made him look even kinder and ten times more mature and masculine by comparison. The intensity of this man's scowl made Joanna shiver.

"Don't mind Finn." Aiden's comment carried on the breeze. "He's got a lot to learn about life and manners."

Across the yard, Finn muttered a terse answer that was drowned out by the harsh clatter of his boots on the steps. Anger emanated from him like heat from a stove. Joanna took one look at him and stayed where she was.

"Don't blame you for not wanting to cross his path." Aiden had hunkered down on the stool beside the cow. "When Finn's got his dander up, he's meaner than a rattler trapped in a brush fire. I apologize for him."

"There's no need. I'm the trespasser here."

"You've gone pale. He upset you."

"No, he reminded me of someone. M-my husband."

That explained it. Aiden didn't need to know anything more to see how her life had been. Sourness filled his stomach. Life was hard enough without such people in it. "Finn would make a poor husband."

She didn't comment, but the way she tensed up, as if she were holding too much inside, let him know more than her answer ever could. "Come by in, say, thirty minutes and I'll have breakfast on the table. Your young ones might as well eat while we figure out what you and I are going to do."

"About what I owe you?"

"No." Tied up inside, he said the word with all the patience he had. "You have to go somewhere, Joanna. You can't keep living out of your wagon."

He could see her face beneath the shadow of her bonnet. Really, she was very lovely; her forehead and nose, cheekbones and chin were so fine they could have been sculpted of porcelain. Her big blue eyes were as pretty as cornflowers and her mouth looked soft and cozy, as if she had spent a lot of her life smiling. Once upon a time.

Her brows knit and her chin shot up. "Plenty of folks live out of their wagons when times get hard."

Pride. He knew something about that. "I wasn't criticizing. Only saying that eventually winter is going to come. Maybe I can help you with that."

Her throat worked at the word *help*. Pain shot across her face. Whether she suspected his motives or wanted nothing to do with his help, he couldn't know. She gave a nod of acknowledgment—not of agreement—and went on her way through the growing, seed-topped grasses.

Painted with dawn's soft golden light like that, framed as she was by the crisp lush green of the prairie, Aiden felt he was seeing her for the first time. She was a truly lovely woman. He might even say beautiful.

He wasn't proud of himself for noticing.

Joanna kept swallowing against the painful burn in her throat as she whisked a dollop of milk into the egg batter. *Eventually winter is going to come.* Aiden McKaslin's remembered words made that pain worse. *Maybe I can help you with that.* Charity. That's what he saw when he looked at her. A woman to be pitied.

Shame filled her, because it was the worst sort of criticism. She stopped whisking to flip the thick-cut bacon sizzling in one of the frying pans. Charity was all pretty and tidy and wrapped up real nice when you were the one giving it. It was different when you were on the other end. She'd been able to keep her chin up before, because she had been doing her best. There had been solace in that.

Now he thought she expected his help, that she would accept it. He meant well, but she was afraid of being in a man's debt. Even in a *good* man's debt. Anyone could see that Aiden McKaslin was a good man.

"Ma." Daisy gave her rag doll a squeeze where she

sat on a chair at the round oak table. "Can I get a drink of water?"

"You just had one, baby." Joanna knew the child wasn't asking for water, but to be able to get down from the chair and move around. "This isn't our home, so we have to mind our manners. I want you to please sit there a little while longer."

"Oh. Okay." The little girl sighed and squeezed her doll harder.

"Ma?" James fidgeted in his chair and swung his feet back and forth. "I'm awful hungry. Especially for some of that bacon."

There was no missing the hope on his face. Real bacon. They'd had such a luxury when they had their own little plot of land and their own pig to butcher. Joanna sighed, remembering those times, harder in some ways, better in others. "This is Mr. McKaslin's breakfast. We ate in the shanty before we came here."

"I know, but I was hopin'…" He left the sentence dangling, as if afraid to ask the question he already knew the answer to, but wanting to hold on to that hope.

She couldn't blame him for that. "Maybe there will be a surprise for two good children later on. How about that?"

"Yes, ma'am!" James stopped fidgeting and sat up soldier straight, eager at the thought of a surprise.

"Oh, yes." Daisy offered a dimpled smile.

It took so little to please them. Joanna's heart ached as she poured the eggs into the waiting skillet. If only there was something more than another few pieces of saved candy for them. They deserved more than she could give them—at least now, anyway. In a month's time, there would be fieldwork to do. It was hard labor, and she still didn't know what to do with her babies while she worked, but at least she could hope for real wages. Hope for a betterment of her children's lives.

The eggs sizzled and she whisked them around the pan, reaching for the salt and pepper. She surveyed her work in progress. The bacon was crisping up real nice, the tea was steeping and the buttermilk biscuits in the oven were smelling close to done. Cooking for the man wasn't much of a repayment, but it was all she had to offer.

The back door swung open and there was Aiden, leaving his boots behind in the lean-to and staring at her with shock on his stony face. The kindness she'd come to see there vanished, replaced by a cold blast of anger.

"What are you doing?" His voice was loud enough to echo around the room. He came swiftly toward her, with raw fury and full power. "Get out of my kitchen."

She'd expected him to be happy that she'd cooked for him, saving him the chore. She kept stirring the eggs so they wouldn't congeal. "In a moment. I'm nearly done here. I didn't mean to intrude. I know it was forward of me, but—"

"I want you out." He drew himself up as if ready for a fight.

Yet she was not afraid of him. She heard Daisy crying quietly at the table and James hop off his chair to come to her aid.

"Outside, both of you." She laid down the whisk. "Aiden, the biscuits are ready. Let me take them out of the oven."

"Now, Joanna." The words came out strangled.

He was not angry at her, she realized. There, behind his granite face, she thought she caught something terrible—grief and sorrow—before that glimmer of emotion faded from his eyes. He stared at her, cold and imposing. He did not have to say another word. His face said it for him. She was not welcome here. Coming had been a mistake. An enormous mistake.

Miserable, she turned away. She had to detour widely to avoid bumping his arm with her shoulder, for he'd planted himself in the middle of the kitchen. Shame made her feel small as she hustled to the door, where her children waited, wide-eyed and silent, in the lean-to.

So much for her brainy ideas. She took James with one hand and Daisy with the other. They tumbled into the blinding sunshine together. Dust kicked up beneath their shoes as they hopped off the last step and into the dry dirt. To the right lay a garden, the vegetables small and stunted, wilting in the morning sun. Duty cried out to Joanna to water those poor plants, for their sake as much as for Aiden's. She glanced over her shoulder, remembering the awful look on his face.

She could see him in the shadows of the kitchen, standing where she'd left him, his shoulders slumped, his hands covering his face.

She'd never seen a man look so sad. Her feet became rooted to the ground, even though James was tugging at her hand. Something held her back. Something deep in her heart that would not let her leave the man behind.

He'd loved his wife. He really had. Joanna stared at him, transfixed by the shadows that seemed to surround him, by the slump of defeat of his invincible shoulders and the hurt rolling off him like dust in a newly tilled field.

She could see as plain as day what she'd done. Had there been another woman in this lovely house he'd built for her since her death? Probably not. He'd simply walked with no warning into the kitchen from his work in the barn to see a woman standing where his wife had once stood, cooking his breakfast.

Sympathy flooded her. Joanna hung her head, staring at her scuffed and patched shoes dusty from the dry Montana dirt. What she'd done with the best of intentions must have cut him to the soul.

How did she make this right? Would it be cruel to try to stay and work off what she owed him, and put him through this kind of remembering? Or was it better to pack up the children and leave? Which would be the best thing to do? There had been a time in her life when she would have turned to the Lord through prayer for an answer.

Now, she merely felt the puff of the hot breeze against her face and the muddle of agony in her middle. It was strange that Aiden's hurt was so strong she could feel it as easily as the ground beneath her feet.

"Why's he so mad, Ma?" James asked quietly, his hand tight in hers.

"He's had a great loss."

"Oh. Does that mean he had a funeral?"

"Yes."

"He's sad. Like I was when Pa died." James's breathing caught in a half sob, and he fell silent.

Joanna had never known that kind of sorrow, one that was deep and strong enough to have broken a person in two. Out of respect for Aiden's privacy, she turned away. She made her feet carry her forward, past the garden and those tender parched plants, and she did not look back. Although not looking made no difference. She could feel the powerful image of him standing motionless while the bacon popped and the eggs cooked in that lovely kitchen he'd no doubt built with love and his own two hands.

As Aiden set several biscuits on a platter, Finn banged in from the lean-to wearing his barn clothes and a scowl. His brother took one look at the buttery biscuits and the fluffy eggs on the table and shook his head.

"What did I tell you?" he grumbled as he poured himself a cup of tea. "Hooks."

Guess there was no need to mention who had cooked breakfast. And a mighty fine one, too, judging by the smell of things. He'd loved Kate dearly, but she was not a good cook—not even a passable one. But Joanna, why, she could put his ma to shame in a cooking contest.

"I'm just glad not to have to fix breakfast," he told his brother. It was partly the truth—close enough—but not the whole truth. It still hurt to remember how she'd been standing at the fancy range he'd ordered in to surprise his wife.

"This is how it starts." Finn's scowl turned to a grimace as he drew a chair back with his boot and slumped into it. "She's gettin' into your good graces. Treating you to a meal so you can see what a good wife she'd make."

"I suppose the fact that she's been living without paying rent on the back pasture, and wanted to do something in return, has little to do with it." Now that Aiden's mind had cleared, and the agony was gone from the empty place in his chest where his heart used to be, he could see what she might have been doing. For some reason he didn't want to think too hard on, he could understand Joanna Nelson pretty easily.

He slid the platter into the warmer—food he intended to take over to the children later. "She's just doing what she can. Heaven knows I could use having my load lightened a bit."

Finn, as usual, either ignored the comment or didn't figure it applied to him. "See? That's how it'll go. Next thing you know, she'll have this house spick-and-span and her brats—"

"That's enough, Finn." Aiden reached for the teapot. "Mind your manners. Those are good kids."

"—living in the upstairs bedrooms. Watch." Finn took a loud slurp from his cup. "Open your eyes now and smarten up, Aiden. Stop her while you can, otherwise you won't know what hit you. You'll have a wedding ring on your finger and three more mouths to feed, and she'll be gettin' a free ride."

If there was something he couldn't imagine, it was a woman like Joanna behaving in such a way. No, she was quality—simple as that. A real good, hardworking, God-fearing woman. Aiden rolled his eyes and carried his steaming cup to the table. "I don't want you talking about her like that."

"Sure, don't listen." Finn was already crunching on

the bacon Joanna had fried up. "You'll see that I'm right."

"Aren't you forgetting something? How about grace?"

"Why bother?"

Aiden shook his head. The boy was never going to learn. "You might not want to believe in God, but that doesn't keep Him from believing in you. Sit up straight, stop chewing and bow your head."

Finn's grimace darkened but he did as he was told.

"Dear Father," Aiden began, bowing his own head and folding his hands. "Please bless this meal we are about to receive. Thank you for your bounty and keep us mindful of our blessings—"

"Amen," Finn interrupted, with the intent to end the blessing, as if that was about all the religion he could take on an empty stomach.

One day, Finn was going to learn, but in the meanwhile, Aiden added a silent prayer. *Lord, please watch over Joanna Nelson and her children. Show me the right way to manage this.* "Amen."

He opened his eyes, and saw Finn already biting into one of the biscuits, moaning because it was so good. Aiden didn't need to take a bite to know that for himself. The buttery fragrance was making his stomach rumble. He reached for one and broke it open. Light and fluffy, better than even Ma could make.

There, out the window, he could see Joanna crossing the lawn toward the barn. She was walking with a fast stride, her head down, her shoulders set. She looked like one determined woman. One who always did the best she could.

Odd how he could see her so clearly. He slathered butter on the biscuit and took a bite—sheer perfection. No doubt about that. Finn was already digging into the scrambled eggs, and so Aiden did, too. They were light and fluffy, with plenty of flavor. Saying she had a gift for cooking would have been an understatement.

He chewed and chased it down with a gulp of tea, watching as Joanna disappeared into the barn. He stood up, wishing he could take his plate with him.

"Don't you do it, Aiden," Finn warned, as if he were about to take a plunge headfirst off a cliff. "Don't you ask her to stay and cook for you."

"Mind your own business." Aiden didn't look back. He was in no mood to put up with his slacker of a brother, who did the least he could get by with. "I expect you to take a page from her book and work harder at earning your keep around here."

Finn grumbled something, but Aiden gave the lean-to door a slam so he wouldn't hear it. That boy could get his dander up in three seconds flat. Maybe because there wasn't an ounce of appreciation for the roof over his head.

"Joanna?" He wasn't surprised to find her at the end stall, where he'd stabled her two horses. "Don't trouble yourself with the team. I'll bring them out after I'm through with breakfast."

"I would like to get a good start on the day." She gave the lead rope a twist to release it, and tried to back the old work horse into the aisle. "I have the wagon packed, so ten more minutes and we will be on our way."

"To where, Joanna?"

"I shall figure that out on the way there." She gave the gelding's halter a gentle tug. "C'mon, boy. Back up. C'mon."

Aiden laid the flat of his hand on the horse's rump, stopping him before he could move. "I didn't mean to run you off. I never should have spoken to you like that. I was surprised to see you there. Unprepared."

"I understand." She still wouldn't look at him. "I overstepped my welcome. I only meant to do you a kindness, to pay back how you've been kind to us."

"I know that. I've been a widower a long time. Maybe too long." Pressure built in his chest, directly behind his sternum, making it hard to talk. Hard to feel. Hard to do anything. "I didn't mean to be so harsh."

"I said I understand." She sounded a little firm herself.

He hated that he'd done that to her. "That was Kate's kitchen. I wasn't prepared to see—" His throat closed up. The rest of him did, too.

"Another woman standing in her place." Joanna finished for him.

Amazing that she could know that. Amazing that she could see what no one—not even his family—could understand.

"Don't worry, Aiden. I didn't mean to make you remember something that brings you so much pain. I intended to be leaving, anyway. I have a debt to you, and I will pay it. One way or another, you can be sure of that. Now, if you'd let me take my horse, I'll be on my way."

She was such a little bit of a thing, frail for all her strength. There was a world of fortitude in the set of her chin and the steel of her spine, but it wasn't right to send her off just because it would be best for him.

No, that wouldn't be right at all. He squeezed his eyes shut for just a moment, trying to listen to common sense, or maybe to that voice from heaven giving him a little direction. Just one word came to mind. "Stay."

Chapter Five

Had she heard him right? Joanna's fingers slipped from the halter. Dancer stared at her, patiently swishing his tail, as if there was no explanation in his mind to her behavior.

In truth, she couldn't explain why Aiden's kind request turned her to stone. Or why the feeling was worse than the fear gathered up inside her like a hive of angry bees. Being alone in this wide world was not a comfort. But neither was accepting a good man's charity. All she had to remember was the look of horror and hurt on his handsome face to know the right thing to do. "I'd best take the children and move along. You don't truly want me here."

"No," he agreed. "You're right about that. But you owe me, Joanna. I expect us to be squared up before you head off. I don't think I'll get what you owe me otherwise."

"You're worried that I won't keep my word?" Her throat felt tight, her eyes hot.

"Absolutely. You might be the kind of woman who

means to keep her promises, but there's no saying what will happen to you once you're off this land. Hardships come along, as both of us well know."

Kindness rang in his voice like the toll of a church bell. Like salvation on Sunday morning. "Yes," she said quietly. "There is no telling what's up ahead of any of us."

"You might get in a worse situation. Or can't find a job, like you haven't found one in these parts. Then where will I be?" Aiden came close, close enough so that she could see the goodness in the man. Down deep and all the way to his soul.

Oh, she could see what he was up to, finding a way to keep her here without her pride getting in the way. Making it seem as if it was her duty to stay. When the truth was this had to be costing him something terrible.

She swallowed hard against the pride building in her throat. "So this is about money."

"It is." The softness in his eyes—and the sadness— said something different.

So did the twist of her soul. She was awestruck by this man's generosity. She was touched by the chance he was offering her. "What will it take for me to pay back what I owe you?"

"I'd expect meals cooked or at least made up ahead. Maybe some cleaning and laundry. Heaven knows the garden needs someone interested enough to tend to it every morning."

"Heaven knows," she agreed, understanding a deeper meaning. He was offering a hand to a drowning woman. She thought of the hot dusty miles, the crack in Dancer's left front hoof, the weeks—maybe months—on the road and how hard that would be on the children. She would have to travel until she found work. Who knew how long or how far away that would be? Times were hard in Montana, true, but the drought had stretched beyond the territory's borders.

"At harvest's end, you and I will talk. If we can find you a paying job for a few hours a week, which I think I can do, then you ought to be set to move on then, wherever you have a mind to." His jaw tensed, betraying him.

This wasn't easy for him. Nor was it for her. She took a ragged breath. The gelding lipped her bonnet brim, and she rubbed her hand along his warm, sleek neck. How could she say no? She'd be able to work off what she owed Aiden. She'd have a real roof over the children's heads and a stable for the horses. The crack in Dancer's hoof might have time to grow out. She might have the chance to work for cash in her pocket. Money for good meals and new shoes for the little ones. A little savings to put by for a trip.

He was offering her so much. But saying nothing about himself, about how hard this would be for him. That meant staying was not the right answer, either. Yet it was best for her children. She thought of James and the unspoken sadness in his eyes at having to leave another house. She thought of Daisy, too little to understand, but needing security and comfort all the same. Joanna thought of how hard she had wished for just one chance to improve her life. This was certainly a chance she had to take.

Then she studied the man in front of her. His eyes were dark and bleak. His presence like stone, cold and remote.

"How can I say yes?" she said into the silence that had grown between them. "My being here upsets you."

"I know." His hands curled into fists. "But I have my sense of duty."

"You pity me. That's not reason enough." Everything within her longed to stay. To repay him for his kindness at giving them lodging and supper. To have the chance to provide better for her children. But at what cost to him? "I saw you in the kitchen after we left you. I've never seen that kind of emotion."

His knuckles turned white as he clenched his fists. It was as if his sorrow began to bleed. "What I lost is in the past. Perhaps God has put you in my path to teach me."

"That sounds harsh." She hated to think that life—and God—were so brutal. That love lost was like love never felt. That hardships and loss were only meant to teach lessons. Maybe that was why she'd stopped hoping prayer could help her. Why she didn't believe God would.

Aiden shrugged one brawny shoulder. "What if I had been the one to die? What if I had left Kate widowed? I want to believe there would be someone out there man enough to help her and protect her. To make sure she and my boy would be safe and fed."

His words were like a knife to Joanna's heart. She blinked away the tears from her eyes, feeling pain take over. The poor man.

A muscle worked in his neck, perhaps his attempt at controlling his emotions. "Will you allow me to help you, Joanna?"

"I'll allow you to help my children." It took all her

dignity to keep her chin up. "I appreciate your offer, Aiden."

"Good." His fists loosened. "Your gelding needs care. The balm you're using is what most folks use, but I've got something better."

"I noticed that you had done something different to it. Thank you for that."

"It was no trouble. You'd best be leaving the gelding here, as you're staying. I'll be by after I'm done in the fields to help you unpack your wagon."

"I hate to trouble you, Aiden. I suppose you have fence work to do, and haying?" She said the last like a question.

"You were a farmer's wife."

"And a farmer's daughter. If you need an extra hand, I can drive horses, turn hay and I'm good at pitching."

"I never would have guessed that." He had his opinion about women working in the field—he had never wanted his wife to labor that hard—but Joanna spoke of her experience with a hint of pride. He had to admire a good work ethic.

"I have a certain knack with topping haystacks. I'd be happy to help. I have the children, but…" She stopped, leaving the question unasked.

He had his beliefs, but he wasn't about to deny her the chance to make her life right again. "I reckon we will figure something out. Perhaps my ma wouldn't mind keeping an eye on them. We'll see."

"That would be wonderful." Tension rolled off her. She smiled up at him, and in the dappled stripes of sunlight coming through the plank walls, she seemed transformed. Young and dainty and softly beautiful.

Aiden felt his throat tighten up with too many emotions—too much feeling for a man who'd lost his heart—and looked away. "Where are your children?"

"Playing in the yard by the wagon. I can see them…" She glanced through the slatted walls. "James is watching his sister."

Aiden managed to nod and to keep his eyes down on the straw at his boots. It was easy to hear the affection soften her voice. He figured love would do the same to her face. Best not to be noticing that. He took a step back. "Why don't you bring your children up to the house? There's a platter in the warmer for them."

"We ate."

Toasted bread, or oatmeal, was his guess. "Treat them to the food you fixed. There's plenty, and make sure you feed yourself, too. I mean that, Joanna. Then clean up the kitchen when you're done."

He winced inside at the sound of his hard tone. He didn't have much of a choice. He couldn't allow himself to soften toward her. He ignored the ache in the hollows of his chest and took the gelding by the rope.

He could feel her gaze searching his face as he turned to the horse, pretending she was already gone from the barn and on her way to follow his orders. But she wasn't. She stood in the aisle, her presence as sweet as morning light. He could feel the radiance of her smile, sweeter than spun sugar, before she turned and hurried away.

"Ma! Ma! Look at me!" Daisy sang out as she climbed a boulder at the edge of the field, her little blue dress snapping in the breeze. Sunshine glinted like gold in her hair as she followed her brother to the flat top of the large rock. "Look, Ma!"

"I'm looking, sweet girl." Joanna laughed as she hefted the crate off the wagon's tailgate. She had already put in a hard day in Aiden's kitchen, first cleaning up the breakfast dishes and then baking and cooking and cleaning up after that. Then there had been the shanty to scrub clean—it was surprisingly dusty, with a thick layer of dirt in the corners. Now there was the wagon to unload, and she wasn't about to wait for Aiden to come in from his work. He'd done more than enough for her already.

"Ma! I'm gonna jump!" Daisy crept to the edge of the rock, afraid but determined. She grasped her brother's shirtsleeve with fisted hands.

James looked burdened. "Ma! She's on my fort."

"I see that. You're a good boy to let her play with you."

James didn't say anything to that, but the look on his face was one of adorable resignation. He clutched a wooden horse, as if he'd been about to set up his horse corral on part of that boulder top.

Joanna carried the crate across the ripening grasses, keeping a watchful eye for Daisy's courageous jump. It was good to see them so happy. James had been such a good boy, watching his sister play with her doll by the shanty door all the while Joanna had been cleaning. Her son looked more secure as he leaned close to whisper something in his sister's ear. Daisy lit up with a huge smile and then bunched up before leaping off the rock. She landed on both feet, squealing.

"Ma! Did you see? I jumped!"

"I saw. That was the best jump I ever saw." Joanna loved knowing that her children would have the security of home. That for now, for a while, they could play in this field and jump from that rock like normal kids. They were no longer homeless. It hurt to accept Aiden's charity, but looking at her little ones, she had no other choice.

"Ma!" Daisy came racing through the grass, hardly visible, it was so high. "Watch. I'm gonna do it again. James! James! Are you gonna jump, too?"

James had that put-upon look again, but good boy that he was, he merely blew out a breath. "Yes, Daisy. Now, stand back."

Joanna stepped into the shanty's shadow and suddenly felt that she wasn't alone.

"That looks heavy. Let me get it." Aiden stepped into sight in his work clothes and heavy boots, dusted with bits of cut grass. He smelled sweet with it. "I thought I asked you to wait for me."

"I'm not so good at following orders, as my former husband learned to his great dissatisfaction."

"Did he now? I did not have the best success with my Kate." Aiden took the crate out of Joanna's hands. "Why don't we make a bargain? If you don't mind fetching me some cold well water, I'll empty out your wagon."

"You're trying to keep me busy and out of the way."

"I'm thirsty," he corrected, and it was hard to tell if he was unhappy with her or simply being his stoic, reserved self. "And I don't take to women doing heavy lifting. Next you'll be telling me you're capable. I don't doubt it. But a man ought to make a woman's load lighter, even if they're strangers to one another."

Joanna took a step back to study the man before her, damp with a hard day's sweat in high temperatures. He did look intimidating. But there was kindness on his face. It was an attractive combination. She shook her head. "You have some mighty strange notions, Aiden McKaslin, but I do happen to like them."

"What's mighty strange about them?"

He didn't seem to know, she marveled, wondering how on earth he could be real. But he was a flesh and blood man standing before her, of that there was no doubt. She headed for the shanty. "I'm used to men trying to get out of work, not stepping up to do it."

"I'm not afraid of a little hard work." He didn't crack a smile, but he sounded slightly amused, although it was hard to tell with his deep, wry baritone. "I see that you watered the garden, so I know you found the well."

"I did. Don't worry. I'll fetch your water."

"I had to wonder, since you were heading in the opposite direction from the well."

"To grab the water pail." She snatched the bucket from just inside the shanty door, and took off toward the main house. On the rising slope of land, she had a better view of her children. James had turned to watch her with careful, inquisitive eyes, just making sure. She hated that he worried so. One small change—her stepping away to fetch water—and he went from a carefree little boy to a burdened one. She lifted her hand in a wave to show him everything was fine. After a moment he went back to play, paying attention to Daisy, who tugged on his hand.

When Joanna knelt at the well to hook the bucket onto the end of the pulley, Aiden had emerged from the shanty, his arms empty of the crate. He was a big man, even from a distance. He had a long gait, steady and strong, and did not swing his arms when he walked but kept them at his sides. His wide-brimmed hat shaded his face as he hauled a straw tick from the wagon bed. He easily carried the awkward mattress, quickly disappearing into the house.

What I lost is in the past. Perhaps God has put you in my path to teach me. She could hear again his words and see again the look of desolation on his face. She ached for him. He'd shown her kindness when she had been sure there was no more of it left in the world. He was a good man, and in her experience, those were rare. She intended to do the best possible job for him. She was going to work harder than she ever had. He deserved nothing less.

"Ma!" Daisy ran ahead of James, who had come close to watch the unloading of the wagon. "Can I have a drink of water, too, please?"

It was impossible to look into those pretty eyes and say no. Joanna unhooked the bucket of crystal-clear water and held the full dipper for her daughter. Smelling of fresh grass and sunshine, Daisy leaned close and sipped daintily. Joanna smoothed the fine tangle of platinum hair that had escaped from her daughter's twin braids. It would need a good brushing later.

A movement blurred at the edges of her vision. It was Aiden reappearing from the shanty, bringing the shadows with him. He cut a dark figure across the lush green prairie. His wide hat shaded his face, but she could feel his gaze on her like the tangible rays of the sun.

"Come on, baby." Daisy was done, so Joanna took

the dipper and dropped it into the bucket. "Let's take this to Mr. McKaslin."

"Okay." Her daughter bobbed to her feet and skipped through the tall grasses. Her happy gait lifted Joanna's heart another notch.

Aiden had already hefted the second straw tick from the wagon box and was halfway to the shanty. This time James trailed after him and hesitated on the front step, peering in. Joanna set the small pail on the open tailgate. "James? Don't pester Mr. McKaslin, honey."

"But I gotta thank him for the bacon!" Earnestly, the little boy planted both dusty feet.

"No need, little man." Aiden filled the shaded doorway.

James hopped back, his head tilted to gaze up at the tall man. "I can help. I'm real strong."

"I see that."

Aiden's tone might be gentle, but she could see his white-knuckled fists and the cords tight in his throat as he marched back to the wagon. She didn't get the feeling that he disliked children—no, not that. She thought of what he'd told her, and wondered if her children were a reminder, too. Her spirit ached for him, and she laid a hand on Daisy's little shoulder, pulling her close to her skirts.

"James," she said softly. "Keep out of Mr. McKaslin's way."

"But I'm helpin'." James proudly climbed into the wagon box.

"James." She loved him for his good heart, but the last thing she wanted to do was cause Aiden more pain.

"It's all right, Joanna." He swept off his hat, stopping to take a long cold drink. "Thank you kindly, for I've been thirsty. I see you already carried in what you could. I'll finish up bringing in the furniture, if you want to help yourself to my kitchen and start on dinner. Finn and I will be in the field until dark. If you don't mind, if you could bring our meals out to us."

"And water, too," she said with a nod.

"That would be greatly appreciated, ma'am." He dropped the dipper back into the bucket and the hat onto his head. He had a fair piece of work ahead of him if he wanted the last of the south field cut before the Sabbath. "I'd best get crackin'."

"Come help me in the kitchen, James." Joanna held out her hand. The boy gave a sigh but did as he was told, and followed his ma and sister through the whispering grasses.

This wasn't going to be an easy thing, having her here. Aiden steeled himself and held his feelings still. This was going to be tough on him. He'd learned that the right thing rarely was the easy thing. God was surely handing him a challenge when he'd put Joanna Nelson in his path.

I hope I don't let you down, Lord. Aiden slung a wooden rocking chair over his shoulder, rockers skyward, and lumbered back to the shanty.

Already she had changed it. He set the chair down by the window. There was something different about a house with a woman in it. It smelled pretty, looked tidy, felt peaceful. The old tick on the bed was made up as neat as a pin with a colorful ringed quilt. A tiny crate of blue dishes sat on the floor next to the table. A towel embroidered with roses at the hem hung on the bar next to the water basin.

The sound of children's laughter drifted on the wind. Why that picked his spirits up, he couldn't quite say. He stacked Joanna's straw ticks and laid them flat next to the bed. She would be more comfortable with the second mattress between her and the hard dirt floor.

The shanty wasn't much, but it had housed his family just fine when he was a boy. The roof needed a bit of work, he thought as he stepped outside, but he would get to it before the next heavy rain. As he hiked up the rise, he caught sight of the children running in the grass outside the main house's back door. The little girl gave a musical giggle and the boy let out a whoop as he carried his wooden horse high.

Aiden tried not to think of the son he'd buried. The little boy he had never gotten to know. He swallowed his emotions, skirted the house and cut behind the barn. The sounds of the children seemed to follow him, those carefree, innocent sounds, teasing at the lost places within him.

What was he going to tell his family? They were bound to find out come church tomorrow. This was only the start of speculation, he knew. His ma and middle brother, Thad, thought he ought to get married again. His mother would especially start quoting Scripture on the subject. Now, he wasn't objecting to the Scripture as much as to his ma getting her hopes up. Ever since Thad and his wife, Noelle, had gotten married earlier in the year, she had hopes for grandchildren again.

Hopes Aiden could never see clear to fulfilling. Love could put softness into a man's life, and that was nice.

Real nice. But it left him wide-open and vulnerable, without a single defense. He'd been broken clear to the quick. There had been no way to prevent it. When Kate and his son died, it had cost him too much. There was no color in Aiden's world, no gentleness, no music. There would never be again. His ma wouldn't understand, nor Thad, either.

But perhaps Joanna did.

If he glanced over his shoulder, he could see the kitchen windows clearly. Sun streamed into the room, backlighting the woman there. She was searching through the cabinets for something...she went up on tiptoe and brought down a large mixing bowl.

He could not say why he lingered to watch her as she set the bowl on the counter. Her long skirt swished around her ankles as she headed to the pantry. She stopped by the door, disappearing from his sight, perhaps to check on the children. Sure enough, both the girl and boy stopped playing and called out to her in reassurance that they were staying close by, before she swept back into his sight with a small sack of sugar.

He could not say when it happened. He only knew the sunshine felt warmer on his face and the hollow where his heart used to be felt less cold.

Work was waiting, so he turned and headed back to the south field.

Chapter Six

It was a beautiful morning, Joanna decided as she wiped the last ironstone plate dry and stowed it on the shelf. She laid the dish towel over the top rung of the ladder-back chair and carried the washbasin to the doorway.

The children were playing outside in the sun. Their innocent laughter brought joy to her heart. They were her greatest blessings. The best things that had ever happened to her. Since it was Sunday, it was a good day to make a list of her blessings. It had once been a short list, but now it was much longer. Because of Aiden.

She sent a sparkling arc of water flying into the brilliant sunshine beside the path to the door. There was Aiden McKaslin driving a wagon behind his matched set of black Clydesdales. He was dressed in his Sunday best, a tan hat, a blue shirt and tan trousers. He was a fine-looking man.

He reined the horses in and studied her a moment from the high seat, his gaze stony.

She felt plain in her best sprigged calico and with

her braids pinned up in a simple coil. "Mr. McKaslin. I was just about to come find you."

"Guess I saved you the trouble." The brim of his hat shaded his face, and so his expression remained a mystery. "I wasn't sure, but I thought you were a church-going woman. Wanted to ask if you and your children wanted a ride in to town."

A ride? With him? She gripped the ironware basin so hard the rim bit into her fingers. In the background, her children had stopped playing, to watch the man with guarded interest. "We planned on walking."

"That's a mighty long distance for your wee one."

"I was going to carry her."

"Carry her? That's a far way." His jaw snapped shut and tension bunched in the corners. He looked out at the prairie stretching off toward the mountains, toward town. "I know you want to save your horse's hoof. I suppose the other one doesn't drive well alone?"

"That's right." Joanna wondered what was troubling him. "I did not accept your offer to cause you more trouble, Mr. McKaslin. I can see what you're about to ask. I know you feel your Christian duty deeply, and I respect you for it, but not if it causes you pain. I'm not here to bring you more trouble."

His midnight-blue eyes snapped to her, studying her bare head—she'd not put on her bonnet yet—and her feet peeping out from beneath her skirt ruffle. Again, she felt oddly plain, and that made no sense. She knew she'd always been a plain woman. But now watching Aiden up on that high seat, looking handsome and powerful with that backdrop of rich blue sky and pure white clouds, her breath hitched in her chest a tad. Soft feelings—kind feelings—rushed into her heart for this man.

"I don't mind a little trouble, Joanna." Aiden knuckled back his hat.

She remembered the image of him in the kitchen with his hands to his face. Surely the feelings swirling to life within her were deep admiration and respect for him. Surely that was all and nothing more.

"As I'm already here and we're both going the same way, you may as well come along. Is that all right with you?" He leaned forward in the seat, his gaze on hers, his strong frame tensed.

Realizing she had been staring at him for too long, she blushed and ripped her eyes away. She glanced down at the basin she was gripping with white-knuckled fingers. "Y-yes. It would be better for the children."

"Fine, then." He leaned back against the seat and crossed his ankles, as if setting in for a pleasant wait.

I've never met a man like him before. Her eyes found him like sunlight found the earth. The feelings within her sweetened. Surely it was impossible not to admire him. There was nothing wrong with a little admiration for the man who had done so much for them, right?

Right. She whirled around and hurried into the shade of the shanty. Every step she took, she remained aware of Aiden high up on his wagon seat behind her. She thought of his brother, who usually accompanied him to town. Where was Finn? Had she caused trouble between them? Worry curled in her stomach as she buttoned up her shoes. And what were folks in town going to think when she walked into the church vestibule with him?

People were bound to talk; it was simply human nature. And without a doubt, that talk, that speculation, would hurt Aiden. As if a man who had loved and lost as deeply as he had could simply start courting again. No one in his or her right senses would ever mistake his sense of kindness for romantic interest.

Joanna set the sunbonnet on her head and tied the ribbons beneath her chin, glancing in the small mirror. She was too thin, too peaked, too ordinary. No man was going to love her. She'd learned that the hard way.

"Ready?" Aiden called from the wagon seat.

"Yes." She closed the shanty door, turning to call for the children, but they were already close, standing at the edge of the grass with quiet, solemn expressions. Bits of grass clung to Daisy's pink gingham skirt, and dust streaked James's cheek, but they still looked presentable.

She held out her hands. "Isn't this a treat? We get a ride to church."

Daisy galloped forward and grabbed her mother's fingers. James looked up wistfully at Aiden and took her other hand. She was surprised to hear the seat springs squeak faintly. Aiden's shadow fell across her as he descended. She felt a shiver at his closeness, for he brought the shadows with him.

"Let me help them up." He spoke to her, not the children. He lifted Daisy into the back, where two board seats had been carefully anchored, and then James.

Such thoughtfulness. He took care with them. Joanna felt the wedge of gratitude take a bigger piece of her soul.

"Your turn." Aiden held out his hand, palm up. "I reckon you want to sit with your kids?"

"Yes." She felt like a lady at his kindness. She reached out to place her hand in his. Her fingertips grazed his palm, and it was like touching winter's frozen ground. Sympathy filled her as he helped her up over the board side of the wagon. Her shoes thudded on the wooden box and her skirts swirled around her ankles, but she was only aware of Aiden's lost heart.

He released her hand without a word and turned his back, as if he were unaware of the moment. The lark song came again to her ears and the blinding glare of sunlight to her eyes, and yet still she felt cold as she settled with the children onto one of the seats.

He's without hope, she realized. She knew that place of darkness. It was like being in a blizzard, pummeled by the wind and battered by the ice-sharp snow, unable to see. Perhaps that was why her soul recognized his.

Looking at him, you would not know it. Her gaze caressed the strong straight lines of his shoulders and back, the determined set of his hat and the purposeful way he held the reins. The wagon bounced and jostled through the grass, perhaps following a road that once had been there, to the main driveway, where wild rabbits darted out of sight and gophers popped up out of their holes to watch the travelers rolling by.

Joanna thought she heard something in the whisper of the wind, like a voice just out of reach. The sunshine blazed, the seed-topped grasses stretched like a long ocean of green around them and the music of the birds filled the morning like the sweetest hymn. She knew, impossibly, that Aiden needed far more help than she did.

* * *

Aiden halted the horses along the tree-shaded town street, hardly having the room in his thoughts to be glad for the handy parking spot because he felt the weight of so many eyes. He felt the curious looks as surely as he did the hot wind puffing at the back of his neck. This wasn't the first time he'd been a source of speculation. He gritted his teeth, told himself he didn't much care and set the brake.

"Those are mighty good horses you got."

The little boy was standing right behind him, chest up, hands fisted. Aiden swallowed hard, forcing himself to answer. "Clyde and Dale are getting along in years, but right you are. They're good horses."

"Clydesdales." The little boy's serious eyes lit up with excitement. "My pa used to have one once, but we had to sell him."

Little boys liked horses, Aiden told himself as he knotted up the reins. That was all it was. No need to look at the fatherless boy. No need to think the lad was needing something in return.

"James, come." Joanna laid her hand on her son's shoulder, speaking in that soft way of hers. "Goodness, you're as windblown as a tumbleweed. I can't have you going into church like this."

Aiden swung down, not wanting to see the motherly way she dug a comb out of her reticule and smoothed down the boy's hair. Nor did he want to see the snap of her skirts in the breeze, or the way she smiled as she worked, or the love on her face making her beautiful.

He swiped his hand down Clyde's neck, concentrating on the horses. Over the angled line of their manes he could see a buggy roll to a stop and the delight on his ma's face as she hopped to the ground, hoopskirts swaying. Delight. That hit him deep. Yep, this was going just as he figured. His ma, wearing a grin twice as big as the Montana sky, was hurrying across the street.

"Aiden!" Ida McKaslin had had a hard life, and the worry and a lifetime of troubles had etched deep into her face, but she was still lovely. Smiling, she raised her arms and pressed her hands to the sides of his face. "Look at you. I can't get over how much I miss seeing you every day."

Aiden's chest knotted up with failure, with emotion he could not let himself feel. "Ma, you look as if Thad and his wife are treating you well."

"They are spoiling me. That's never good for a soul, but I am not about to complain. I'm settling into my new little house just fine." His mother looked to be bursting with the next question. "Introduce me to your lady friend."

Yes, of course that's what his sweet ma thought. No amount of explanation would talk her out of it, either. He might as well face the music. "Joanna has come upon hard times and she and her kids are staying in the shanty for a spell."

"I see." Ma's eyes lit up even brighter. Judging by the look of her, she didn't understand at all.

"Oh, no, Mrs. McKaslin." Joanna came to his rescue. "I'm not his, well, his friend. It's a business arrangement. I'm working in exchange for rent."

"Can't be much rent he's charging you. Or he'd best not be. You are being fair to her, aren't you, Aiden?"

He rolled his eyes. "Yes. Ma, does Thad know you ran off? He's probably looking for you."

"Joanna." Ma was hardly paying him any mind. She was setting her sights on Joanna. Probably measuring her up as future daughter-in-law material. "Your last name is Nelson, isn't it? I've seen you around, but I don't think we've ever been introduced. Your father, rest his soul, was never on speaking terms with our family."

"I understand that half of Angel County was not on speaking terms with my pa." Joanna, with a child in each hand, smiled kindly toward the fragile older woman. "It's mighty nice to meet you, ma'am. You have a fine son in Aiden. You must be very proud of him."

"I surely am not." Her twinkling eyes said otherwise. "I am about to take him to task for not telling me all about you before this."

"I'm only here for a short time, then I'll be moving along." Joanna shot him a look as if to say, *I'm trying to make her understand.*

"Don't worry, Joanna. My ma is a hopeless case. She's overly optimistic, and it's my opinion that is not good for a person." He gave his mother a severe look, but it apparently bounced right off of her.

"Come, Joanna." Ma reached right past him as if he didn't exist. "Your little family must join ours. Aiden, I take it Finn will be along?"

"That's my understanding." He watched, helpless to stop it, as his mother drew Joanna into a quick embrace, and fell in stride with her and her children. They were talking about the little ones. The boy smiled up at her. The girl skipped at Ma's side.

"She's already wondering if one day they will be her grandchildren," a voice quipped behind him.

Aiden didn't need to look over his shoulder to know his brother wore that irritating know-it-all grin. "You aren't helping matters, Thad. You broke down and got married, and now Ma will think I'm likely to be next. Good day, Noelle."

"Hello, Aiden." Thad's pretty new bride clung to his arm, as lovely as could be. Her emerald eyes sparkled up at him with happiness, although she could not see him, as she was blind. "I'm eager to meet your new lady friend. I would like to invite her to join my sewing circle."

"I'm not courting her." He had to make that clear. They were just a few paces ahead now. The wide brim of Joanna's sunbonnet hid most of her face from him, but he could see the delicate angle of her jaw, and the corner of her mouth was drawn up in a smile.

She was being kind to his mother. His chest muscles twinged and his knees felt a little watery. Maybe it was gratitude. He was even more grateful when the wind carried a snippet of Joanna's voice. "No, ma'am, I am not sweet on your son."

"Well, you might not see it, dear, but I can." Ma sounded pleased.

Yes, he thought, it was just as he feared. "Ma, do go easy on Joanna. A pretty woman like her isn't looking to get tied down with a dour old man like me."

"That's exactly right." Joanna's tone was very serious.

He couldn't say why that gave him a pang, seeing as the last thing he wanted was a woman's affections. He

drew himself up, ignored the smarting of his pride—
at least he wanted to believe it was his pride hurting
him. Then she glanced over her shoulder at him, and
her soft smile said more than words and simple assurances could.

He wished he could thank her. He wished he knew
how to express what was fighting to life within him.
But they were hardly alone, and as they approached the
front steps, even more people were around. Besides, if
he reached out to her, it would take him one step closer
to her, the last place he wanted to be.

That didn't mean he wasn't grateful to her.

At the bottom of the steps, Joanna turned to him.
"I'm sorry, Aiden. I'm doing my best."

"Not to worry. I fear it's a lost cause."

She smiled up at him, with both children in hand. For
a moment, the sunlight framed her with gentle golden
light, burnishing her blond hair and lighting her up, as if
from within. Air caught in his lungs. Stunned, he could
only stare at her, lost in her smile. In that instant, the
pain of the hopelessness inside him eased.

Joanna turned away and followed the line of church-
goers into the building. She swished forward with a
twist of her skirts, her children quiet and wide-eyed
at her side. Aiden's feet felt rooted to the earth as he
watched her disappear into the serene shadows of the
church. She seemed to take the sunshine with her.

Aiden was a genuine blessing in disguise. Joanna
could see him at the end of the pew, on the other side
of his sister-in-law, faithfully singing the closing hymn.

He seemed like a hard man, standing so straight and severe, brooding with a keep-away look.

But she saw a different man now. Because of him, she had a little more faith in humanity than she'd had a few days ago. That had made it easier to sit through the service and feel included in the minister's sermon. God had felt so far away for so long. He still did. But she no longer felt alone.

The hymn ended. The service was over. James took her hand solemnly, his gaze fastened not on her, but on the tall man at the end of the row.

"Ma." Daisy clung to her skirts. "I'm awful thirsty."

"Me, too, baby. We'll get you some water before we start home." She lifted her daughter into her arms and tugged Daisy's little sunbonnet back into place. She needed to get a hat for James. She smoothed his hair absently as she inched down the row, where Aiden stood like a sentry, waiting for her.

He was as severe as ever, but his eyes warmed when she came closer. "Ma has invited all of us to Sunday dinner. Including you. Will you come?"

"I suppose so, seeing as how you have the horse and wagon."

"Then you're at my mercy."

"Yes. That has not been a hardship." She wasn't certain, but thought he almost smiled. He waited for her to step into the aisle before he followed her. With every step she took, there he was, at her back. She could feel the faint flutter of his breath against her nape and his significant presence like a shadow.

"Who is that woman with Aiden McKaslin?" A sharp

whisper cut through the rustle and muttered conversations of the other worshippers heading for the exit.

She heard nothing more, but her face heated. Had Aiden heard? She could not tell. His step didn't falter. He remained silent, as if nothing had happened. She knew without asking him that the last time he'd brought a young woman with him to church, it had been his wife.

"If he's looking for a woman, he could do much better than her." The whisper was louder this time, sharper.

He had to have heard that. Joanna winced. Her face burned. She was glad that her children could not understand. She wanted to turn around and tell whoever was speaking the truth, but perhaps that would make a bigger scene. Already the line was moving on. She could only hope the rest of the McKaslin family, who were in front of her in the aisle, had not heard. She glanced down at her plain dress, patched discreetly in places, and at her son and daughter, who were good and sweet, and told herself it didn't matter what others thought.

Aiden's hand settled on her shoulder and stayed there. What a comfort to have him behind her, his unspoken act unmistakable. She swallowed hard against the emotion balling up hot and thick in her throat.

Yes, Aiden McKaslin was a fine man. Far too fine a man for a plain woman like her, but that didn't stop her from admiring him. It was the sudden glare of the sun that had her blinking hard as she followed Ida down the steps and into the churchyard—nothing more.

"I'll get the children water," Aiden said before he withdrew from her, leaving her alone.

She had no time to thank him or to go with him. She

glanced behind her to see a young woman in a lovely blue dress and fashionable hoops, with her hair done up in stylish ringlets, watching her through narrowed eyes. The whisperer, no doubt. Joanna lifted her chin. She had nothing to be ashamed of. She watched as the woman in blue sauntered past with a dismissive look.

"I heard Aiden invite you to supper." Ida turned to Joanna, after chatting with Noelle and Thad. "I'm so pleased you and your children will be joining us."

"It's kind of you to have us." She kept James at her side and Daisy on her hip, waiting for Aiden to return. The church crowd was thinning as people hurried home. She spotted him approaching holding a big dipper, which he handed to her.

"Sorry, there was a line." He said nothing more, but waited, staring off down the road, while the children each took a turn sipping from the cold, fresh well water.

"I'll take it back. You go on ahead to the wagon. Get the kids out of the sun. I'll be along in a few shakes. Don't drive off without me."

"Maybe I will. Maybe not. You'll just have to find out."

"What?" He couldn't have heard her right. Perhaps it was the hustle of other folk around him in the churchyard or the noise of the road traffic. He saw amusement melting the strain on her pretty face. Was she joking with him? Well, he could kid, too. "Sure. Horse stealing is still a hanging offense in this part of the country. I'd be careful if I were you, ma'am."

"Oh, I'm not worried one bit. Your bark is worse than your bite, Aiden McKaslin. I *might* stop the wagon for you. I might not. It depends."

"On what?"

"How fast you can run after us." She turned with a flick of her skirts.

A chuckle rolled through him. Who would have thought the serious widow could make a man like him laugh? He shook his head, watching her walk away. There was something stunning about her, but he couldn't put his thumb on it.

The dress she wore was simply cut and sewn, without anything more than a modest ruffle at the hem, and none of the hoops and frills and lacy things females added to fancy up their dresses. Joanna was enough without all that. Her walk was a sensible, no-nonsense gait that was still feminine and dainty. With a child on her either side, she could not be mistaken for a captivating woman.

Yet she drew him all the same. How about that? He spun on his heels and marched back to the well. Only a few people remained gathered in the yard, and he nodded a greeting to the minister, who was in a deep discussion with a man in a dark shirt and trousers. That was his new neighbor, Aiden realized as he dropped the dipper into the pail with a splash. He didn't know them like he should, but he gave another nod as he went past the minister and Franklin—that was the man's surname.

Joanna. He couldn't get over her quip, if it had been a quip. He might not know her well, but he had a suspicion she had been half-serious. He strained to look around the copse of cottonwoods and up the road. There she was, graceful and wholesome in her red calico, as she held a water bucket for Clyde. She made a pretty picture standing willow straight, chatting first with the horses and then with her kids, who sat safely inside the wagon.

"Aiden!" someone called out. Footfalls padded behind him.

The minister. Aiden came to a halt, noting the man's urgency. Oh, this was about Finn. "My brother missed church, unless he came and I didn't see him."

"No, Aiden. I didn't see him, either." Pastor Hadly seemed very grave. Concern was etched into his grandfatherly face, but it was his eyes, full of sadness, that startled Aiden.

"You know something about my brother." He hated saying those words. Once, he had been protective of his littlest brother, and defensive, insisting that Finn would grow out of his rebelliousness. That the boy was simply spirited.

But manhood had not mellowed Finn or put sense in his head. Not even the second chance Aiden was giving the boy. Finn was going to find himself back in the territorial prison if he didn't smarten up. Aiden braced himself for whatever hard news the minister had brought. "Do you know where Finn is?"

"No, I don't. This is about you, Aiden."

"Me?" Not again. Now and then the kindly minister felt he had to offer help. Some folks saw Aiden's self-imposed isolation as grief. No, grief had come and gone. It was what was left in its wake that was the problem, and what could be the solution for that? Aiden turned away. There was Joanna, holding the bucket for Dale. Dependable, that's what she was. A reasonable, sensible woman who knew what mattered. "Now's not the time, Pastor. Sorry."

"There is a season for everything, Aiden. Come stand in the shade and speak with me."

"Finn is heading down a path that will lead him straight to trouble, and I can't stop him. I can only pray that you can."

"I'll speak to Finn, don't you fear." Pastor Hadly took refuge from the blazing sun in the shade of the trees, and his expression grew grave. "What is this I hear of a woman living with you?"

"With me?" That was like a slap on his face. He recoiled and shook his head. Was that what people were thinking? And didn't they have anything better to do than talk? "No, I assure you that is not true. Joanna Nelson had no place to go. She was living in her wagon in my back fields, so I offered her the shanty."

"But the shanty is on your land. Rather close to your house, as I remember it."

"A couple acres away, I guess. Far enough to make us neighbors not sharing the same house. *This* is what you want to talk to me about?" Anger beat at him. He wasn't mad at Hadly; the man was just doing what he saw as his duty. "Joanna is a widow with two small children. I'm not the sort of man who takes advantage of that."

"Easy, now. I'm only saying the look of it isn't right."

"I don't care about the look of things."

"Aiden, I'm telling you this for your own good. Maybe there is no need for concern yet, but temptation being what it is—"

"Perhaps for some people, but not for me." He rubbed the back of his neck, turning to watch Joanna replace the bucket in the watering trough up the road. He tamped down his anger, knowing the minister had a fatherly concern for him. Always had. "You of all people should know how strong my faith is, Mel."

"I do. Kate's death and your son's loss strengthened your faith. There aren't many who can say that."

Heat built in his chest, but it was no longer anger. Aiden drew in air to try to chase it away, but it remained hard and hot like a fist. He turned his back to the minister, fighting for control of emotions best left unfelt. Joanna had climbed up into the wagon box, tender with her children, who were talking rapidly and vying for her affection.

She really was a beautiful woman. Maybe more beautiful for the love he saw on her face as she gazed at her little ones.

The pieces inside him felt raw-edged and throbbed like a broken bone unable to heal. Yes, he had to believe that this was all part of God's plan. That he'd done right in having Joanna stay. That this wasn't the start of one big mistake. He'd had enough heartache in his life. He wasn't looking for more.

"If anyone questions my integrity, Pastor, then you point 'em to me." Aiden meant it; his soul resonated with the words. "The day that helping a fellow Christian down on her luck is wrong because of how it looks to some people, well, that is a sad day for heaven."

"Aiden, I have Joanna's concern at heart, too—"

"Sure. I know." He was already walking away, wondering how many people knew she'd been living with her children out of the back of her wagon. Wondering how many of those who knew had not offered help of any kind, not a handout, not a meal, not a job, not even kindness.

He was halfway to the wagon before he realized he'd stalked away from his minister, who was a good man. Suddenly, there was Joanna, her laughter, light and sweet, falling around him like dappled sunshine. A hot breeze puffed through the trees, and he'd never seen a sky as blue.

"It was tempting to leave you behind," she told him as he hiked himself up onto the high seat. "But I've developed a surprising respect for you, so I didn't want to make you walk all the way to dinner in this heat."

As if she would have stolen his horses. He smiled, really smiled. "That was mighty kind of you, considering I don't believe you one whit."

"Yes, but it made you smile. You looked unhappy, Aiden. I just thought…" She shrugged a slim shoulder, looking like pure goodness itself with the sun kissing her and the breeze tangling the delicate tendrils of her perfectly gold hair.

He did not know what it was about her, but he felt more like himself than he had in a long while.

He unknotted the reins and released the brake. The horses plodded to life, drawing them past the church, where Pastor Hadly stood, watching with grave eyes.

Chapter Seven

Noelle's kitchen was bright and sunny. The windows and doors were open to the breeze off the falls and displayed a view of the wild mustang herd in the far pasture. It was the perfect place to whip together the ingredients for a pie. Even more perfect to get better acquainted with Aiden's ma and sister-in-law.

"My mother's rule," Joanna explained as she brushed milk over the top crust. "I've never tasted a better strawberry pie. I always sprinkle sugar and cinnamon on it, too. You wouldn't happen to have fresh cream in the cellar, would you?"

Noelle, seated at the table, smiled. Her fingers were busy crocheting a delicate lace tablecloth. She was a beautiful lady with bright green eyes and a cheerful manner. "I'm sure we do. You have my mouth watering, Joanna, and the pie isn't even in the oven. Which reminds me, Ida, what about the roast?"

"We have a few more minutes to go, but it smells done, doesn't it?" Ida wandered over to peek in the oven.

"It's nearly there. I think the men are hungry. Look at them, Joanna."

Joanna finished sprinkling the cinnamon and set the pie on the counter, ready to go in when the roast came out. The window framed Aiden and Thad as they talked together, standing side by side, hats shading their faces, their wide shoulders braced. You could tell they were brothers. Aiden was slightly taller, brawnier and more mature looking. But they shared the same posture, the same rugged, strong jaw and chiseled cheekbones. "They keep looking at the kitchen door, waiting to be called in."

"Talking about horses, no doubt." Noelle's needle paused as she stopped to count the tiny stitches with her sensitive fingers. "And trying to avoid talking about Finn."

"They *are* men, and that's what men tend to do." Fondness warmed Ida's voice. There was no mistaking her motherly love as she gazed on her two oldest sons. "They don't talk much about what matters, but that doesn't mean they can't feel it. Finn has a powerful temper on him. He was a good little boy, always polite and quiet. He never got over his pa's death."

Joanna found herself listening harder. Her hands stilled as she tidied up the workplace at the table. How had his father's death affected Aiden? she wondered, but hesitated to ask.

"That was a hard time for us," Ida said as she checked one of the pots boiling on the stove. "We were mortgaged up to our chins. There were even loans on the horses. We had five poor years of crops, followed by a complete drought one summer. We didn't have a single crop that year. My, that hurt. We were lucky to keep the garden alive and producing, and it was sparse at best."

"My last year on our farm, my husband's land," Joanna explained, "was like that. In Dakota Territory. It was a struggle just to scrape enough off the land to survive the winter."

"Then you know how it was for us." Ida set the pot lid into place. "Noelle, you were a schoolgirl at the time, living in town. I'm sure the weather brought no trouble to your family, and I'm grateful for that. But my man took off that autumn. Finn was too young to know. Thad only thirteen. Aiden was a big, strapping young man. I had hopes of him finishing up and graduating from the school in town. I wanted him to have a real fine education. He had the mind for it."

"I can see that," Joanna found herself saying.

"It was a sadness that he had to find a job instead. He has been working winters at that mill up north since he was sixteen, and growing wheat the rest of the year."

"He has a winter job, too?"

"Yes, dear. Didn't you know?"

She shook her head, her mind spinning. She could see clearly how Aiden had stepped up to take on the burden of his family. It did not surprise her. As she piled the measuring spoons and cups, the wooden spoon and knife into the mixing bowl for washing, she could see what had made Aiden the man he was. His mother's gentle love, his sense of duty and his faith, which kept him strong even in hard times.

She wished she could say the same about her belief.

"My Aiden worked long hours six days a week. We had fuel and food enough through the winter, thanks to him." Ida gave a soft sigh, a sound of love and gratitude. "He and Thad worked beside me in the fields come spring, and we drew in a crop that harvest. It took all of us working, but Aiden made the difference. He is a good man, Joanna."

Oh, the point of the conversation. She carried the bowl to the counter. "You don't need to convince me, Ida. My opinion of Aiden is already sky-high."

"He's a rare one, just like my Thad." Noelle chimed in, rising from her chair, using her fingertips to guide her along the table's edge. "Aiden tells me you are available for hiring. Is this true?"

"Yes. I sound too eager. I'm sorry." Joanna's knees had turned watery and she leaned on the counter to steady herself. Work. She had stopped praying long ago for a job. A woman could get her hopes only so high before she realized they would just come crashing to the ground. And yet here it was, the hope she had been afraid to feel. "What kind of work?"

"Didn't Aiden tell you? Oh, isn't that just like a man." Friendly and so wonderfully gentle, Noelle came over to the counter as if she saw just fine. "I have been looking for someone to clean and do laundry for me. Maybe help Ida out in the garden, since I am a hopeless gardener, not being able to see one plant from another."

"That makes it very hard to garden, dear." Ida's merriment was lovingly meant. "I think Joanna would be just right for us. I would be happy to keep an eye on your children. What treasures they are."

"I would love that." She had a job. Her worries about her children's care were solved. Their future had changed. Just like that.

Thank-you seemed too small of a word for what Noelle and Ida were offering her. Gratitude built within Joanna like a rising dam. This was because of Aiden. Because of him, she no longer felt alone.

"We're starving out here." Aiden filled the doorway, wry humor in his half grin. "How much longer is it going to be?"

"We're setting the table now," Noelle said cheerfully as she counted out dinner plates from her glass-fronted cabinets. "You go back outside, wash up and take the kids with you. You men may as well make yourselves useful."

"Yes, ma'am." Aiden saluted her, then his gaze swept right past her.

Joanna felt the impact of his eyes, but it was a welcome thing. Here, with his family, he seemed happier, as if a little more life had crept into him. As if the hopelessness he was drowning in had ebbed away for now. Her heart filled with admiration for him.

In truth, maybe it was a little more than admiration she felt for him. A smidgeon more than respect.

"I'll make sure the little ones are washed and ready for dinner," he told her over the kitchen noise, his gaze meeting hers and shrinking the distance between them.

Her pulse stopped; her world stilled. The sounds of Ida taking the roast out of the oven and the clink as Noelle set the table faded into silence. There was only the man tipping his hat to her, only Aiden, his dark blue eyes holding hers a moment too long.

It was like eternity. Like hope found. Her unprotected heart tumbled a notch. She gripped the counter more tightly, afraid her feelings showed on her face.

Afraid that he would look at her and know. Because she was certain now that this *was* more than plain admiration she had for him, more than simple respect.

"Ma!" Daisy squeezed past his knee and tumbled into the kitchen, breathless, with daisy petals clinging to her little pink pinafore. She held up her hands, full of wildflowers. "I got enough for a necklace!"

Aware of Aiden watching her, Joanna gulped hard and struggled to sound normal. "Come here, honey, and give them to me. It's time for dinner. We'll make your necklace after we eat."

She knelt, feeling Aiden's gaze like an unspoken question. She did not know what he was thinking, but whatever it was, the rare humor had faded from his face. His eyes were shielded, his mouth a hard, unyielding line. Her hands trembled as she collected Daisy's prize of picked flowers.

"Ma!" Her baby's eyes went wide. "Is that real butter for the potatoes?"

"Yes, sweetie." Real butter had been a rarity before and nonexistent lately.

"Goody." The little girl sparkled with excitement.

"Go with Mr. McKaslin and get washed up." Joanna swallowed down the lump in her throat. "Tell James, too."

"Okay." Good girl that she was, Daisy pranced off, shoes tapping on the wood floor, and raced out the open door.

Aiden was gone. He hadn't heard the butter comment. Joanna rose on her shaky knees, relieved that she didn't have to see that look of pity on his face or, worse, one of understanding. He knew what hardship was. Perhaps that was why she liked him so much. He understood that you could do your best, do everything right, and it could still go wrong. At least she didn't have to look at him and wonder what he'd read on her face.

"What a precious child," Noelle was saying. "And your little boy is adorable. I heard him pretending to round up wild horses outside the door. We should tell Thad. He and I have a new herd of mustangs that were captured on the prairie. Perhaps he would like to look at them, although they are not tame, I'm afraid. The stallion is very protective of his herd."

"I'm sure he would love seeing them. We have already met Sunny."

"Sunny is exceptional. He loves children. He's been Thad's horse for many years."

Joanna adored this woman—practically a stranger—for her kindness. She had forgotten there were such people in the world. She had forgotten what a difference kindness could make.

She would never let herself forget this moment, these people. Just as she would not forget what she saw when she looked out the open door: the image of Aiden watching over her children at the pump. He held the soap for them and handed James the towel. He was a caring man, despite his gruffness and distance.

Kindness was one thing she could give him. She circled around Ida and slipped the pie into the oven. She owed Aiden McKaslin more kindness than she could possibly repay, but that wasn't going to stop her from trying.

"She sure bakes a tasty pie," Thad said as he clipped the lead rope on his mustang's halter. Sunny, a palomino paint, tossed his head and looked over the fence rail at the little kids on the other side. The horse gave a snort as if scenting the air, trying to make up his mind about the children.

He was a gentle fellow. Aiden ran his hand down the mustang's neck. Thad was trying to get more information about Joanna. He was fishing around, suspecting more was going on than appeared at the surface, just as their mother did.

Frustrated, Aiden shook his head. "That's why I hired her. She makes the best biscuits I've ever tasted and her pancakes are better than Ma's. It took one bite to know I would be a fool if I didn't hire her."

"And she just happens to move into the shanty a stone's throw away from you." Thad tossed him a smile over the top of Sunny's mane. "That's mighty generous of you."

"She and her kids have been living out of their wagon since her pa died."

"Back in June?"

"Yep. Good thing it's summer. A few more months and then what would they have done?" Aiden opened the gate into the training corral he'd helped Thad build a few weeks before. "I know what you're thinking, and stop it. The minister has already let me know how this looks."

"What? I was only thinking I'm glad you found someone to cook for you. I was feeling mighty guilty taking Ma off your hands."

"Noelle needs her help, we both know that, and it's been good for Ma, too. You know how she likes to be needed." He glanced toward the small rise where the new house stood, windows open to the warm breezes. He searched until he found Joanna in the kitchen, washing dishes and handing them to Noelle to dry. She was talking away like women were wont to do.

Joanna seemed relaxed and happy, the exhaustion gone from her face, replaced by a healthy glow to her pretty complexion. She looked good—more than good. Funny what a handful of nights with worry-free sleep and plentiful meals, would do.

He was doing the right thing, whatever anyone else thought, even his trusted minister. Pastor Hadly had helped him get through his grief, but nothing—not even his stout faith—could begin to help Aiden cope with what had come after the grief. Life hadn't been the same. It would never be the same.

Not until this moment, watching the pretty woman as she hefted the dishpan and disappeared from the window, did he feel life calling to him once again. Like the murmur of the nearby waterfall, he could hear the whisper in his soul. It grew stronger when she appeared on the back porch, marched down the steps and tossed the dishwater far out into the grass. When she turned, she smiled at him.

He found himself smiling back.

I have Joanna's concern at heart, too. The minister's words came back to him, stirring the anger like a hard fist in his chest. Already people were talking. He should have considered this before he asked her to stay. What would be the consequences for her?

"Ma!" The boy's call rose on the wind, echoing on the vast prairie. "Look what I get to do! I get to ride a real mustang."

"Me, too, Ma!" the little girl shouted.

Aiden did his best not to look at them, so small and vulnerable, with no man to protect and provide for them. He closed off his feelings, knowing full well that he was a man prepared to protect and provide—with no wife and children to look after. It was hardly fair to either of them.

"Are you being trouble to Mr. McKaslin?" Joanna set the dishpan off to the side of the walkway and hiked through the knee-high grass. "Thad, you oughtn't to feel obliged to let them ride your horse."

"I don't mind, Joanna." Thad seemed to hold back a lot of amusement.

Aiden frowned. Sure, his brother might say he understood, but he was understanding the wrong thing. Now what was Aiden going to do? Even Thad believed he was sweet on the widow.

Aiden steeled himself as she swept closer. The sunlight seemed to find her and follow her, and she was pure golden goodness as she swept the little girl into her arms and onto her hip.

"You two be sure and do exactly what Mr. McKaslin says when you're up there on that horse." She straightened her daughter's flower necklace. "And remember to stay away from the wild horse pasture. And to thank Thad kindly when you're through."

"Yes, Ma." James climbed up onto the bottom rail, excitement vibrating off him. "I want to thank you right up front, Mr. McKaslin."

He was a sweet, sincere boy. Aiden had to look away.

It was Thad who answered. "You're welcome, little buddy. You know how to approach a horse?"

"Yes, sir. You stick out your hand."

"Yep, so he can scent you. That's how he learns who you are. That's right, but put your hand the other way. Palm up."

Not to be left out, the girl leaned in her mother's arms to stick her hand over the fence. She was a darling thing, a lot like her ma. Light haired and wide eyed with a button face. So little and trusting.

Aiden tried to glance away, but Joanna held him captive with the love on her face. A softness came over her as she watched her children. She was tenderhearted and a sensible woman, not pining after frills and frippery. Content with the simple necessities of life—a shanty roof over her head, food on the table, security for her young ones.

He hadn't known too many women who were like that. Joanna was a rare one. She'd certainly made his life more comfortable, maintaining a clean and polished house from top to bottom, true to her word. She brought cold water to the field straight from the well, a luxury for a man who did not like to put down his work. Her cooking was some of the best he'd tasted. The garden was thriving. All of that, and he hardly knew she was there. She was making her presence in his house as easy for him as she could. She understood how tough the situation was for him, when not many people seemed to. His family included.

"I'd best get back to help out." Joanna set her daughter on the grass. "Do you want to come with me, baby, or stay here?"

"I wanna ride the pony, too, Ma."

"It's all right, Joanna." Aiden found himself reassuring her as he took the halter rope from Thad. He'd let his brother lift the children onto the horse and steady them. He'd do better leading the horse. "Sunny is as trustworthy as could be."

"I trust you." Her smile was for him alone, quiet and gentle as her soul. "You hold on tight, James."

"I will, Ma." The little boy clung to the fence. "Can I come in, sir?"

Aiden glanced down at Joanna's son. "Sure."

The broken bits of him hurt as he nodded to the boy and noticed his eagerness and his earnestness. The kid ducked between two rails and landed with both feet on the ground. His shoes were patched in the toes, Aiden realized, carefully done to allow more room, which meant they were too small. Joanna had been making do on very little for far too long.

This was such a hard world, he thought, watching her wait while Thad lifted her son onto Sunny's back. Such a hard world. Perhaps he ought to do what he could to change that.

"Ma! Look! I'm on a real wild horse."

"I see," Joanna said as she backed in the direction of the house, surrounded by the deep green of the field and the dotted brilliance of wildflowers. "You look like a wrangler to me."

"Yep."

The little boy brimmed with excitement. He filled his fists with the mustang's white mane, listening to Thad as he told of how he'd found Sunny as a colt on the wild plains. Joanna's son was clearly awestruck. The little girl was swung up behind her brother.

Aiden looked away, quieting his feelings. Best not to think of what might have been.

"All right, our wranglers are mounted." Thad cut into his thoughts. "Aiden? You all right?"

"Sure." He almost believed it as he led the mustang forward. The boy gasped in delight; the little girl gave one excited shriek. Sunny calmly kept walking, quite aware, Aiden believed, of the value of what he carried on his back.

It was the sun making his eyes smart. He blinked hard and kept going. His gaze went to her, to Joanna, as she bent to lift the dishpan from the ground. With one last look in his direction, she spun with a flourish and skipped up the steps.

He could not know for sure, but he felt that she'd been watching him, just as he had been watching her.

Chapter Eight

"Are they asleep?"

Aiden's low question seemed to come out of the twilight. Joanna padded barefoot across the shanty's floor and stepped outside, drawing the door shut behind her. There he was, a shadow in the gathering darkness. She kept her voice at a whisper. "Their eyes were closed the second their heads touched the pillows. They haven't had such a nice day in a long while. I don't know how to thank you."

"No need. It was mainly Thad's doing."

"Yes, but your idea." She made her way toward him through the grass. The soft blades tickled her feet and rustled against the hem of her skirts. "James was so excited to have met a real wild horse that he couldn't stop talking."

"Yep, it was hard not to notice." Aiden's baritone rumbled with humor.

"Even as he was getting ready for bed. He fell asleep midsentence." It had been such a good day. She glanced back at the shanty, dark and quiet, where her treasures slept. "Daisy is in love with your ma. It was kind of Ida to sit on the porch and play dolls with her."

"You seemed to get on well with Noelle. I hear she hired you."

"Three afternoons a week. You don't know what this means to me. I'll have real wages, money for my children. Because of you."

"No. Because of *you*. If Noelle didn't like you and didn't feel comfortable with you, she wouldn't have hired you."

What was she going to do with this man? He could not accept a compliment. The twilight was giving way to night, taking the shadows with it. Darkness wrapped around them both, making it hard to see him. "Has your brother made it back home yet?"

"Not yet. I imagine he'll roll in sometime tonight. All I can do is apologize for him. Finn has a powerful weakness for whiskey."

"My husband did, too."

"Then you understand."

"More than you know. There's nothing you can do to stop him. It's painful to watch him destroy his life one swallow at a time, and it's impossible to make him see what he's doing."

"Yep. That about sums it up. It didn't work with my pa and it's not working with Finn." Aiden turned toward the east, where the first stars were struggling to life. "I'm at a loss. I know Finn's gonna do what he's determined to do, but I keep thinking I've got to stop him or at least slow him down some."

"You love him. You feel a duty toward him."

"I've been looking after him since our pa took off. It

wasn't a month later that he died. We don't talk about it much, but the truth is Pa died in a tavern brawl in a little no place town south of here. It's a shame to him. It's a shame to the family." He didn't know how to put it into words. "There's enough hardship in this life without making more for yourself on purpose."

"That's how it was with my husband, Tom." Her voice wavered. "I didn't know of his problem when we married. He hid it from me, and by the time I realized that he would never care for me the way he cared for his liquor, there was nothing but one problem after another."

"It's a hard way to live. I watched my ma go through it." Aiden could see how it had been for Joanna, too. Her hardships had begun long before he met her. "You were not happy in your marriage."

"No. I wanted to be, but life doesn't turn out the way you want it."

He thought of those two grave markers on the hill and gave thanks for the night that hid them. Somewhere a coyote howled, and the forlorn sound echoed across the prairie. "No. Life never turns out the way you want it. It is not our lives, but God's for us."

"How do you keep your faith with all that's happened to you?"

"I guess the question is, what kind of faith would it be if I could not? Real faith isn't something you put on and take off like a boot."

"No, I suppose not."

Silence settled between them. Night had come to the high plains. The vast sky stretched out over them, rich with thousands of diamond-white stars. Starlight dusted the crests of the prairie rises and the glacial peaks of the Rocky Mountains. An owl glided on silent wings in front of them. Aiden tried to draw the peacefulness into himself, but no luck. The tight coil remained knotted up in his chest.

There were questions he had to ask. Things he had to say. Putting them off wasn't going to get the answers he needed. "How long ago did your husband die?"

"It was more than a year and a half ago that Tom finished a bottle of whiskey at the kitchen table, fell asleep and didn't wake up." She looked down at the ground. Her braids fell over her shoulder and her hair shone like platinum in the starlight.

It wasn't sadness she felt, and he understood. "You did not love him."

"I did or I never would have married him. I did not have the kind of marriage you had."

He squeezed his eyes shut. The darkness within him was complete. "I was blessed for a time. But I do not think something as fragile as love can last long in this world. My chance to love has passed."

"Mine, too."

"Is that why you haven't remarried?"

"Me? Remarry?" She wrapped her arms around her middle. "Available bachelors are not lining up to court me. A woman with two small children? I have little to offer a man. No, I can't imagine that. Not unless he was admiring how hard I work, but I would not marry such a man."

"Then you plan to raise your children alone?"

"Somehow." The darkness continued, deepening its hold on the land, on the night. "I don't see what other choice I have. I know staying here is just a temporary solution, and I am so grateful. Your help is like a burden off my soul. Maybe now our fortunes will turn, and if they do, you are responsible. I will always be grateful for that."

"You give me too much credit, Joanna."

"You do not give yourself enough." She could make a long list of Aiden McKaslin's outstanding attributes, but then, she had grown a bit biased. Starlight brushed him with a silver glow, and her eyes had adjusted to see the proud lines of his face.

She liked him more than she should, she realized. Much more than she felt comfortable with. She wished that it was a black night with no stars to shine on her face and reveal the feelings she feared were too strong to hide.

"Joanna?" He shuffled closer, his focus on her now, the dark pools of his eyes unrelenting.

She shivered at the power of his glance. She wanted to lift her chin and keep that easily imposed distance between them, but where had it gone? And when? Suddenly she was intensely aware that they were alone, as if they were the only two people for miles with nothing but the stars as chaperones. The children were asleep; it was late. Her better sense told her she ought to say good-night and head back to the shanty—except for the tiny problem that she could not seem to make her feet move.

A little flurry of panic broke out behind her ribs. She trusted Aiden. She trusted herself. But something frightened her. Maybe it was because he'd taken another step closer, so that she could hear the faint rhythm of his breathing and smell the hay on his clothes, which lingered from his evening barn work for the horses.

"What if this is not a temporary solution?" He took her hand in his. His big, work-roughened, warm hand seemed to engulf hers.

His eyes were shadows, his face as shielded as granite. It was too dark to see what he meant, and not dark enough, because she felt exposed and vulnerable to him. "Wh-what do you mean?"

"You could stay here."

"No, I couldn't impose on you like that. It is one thing to accept a little help for my children's sake, but another entirely to take advantage of your generosity. I've got a paying job. Soon the fields will need harvesting and perhaps I can pay Ida to watch the children for me. If I work hard enough, I could have money for a new start."

"That wouldn't be much of a start. The farmers don't pay that well."

"Well enough for me."

"I admire your sense of duty." His baritone rumbled, deep and strangely intimate. "You are talking of long days, maybe sixteen hours or more, working in the cornfields in the hot sun, day after day until the crop is in. That won't be easy."

"I don't mind, Aiden. If you are concerned I might fail and you will be stuck with a woman and kids in your shanty all winter, I promise you that can't happen. I won't let it. I refuse to let my children down."

"I know that." His voice came warmer this time, deeper, and his hand wrapped around hers tightened gently.

Emotion kicked to life within her. A little flame of caring she could not stop warmed her heart. "You have my word, Aiden. I know what some people must think—your brother Finn, for instance. I see how he looks at me."

"And that woman at church?"

"Yes." She bowed her head and winced. "You heard that?"

"Hard not to."

She broke a little inside. Was this why he had been asking about her plans? About her not wanting to remarry? Did he suspect her motives? The night's hot wind wheezed over her, stirring the dust in the air and making her eyes smart. "I promise you that I do not have designs on you. I hope you don't think—"

"No." His answer came swift and sure, cutting her off. "I'm not worried about that, Joanna. It's easy to see the kind of woman you are."

The kind a man like Aiden would never be interested in. The kind of woman, Joanna thought, who did not inspire real love in a man. It hurt, sure, but at least he didn't believe the worst about her. That was some consolation. She brushed at her watery eyes. "I'd best turn in."

"It's late, but I have one more question."

As if she could take any more. "It's been a long day. Can it wait for tomorrow?"

"I'm not sure I will have the gumption tomorrow." He kept hold of her hand, so small and fragile within his big rough one. "I don't know how to go about this, so I'm just going to say it. You don't have to answer right away or even anytime soon. This is just something for you to mull over, and when you are sure of your answer, then let me know."

"I'm not sure I'm going to like this question." She gazed up at him with so much worry on her face.

It was easy to see her fears. She had gotten so used to one hardship after another that it was all she expected. He knew, because life had become that way for him, too.

"This isn't easy for me," he choked out, hating that the words were so hard to say. His pulse began to hammer. He felt as if he'd fallen into a fast and deep river and was about to be carried right over the crest of a deadly waterfall.

Just say the words, he told himself. He took one last breath and let the current carry him. "Marry me."

"M-marry you?" She jerked her hand from his.

He could see he'd surprised her. His hand felt empty. He felt sorely alone. How did he tell her that? "I haven't given it much thought yet, but I believe it is the right thing."

"How can it be right? I don't ever want to be beholden and bound to a man who doesn't love me. And I know you don't, Aiden. You can't."

"No, I don't love you. I can't. That's true." He fell silent, at a loss over how to say what he meant. He didn't even know. "Folks are going to start talking about you, and it could get ugly."

"I have nothing to be ashamed about." Her chin went up. She was so full of dignity, and yet so fragile. "Let people talk, Aiden. I would rather leave than cause you any shame. Maybe that is what I should do."

"We both know that's not wise. You need to stay for your children's sake."

"Yes, I do. But then what do I do about yours?"

He squeezed his eyes shut, not wanting to see the concern on her pretty face. Yet even with his eyes closed, he could still see her wide caring eyes.

"It would not be a real marriage," he found himself saying, snapping open his eyes, because he found he did not want to look within, either. The fields of wheat beyond the fence waved gently in the breeze, graced with starshine. "You and your children would have security and I would…"

No longer feel so alone. He hung his head, unable to say the words. Hoofbeats broke the stillness. Divine intervention. Grateful, Aiden moved away. "Just think on it some. Maybe you'll get used to the idea. If you do, then let me know. I'd best go face up to Finn. He and I have a few scores to settle. Good night, Joanna."

She didn't answer as he walked away. He knew he had surprised her, just as he'd surprised himself. When he glanced over his shoulder to check on her, she was still standing where he'd left her. He wanted to think it was surprise, anyway, and not shock at assuming she wouldn't mind marrying a worn-out, average man like himself who was missing more than his heart.

In retrospect, maybe he shouldn't have asked his question. He'd proposed to her. Maybe a measure of how frozen he'd become was that he didn't feel a thing about it. Not at all. In fact, every step he took away from her made him more like the night—full of shadows and without a speck of light.

At least he wasn't as far gone as Finn. He found his brother in the barn. All he had to do was to follow the noise, the muttering and the smell of cheap whiskey.

Finn had lit a lantern at the end of the main aisle, and he didn't look up as he knelt in the shadows loosening the cinch. The horses, in their stalls for the night, were agitated. Clyde's skin was twitching.

Aiden halted at his gate. "Easy, old fella. You know you're safe here."

The gentle giant nickered low in his throat and leaned over the bars of his gate, seeking reassurance. Aiden rubbed the horse's nose and ears while he watched his youngest brother heft the saddle from his horse's back. A little rough, in his opinion. "Remember I bought that gelding. I see you treating him like that again, and you'll be walking back and forth to town."

"Yeah? Go ahead and do it." Finn tossed the saddle and blanket on the ground, his stance aggressive, his jaw jutting stubbornly. When he stood like that, he resembled Pa. "I'd like to see you try. I'm younger and I'm stronger."

"I wouldn't be too sure about that. I have sixty pounds on you and three inches. Add the fact that I'm not drunk, and I'm sure to be the winner."

Now that Clyde had settled, Aiden gave him a final pat and ambled down the aisle. "I told you how things were going to be if you wanted to live here. Staying away from the closest tavern would be one condition. Attending church every week would be another."

"So? Why should I go? I've been going since I was a kid. It's not like that old minister is going to say anything I haven't heard before. And neither are you." Finn tossed down the bridle. "I saw you with her in the field when I was riding up. You two looked mighty cozy.

She's already got you holding her hand. Next thing you know, she'll be—"

"That's enough." Aiden didn't want to hear it, whatever it was. "You don't know what you're talking about."

"I saw plenty."

There was no reason for him to defend his behavior, and he wasn't going to try. Aiden bent to grab the match tin from where it had been tossed onto the floor, with the dead match on top. He didn't comment on that, either, mostly because he knew Finn well enough to know he had done it on purpose. He had a lot of anger about rules, even if they were only common sense.

Sorrowful, that's how he felt, for this boy in a man's form who refused to grow up. Well, he would have to learn sometime. Aiden put the tin on a nearby shelf, close enough now to see the glaze of alcohol on his brother's face and how clumsy he was as he fought with the latch and threw open the stall gate. It swung hard and banged against the wall. The noise startled the gelding and sent neighs of alarm through the barn.

Finn swore at the horse, but Aiden was quick. He laid his hand on the old fellow's jaw and cheek and talked him back into the stall. The gelding just needed a reassuring word and touch, and he was relieved to be back home in his stall. Aiden kept Finn in his sight as he closed and latched the gate. He saw the grimace his brother gave him before he lumbered drunkenly down the aisle.

"Hey, Finn. Where are you going?"

"To bed. I'm not in the mood for any of your grief, either. I don't need a lecture."

That was a matter of opinion. Aiden crossed his arms over his chest. "You aren't sleeping in my house."

"It's my house, too."

"No it's not." He hated to do it. It killed him to do it. "I warned you, Finn. If you came home drunk, then you are off this property."

"You wouldn't toss me off this place. Where am I going to sleep?"

"That's not my lookout. It's yours." Aiden gulped down enough air to force the next words out. "You're a grown man. It's time you started acting like one. Ma and Thad and I have done everything we can to help you get back on your feet after spending two years in prison."

"It wasn't my fault." Finn lashed out, just as he always did. "I didn't know what I was doing. Even the judge agreed I didn't know I took the blasted wrong horse from the hitching post. C'mon, Aiden—"

Typical Finn. Arguing a point that had nothing to do with the real issue. "You were drunk then, and you're drunk now. I won't have it. If you want to throw away your life, then you do it somewhere that I can't watch. I won't be responsible for helping you do it."

"Fine. I'll just take my horse—"

"*My* horse. And anything you have in my house is what I bought you. That makes it mine." Aiden wished his brother would see reason. He wished Finn would turn his life around. But he had to be tough about this. Finn's future was at stake. He took a ragged breath; he dreaded what he had to say. "Start walking. You take nothing but the clothes on your back, same as when you got here."

"But what about—"

"Don't care." He cut his brother off, tired of excuses, tired of everything. "I've got a ranch to run, crops to bring in and Ma to help support. You are not my responsibility. Now, go."

"I could fight you for the horse."

"You could, but let's be clear. I won't let you steal this horse. I have to think of his welfare, too. You won't take good care of him. You don't deserve him."

"I should have expected this from you." Finn's temper flared, predictably, turning now to blame whoever he could. "It's that woman. You don't want me around because—"

"Go." Aiden couldn't stomach it. He took Finn by the shoulder and gave him a calculated shove. Not too hard, because Finn was much drunker than he thought, and he might fall and hurt himself, but hard enough to get him out of the barn. Aiden shut the door tight. "I want you gone, Finn. Don't come back unless you will follow my rules."

"Don't worry, I won't be back." Rage now, and it was ugly. Aiden tried not to remember when Pa was like that, blaming Ma for bringing him down and his sons for being a burden to him. "It's a sorry day when a man chooses a woman like her over his own brother."

Aiden clamped his jaw hard so he wouldn't rise to Finn's bait. Anger beat at him while he huffed in one breath after another, trying to keep control. He hated how his brother was living. He wished he could shake some sense into him. Prayer hadn't helped. Talks with Pastor Hadly hadn't helped. Not even Ma's pleas to Finn had made a bit of difference in the end. Aiden had done all he could for the boy ever since he had come home last February. There was nothing more he could do.

Now Finn was disparaging Joanna, getting in what licks he could as he staggered away. Aiden felt tired, deeply tired. Her words came back to him as softly as the night breeze. *Maybe now our fortunes will turn, and if it does, you are responsible. I will always be grateful for that.*

There was a difference he could make, if Joanna would let him.

He followed the roll of the prairie past his house toward the shanty. Its small peaked roof was topped by the stars' lush glow, and he thought of Joanna there. She was no longer in the field, at least that he could see. Was she thinking about him, too? Wondering about his proposal? Or was she not interested in marrying a washed-up man like him?

He opened the barn door to give the horses the benefit of the breeze, sure now that Finn was gone. He was only a faint blur of movement far down the road. Another blink, and he'd disappeared.

Watch over him, Lord. Wearily, Aiden headed back to the house through the grass, feeling as if the light could not touch him. It was as if night had fallen inside him, too.

Chapter Nine

"Ma! Look!" Daisy's high sweet voice rose above the music of the wind and the whirring sound of the cutter. She held up a handful of cornflowers. "I want a purple necklace, please?"

"All right. We can make it after we deliver this to Mr. McKaslin." Wearily, Joanna checked over her shoulder. It had been a long, sleepless night and a hard morning of work. There was James, bringing up the rear, packing the ceramic water jug, which he had insisted on carrying. "Are you sure that isn't too heavy for you?"

"I'm sure, Ma." James's chin stuck out and he frowned with intense focus. He clutched the jug with both hands. "I'm gonna be a rancher one day with lots of mustangs. I'll have to carry a lot of water. I'll get to cut hay, too. There he is, Ma! It's Mr. McKaslin!"

Yes, it certainly was. He was up ahead, walking beside the horses as they pulled a mowing machine. He had the reins knotted loosely around his neck, and although his hat hid most of his face, his strong jaw was squared with concentration. Bits of grass floated in the air and clung to him like dust. Why did that only make him more handsome to her?

She had no answer to that. Last night's question had unsettled her. She'd had the good luck of avoiding him at breakfast, and had left his and Finn's food in the warmer. He and his brother must have eaten quickly and headed out to their work in the fields, because when she came in later to clean up the kitchen, the tea had gone cold. All morning she had been safely in the house, cleaning away, but now there was no avoiding him. Her feet seemed to drag with every step she took through the sweet prairie grasses.

How was she going to face him? She would have to look him in the eye and know that he'd offered to marry her out of charity. Pity. A sense of duty. And that made her feel two inches tall.

If only there was a way to leave the basket without meeting up with him. With any luck he would keep right on working and miss seeing her entirely. She could leave the food on the fence post and leave. They wouldn't have to talk.

Luck wasn't with her. Aiden spotted her. Even across the expanse of the field, she could feel the impact of his gaze. Not full of pity for her, as she expected, but as stoic as the ground at her feet.

He chirruped and the big horses stopped. The cutter's blades went silent. Her pulse began to thrum in her ears and she went hollow with dread. She watched the capable way he unwound the reins and patted the horses before he ambled through the fallen stalks of mown hay.

All night she'd been up, her mind whirling. What if she turned down Aiden's offer? Did that mean it would be best if she left sooner rather than later? Even if she had some wages in hand, would the money last long enough for her to find another job? And if she did, what would it be? Without a doubt, she would be cooking or cleaning for someone else. And if that were the case, then why not stay? Staying might be better for the children.

If only that was all she had to consider. She remembered how Aiden had caught the eye of several women in church on Sunday. Not that she blamed them one bit for being sweet on him. No, she thought as he stalked toward her. He was more than simply good-looking. When he walked, he radiated strength. When he studied her, as he came to a stop before her, he radiated kindness. What a combination.

"That basket is a welcome sight." He broke the silence between them. The way he rubbed the back of his neck might be a sign he was as uncomfortable as she was. "Seems I've worked up quite an appetite."

"Then it's a good thing I brought lunch early, because I need to head over to Noelle's." She stared down at the basket. It was safer looking at the wicker top than at his guarded eyes. "I assumed you and Finn would be together. If he's working in another field, I could take his share out to him."

"Finn is gone." He looked past her toward the house, and then out at the western horizon, where a few lazy clouds were gathering. "He left last night."

"Left?" So that was why there had been a lot of breakfast leftovers. She had assumed Finn might have been feeling poorly this morning. "But he'll be coming back?"

"That's up to him." Aiden swept off his hat and pulled his handkerchief out of his back pocket to wipe the grit from his face. He said nothing more, standing like a giant with the sun at his back and the deep blue sky stretched over him like a dream.

"I brought your water, sir." James had finally caught up and lugged the container to Aiden. He held it out carefully with both hands. "It's still real cold."

The man hesitated, studying the boy quietly before he took the jug. "That's real fine. Thank you."

"You're welcome. Can I go pet the horses?" So much need in those pleading eyes. So much more in those words than the question.

The poor boy, wanting approval from the man. Looking for a father. Joanna felt her anxiety slip away. And poor Aiden, trying not to think of the son he'd lost as he set eyes on the boy. Sadness tugged at her soul, making her helpless to do more than put her hand on James's small shoulder. "Come, let's you and I go look at the horses together while Aiden cools down. Daisy, are you coming?"

"Yes. And my flowers, Ma."

"I haven't forgotten, baby." Every fiber of Joanna's being was aware of Aiden. Last night stood between them as unmistakably as the sun-baked earth at their feet. She felt small—very small—as she set the basket into the soft grass and walked away from him. If only she could walk away from the memory of his proposal as easily, but, no, it loomed like a weight on her shoulders.

Did he think she was the type of woman who ingratiated herself to a man, cooking and cleaning for him, making strawberry pie for his family, so that he might see how handy a wife she would make him?

You know that's not what he thinks, Joanna. She kept her back to him, walking steadily after James toward the standing horses.

"Ma! He likes me. See?"

Joanna blinked, pulled from her thoughts. There was James, alive with excitement, while the gray-whiskered giant fondly nibbled his hair. James laughed, simply, easily, without a care. He was like a whole different boy. He held out his hand, still laughing, as the horse stopped nibbling and snorted into his palm.

"Me, too!" Daisy raced up, her bare feet pounding on the hard earth.

Joanna reached out for the Clydesdale's bridle bits, but he placidly turned in his collar to give the little girl a snort, too, so Joanna settled for patting his velvety neck. The second horse was as gently tempered. The two were gruff and imposing looking, just like their master, with hearts of gold.

Boots crackled in the grass behind her. "You needn't have any worries around these fellas. We've had them since I was a boy, and I've never seen either of them startle or work up a temper about anything. Not even a rattler, once, that came out of the grass at them. Clyde just tossed him out of the way and kept on pulling the plow. He didn't hurt him, either, just stunned that snake so that he was too afraid to move. A good part of an hour passed before he slinked away."

"That is a good horse," Joanna praised, glad to know it. "They seem to like kids."

"They watched the three of us grow up. Finn was just

about as little as your girl there. Clyde took to watching over him like a papa. No need to worry if Finn was off getting into trouble. The horse would give a sharp whinny, stomp out of the field and go after him."

She couldn't think of a thing to say to that. She had so many thoughts bubbling below the surface, she didn't know where to start. She had to turn down his offer. She had learned the hard way she had to rely on herself. That sooner or later a man let you down. She'd seen it happen to her ma, and her own marriage had been one heartbroken disappointment after another.

No, it was best she stand on her own feet. Joanna drew herself up, her decision made. And yet there he was, like the salt of the earth. When she looked at him with her heart, she saw more than his goodness. She could see her dreams: a stable life for her children. Security for them. They would never have to live out of a wagon again.

How could she not accept his offer? Worse, how could she?

"Here, I want you to take this." He pulled a handful of coins from his pocket and shook them around to count them. Five dollars. "You'll be driving through town. On your way back through, I would like you to stop and do some shopping. That money is just in case. I'll try to drop by and put your name on my account, but I can't say for sure if I'll make it before you do. I plan on stopping by the church to chat with the minister later today, and there's no judging how long that'll take."

"About your brother?"

His throat worked and he looked away.

He was more upset than he was letting on, she realized, and that came as no surprise to her. Was he regretting last night? Did he wish he could take back his offer? Her stomach coiled up into a worried ball. Was it his question last night that had changed things between them? Or was it her silence that answered his question?

"I'll be glad to stop by Lawson's store and do your shopping." She had time enough to make a list before she left for Noelle's. "What do you need?"

"Just regular groceries. Whatever you want for the kitchen for the week." He fisted his hand around the coins. "Wouldn't mind if you got some pie-making ingredients."

"You like strawberry pie?" The coins tumbled onto her palm.

"I would like anything as long as you baked it."

"Was that the real reason behind last night's question?" The words were out before she could take them back. In her mind they'd been light, but spoken, they hung in the air between them like a swirling tornado.

"Possibly." Aiden grinned slightly, but his eyes remained sad. "There are other reasons I asked what I did, you know."

"I'm a passable cook."

"A mighty fine one in my opinion. But there are more reasons, too." He glanced at the kids and said nothing more.

She heard what he didn't say. Daisy had taken to hugging Clyde's front leg. The other horse held his head low enough so that James could pet his ears. Her children were happy and giggling.

They were what mattered most.

* * *

Aiden was still at the center of her thoughts at day's end. She was driving toward town. Her first day working for Noelle had been the best job she'd ever had. She had helped Ida in the garden and spent another pleasant hour washing down Noelle's lovely new kitchen. Ida was glad to keep an eye on the children, who wore themselves out running in the wild grasses. Joanna was looking forward to returning on Wednesday afternoon to help with the weekly baking.

"Ma, why are you doing that?" Daisy bounced closer on the wagon seat. "How come, Ma?"

"It's a hem," James said from Daisy's other side. "From church."

"A hymn," Joanna gently corrected him. "I guess I was humming, Daisy."

"I can, too." Daisy clamped her lips together and gave it an off-key try.

James covered his ears. "Oh, brother. Do I gotta listen to that, too?"

"Yes, you do." Sympathy filled Joanna. She had been the oldest, as well. She knew how hard it was to always be patient.

As she turned into town, she couldn't help but notice one of the local saloons. Aiden had tried not to seem affected, but she knew him better than that. He had to have taken his brother's leaving very hard, which was why she had quietly mentioned Finn's departure to Thad. Maybe this was one heartache Aiden wouldn't have to shoulder alone.

She pulled the horses to a stop outside the mercantile. It had been a good month since they had all been inside the store. She had bought beans, cornmeal and flour, counting coins out of the bottom of her reticule to pay for them. "I want you both to remember to mind your manners."

"Yes, Ma," James said seriously.

Daisy's head bobbed in agreement.

Joanna thought of the few extra coins she had now as she climbed down from the wagon. Her little ones were so dear, sitting there as neatly as could be. Daisy's twin braids were tidy and her little pink calico dress made her look adorable. James had a grass stain on the knee of his denims, but that aside, he was a little gentleman. Her heart swelled with love for her babies. She held up her hands to lift Daisy from the seat.

She set her daughter on the ground and let James hop down on his own, as he insisted. But she kept a hand out to catch him just in case. He landed with a two-footed thud in the dusty street. She looped the reins around the hitching post and let James lead the way onto the boardwalk.

"Do you know what I have for each of you?" she asked just outside the door. "A penny. After we get all of Mr. McKaslin's groceries, then you each can pick out candy of your own."

"Really, Ma? Honest?" James's smile lit up his face.

"I want the striped kind," Daisy decided at once.

Together they went into the store, hand in hand. The pungent brine of the pickle barrel, made stronger by the day's heat, wafted toward them the instant they stepped through the door. It wasn't busy. Most folks had probably already done their shopping in the cooler part of the day. Joanna dug through her reticule for the list she'd made before leaving Aiden's house.

Mrs. Lawson had her back turned, kneeling to sort through a few low shelves behind the long front counter. She seemed terribly busy. Joanna lifted a small sack of white sugar from the stack against the wall and chose a can of baking powder from a nearby shelf. She felt a tug on her skirt.

"Are you done yet, Ma?" Daisy whispered.

"Not yet, baby. We just need a few more things." Like a sack of beans, a tin of tea and a few bars of lye soap, which she carried to the front counter.

Mrs. Lawson didn't seem to notice her. Joanna waited, realizing she might be filling someone's order. She slipped her list back into her reticule.

"Now, Ma?" James asked politely.

"You may look." She hadn't gotten the words out before both kids were off, rushing across the floor toward the glass display of candy next to the door.

"Don't touch," she reminded them just as Daisy's fingers were about to reach out and smudge the spotless glass.

"I'll watch her, Ma." James, resigned to his fate, took guard over his little sister.

He was such a good boy. She was thankful for the new job because now she had a few pennies to spare. Now, if only Mrs. Lawson would be free to fill the rest of her order, they could have their candy and be on their way home. Home. A rush of relief swelled through her at that single word. Already that little shanty had become a safe place all their own.

"They have the striped ones." Daisy's whisper to her brother carried in the still hot air.

"And the lemon ones." James held his sister's hands to keep her from reaching out.

It seemed as if they had been waiting awhile, and no other customers were in the store. "Mrs. Lawson?"

"I'm busy, Joanna." The woman's tone was sharp and her hand faltered. A bobbin of thread tumbled to the floor.

"I know, and I hate to bother you, but I need a few more things. A pound of bacon and a large sack of flour."

Mrs. Lawson snatched the thread off the floor. Her gaze was as hard as her frown. "You'll have to take your business elsewhere."

"Excuse me? I thought you closed at five o'clock."

"Oh, we're still open."

"But—"

"I don't need your kind in here. Women like you." Mrs. Lawson nodded toward the door. "Good day."

Joanna felt her jaw drop. *Your kind,* she'd said. What kind was she talking about? Oh, maybe it was because of last time she'd been in. She had to count pennies and put back two items before she could afford her groceries. She felt every stitch on every patch of her dress. Shame bit her hard, and she lowered her voice. She tugged open her reticule. "I can pay for this. It's for Mr. McKaslin. He gave me enough for—"

"Whatever he gave you is none of my concern, I can assure you." Mrs. Lawson sounded scandalized. Worse was the harsh judgment on her face. She lifted her lip as if she smelled something foul. "Your money is no good here. Please leave."

"But—" Shock washed over her. She stared down at Aiden's silver dollars at the bottom of her reticule. *Please leave.* Those words echoed in her brain over and over. *Your money is no good here.*

"Try the general store over on Eighth Street. Right next to Steiner's Saloon." Mrs. Lawson marched around the end of the counter. The strike of her shoes sounded like a gavel of judgment.

"But that's a bad part of town."

"Exactly." Mrs. Lawson seemed perfectly aware of that as she yanked open the front door. "They serve your kind there. Take your children and leave. Now."

What kind of person did Mrs. Lawson think she was? Bewildered, Joanna left the groceries on the counter and forced her feet forward. She could feel the shopkeeper's disdain, as if she were little more than those unfortunate women who worked on Eighth Street. Was that what folks were thinking? That she was— No, she couldn't even think the words. Her mind closed off, her heartbeat lurched to a stop and she took each child by the hand.

"Come," she said quietly, struggling to keep her voice steady, although it did wobble a little. "We need to go to another store."

James hung his head, as if to hide his disappointment. He took one last long glance at the lemon drops. "Yes, Ma."

It broke her. James came along at her side, as if resigned, but his hurt seemed to hang in the air. He did not deserve this. Her eyes blurred and she blinked hard to keep control of her emotions. "Come, Daisy."

"But, Ma." Big blue eyes filled with tears. "I got my pieces all picked out."

"I know, honey." Joanna ignored the store owner's gaze boring into her back, and knelt down to kiss her baby's cheek. "Come, we have to go."

Daisy sniffled. "You said, Ma. You said we could."

"I was wrong. I'm sorry." Anger beat at her, because it wasn't right, denying her children. They might not have much, but they were good and honest. She mustered all the dignity she could and led her family out of that shop, shielding them the best she could from Mrs. Lawson's bare disdain, and started blindly down the boardwalk. She couldn't seem to think what to do next.

There. Her vision cleared enough to spot the dry-goods store at the end of the block. "We'll try in there. I know they have a good selection of candy."

"It don't matter, Ma." James fought to be brave, although the choked sound of his voice gave him away. "I don't want any candy. We can't afford it."

At least her children were spared the understanding of what had happened. How could Mrs. Lawson think such a thing? Joanna glanced around at the busy boardwalk, realizing that a woman she recognized from church was giving her a wide berth as she passed. No nod of greeting, no smile, nothing. Mrs. Collins deliberately looked the other way.

Apparently Mrs. Lawson was not alone in her judgments. Joanna withered inside, not at all sure what to do. What if she was turned away from the dry-goods store and the other stores on the good side of town?

She told herself that she didn't care what others thought; she knew the truth. But as another woman she didn't even know purposefully avoided her on the boardwalk, shame washed over her.

She stopped in the shadow of the barbershop's awning and dug two pennies out of her reticule. They shone coppery in the sunlight, winking like a promise. She handed one to each child. "Now don't drop yours, Daisy. Hold on tight. We'll go in and you can buy your own candy."

She wasn't sure it would work, but it was worth a try.

Chapter Ten

Joanna was like a godsend in his life. Aiden led the way out of the minister's office and into the sweltering sunshine, glad for the drum of footfalls following him. He wasn't alone, because Joanna had mentioned his meeting to Thad. Thad had come, dutiful Thad, and he was going to take over the reins.

Aiden knuckled back his hat to take a long look at the sky. Storm clouds were gathering in the west, blocking out the lowering sun. He judged it to be near four o'clock, maybe a few minutes later. Those thunderheads might hold some rain, he figured, but it would take until dark before they would see any. It would blow on northeasterly, was his guess, and the hay drying in his field would be safe.

"I wish I could come along," he told Thad.

"Me, too, but something tells me Finn might take one look at you and lose his temper." Thad glanced over his shoulder, waiting for the minister to join him. "We'll stop and get Hadly's son to help out. There are only four saloons in town. Finn is likely to be in one of them. Don't worry, I'll take care of him if I can."

"That's a load of worry off my chest." Aiden had hardly slept last night, torn between standing his ground and riding to town to search for him. He feared what choices his youngest brother was making—his baby brother. "You'll send word if you find him?"

"I will." Thad's seriousness eased a fraction. "No one could have done as much as you, Aiden. Finn has to know that somewhere deep down. This will right itself in the end, I know it. Now, go find that woman of yours—"

"She's not my woman."

"Sure, fine." Thad didn't look as if he believed it. "You go have a nice evening. Maybe she'll bake you another one of those pies. Best dessert I've ever tasted."

"You and me both." Aiden loosened Clyde's reins from the post. Dust scudded in whirlwinds down the street. He figured he had a chance of making it to the mercantile before Joanna did. "There's something you ought to know. I suppose you could call it news."

"That's no surprise, considering. Glad you're getting around to telling me." He gathered Sunny's reins and mounted up with a squeak of the saddle. "Are you going to marry that woman?"

"I asked her." Aiden slipped his foot into the stirrup and swung into his own saddle. "How did you know?"

"I figure that's why you wanted us to meet Joanna."

Aiden didn't correct him. His throat clenched up tight. He'd brought Kate home to meet his family right before he'd got down on his knees and given her his ring. He couldn't seem to find the strength to say it was different this time. This wasn't love. This wasn't foolishness. It was practicality. He wanted to say he was doing the right thing for Joanna, but his proposal wasn't that selfless. He would be getting something out of the deal. Not his heart, that was for certain, but maybe his soul.

"I got to tell you, Aiden, I didn't think this day would ever happen." Thad drew Sunny around. The gladness on his face was easy to see.

Aiden struggled to breathe. Tangled pieces of too many broken feelings seemed to jam up, leaving his voice strained. "Don't say anything. She hasn't said yes."

"I can see why she might hesitate. She's a sweet-seeming woman, and you are no catch, big brother."

So now the teasing was going to start. Aiden rolled his eyes and guided Clyde into the street. "I guess that makes me a lucky man that she didn't say no right out. I'll try to catch up with her at the mercantile."

"Guess even the tough fall in love." Thad winked, and there was no hiding the grin on his face. He was enjoying this.

Aiden cringed, remembering how adamantly he had insisted he would never marry again. He supposed he deserved the brotherly ribbing. "Speak for yourself, Thad. I hope you can talk some sense into Finn. Good luck."

"Thanks. I'm going to need it and a whole lot of divine intervention. There's the minister." Thad rode off toward the narrow alley next to the church so he could join Hadly on his white mare.

Aiden was mighty grateful to have their pastor's help

on this. It was a perilous road Finn was walking, and if he didn't make a real change, then Aiden hated to think what would become of his littlest brother. He disliked feeling helpless. He wished there was something more he could do to change things. The failure ate at him.

There was Joanna's horse and wagon right in front of the mercantile. Looked like he'd lucked out. The prospect of seeing her again put a little spring into his step as he left Clyde at the hitching post.

His eyes were already searching for her through the wide front window. His ears were straining for the gentle music of her voice. When he heard it, his hand was on the door handle. Something was wrong; he could feel it like a cool breeze skittering down the back of his neck.

"But I wanted the candy, Ma." The daughter's face was streaked with tears.

"I know, baby. I did my best." Joanna scooped the child up into her arms, balancing her on her slim hip. She kissed away her tears. The boy was looking down at the cracks between the boards, his shoulders slumped.

What was going on?

"Joanna?" Aiden was halfway to her before he realized it. A few more steps and he was close enough to see the tight control around her mouth and the hurt in her eyes. It was all he could see—that hurt. He drew himself up tall, hands fisting, stunned by the overwhelming impulse to protect her at any cost. "What's wrong?"

"Aiden." She gazed up at him with regret—it could only be regret—as if she didn't want to be seen with him. Her face was pink from emotion and her delicate jaw set like steel. "I—I was just trying to get groceries."

"At the dry-goods store?" That didn't make any sense. He looked at her arms, empty of packages. He glanced toward the back of the wagon and didn't see a single sack of staples. Why did she look ashamed? "Come with me into Lawson's."

"No." She stopped, bracing both feet. "I don't want to upset the children. I'm sorry, Aiden, but I can't do your shopping. The only store that will probably serve me is one I don't want to go in."

This still did not make a lick of sense. "Why won't they serve you?"

"It doesn't matter, Aiden. I'll take care of it later."

"No. We'll take care of it now." He drew himself up taller, all might. All fight. "This better not be what I think it is."

"They don't serve my kind, according to Mrs. Lawson." Joanna wouldn't meet his gaze. She kissed another tear from her daughter's cheek and smoothed the boy's windblown hair with her free hand.

"Your kind?"

"That's what she said." Shame ate at Joanna. What more could she say? She could see Mrs. Lawson watching through the front window, tsking as she shook her head slowly from side to side. *We don't do business with your kind,* she'd said. *Women like you.*

"Ma?" James asked. "Are we gonna go home?"

"Yes, baby, we are." Humiliation had turned her mouth bitter, and her face felt sunburn-hot. She fought hard to keep her voice calm and her upset locked up tight, for her little ones' sakes. "Let's go to the wagon now."

"Okay, but you should have my penny." James held

it out, trying so hard to be good, her dear little boy. "I don't need any candy."

"I do," Daisy hiccuped.

Joanna's heart just kept breaking off in pieces. "Baby, you keep the penny."

She didn't see it as much as felt it, the way Aiden seemed to swell up even taller, like a bear ready to fight.

"Stay here," he told her, already stalking toward the mercantile door. "I'll be right back."

"No, it's not—" *worth it*. She didn't have time to finish, for he'd already jerked open the door and disappeared inside. There he went, a big bear of a man, hunting down Mrs. Lawson.

"Is he getting my candy?" Daisy asked.

"I don't know." The last thing Joanna wanted was a scene. It was only going to make people like Mrs. Lawson think whatever they knew about her was right. That would only affect her children more. All she wanted was to go home. She would fix dinner—Aiden had enough on his pantry shelves for her to make supper—and she would come back and try again tomorrow. Maybe Ida could watch the children again.

"Come." She took James by the hand. "Let's get into the wagon."

A man came out of the barbershop, gave her a friendly look that lasted a bit too long and wasn't nice at all.

She cringed. The shame inside her doubled, and she jerked her gaze to her feet, studying the tips of her shoes as he sauntered past. She had never in her life wanted to disappear more than at this moment.

She helped James climb onto the high wagon seat, and hefted Daisy up after him.

"Hey, Ma." James settled onto the edge of the seat. "Mr. McKaslin looks awful mad."

He did. She could see him clearly through the glass. She had never seen a man look more intimidating or more controlled. He towered over the counter, tensed as if for a fight, but there was no threatening gesturing or temper. That was a surprise, since that was her experience with angry men. Aiden was merely speaking with Mrs. Lawson with a quiet firmness. Mr. Lawson came out of the back of the store to the counter and joined the discussion.

Aiden was going to make this right. Wonderful Aiden. He was standing up for her. No man had ever done that before. Places in her heart warmed—places she didn't know she had. The sunshine seemed brighter and the air more sweet. The backs of her eyes smarted as she watched Mrs. Lawson pull items from the shelves. Mr. Lawson went to the candy case and put several pieces into a brown paper bag.

"He got some lemon ones," James announced.

"How about the striped ones?" Daisy asked.

"Yep."

Aiden strode out of the store with a big brown package in his arms—the wrapped groceries. Mr. Lawson followed with two bigger sacks.

"Ma'am." He nodded cordially as he passed, and set the flour and beans into the wagon bed.

Joanna couldn't speak, so she bobbed her head, her pulse pounding nervously as he went back to his store.

There had been no more judgmental looks. Nothing uncomfortable.

"I got things set right," Aiden told her as he put the package in the wagon bed. He held out the sack of candy. "For your little ones."

Joanna heard two excited gasps behind her on the seat. She took the bag. Her heart began to melt just a little. Maybe it was the way the sunlight graced his broad shoulders and the brim of his hat, but he seemed bigger to her. In her eyes, there was no one better. Caring swelled through her in the sweetest way.

"Thank you." Again, the words were far too small for the great kindness he had done for her and for her children.

"It was no trouble at all. You go on and climb up." He took her elbow to help her.

Her heart took another slide. It was no longer gratitude she felt, no longer simple respect. Her feelings for him had multiplied, taking on depth and layers. She let him boost her up, and she settled into the seat. Silence filled her as she waited while he untied the horses and handed her the reins. She cared for him very much.

Too much. She took the reins from his gloved hands, avoiding his gaze. There was too much swirling around inside her that she didn't want him to see. Too many emotions she was afraid to examine closely.

"I'll see you at home?" he asked, but the question in his eyes asked more.

That was a question she could not yet answer. Look how this afternoon had turned out, and what folks already thought. She might not care, as long as it didn't harm her children, but those opinions also painted

Aiden in a poor light. How could she allow such a thing? As long as she was in his life like this, those rumors were not going to stop. Simply accepting his proposal might not make them stop entirely. Maybe it would be best for Aiden if she packed up the kids and rode out of his life.

"I'll be right behind you," she told him, instead of the yes he was waiting for. "You go on ahead."

"All right." He winced a little, as if disappointed.

She hated that. Guilt crept into her. She straightened the reins and released the brake, waiting as Aiden ambled to his horse and mounted up. His movements were sure and controlled. Maybe it was the shadows making him look so weary. Maybe it was her imagination, what she wished she would see.

The truth was, she was troubled by these rumors. She didn't want to leave; she felt she needed to stay. Because if she did, then she could do everything possible to make his hard life easier. She wanted to repay his kindness. She longed to have her children know security and stability and the care of a strong man who would not let them down.

"Ma?"

"Yes, James?" Then she realized she was still clutching the bag of candy. How on earth had she forgotten? She transferred the right rein to her left hand and held the sack out. "One apiece so you don't ruin your supper."

After James had chosen a lemon drop and Daisy a striped peppermint ball, Joanna tucked the sack into her skirt pocket. She gave the reins a firm snap. The horse plodded forward and the wagon wheels creaked.

There was one more truth rising up from her heart, a truth she could no longer ignore.

She was a little sweet on Aiden. It was hard not to be.

Storm clouds had turned the northeastern sky coal-black and sent a cool wind skittering through the fields.

Aiden pulled up the horses, let the welcome breeze blow against him, and gave thanks for it. That felt good, for he was blistering hot. He'd been pressing hard since he'd gotten back from town, mostly because he had twice the work to do now that Finn was no longer here to pitch in. But the truth was, as long as he was working hard, he didn't have to think about what had happened in town today. He didn't want to speculate about how those rumors got started in the first place. He feared that Finn had been drinking and talking up a good story at one of the saloons. Aiden shook his head, remembering the hurt look on Joanna's face.

Yep, just thinking about it got his guts knotted up and put his chest in a tangle. Too many emotions blew through him and he fought them down. He didn't like feeling this much. He dragged in a long breath, took off his hat to let the breeze cool his head. Joanna and her kids were coming his way, bringing his supper.

The family was a pretty sight. The little girl was skipping ahead to collect wildflowers. The boy trailed after Joanna, carrying the big water jug. It looked to be pretty heavy for a kid that size, but his jaw was set with determination. In that way the boy was a lot like his ma.

Then Aiden looked at her. At Joanna. With her sunbonnet down and her braids uncoiled from her proper topknot, she was a sight to behold. The wind danced through loose wisps of blond hair that had escaped, and she could have been a ray of sunshine come down to earth for all her innocent beauty.

It wasn't a puzzle to figure out why she might not want to tie herself to a man like him. He felt like the dark side of sunset as she lifted a hand from the basket handle and waved in greeting.

His hand was up and waving in return before he thought about it. There was that tangle in his chest again, the one he'd do best to ignore. He left the horses to rest and headed toward the creek. By the time he had washed most of the grime off his face and neck, Joanna was there, handing him a small towel from inside the basket.

"I brought pie for dessert, just as you asked." She hardly looked at him.

"Did you now?" He dried his face with the soft cloth, feeling her distance and his. "I'm real partial to apple pie, too."

"I'll keep that in mind. I noticed the apples in the orchard are starting to ripen."

"I'd be mighty obliged." He folded the towel. "What else do you have in that hamper?"

"Sit down and find out." She shook out a blanket and let it settle on the creek bank, keeping her back to him as she smoothed away the wrinkles.

Yessir, he reckoned he had her answer to his proposal. He'd seen it in her hurt eyes in town as she sat on that wagon seat, holding the bag of candy out to her children. Being associated with him had brought harm to her reputation. There was no way she was going to accept him now. Why that hurt like a blow, he couldn't rightly say. He only knew his life was better with her near.

It was her cooking. At least that was the simplest explanation and the only one he would allow himself to think about. He knelt on one corner of the blanket, his mouth watering at the scents coming from the tin containers Joanna was opening. Buttered carrots; must be the first from the garden, since they were so small. Butter melting off the tops of fluffy buttermilk biscuits.

He couldn't believe all that she had done. "Is that chicken and dumplings?"

"Your ma made a point of telling me all your favorites." She placed the largest container in front of him, full to the brim. Joanna didn't look up or acknowledge him as she kept working, setting out the delicious food. "Ida wasn't even ashamed of herself, as if my cooking would be enough to, well, you know."

"Hook me?"

She hung her head. "I made something I knew you would like, because of what you did for us today in town. To thank you."

"I understand." He wanted her to be clear on that. He didn't want her to think he believed any part of such nonsense. "You won't have any more problems at the mercantile. I've made sure of that."

"I know." She turned pink, as if she was still ashamed.

"It's a hard thing having folks think the worst of you, I know." He paused when the little boy made his way up to the blanket, sweat dampening his flyaway hair.

"Here." Joanna's son set the jug on the ground. "I reckon you gotta be mighty thirsty."

"I reckon so." Aiden couldn't look at the boy. He wanted to; he just couldn't. "Thank you kindly."

"Here." Now that his hands were free, the kid reached into his trouser pocket and held out something on the flat of his palm. It winked in the sun.

A copper penny. "What's that for?"

"For the candy." Such a solemn little boy. "Thank you, sir."

"You're welcome, but you keep the penny."

"Nah." The kid shook his head. "Ma always says you gotta pay for what you get or it's the same as stealing."

What does a man say to that? "You have a wise ma. Then will you give your penny to your ma for me?"

"Yes, sir." The boy ambled off to hand over the bit of copper to his mother.

Nice boy. Aiden had to glance away. Joanna's daughter was at the creek's edge, reaching out to dip her fingers into the clear, shallow water. It was easy to see that Joanna had an eye on her as she took out a napkin, a fork and the final tin—no doubt holding the fresh piece of pie.

"Looks like a storm is blowing in." She handed him the knife and fork rolled up in a napkin.

It was hard facing her. Resolutely, Aiden steeled his spine. Last night the darkness had been a safe haven, but in the unforgiving light of this day, she had been able to get a real close look at him. At this man who had offered marriage to her—not a real union, true, but a marriage nonetheless. Last night he had been fairly hopeful, but he knew now that she was going to reject him. After what happened at Lawson's store, she was going to pack up her things and leave him.

He unrolled the silverware, hoping she couldn't see—that she would never guess—how lonesome he was going to feel without her.

"I think just north of here is likely to get a hard blow. Maybe some hail," he said practically. He was, after all, a deeply practical man. "My hay should be safe for tonight."

"And your wheat, too. You have a fair-size crop."

"Enough that it'll be a tussle getting it harvested in a day." He stared off at the horizon and thought about that storm gathering strength. About the lightning ready to strike. "Finn could have helped with that, but it's no matter. I've got neighbors, and Thad will come help me."

"You have a good brother in him."

"That I do." Thad was good to the core. Dependable. Aiden was blessed to have a brother like him, and he knew it. "I don't suppose he dropped by word about Finn?"

"No, I would have told you."

"Yeah, I knew that. I had to ask."

She nodded with understanding, rising lightly to her feet. "Where did you put the pitchfork?"

"Uh, over against the corner post. Why? What do you need me to do?" He was already rising, but she waved him back.

"No, you stay and eat. You can help me by keeping an eye on the children." She was already walking away, a pretty willow of a woman in a patched, pink calico dress. "You can join me when you're done."

"Done, what?" She was the most puzzling woman. "Joanna, what are you going to do?"

"I'm going to start turning the hay."

"Whoa, there." Why should she do such a thing? What had given her such a notion? He got to his feet. "The work is too hard for you. Besides, I don't take to a woman helping me in the fields."

"Too bad. You will have to get used to it, as these will also be my fields very soon." She tossed him a small smile as lovely as the wildflowers nodding in the wind. "I've decided to marry you."

Chapter Eleven

"Are they asleep?" Hours later, Aiden's voice floated out of the darkness.

"Finally." Joanna left the shanty door open to the breeze and padded barefoot in his direction. Her muscles ached from the difficult work of turning the mown hay over so it could dry for stacking. She didn't mind hard labor and she hadn't minded the company, either.

Grasses tapped against her skirt hem as she made her way through the night shadows. "You were right. The storm is staying north of us."

"Good thing, or we'd be getting wet about now. It's a pretty sight from here, though."

"Yes." She followed the sound of his voice.

There he was, hunkered on the porch step, as still as the shadows. She eased down beside him. The thick clouds blotted out the sky and glowed with the sparks of lightning. Like black opals, they shone with a dark incandescence.

"I love watching storms," she confessed, "as long as they are a goodly distance away."

"Me, too. The lightning has just started." He nodded toward the far north, where a jagged trail of blue-white light snaked and crackled across the angry clouds. "Have you always like watching storms, or is it a recent inclination?"

"It goes as far back as I can remember. When I was a little girl, my ma would wake me and we would go watch the lightning together."

"Kind of like this?"

"Exactly like this." Her voice softened at the memory. Her ma had been a good woman, loving, hard-working and endlessly kind. "When I was James's age I would rush from one window to another trying to see the next lightning strike through the downpour streaking the glass."

"I would head out to the barn."

"I can't imagine your ma letting her little boy outside in a lightning storm."

"I wasn't so small, I guess. Twelve or so, and older. I still do it. I climb up and sit in the haymow. I can see the whole of Angel Valley from up there."

"And a lot of lightning."

"A few twisters," he added. The wind gusted through the grass like an ocean wave. He waited while another streak of light crackled through the clouds in one long bolt. That was quite a sight. And judging by Joanna's rapt attention, she thought so, too.

His eyes had adjusted to the dark so he could see her against the glow of the clouds. She had a sweet profile with a cute slope of a nose and a daintily cut mouth and chin. The tangle of her golden hair curled over her forehead and framed her face. He remembered how hard she had worked in the field beside him, tirelessly and without one complaint. She had kept one eye on her children while she flipped shank after shank of cut hay, and expertly, too.

"You helped me more in one evening than Finn ever has." It had taken a chunk of his pride to allow her to work. No, he wasn't one of those men who believed a woman had her place, but he didn't think a woman ought to work that hard.

As a boy, he had watched how hard his ma had worked in the fields when Pa had been passed out. She had ruined her health, working herself to the bone. He had helped all he could and that made a difference as he had gotten older. He thanked the Lord he was built for hard labor. By the time he was twelve, he was doing a man's work in the fields so his ma didn't have to.

It had been difficult to keep quiet this evening, but he'd done it. Joanna had agreed to marry him. And he hadn't wanted to give her a reason to change her mind.

"Then your offer still stands?"

"You know it does." He smiled some. She was humble, and it was endearing. "After that supper and dessert, no man in his right mind would turn you down."

"At least I have something to offer you in our arrangement. It feels one-sided to me."

"It's not, believe me. But your cooking is not why I proposed." He paused, gathering up his courage. It was hard for him to talk about the things that mattered. "I hope you know I don't look at you and see all the work you could do around here."

"Yes, I know that, or I wouldn't have agreed to marry you." She sounded young, suddenly, and vulnerable.

He bowed his head. It wasn't that she was so very young; it was that hardship had worn on him. His existence, numb as the frozen ground at winter, had aged him more than he liked to admit. Hopelessness could do that to a man.

Joanna seemed to understand what he couldn't say. "I know you need help around the house, and that's only sensible, as you work hard all day to make a living off this land. But your proposal is a practical solution, too. As are my reasons for accepting."

"Yes." He cleared his throat, glad that they had this understanding. "You know I'm not about to follow Finn to the saloon and leave you to bring in the crops."

"I do. My children are children again. I can't tell you what it means. James is no longer so worried. Daisy isn't as clingy." Joanna looked away, blinking fast.

She was trying not to cry, he realized. "I have an inkling. If the good Lord would have seen fit to make me a pa, I would have moved mountains if I had to if it meant my son would be safe and secure."

"You mean, those mountains?" She gestured to the west, where the great Rocky Mountains rose up like a fortress out of the prairie floor.

He nodded. Love was a tricky thing. All these years had not diminished what he'd felt for the son he'd never met.

"I believe you, Aiden." Her understanding mattered. "You would move the entire continental divide rock by rock if you had to."

"I'm not alone in that kind of determination." It was why he admired her, not that he was able to tell her that. Joanna had a good heart, and in this world that had to be protected. That was his opinion, at least. "I've been thinking some tonight when we were working. That shanty is awful small for the three of you."

"Aside from my pa's farmhouse, a shanty is all my children have ever known. We're snug in there and I'm grateful, Aiden. More than you know."

"Winter will be here and the shanty won't be as snug. The main house will be warmer for you and the little ones."

"I'm not sure our moving into your house is a good idea." She swiped at the stray curls the wind was blowing into her face. "I figured we would keep things the way they are. I'm satisfied with that."

"I see." He nodded as if he understood. "You're afraid that I'll be upstairs in that house with you."

No, I'm afraid for you. She remembered how he had stood in the kitchen that first morning when she had made him breakfast. In her mind's eye she could still see him with his wide shoulders slumped and his face in his hands. She hurt for him. "This has to be hard for you, Aiden."

"I will be all right." His words were firm, but his voice sounded lost.

He would always do right, she realized. It was good to see that some men were really like that. Her spirit ached with hope in all the sad places life had created. "You have done so much for my children. The last thing I want is to cause you pain."

"Pain is part of living. It lets you know you're alive. I suppose that's a good thing." He rubbed the back of his neck, as if he was thinking, or trying to brush away what was past. "I told you this would be a practical solution, nothing more."

"That is why I'm agreeing to it." There were so many assurances she could give him, but she chose the most sensible one. "This is for my children."

"I know that, Joanna. I'll make certain they are always fed and sheltered and safe. You have my word on that."

"I already know that for sure." Gratitude filled her up until she brimmed with the burn of it. She blinked hard, fighting more than tears. What was she going to do about her feelings for this man? He had her endless devotion for his promise. He broke her heart with his vow, and she understood why. He had not been able to provide for his child, so he would provide for hers.

She swallowed, fighting to get the words out. When they came, they were shaky and thin with emotion. "You have my word that you will never regret marrying me. But I'm worried what certain people will say about you. When we wed, they will think those rumors are true."

"It's not my worry what others choose to fill their minds with." Aiden shrugged away her doubts with a quick movement of his shoulders. "I know the truth. You know the truth. That's what matters."

"As long as you're sure."

"Absolutely." He did not pause. "When do you want to have the ceremony?"

"The sooner the better, but you are in the middle of haying." She stopped to watch another streak of light splinter the endless sky. "I don't think we should interrupt your work. What if the next storm comes this way? We might regret taking that time to get married."

"You're worrying about the hay?"

"I worry about a lot of things, Aiden. How about this? I'll be ready whenever it is best for you."

"You are a peculiar woman, Joanna." He chuckled, and it was a cozy sound, like a warm blanket on a cold winter's day.

"Peculiar? I don't like the implications of that. Is this the way it is going to be? You're going to change into a different man because we're married?"

"No, no. I'll always be the same, Joanna. Always have been, always will be." He shook his head, as if he couldn't win no matter what he did. "I meant to compliment you. There aren't many sensible women in this world."

"That's what a woman likes to hear from the man she's about to marry. That she's sensible."

"I mean that as a compliment, too. I loved Kate to the depths of my soul, but she was as impractical as the day was long. It took her a good part of five months to plan our wedding." He chuckled again. "And here you are, willing to get married around my haying schedule."

"You said this was a practical arrangement." She was laughing, too. "I could plan a big to-do, but I didn't suppose that would be fitting or a wise use of time or money."

"I'm a busy man and I don't have much money to spare. I appreciate your view, Joanna."

"Good, then it's settled." Soon, she would have the right to care for this man, to repay his kindness and his generosity. She had no wish to put that off. She intended to place him right up there with her children in terms of what she valued. "Are you sure you want me living in your house, Aiden?"

"I'm sure." And he sounded certain. "How about Sunday after church? We'll be in town anyhow, so it will save us a trip there."

"Sounds practical to me." Maybe it was far from romantic, but that set with her just fine. "I had such high expectations when I got married before. It was as if I was the lightning up there, glittering high above the earth."

"That's the problem with love. It's impractical, and it can't last."

"It devastates you when it's gone."

They sat in quiet agreement and understanding, the pain of their pasts between them as surely as the cool wind whipping by. Far in the distance the lightning flashed again, growing worse now, streaking the roiling black sky. White-blue cracks of light flared to life and faded.

"Did your work go all right for Noelle?"

"Very well." She said that with a sigh of relief, as if glad for the change of subject. "Noelle asked me to join her sewing circle."

"That's just like her." It didn't surprise him a bit. He remembered how his sister-in-law seemed to take to Jo-anna on Sunday. "You should go."

"I haven't made up my mind about it. There's so much to get done here."

"It will all get done eventually. You go." He watched the lightning instead of her. "There's something else I want you to do."

"For you? Name it."

"Tomorrow, head into town and go to Cora Sims's dress shop. Tell her you need something nice to get married in and to bill me."

"What? Oh, no, Aiden, I don't feel right about that."

He winced. She sounded sincere and stubborn. How did he tell her what he meant? He had no notion how to say it, so he made light of it. "Do you know how mad my ma is going to be at me if you get married in a patched calico work dress?"

"I have a Sunday best dress."

"I know, and it's calico, too. And patched."

"There's nothing wrong with that." Her chin went up.

"I'm not saying there is. I want you to have better, Joanna."

"You do?" Her throat tightened and she turned away.

"You have been struggling alone for a long time, but I want you to know that's over. You're not alone anymore." He meant that. "You go buy yourself a nice dress. It's what I want."

He didn't know how she was going to take to that order, or if she would give him her opinion, as he had already learned she was quick to do. But then he realized her silence was because of something else.

"Thank you, Aiden." Her voice was thin and vulnerable. She, too, watched the lightning in the distance, but he heard what she didn't say as a comfortable stillness settled between them.

He did not want a wife. He did not want to marry again. But helping her was the right decision. He could feel it with all the pieces of his soul.

* * *

Dread. Remembering her experience with the Lawsons at the mercantile, Joanna was not looking forward to pulling open the dress-shop door and facing another woman from town. But Aiden had asked her to. She couldn't let him down. When she stood up with him before God and his family, she did not want to embarrass him in her Sunday best calico dress. He was right— even that dress had been patched.

Thinking of him, she gripped the handle and pulled open the door. "Come in, you two, and remember to keep your hands to yourself, please."

"Yes, Ma," they said in unison, and followed her into the beautiful dress shop. James glanced around, already bored, but good boy that he was, he didn't say a thing. He squared his small shoulders like a little man, determined to make the best of the situation.

"Look!" Daisy let out a gasp of delight. "Ribbons, Ma. Look!"

"Yes, aren't they pretty?" She had never seen so many ribbons set out in a display, in so many beautiful colors, from sensible brown to candy pink.

It was a fine shop and far too fancy for her to ever afford. Perhaps Aiden did not know how much things were likely to cost in a place like this, especially the ready-made dresses she saw hanging along the back wall. She hated to think what those cost. Likely as not, they were far too fancy for her to feel comfortable in.

"Hello." A pleasant-looking woman in a finely tailored lawn dress rose from a chair at the farthest window and set her sewing aside. "I'm Cora Sims. Welcome to my shop. Are you Joanna, by chance?"

She noted the shop owner's earnest smile and took that as a good sign. Maybe not everyone in town had heard or believed those horrible rumors. What a relief. "Yes, I am. You have a beautiful store."

"Thank you. Ida McKaslin told me all about you at our church meeting this morning. It's lovely to meet you." She lifted a small basket on the front counter and smiled at the children. "You may each have one piece. Well, as it's a slow morning, perhaps two."

Bless Cora Sims. Predictably, James chose two lemon drops and Daisy two peppermint balls.

"Thank you, ma'am," her son said politely.

"Thank you!" Daisy practically hopped in place, her platinum-blond ponytails bouncing.

"You're welcome. What good children you are," Cora praised. She was truly kind. "Now, Joanna, can I offer you something cool to drink? It's a scorcher out there, isn't it?"

"That's kind of you, but I'm fine. I've come for a dress." Here was where things got tricky. "Aiden wanted me to have you bill him."

"Ah, I see. Of course." Cora's smile deepened. "You need a dress for your wedding."

"How did you know?"

"You would be surprised. I am one of the first people to know when a couple is going to be married. When is the big day?"

"Sunday." Joanna braced herself for that welcoming smile to fade. She knew how it must look. "They say marry in haste, repent in leisure, but we need to be practical. Harvest season is coming soon."

"Yes, and then Aiden will be too busy to even think

about getting married." Cora didn't seem at all surprised by this. "My parents were farmers, too. I know how demanding it can be. You will need a ready-made dress. I believe I have several that ought to be about your size. Come in the back and see."

Joanna herded her little ones ahead of her, around a colorful table of embroidery threads and past racks with thick bolts of rich fabrics.

"Ma! Look!" Daisy stopped licking her peppermint piece long enough to exclaim, "Look at those buttons!"

"I see." She was amazed by that glass display case of hundreds of buttons on little paper plackets. Mother-of-pearl buttons, carved buttons and ones in shapes like roses, a teddy bear or a castle. "You may go look and not touch, if James will watch you."

While Daisy gasped gleefully, James gave a sigh of resignation. Dutifully, he trudged toward the case. "C'mon, Daisy."

She raced to keep up.

"I also have some little girl dresses. Would you be interested in seeing those, too?" Cora chose a dear little butter-yellow frock from among the others hanging on the rod.

Joanna stared, awestruck. There were ribbons of lavender and blue accenting the puff sleeves and tiered skirt. A row of daisy-shaped buttons marched down the front of the bodice. She'd never imagined anything so fine for Daisy.

"I just finished this yesterday," Cora explained. "Of course, you may have something already in mind for your daughter to wear at the wedding, but with her coloring, I thought of this dress instantly. It would look adorable on her."

"Yes, it sure would." Joanna stared at the dress longingly. She knew without asking that the price was something she simply could not afford, and Aiden had said nothing about buying a dress for Daisy. Joanna had never wanted anything more than that beautiful frock. She tried to tell herself that it would make a good Sunday dress and would wear well, but it made no difference. No amount of reasoning could make up for the fact that she did not have the money for it. And she would not take advantage of Aiden's generous nature.

Cora slipped the lovely garment back onto the rod. "Did you have anything in mind for yourself?"

"I don't suppose you have anything calico." It would be sensible, something she could wear to church on Sunday, too.

"No, I'm sorry. If I had more time, I could make something for you." Cora turned to the women's dresses; there were several dozen of them, in all colors and sizes.

Joanna's heart sank. Every one looked far too frilly to suit her, with expensive details like silk ribbons and lace and embroidered embellishments. She had no need for such a gown.

"Here, what about this lawn?" Cora pulled a dress out from among the others. "It's perfect for this summer weather we're having. It's simple enough to be serviceable, and yet fine enough to be special. What do you think?"

Joanna simply stared at the finely woven ivory fabric dotted with tiny green leaves. The style was tailored, the lace edging the collar and sleeves was the nicest she had ever seen, and pearl buttons accented the bodice. It was a fragile, beautiful dress and she loved it.

"The look on your face is answer enough." Cora held the gown up. "I think it was meant for you."

Joanna's hands shook as she took the fine garment. She had never owned anything so nice. But it wasn't the dress she wanted most.

She glanced over at her daughter. Daisy was still absorbed in studying the buttons. Joanna feared she already knew the answer, but she had to ask, anyway. "There wouldn't be a way to make payments on that child's dress, would there?"

"No, I don't take payments," Cora said gently. "Usually. But I'm sure we can work something out."

"Really? Oh, thank you. I'll take it." She hesitated. "And maybe some fabric suitable for a new shirt for James?"

"I'm sure we can find something. You'll need a few things to go with your new dress. How about a nice bonnet to match?" Cora wandered toward the shelves of beautiful hats. "I'm sure Aiden would want it for you. He'll expect you to be well appointed."

That was true. He would be sure to comment on her patched sunbonnet, if she showed up to marry him in one.

"You are getting a fine man for a husband." Cora was friendly as she led the way to the hats. "You must be so thrilled, getting married in, what, just five days?"

"Yes," she said simply, stopping to study a lovely ivory bonnet.

Thrilled? Only for her children's sake. She did not love Aiden McKaslin and could never let herself. He had been honest with her. He would never be able to love her, and she was not surprised by that. No amount of fine lace and silk ribbons or this nice dress would change who she was, inside and out. She was not the kind of woman who inspired love in a man.

Maybe it was better this way, she thought as she glanced over at her little ones. This union wasn't based on some false romantic notion that would only bring her mountain-size disappointments. No, this marriage would be based on what was real, what was most precious to her. While she was not marrying Aiden for love, she was marrying because of love.

That had to be better. Her heart brimmed as she watched Daisy telling James about the pony-shaped buttons, and they both knelt for a closer look. She wanted better for them. She would do her best for them. She prayed that the Lord was up there somewhere watching out for them all. This marriage was a big step she was taking—one built entirely upon hope and faith.

Aiden put down his pitchfork the moment the horses and wagon pulled into the yard. He knew Thad was going to notice how he had stopped work at just that moment, as if he'd been keeping an eye out for her. It was true, but probably not for the reason Thad might think.

"Look who's back." His brother grinned at him from the other side of the wagon bed. "Has she made up her mind about marrying you yet?"

"Apparently. I still can't believe she said yes." Aiden flipped off his hat and pulled his handkerchief from his back pocket. "It's happening this Sunday after church."

"Congratulations." Thad was grinning from ear to

ear as he pitched a forkful of hay into the wagon. "I'm glad you could find someone again. I was afraid that wouldn't happen for you."

"Me, too." That at least was the truth. Years had passed and he'd never considered marrying again, but Joanna had changed all that.

The trip to town must have gone well. She smiled as she lifted her daughter down from the wagon seat. He had to squint against the sun, but he could just make out a big package wrapped up under the seat beside a hatbox. He was glad about that. It looked as if Joanna had found what she needed.

Bless Miss Sims. He'd figured she would help Joanna, as she was too classy of a lady to listen to the terrible rumors Finn had started. Finn. Aiden took a deep breath, trying to squeeze out his sorrow. They knew this for a fact, now. Neither Thad nor the minister could lure him from the saloon or talk him out of his destructive choices.

"Maybe you ought to go check on her." Thad seemed mighty pleased with himself as he kept pitching. "I'll finish up filling the wagon, don't you worry. Go on."

He could see as plain as day what his brother was thinking. "This is an arrangement I have with Joanna, nothing more."

"An arrangement? I don't understand."

"I'm marrying her because she needs help." How clear did he have to be? "That's the only reason we are marrying."

"That's it?" Thad looked mighty perplexed. "You don't love her?"

"No, and she knows that." Aiden slid his pitchfork

against the tailgate, feeling that he ought to be honest. Thad was thinking one thing about this marriage that wasn't true. "She's not in love with me, either."

"Then why are you getting married? Wait, I know." His brother shook his head. "Don't worry, Aiden. No one worth their salt believes any of those rumors. Besides, they are already dying down. I've done my best to make sure of it."

"I appreciate that." Aiden turned away, dreading what his brother was going to say next, no doubt something about love needing to be a part of marriage.

There was Joanna's son petting the horses, while she unbuckled them from the traces. It was hard looking at that boy. The kid was about to become his son, and Joanna his wife.

His wife. The emptiness within him hurt like a broken bone. No, he would do best not to think of her as that. He wiped the sweat from his face and neck, trying to figure out what to say. "Joanna needs help, and I'm helping her. That's all there is to this. She'll be moving into one of the upstairs bedrooms in the house, and I plan on sleeping in one of the downstairs rooms, or the shanty. I'm still deciding."

"The shanty? You're serious, aren't you?"

"Yep." His voice sounded strained and he knew it, but he was managing this the best that he could. "After what I lost, I don't have it in me to love again."

"C'mon, big brother. I don't believe that."

Aiden shrugged, at a loss. "It's just not there. I broke after I lost Kate and the baby. My heart, my soul, they're ashes now. There's nothing left."

"But—"

"There are no buts. There's nothing to argue about, Thad." He stepped away from his brother and the painful conversation.

Joanna was taking the horses to the barn now, with the girl on her hip and the little boy leading the way. She was as wholesome as could be in her pink calico dress and matching sunbonnet. The sun seemed to follow her and grace her, as if heaven were watching over this good woman.

"Aiden, I still don't understand. This could be a second chance for you," Thad argued.

He cleared his throat in order to say what he had to say. "Think of how deeply you love your wife. Now, think of your future without her."

As if struck, Thad bowed his head, silent, his wide shoulders slumped. He looked as if he'd been hit in the chest with an anvil. It was like the sun going down, Aiden knew, never to rise again.

Without the need to say more, he grabbed his hat. "I'll see if Joanna needs anything. I'll be back in a bit."

Thad still didn't say anything, as if he were unable to move.

Aiden found her in the barn, rubbing down the horses, although they were not in a sweat. She sure took good care of her animals.

He hefted the water bucket from the corner and hauled it over to the stalls. "How's his hoof looking?"

"Better, I think. He made the walk to and from town just fine." Joanna looked at Aiden over the horse's smooth rump. "I don't think it's tender at all."

"Good. He'll likely be just fine. I'm having the blacksmith out next week, and he'll take a look. New shoes might help, too."

She nodded, folding up the towel. "How much will that cost?"

"You and I haven't talked about what we are going to do about money after we marry." His lungs felt empty, as if he couldn't get in enough air. The boy was walking down the aisle, peering into the empty stalls, as if dreaming of horses. The girl was staring at something small she held in her hand. He did his best not to notice. "It will be like any marriage, Joanna. I'll pay for what you and your children need. The horses, too."

"But that's not fair to you." Her jaw tightened and her chin went up in the air. "That isn't why I'm marrying you, so you can pay my way. I plan to keep my job with Noelle and maybe pick up some other work in town. Cora Sims has need for an extra seamstress. I'm going to work off a few things I bought for the children."

"I don't think I can stand for that."

"You'll just have to." She had character, he had to give her that. She stood up to him and met his gaze as if she had no intention of backing down. And she didn't. He could see that.

He held up his hands. "Whoa, there. No need to get all mad at me."

"I think there's plenty of need. I'm not marrying you to take advantage of you, Aiden, and if that's what you think, then I'd rather not marry you."

Yes, this was what he remembered of being married. Women, he thought, shaking his head slowly, wishing he could understand them enough to know how to avoid this type of thing. "I only meant I don't want you to work so hard, Joanna. First the fields. Now working for pay. I'm not used to that, is all I'm saying. I never allowed my wife to work."

"And neither did my husband, at first, and look where that got me." There was hurt in Joanna's eyes, creeping in like shadows. "I will always be grateful to you for my children's sake, but I have to know that I'm making a difference for you, too. That I'm making your life a little easier."

His throat choked up. He could not bear to feel one single emotion struggling to life within him.

"It's up to you." Those were the hardest words he had said in a long time. Marriage was like that, too, he remembered. "I don't want you working so hard, Joanna. You need to take better care of your health for those children."

She nodded, avoiding him, too. Silence settled between them, heavy with all they were both unable to say.

He filled the water troughs with a few splashes of water, just enough to wet the horses' tongues until they were a mite cooler. "I'll finish up the work here."

"Then I'll get supper ready for you and Thad." She took Daisy by the hand. "C'mon, James."

The woman left him standing in the aisle, alone in the waning sunlight, still a little surprised. She was going to be his wife.

Chapter Twelve

She'd said yes. Aiden still couldn't believe it, not even standing in church before the minister and most of his family. He was looking right at her and the shock was still with him.

Maybe because there was so much shock, for so many different reasons. He'd never figured he would marry again. He couldn't believe a good woman like Joanna would want to be stuck with a man like him. But mostly he was shocked because the lady in ivory and gold at his side had been hiding her beauty from him.

She wore a simple dress by most standards, but the light color brightened her like a moonbeam. Her golden hair was knotted up primly and properly except for the stray tendrils that curled around her soft face like fine silk. She was luminous in the light of the sanctuary. Her hand held his tightly, and he could practically feel her hope.

Lord, don't let me fail You, he prayed silently. *I'm trusting You to lead me from here.* Only God knew how hard this was for him.

The last time he had been standing in this church and slipping a ring on a woman's finger, he had been so in love his spirit had hurt with the power of it. Never would he have thought his life would bring him here, back to this place.

Pain had a sharp edge as he tried to swallow. He tried not to think back on what he'd lost. He saw instead what he had to gain. A helpmate for his life of hard work. A purpose for his existence. Hope, however small, that providing for Joanna and her children would somehow make up for the loss of his own. Nothing could bring his heart back, he knew, but maybe he could bring life back to hers.

"I now pronounce you man and wife." Hadly, who should have been somber, was grinning. "Aiden, you may now kiss your bride."

"Kiss her?" he repeated, not quite understanding. Kiss her? Why, he had forgotten this part entirely.

"It's all right," Joanna was hastily saying. "It's not required, is it?"

"There's no reason for you two to be shy." The minister closed his Bible, cradling it in his hands. "You're allowed to kiss."

"Oh, my." She turned toward him. "I was so nervous about the ceremony that I forgot we're expected to—"

"Yes, the ceremony's over now." He towered above her, moving a tiny bit closer, and whispered, "I think one kiss would be okay."

"You do?" She discovered she was leaning a tiny bit nearer to him, too. Nerves skittered through her. She did not love Aiden. She did not want to kiss him. They were standing before God, their vows spoken, and his mother watched expectantly with happy tears in her eyes. Joanna felt the pressure of Ida's hopes as surely as the muggy air inside the church.

Should they kiss? No one here, including the minister, believed their quick marriage was anything less than love at first sight.

"I do." Aiden looked solemn as he cupped her face with his big hands. His eyes were as dark as that stormy night sky without the cracks of lightning in it as he leaned forward and kissed her cheek.

Sweetness filled her. In the distance, Ida sighed with happiness and told Noelle, who gasped with pleasure. But it was hard for Joanna to hear over the rush in her ears. The way he looked at her with a question, as if asking permission, made that rushing sound a little louder. The sweetness within her swelled until she felt near to bursting.

"Thank you," she whispered, so that only he would hear.

"You're welcome." He took his hands from her face, but the caring in his eyes remained. "Now neither of us is alone."

"Congratulations," the minister said, beaming. "I pray that you two will always know more happiness and less hardship. Look at poor Ida. She is overcome. Aiden, you made her proud today. I don't think she ever thought this day would come for you."

"It surprised me, too." He stood straight and manly, leaning down to accept his mother's tearful hug. No one would guess by the small smile he managed and his stately acceptance of well wishes from Thad and Noelle, that he was hurting inside.

Only Joanna knew.

She felt a tug on her skirt. Daisy, looking dear in her new dress, gazed up at her pleadingly. "Ma, I have to go."

"All right. We'd best hurry outside." She took her little girl by the hand and turned toward Aiden, but he was already nodding to her, acknowledging that she was leaving, letting her know he would wait for her to come back.

Another piece of hope dammed up the broken pieces of her heart, and Aiden was the reason.

"Welcome to the family, dear." Ida wrapped her in a big hug right in the middle of the front yard. "I can't tell you how pleased I am to have you for a daughter."

A mother-in-law. Joanna hadn't thought that while her marriage to Aiden might not be real in the romantic sense, her relationship with his family could be. "I don't think I could have a better mother-in-law."

"There is no in-law, you hear me, young lady?" Ida was pure loving warmth. "You will be like a daughter to me, the same way Noelle is. Tell her, Noelle, that you can't get rid of me."

"Yes, that is very true. Lucky me." Noelle climbed down from the wagon into her husband's arms. "Ida, you are like a mother to me, you know that. Joanna, prepare to be spoiled."

"That sounds good to me." It was hard to believe her good fortune. That suddenly, with a few vows, she was here, surrounded by family. She lifted Daisy onto her hip. "Please come in. I have dinner ready to warm up."

"As if I'm going to let the bride do all the work!" Ida,

apple-cheeked and rosy, reached out to take Daisy into her arms. "Why don't we go into the kitchen? Noelle, did you remember the baskets?"

"Of course!" Noelle was a wonder, cheerfully feeling her way along the wagon sides, her fingers lightly skimming the boards. "Aiden, come help Thad lift all this stuff. We brought wedding presents."

"And cake." Ida gazed down at the little girl in her arms. "And presents for my grandchildren."

"I got a new button for my collection," Daisy told Ida. "I have eleven now, all of my very own. Do you want to come see?"

"Yes, I do." Ida positively beamed.

She was a born grandmother, Joanna decided, feeling overwhelmed. Maybe it was the scorching heat of the day or the muggy weather, but her knees felt weak and her bones like water. Her children had never known a grandmother's love; her mom had died before she had married Tom, and his mother had no interest.

James had perked up at the word *presents.* He watched the older woman closely, as if afraid of believing what he had just heard. Gifts had always been strictly Christmas and birthday events. Until now.

Ida held out her hand, James took it and the three of them disappeared into the house. A kind grandma. Now, that was more than a blessing, it was divine gift. The hot breeze swept around Joanna, twirling her skirts and skimming her face. The gentle lilt of Noelle's quiet alto and Thad's rumbling bass made a cozy duet as they talked low together at the far end of their wagon. They obviously had a happy marriage, another rare blessing.

Aiden was one of those, too. Not only a gift, but a

once-in-a-lifetime kind of man. Joanna's heart swelled
tenderly as she searched the yard for him. There he was,
standing at the far side of the house with his feet braced
on the land like some western myth, watching the white
puffy thunderheads building in the southern sky.

He didn't turn as she approached, but began talking, so he obviously knew she was close. "We might
get a hard blow. I've got yesterday's cut hay drying in
the field."

He seemed distant and motionless, as if made of
stone. Alone, as if he were always destined to be. She
ached, wishing she knew how to ease his pain. "Do you
need some time? Or should I start setting out the meal?"

"Go ahead and eat." His throat worked, the only sign
that he was made of flesh and bone and not granite. "I'll
come in when I can."

She thought of Ida fawning over her grandchildren.
Of how happy his family was for him. It had to be a
painful reminder of the time he'd brought his Kate home
after their wedding, and of Ida's first grandchild, who
hadn't lived.

Now neither of us are alone. His words in the church
came back to Joanna and touched her anew. How alone
he must have felt all these years. When she laid her hand
on the steely curve of his shoulder, he let it linger for a
moment before he turned away.

"I've got to take care of the horses," he said hollowly.
"I need to keep an eye on the storm."

The ring on her finger was a reminder that she was
more committed than before to making this man's life
better. But how? She was at the end of her rope. She
had done everything she knew to do.

Lord, show me. Please. It was on faith she prayed, for she had no one else to rely on. Not even herself. She did not know how to help him. She didn't know if anyone could.

"I'll be inside if you need anything, Aiden." It was hard to force her feet to carry her away from him. She had so many things to do: change into her work clothes and get the little ones out of their new things, put the meal on the table, make sure everyone was fed and comfortable and happy.

"Joanna, dear, there you are." Ida was on the kitchen steps. "Does Aiden think bad weather is on the way?"

"Yes." She glanced over her shoulder, nearly missing her footing. He still had his back turned, watching the storm clouds gathering. She longed to draw him away from that lonely field and take him into the house where his family waited for him. She knew she did not have that power.

"Then we'll leave him to his weather watching." If Ida was troubled over her son, it didn't show except in the tight lines around her mouth. "He'll join us when he's able. Come see what present we brought for you."

"For me?"

"Why, yes. You are the bride, are you not?" Ida took her by the arm and led her through the lean-to into the kitchen. "Don't make the mistake of thinking that this is no big occasion, being a second marriage for both of you, because you would be wrong. Come into the parlor."

Joanna noticed the leaves had been put into the table and it was set for seven. The stove had been lit and pots were sitting on top, heating up. The dinner rolls she had baked yesterday were spread on a sheet, ready to go into the oven. Ida had already taken care of heating up the meal.

"Ma!" James jumped to his feet and came running across the parlor. Excitement sparkled in his eyes and he appeared happier than she could ever remember seeing him. "Look what Uncle Thad made me. A real mustang."

Joanna glanced at the carved wooden horse with mane and tail flowing. She had to blink hard to keep her eyes from burning. "He looks just like Sunny, doesn't he?"

"Yep. That's what I'm calling him. I got another one, too." He pointed to the second horse he had been playing with on the floor. "That's Sky. They are best friends."

"Did you thank your uncle?"

"Yep. About five times." James wrapped his arms around her in a quick hug.

There was Daisy, on the sofa next to Noelle. Together they were dressing her rag doll in new calico dresses. "Ma! Look! Anna has lots to wear. And a nightie, too!"

It was like Christmas morning. Joanna didn't need anything more than this, to see her little ones so happy. Material things were not what mattered; she knew that more than most. But the loving people around them, welcoming them as family, were worth everything. More than she had ever dreamed could be.

She had been on her own for so long, even in her first marriage, that she had forgotten the comfort of a caring smile against the cruel harshness that came to a person's life. She had forgotten the simple pleasure of having someone hold out a hand, wanting her to join in.

"Come over here with us and see," Noelle offered.

Joanna picked her way around the pasture James had made on the center of the floor and left him there to play. Thad had also carved fence posts and a gate. There were other little things for Daisy, Joanna saw as she settled down beside Noelle. A doll-size knitted blanket, a calico sunbonnet and a ruffled apron.

"Thank you," she told them all. "This is...unexpected but wonderful. Too much, but wonderful."

"I had the most fun crocheting and knitting up these wee things," Noelle confessed.

"So did I." Ida smiled in her infectious, beaming way. "Noelle, this is good practice for you. You may be making a lot of wee little things of your own one day. You never know."

"Wouldn't that be a blessing?" Thad's wife lit up at the thought. "In the meantime, this was great fun. Joanna, we have something for you, too. You have no notion how Ida and I had to hurry to get this done in time."

"We weren't sure we would," Ida interjected. "It was nip and tuck. But we did it."

"Here, this is for you." Noelle lifted a wrapped bundle from the cushion at her side. "We are so happy for you and Aiden."

She said it with great conviction, as if she had no notion that this marriage was not genuine. Joanna's hands trembled as she tugged at the white ribbon holding the wrapping together. The tissue paper fell away and on top was a beautiful, snowy-white bedcovering, crocheted in a breathtaking pattern of rosebuds and leaves. Beneath that were folds of matching lace scarves for the bureau and bedside tables, and delicate curtains.

Tears swam in her eyes.

"We understand what Aiden told Thad," Noelle said gently. "That this was an arrangement between you. But it is my wish for you both that one day, along with great happiness, you will find great love. Ida and I put our hopes and prayers into every stitch."

A movement beyond the doorway caught Joanna's eye. It was Aiden, standing like a shadow. Then he stepped forward, into the light. There was pain etched in his face, but it was a different pain from what it had been there before. As if he were forcing himself into living again, he eyed the folds of soft, frothy lace and nodded once—just once.

"So, this is where everyone is," he quipped. "Can't a starving man get a meal around here?"

"Yeah," Thad agreed with a wink. "Where's the food? I'm looking forward to dessert. Ma made angel food cake."

"You'll get it when we're good and ready, you two," Ida quipped right back. "Mind your manners."

"Manners? I don't have any. It's my ma's fault. I was raised up terrible." Tiny smile lines creased the corners of Aiden's eyes.

The warm glow of caring Joanna was trying to ignore sparked a little more brightly. Like morning after a long hard night, that's what Aiden was for her. She gently refolded the exquisite lace. He could not know what she was beginning to feel. That the brand of caring she held in her heart was changing into something richer.

She rose, striving to hide her affection. Tucking away

what she did not want seen, she slipped out of the room and followed Ida to the safety of the kitchen.

"You should have seen the looks on those boys' faces." Ma paused over her slice of cake to laugh with the memory. "There they were, swooping blueberries into their little pails as fast as they could go. Thad would shovel a handful into his mouth every once in a while. His mouth was stained blue."

"I'm sure it wasn't *that* much." The man was blushing, fidgeting in his chair at the table, looking sheepish.

"It was, too," Aiden insisted, pointing at him with his fork. He remembered well all the faults of his brother. It was an older sibling's right, after all. "It wasn't just your mouth that would be blue, but your chin and the front of your shirt."

"I was seven years old." Thad laughed good-naturedly.

Ma continued to regale Joanna with the family story. "There I was, trying to keep an eye on Finn, but he was running everywhere, and faster than greased lightning to boot. I had one hand on my pail, the other stripping berries from the bush, all the while looking over my shoulder at my youngest. Then I look the other way to check on my older two boys and I see this big grizzly sitting up on his haunches, looking at them with the most puzzled expression you ever saw."

Aiden watched Joanna's jaw drop. "But weren't you terrified?" she asked.

"Worse than terrified." Ma delighted in telling a good family tale, and she sparkled with the fun of it. It was great to see her looking truly happy. "In my mind's eye I already saw that bear munching down Thad like one of those berries, and holding Aiden in the air with his enormous, dangerous paws."

"Since I'm here," Thad interjected, "you can tell the story ended fairly well."

"For you, maybe," Aiden took the last bite of his piece of cake.

That caught Joanna's interest, because she fixed her gaze on him. Those big blue eyes of hers seemed to reach out to him, so full of life. He felt dark and dour by comparison. He couldn't help feeling that she had gotten the short end of the stick in this marriage deal, but he was going to do his best to make it up to her.

"I think that bear had never seen little boys before," Ma continued, putting down her fork, leaning forward, getting into the spirit of the story. "He watched them, a little aghast, as if he was trying to figure out if they were a different kind of rabbit or something."

Joanna laughed, a light musical sound, and Aiden studied her. She looked so different from the sad-eyed woman he'd seen that day at her pa's wake. She was no longer so painfully thin, and color had come back to her complexion. The heat made her hair curl up around her pretty face, and there he went, feeling drawn to her again. He pushed back the chair and rose to his feet. Time to get another cup of tea.

"Then he must have realized that most of his berries were gone from his favorite bush," Ma was saying. "Why, I had grown ten feet, or so it felt like, and I don't even remember dropping my bucket or crossing those few yards of that hillside, but suddenly I was right in front of that bear. He was enormous, bigger than a man by far, and I remember looking down at him."

"You were fearsome, Ma," Thad stated in that easygoing way of his. "Joanna, I remember being too scared to move. I froze with a big handful of berries in my mouth. I was no help. Aiden, he grabbed a stick and went up to help Ma, but he was too late."

"I'm not sure what good that stick would have been against that bear if he had a mind to take offense at us." Aiden lifted the cool pitcher from the counter. "I remember thinking that animal was going to hurt Ma."

"He wouldn't have dared." Ma pointed her finger, in the way of scolding mothers everywhere. "I shook my finger at him and I said, 'Now, you leave us alone. You go eat your berries somewhere else.' He looked me up and down, bowed his head and waddled off."

"He left? Just like that?" Joanna asked.

"Thank the Lord." Ma nodded. "I was shaking so hard afterward I sat down and couldn't move for a good twenty minutes. Aiden had to help me get back to the wagon."

He heard his brother answer, his sister-in-law comment, which made them all laugh again, but he wasn't really listening. Outside, the clouds were building fast and coming closer. He thought of the field of cut hay drying in the summer sun, and the forty acres of growing wheat. He prayed there was no rain in those clouds, or hard wind and hail that would damage his main crop. He had to make sure Joanna had the security she needed. It was the one thing he could give her. The only thing.

He took a long pull of tea from his cup before setting it down on the counter. "I'm going to head out and start bringing in the hay."

"But, Aiden, it's your wedding day," Ma protested. "And it would be breaking the Sabbath."

"God will understand my need to save my hay. Is this all right with you, Joanna?"

"Yes. You now have two more horses to feed for the winter." She pushed away from the table and stood. "You might need all the hay you can bring in."

"Exactly. There's no telling how long or hard the winter will be. I'm glad you understand that." He was already grabbing his hat off the hook by the door. "See, Thad? She's a sensible woman."

"A real catch." Thad winked at her as he ambled on past and hooked his own hat off the wall. "The question is, if she's that sensible, why did she marry you?"

"That, brother, is a mystery." The men's voices faded as they strode off across the yard.

Not such a mystery, Joanna knew, as she watched her husband go. The gathering clouds were like giant anvils bumping up against one another in the southern sky. But as big as they were and as enormous the sky, they did not diminish the man walking beneath them.

No, not such a mystery at all. Tenderness hit with such force she had to turn away. Letting herself fall in love with Aiden would be the worst mistake.

She closed the screen door, stepped around James, who was on the floor playing with his new horses, and dropped a kiss on Daisy's head as she dressed her doll. Joanna then began clearing the dessert plates from the table.

Chapter Thirteen

Exhaustion had burrowed deep and he felt as if he could never get it out of his bones, but he and Thad had beat the storm, first at home and then at his brother's place. Aiden reined in Clyde at the barn as the first fat drops of rain fell. Good for the land, but not necessarily good for his wheat. He dismounted, knowing there was nothing he could do about that.

"You were a good horse today." He led the draft horse by the ends of the reins, going slow. It had been a long day for the horses, too.

A surprise waited for him in the barn. One of the wagons was empty of hay. It just stood there, as if the wind had blown every scrap from it and left the other wagon untouched. The only telltale sign was the lantern carefully hung from the end aisle post, flickering low.

The rain began pounding like lead bullets on the roof and a shadow raced through the back door and into the pool of light. Dotted with rain and her hair in one long braid, Joanna held his pitchfork in her hand.

"That's really coming down. I got the last stack finished just in time."

"The last stack?" Aiden hadn't realized he'd left Clyde standing in the middle of the aisle. All he knew was that he was already at her side, tight with concern. "It's late. That rain is cold. You aren't telling me that you stacked the hay."

"I told you I'm pretty good at it. I thought, why not? The kids fell asleep early, they had such a busy day. I can see the shanty from here, and I wanted to help out."

She amazed him. He shook his head, flummoxed, feeling a few raindrops drip off his hat brim. "What am I going to do with you? You are supposed to be in the main house, making ruffles or embroidering or something. Not this."

"Are you going to tell me you don't approve of women stacking hay?" Her rosebud mouth quirked up in the corner, and there was no mistaking her challenge.

Yep, she surely amazed him. She was like no woman he'd ever known. He liked her for it. Lord help him, he liked her. "I'm going to allow you to stack hay if that's what you want."

"Allow me?" There it was, the indignation on her face. The quirk of her brows, the rise of her chin. He was glad for the humor sparking in her eyes that told him she knew he was funning her.

He shrugged, removing his hat to shake off the rain spatters. "Am I the man around here?"

A handful of hay hit him square in the face. "Take that, Aiden McKaslin. That's for that big fib you just told."

"I deserved it." He was laughing. Unbelievable, but

it felt good. "I couldn't help it. You're a mighty pretty woman when you get all worked up."

Pink swept across her face. "Now, that's two fibs. What am I going to do with you? I hope this isn't a sign of things to come."

"I wasn't fibbing." Even with her hair wet and plastered to her, she was beautiful. More so every time he looked at her. He reached out, hardly aware of it, his fingers brushing a strand of curls away from her eyes so he could see them better. "My family loves you and your kids. All evening long that's all I heard. I couldn't get away from it."

"I'm sorry. They have hopes for you."

"I know." His fingers lingered at her temple. For some reason, he couldn't pull away. Being this near to her felt soothing to him, when he had hurt for so long. "I heard what they said in the parlor. About the gift."

"You have to know I don't feel the way they do. I know you don't love me. I don't expect that you would." Her forehead creased, and she looked down.

But she didn't move away. The empty places within him stirred like ashes in a winter wind. As if something was there, after all. "My family is hopeful for me, but you have to know something of what I am. You have children, a son. What if that had happened to you?"

Her face crumpled. Her gaze shot toward the barn wall, in the direction of the shanty. "I could not have come back after that."

"No, I can't see as there is a way to be whole. Some things, once broken, can never be put back together again."

"Yes, I think you are right. Not when it's real love."

She gazed up at him, seeing a man more substance than shadow. "I loved my husband in the beginning with all my heart. But the way he behaved and how he treated me wore at my love until it faded away. My heartbreak wasn't sudden like yours. It came one step at a time, like losing little pieces until the polish and beauty of that love was gone."

"I imagine it hurts the same in the end."

"For different reasons." She could see that Aiden had loved deeply and his love had been returned. Hers had not. That was a hard lesson to her. "You are safe with me, Aiden. I don't have your family's expectations."

"You mean, for me to love you eventually?"

"Yes." Sadness filled her, and no small amount of hurt. She caught his hand with hers, remembering how he had kissed her in the church. Tenderness twinkled like a new star in her heart. "I know you can't love me. I don't think it would be good for either of us to think it might be possible. I have my children to raise, and you have this land. We can help each other. That's good enough for me."

He closed his eyes briefly, and she had to guess that it was relief showing on his hard face. "I would give you more if I could," he murmured.

His hand trembled beneath hers, so she let go and stepped away from him. Her skin felt chilled without his touch, and she was aware of the inches separating them. It may as well have been the expanse of the entire western prairie. "It's all right, Aiden. No man could give me more. I'm not the kind of woman a man can love."

"Why do you say that?"

He seemed puzzled, as if he had no notion, and the

caring in her heart for him flared more brightly. It was no longer anything resembling caring. No, not at all. She swallowed hard, trying to deny the truth even to herself. "Being loved is impossible for me. Look at me. All my husband really wanted me for was to ease his burdens in life. He saw me as a maid more than anything."

"When you had loved him."

She spun on her heel so she wouldn't have to see Aiden's face. Would it show pity? Or understanding? Either way, the truth remained. She did not possess great beauty or poise or city polish. What she could do was stack hay to shed even the hardest rain. That rain struck her now as she went to check on her handiwork. Her bare feet squished in the dusty dirt that had been quick to turn to mud. There were her half-dozen stacks, standing as tall and round and whole as the dozens Aiden had already built. She let the wind blow through her, wanting the cool gusts to scatter the emotions inside her. It didn't work. Her love for him clung stubbornly to her heart.

I love him. She swiped the rain from her face and stared out at the dark storm. Once again she had fallen in love with a man who did not love her. She was heading for heartbreak all over again. What was she going to do now?

Deny it, of course. She lifted her face to the sky, welcoming the wonderful wetness. It washed away the sting of tears that could not fall, and the disappointment in herself. It's different this time, she told herself. Better. At least she wouldn't wonder why, in this marriage. She knew.

His hand settled on her shoulder, comforting. His touch could make her spirit lift like birds at dawn.

"I couldn't have built haystacks any better." He moved away to circle the stacks, and nodded once he saw how well they were shedding rain. "Who taught you?"

"My ma. When I was a little girl, I used to help her with the work."

"I'm not surprised by that, as I knew your pa."

"He was not a hardworking sort." She held her hands out, palms up, as if welcoming the rain. It sluiced down her face and dripped off her skirt hem. "I've always liked working outside in the fresh air."

"Have you always liked standing in the rain?"

"You say that as if now you think I don't have a lick of sense. What about you? You are out here, too."

"Well, I'm going in." The haystacks were more than fine, and that was a compliment to her. There was a real knack to it, and he knew plenty of men who couldn't do as well. "Clyde's waiting for me to bed him down."

Rain drummed between them, a thousand drops pinging and pounding all around like a symphony. Funny how he hadn't noticed all the rich notes of the winds in a long time. He hiked into the barn, glad for the shelter. "I'm sorry about this afternoon. I didn't know Ma and Noelle would want to come visit and bring gifts. I can't imagine how fast the two of them had to crochet to get all that made."

"I suspect they already had a start on the project and finished it for me instead of, perhaps, for one of their bedrooms. Noelle told me her house is only a few months old."

"Yes, they got married in late spring." Aiden remembered the hope in his ma's voice. *It is my wish for you both that one day, along with great happiness, you will find great love.*

He grimaced. His ma was a dreamer, always had been and would always be. "I had meant to move you and the kids into the house this afternoon."

"If the mud stays in the field, tomorrow will work out fine. We can move without interfering with your haying." She swiped the rain off her face. "I thought the children and I could share the room at the top of the stairs. It's big and roomy, with plenty of sunshine."

"It's a sensible solution." He held his heart still. "I've decided to move to the downstairs room. It was meant to be something else, but it would serve as a bedroom well enough."

"You had intended it to be a children's playroom for the winter," she guessed.

He nodded, swallowed hard and stripped off Clyde's bridle. "That way you have the upstairs all to yourselves. I won't wake you all when I get up at four-thirty to start the chores."

"You know I get up to start mine."

He knew. There were more reasons, which he couldn't see fit to tell her. "Good night, Joanna. Thank you for all you did for me and my family today."

"They are my family now, Aiden." She padded past him in her bare feet, a perfect picture of a country woman in calico and grace. "You are my family, too. Good night."

What felt like ashes within him, in his heart, in his soul, stirred toward life. He wished he could feel something for her. He wished he had something left inside of him besides the ashes of his heart and the pieces of his soul.

He planned to avoid her in this big house of his, Joanna had guessed, so she wasn't surprised that his chores were done and he was out in the fields before dawn. While the children played on the doorstep, she whipped up a batch of pancakes, fried eggs and bacon. Because he didn't come to the table, she packed up the meal with a small jug of tea, and with James and Daisy trailing with her, headed out to the wheat fields.

The earth was moist and muddy in spots, the air fresh from the storm. A flawless sapphire sky glinted overhead, so blue it hurt the eye. She followed the trail along the fence line until she found Aiden in the middle of a field of wheat, chopping down fallen stalks. The stalks of wheat were tall and nearly ripe this time of year. Most waved softly golden in the temperate breezes. There were acres upon acres lost to wind damage. She saw great swaths of downed stalks, stretching from south to north. A grim sight, to be sure. She was thankful for the crop that still stood.

"We'll stay here," she told the children, who were ready to walk into the field. "We don't want to disturb the wheat."

"Oh." James hitched his arms over a rail and watched Aiden in the field, the man who was his stepfather now. "He looks awful busy."

"You know right before harvest is one of the busiest times for a farmer." She settled the basket on the ground.

"Yep. I know." He sighed anyway.

Aiden must have spotted her. He set aside his scythe, straightened his hat and began heading her way through the knee-high grain. The gentle sunshine seemed to follow him, making him bigger and brighter than she had ever seen him. Maybe, she realized, that was because she was looking at him with her heart. With a new love that had not been there before.

She lowered her gaze, as if that could lessen her feelings for him, and fumbled with the basket lid. Why her fingers were so clumsy, she couldn't say. She had to grab the tin cup twice and suddenly Aiden was there, his deep voice rumbling.

"Let me."

Her heart plummeted to the earth. This was a mistake, she told herself, as she uncapped the pitcher and poured a shaky stream of tea into the cup. She knew too much to fall in love again. But with this man, how could she help it? It was as natural as breathing.

"You are a welcome sight," he said simply as he took a long sip. "That's good after an early start."

"How long have you been out here?"

"It was still dark. I didn't look at the clock. Worrying about the crop, I didn't get a whole lot of sleep. So I got up and made myself useful."

He was tired. She could see the bruises beneath his eyes and the worry etched into his forehead. She unwrapped the clean cloth she'd folded around the food. "We are lucky half the crop was spared."

"I like to think it was more than luck." He took off his hat and hung it on the fence post.

She was beginning to think that, too. It was easier to believe when she was with Aiden, rock-solid in his faith. It made what she was beginning to see much clearer. "Do you think Thad and Noelle's ranch has this damage, too?"

"Hard to say. I've done almost all I can until the fields dry up some, so later on, I'll ride over and see." He took the plate she offered and bowed his head for a quick blessing.

There was a cowlick at the crown of his head. Why she noticed that, she couldn't rightly say. There was so much she didn't know about this man, so many things that she wanted to know and to cherish.

"This looks mighty good," he said when he was done. "Thank you, Joanna."

"You're more than welcome. Is there anything I can do here to help you?"

"No. You come out here and you'll likely get as muddy as me." She was a great cook; he had to give her that. The pancakes melted on his tongue. "This hits the spot."

"I'm glad." She was already packing up, ready to leave him with that gentle smile she always had on her face these days. "I don't suppose you had a chance to check the orchard?"

"Nope. I can only hope there's plenty of fruit left on the trees, as I'm looking forward to fresh pies later this summer."

"Only if you're good." There it was, that flash of mischief in her eyes.

"What does that mean?"

"Just wait. You'll see." She settled the basket on her arm, and with the breeze teasing the golden wisps of her hair and the brim of her pink sunbonnet, she could have been a wild summer rose come into bloom. So vibrant, fragile and alive, she pulled at the shadows within him. Made him feel every emptiness and every broken place.

"The three of us will have the upstairs room clean and waiting, whenever you're ready." She gave her bonnet brim a tug against the low rays of the rising sun. "I plan to go to Noelle's this afternoon."

"We'll do it before you leave then." He winced a little. "And I'll ride over with you."

"It's a good plan." She held out her free hand to Daisy. "I'll come for the dishes later."

"Not to bother. I'll bring them in with me in a bit. I can't do much more out here."

"All right." She wanted to stay and keep him company, but she could see that he was having a hard time. She hated that. She wished she knew what to do for him. "We don't have to move in with you, Aiden."

"My wife won't be living in a shanty if I can provide better." He pinned her with a firm gaze.

He meant it in the best possible way. Joanna could see that plain as day. That still didn't mean it was easy for him. What a blessed woman his Kate was, to have been loved like that. What an exceptional man Aiden was, to have loved with all he had, down to his soul. Joanna could see the pieces of what was left in him. Her heart swelled even more with affection best kept hidden.

"All right," she said quietly, ready to go. Her son hadn't moved an inch. He watched Aiden with more than interest, for surely the boy was old enough to have figured out what yesterday's ceremony had meant. "Come, James. We need to go."

There was a question in his eyes. Such a sweet boy he was. She knew what he was too shy to ask. He wanted to stay in the fields and help Aiden, although he was much too little for that. Aiden would have been the kind of father who would take his son with him just to spend time with him, and teach him by his example and kindness.

If only, she thought wistfully. She had no notion if Aiden would ever come to the place where he could be close to his stepson, so she held out her other hand. "Come, James."

"All right." He hopped down and ran her way, all little-boy energy. He waited until they were a ways off before he leaned close to whisper, "He's our pa now, right?"

"He's your stepfather. Remember I said he and I were married now." She had explained that when she'd tucked them into bed last night.

Daisy seemed unconcerned, but James pursed his lips, thinking hard. "That's like a pa."

"Yes. He's like having a second father."

James seemed satisfied. "Then are we going to stay in his house and not leave?"

"Yes, that's why I married him. So we have a home we never have to leave."

"That's sure good. Cuz I don't want to go back to the wagon."

"I know, pumpkin." She didn't want that for her little ones, either. "We're here to stay."

"I like Grandma," Daisy said, as if that settled it. "She gave me one of her buttons."

Joanna felt an odd tingle at the back of her neck. When she looked over her shoulder, she saw nothing but a meadowlark hopping onto the fence rail near where Aiden had been standing. She searched the meadow, to find him heading back to work, taking his plate and tea with him.

Even surrounded by the bright fields sprinkled with sunshine, and framed by the vivid blue sky, he somehow looked lost. The sunlight on her face was like a gentle touch, like reassurance, helping her to understand. For so long she had been sure that the Lord had forgotten her. Hardships had wedged their way into her faith, creating rifts that grew larger with every difficulty.

Looking back, maybe she could see the purpose behind every trial that had brought her to stay at her pa's house, and then the loss of that, too. God had been there all along, gently guiding her here. To Aiden.

Because he needed her.

Chapter Fourteen

"Where do you want this?" Aiden's voice boomed behind her. He stood in the doorway with the rocking chair hefted easily over his shoulder.

"By the window, please." She was fully aware that she was a sight. Her skirts were damp and strands of hair had come out of her braid, curling every which way.

She stepped aside to make room, but was hemmed in by the bedstead that had already been in the room, which she and Daisy would share. Then there was the smaller bed Aiden had moved in from one of the spare rooms, left over from when he and his brothers were young.

"Sure thing." Aiden passed by, brushing against the hem of her skirts as he went.

What a good husband he is, she thought wistfully, watching him as he carefully swung the chair down. He had a perfect profile, with the spill of his dark hair over his high, intelligent forehead, and a straight nose. His chin and jaw were a strong balance to his other chiseled features. Handsome, yes—she surely thought him so—but he was more. He was built of character, and she ached with admiration. With love.

What was she going to do about that? She could no longer hide from it. Love for him filled her as surely as light coming in the window filled the room.

"You could take one of the other rooms."

"I could," she agreed. It wasn't easy trying to hide how she felt. It wasn't easy knowing her abiding affection for him would cause both of them nothing but grief. She took a step toward the rocking chair, glad that it stood between them like a barrier, creating distance she desperately needed.

She forced herself to look out the window at her little ones playing in the shade of the house, James with his horses and Daisy with her doll.

"You don't have to all be cooped up in one room." He sounded gruff, but there were notes of concern there, too, and, as always, his rugged kindness. "That makes it about the same as the shanty."

"Trust me, this is not the same." Not with the light yellow wallpaper sprinkled with tiny cornflowers, a fireplace in the corner to warm the space on a cold winter's night, the polished wood floor and two big windows. "Was this your mother's room?"

"It was." Aiden faced the window, too, and seemed to be watching the children at play, although it was hard to tell. He was so distant, as if he were looking in and not out. "Maybe after you settle some and feel comfortable here, you'll want your children to have rooms of their own. There's enough for that. Finn won't be coming back."

"Maybe he'll realize the way he's living his life

isn't right and won't bring him happiness. Then he will change. It could happen."

"It could, but I've been disappointed hoping in that before. I wish I could have him back. It's not that I don't want to."

"I know." Even a stranger, someone who didn't know Aiden at all, could see the anguish on his face. Love and life were such fragile things and could be lost in a blink. Aiden had lost Finn as surely as if he had buried him, too. She could see it plainly. "Maybe there's still hope for him."

"Maybe. Pastor Hadly is checking on him as much as he can, and Thad is, as well. Finn is still talking with Thad. That's something at least. Not that Finn wants to stop having fun, as he calls it."

Joanna could feel Aiden's pain. She longed to reach out and lay her hand on his shoulder and somehow absorb some of it. "I don't think even Finn thinks he's having fun. He's escaping from more than the responsibility of working and making a living on this land. He's escaping life."

"I won't argue with you." Aiden winced. "I know you're right."

"You've done so much for him. I wish he could see what I do."

"What's that?"

"How you want to make things right for him."

"Now, how do you know that?" He moved away from the window, away from her.

"It's what I know of you. What I see in you."

"You seem to know a lot about me." There were those

tangled up feelings again, coiling tight in every empty space. "I guess I'm not so hard to figure out."

"No, not at all." There was a smile in her voice and a softness that made him want to turn toward her.

How he wished he could. He fisted his hands, sticking to what was safe, to what was right. "I'm trying to do all I can for him. It's my duty. It's what's right."

"You always do the right thing."

"I sure try. Heaven knows I've made my share of mistakes." He wished he could give Finn another chance, but he knew it wouldn't work. He had to stand firm. He had to let Finn figure out the consequences of his choices, the same as any man. It was the way the Lord intended. A man might have free will, but choosing the easy path was not easy at all. The harder road at first was the easier one in the long run. A man made a lot of mistakes on either path. There seemed to be no help for that other than faith and prayer.

One mistake he hadn't made was bringing Joanna here. At least he felt good about that. She was wearing her green calico dress today, and he was close enough to see all the careful patching she had done to the garment. Matching the pattern of the sprigged calico took great care. He knew, because his ma had done the same to all of their clothes once, when they were young and times were lean.

"You said you're doing piecework for Miss Sims?" he asked, his voice coming out more gruffly than he'd meant.

"I will stop by her shop on my way to Noelle's today, whether you object to my working or not."

He took in the flash of Joanna's grin and shook his

head. No one had ever before disagreed with him so cheerfully. Or gotten around him quite so easily. He had no notion of how to keep her in check. He had a feeling he never would be able to. Joanna had spirit, one that hardship had not dimmed.

He headed to the door, smiling to himself. "Now, I never said I would object. I only meant to say you will get yourself some new clothes, and for your little ones, too. I won't be married to a woman with patched dresses."

"Oh, you won't?"

His smile stretched a little wider, surprising him. He hadn't smiled like this in more years than he could count. "I'm putting my foot down. I don't want to hear any arguments."

"What if I have plenty of arguments?"

"Too bad. You'll just have to suffer in silence." He reached the hall and glanced over his shoulder to make sure she understood what he could not say. "I mean it, Joanna. You'll do what I say."

"Oh, you have a lot to learn." She flipped her braid over her shoulder, as if trying to figure out what to do with a man like him. "Perhaps I'll do as you ask this once. The children are growing so fast."

It was a victory of sorts, and he was pleased with that. "There's something else. There ought to be a few boxes up in the attic. If you want to take the time later on, some of our old toys are crated up. Wooden horses and a barn my grandfather made. Your boy might like 'em."

"I'm sure he would."

He turned before he could see her sympathy, but he

felt it while he hiked down the hall to his room. Here, he was alone, but no longer safe. He no longer felt as hollow. Without hesitation, he hefted the feather mattress off the bedstead and carried it down the hallway.

He was mighty glad to have that moving business done with. Aiden tightened the last of the buckles and gave Clyde a pat on the neck. "Good old fella."

The draft horse nickered and rubbed his head against Aiden's chest, knocking him back a foot. "Careful there, boy. You don't know your own strength."

Clyde gave a woof of expelled air and lifted his head. They had company. There was Joanna's son, standing just outside the barn door. His little shadow fell into the main aisle.

"Does your ma know you wandered away from the yard?"

"No, sir." The boy's voice sounded small and forlorn. "I haven't left the yard. I'm just standing in the dirt is all, instead of the grass."

"You know to keep within sight of the windows."

"Yessir." The boy paled but held his ground. "Ma can still see me."

Aiden took Clyde by the bits to lead him forward. "You know not to wander off, right?"

"Yep. I gotta stay close and watch my sister."

"That's right." Aiden was near enough to see past the narrow angle of the doorway to the span of yard toward the house. There was Joanna's daughter, sitting in the shade, changing her rag doll. "You know there are dangerous animals around. They don't come close to the houses, but I've seen them in the fields now and again."

"Yessir." The boy edged to the side to make room, his gaze and attention switching to the horse. "I reckon you know all the harnessing."

"Yep." Aiden steeled himself because he knew what was coming.

"I sure would like to learn that." The kid breathed that out in a sigh of longing, the question he was too afraid to ask lingering in the silence between them.

He hadn't shored himself up enough; the boy's wish hit him square in the chest. Aiden thought of all the reasons it would be better to ignore the boy and keep on going. All the reasons why it would hurt too much to stop.

His feet made the decision for him. He was handing over one strap of the reins before he had thought it through. "Can you lead Clyde over to the house?"

"I sure can, sir." Excitement snapped across his features. Hope sparkled. "I'll do a real good job, too."

"Walk him slow." He kept his hand on the horse's neck, but there was no need. Clyde gave a snort of pleasure and followed the boy, lipping his hair affectionately. The wagon wheels creaked, the boy giggled and the old Clydesdale plodded toward the house.

"Keep to the wagon tracks," Aiden cautioned, and noticed Joanna on the back doorstep. There was gratitude on her soft oval face and something else that made his pulse skid to an instant halt. Something that made him close his eyes. But the image remained on the back of his lids—the image of her lovely face watching him with adoration.

Maybe it was for the boy, he told himself. Of course she adored her son. That was it, he thought in a panic, opening his eyes and seeing the ground at his feet. Little patches of mud remained from the storm, but already the dust was returning, puffing up with each step he took. He concentrated on that, and when he looked at Joanna again it was to help her into the wagon.

She looked good, and when he took her hand, he felt his spirit stir, as if it was still there, after all, when he had thought that part of him was gone.

It felt right to help her up onto the front seat. "You'll sit up here with me," he told her, and since he now had enough experience with her to know what she might say to that, he added, "please."

That earned him her smile. He didn't think there was a more beautiful sight than Joanna at that moment, grinning down at him from the high wagon seat. The sun sat behind her like a jewel, framing her with gold. She was like a completely different woman. Gone were the lines of strain and worry. Fallen away was the worn-down look of hardship.

It felt good to think he had a hand in that. That his life amounted to something, after all. It was hard to believe an used up man with no life left could make a difference. Maybe God wasn't done with him yet.

She held out her arms and he turned to find the girl at his knee, clutching her doll.

"You're next, little girl." He hiked her up with no effort at all. She was no burden. She went to her mother's arms, leaving him to face the boy.

Aiden held his feelings still, tricking himself into thinking he didn't have any, but before he could offer help, the boy was climbing up on his own, nimbly and easily. Aiden couldn't say why he stood there, watching to make sure the little guy was safely over the rail, before he moved away. Joanna was watching over her son, too, making sure he settled safely onto the backseat. That's what Aiden respected about her most of all—that she knew what was precious in this world.

He gathered the reins together and hopped up next to her. It was strange having Joanna at his side. He gave the leather straps a gentle slap and Clyde ambled forward. Aiden couldn't rightly say why he felt as if a roll of barbed wire was lodged behind his ribs. All he knew was that Joanna was doing this to him, making him ache more with every breath.

"I didn't know where to put the lovely things your mother and Noelle made us." She turned to him, obviously unaware of her effect on him. "I didn't want to put them in my and the children's room."

"You should. It seems fitting."

"Sticky fingers," she explained, and there was that smile again. The soft, captivating look of fondness. "They might fare better in your room."

"I have no use for frilly lace. No offense."

There was her smile again, wide enough to reach her eyes and to touch his worn-out soul. He liked that he could make her smile like that. That meant he'd done the right thing, although judging by how he was feeling, it didn't seem that way.

"I simply wanted to know what to tell Ida and Noelle. Their gift was thoughtful and beautiful, and I wanted to be able to tell them where I intend to display their handiwork. How about the parlor?"

"Good solution." He pushed his hat back and guided Clyde onto the main road, although the big guy knew his way. It gave Aiden something to focus on beside the woman and her smile. Summer had bronzed the prairie. Everywhere he looked was the amber of ripening wheat, the russet of wild grasses and the yellow-gold of wildflowers nodding in the breeze. It would be harvest soon. "I didn't get a chance to look at the orchard."

"Nothing for you to worry about." Joanna glanced over her shoulder to check on her children, safe and quiet on the seat. "The apples were the hardest hit. We picked up what fell, didn't we?"

He kept his attention on the road, but knew the little ones were nodding. The girl's sweet, high voice filled the air and the boy's somber one added a comment or two. Aiden's chest tightened.

He eased Clyde as far to the right as he could go. A driver and wagon were headed their way. It was Stevens. Aiden nodded a greeting to his neighbor as they passed. Stevens waved back, tipping his hat at Joanna, a neighborly show of respect.

Aiden was glad for that. "I don't suppose you met him when you were living with your pa?"

"No. None of the neighbors took a liking to my father. He was a hard man."

"I can't argue with that. Stevens is one of the men I trade work with when threshing time comes. There'll be about six of us plus the hired help to feed. I suspect you know how it works."

"I do." She smoothed the folds of her skirts, as if she was working herself up to say something. "You don't have to worry, Aiden. I was married to a wheat farmer before. I know what's expected. I know the hard work you need done."

"I wasn't saying I needed you in the fields." One day he was going to have to learn how to say what he meant. "I was talking about the meals. Cooking for that many men."

"Me, too." She laughed, a gentle, welcoming sound, one that tugged at the lost places within him. That lured him like the sunlight, like the prairie, into noticing.

She drew him where he could not help following. He felt alive, as if he was breathing in air for the first time.

"For a minute there you had me worrying you planned to be out in the fields helping me." It felt right to laugh along with her. "The joke was on me, I guess."

"I have talked so much about working in the fields. What else were you to think?"

"I'm glad you don't have to work that hard, Joanna. I don't want you to. Do you understand?"

The laughter faded from her face, but not the smile. It remained, wide enough to reach her eyes and real enough to touch what remained of his soul. That felt right, too.

"You have done so much for me and my children, Aiden." Serious now, she laid her hand on his sleeve.

He swallowed at the connection, at the tug of emotion within him he did not want to feel. "I've only done the right thing is all."

"I wish I could do as much for you." Her fingers lingered on his sleeve, and in the heartbeat before she pulled away, there it was again. That fondness he'd spotted before.

For him this time. Clearly for him.

Joanna closed the worn book, quietly laid it on the bedside table and turned down the wick. The lamplight faded into darkness, leaving only the faint light from the sickle moon spilling in through the cracks between the curtains. It was enough to see the shadows of her little ones tucked into their beds. Daisy lay on her side, clutching her doll, looking like perfection, so still and sweet. James, on the other hand, stirred, fighting sleep.

"Sweet dreams," she whispered, and kissed his forehead, hoping that would settle him.

Instead his eyes popped wide-open. "Ma, I can't hardly sleep."

"Yes, but you must. Tomorrow is another good day."

"This sure is a great room." Even in the dark shadows, it was simple to see the contentment on his face and hear the gladness in his words. "I like this house the best. Mostly because we really get to stay here."

"That's right." No more worries for her children. No more want. She thought of the man who had avoided her since he'd helped her from the wagon at his brother's place. The strings of her heart knotted tight. "You get some sleep, now."

"I like my new pa." There was something else there exposed in his words and hidden by the dark. "He let me lead Clyde. Did you see?"

"I saw." She remembered the picture the three of them had made, the small boy, the big man and the giant horse together. "You did a real good job with him."

"I know. I like Clyde. He's a good old fella." James imitated Aiden's intonation.

So much need. How did she explain it to a boy who wanted a father? "It was nice of Aiden to take the time with you, but you know he's terrible busy this time of year."

"I know. That's why he didn't come home with us. Or to supper. He had to help Uncle Thad with his wheat. And tomorrow Uncle Thad is gonna come here and help with ours."

"That's right." She had to find the right words, the right way to handle this. She had to protect James from disappointment. She had to protect Aiden from James caring too much. Tonight, when she knelt down to pray, she would ask for the Lord's help. Just as he had led them here to Aiden, surely he was continuing to lead them.

She brushed James's bangs from his eyes. "We must be careful not to burden Aiden. He did a good deed taking us in. You sleep tight, sweetheart."

"Do you think he's home yet?"

"Not yet." She stood, full of love for her children and for the man who could never love her in return. "For the last time, go to sleep."

James gave a little giggle. "Okay, Ma. I'll try."

She closed the door quietly and padded downstairs. She had left the windows open to the night breezes, and the house was pleasant and smelled of ripening wheat and wildflowers. She went from window to window, closing up before she lit the lamps. There was no tidying left to do in the parlor, and the kitchen was spick-and-span, so she grabbed her sewing basket and sat down at the table to work.

A moth beat at the screen door as she threaded her needle. She planned to work on the fabric she had picked up for James before the wedding. She had not made as much progress on his trousers as she wanted. Ida had pointed out today that school started in town in a few weeks' time.

As she knotted the end of the thread and double-checked the pins on the side seams, she thought of her little boy. He looked up to Aiden. It was natural for him to want a father. Of course that's what he thought Aiden ought to be. He was too young to understand. It was his heart that was wanting what he had never had. Certainly not from Tom, when he'd been alive, and never even from her father in the year or more they had lived with him.

How could James understand, when she didn't understand herself? She didn't know why the heart yearned to love and be loved. It was simply the way God had made hearts. She could not say it felt wrong that a sky-ful of love swept through her every time she thought of Aiden, powerful enough to fill her world from horizon to horizon, and every place in between.

There was no hiding from it. No changing it. No way to go back in time and stop every step she'd taken that had brought her here. She slid the needle into the fabric, basting long, even stitches, working without thought. Her mind was on Aiden. On hearing the plod of a horse in the yard. Seeing his familiar profile as he rode one of Thad's horses through the shadowy darkness. She longed for the moment when he'd walk through the door. She couldn't wait to hear the rich timbre of his voice and simply to have the privilege of making his life easier.

She finished the seam quickly and set down her work. There was the supper she'd saved aside for him, in case he was hungry when he came home. It was a pleasure to set out the big slice of the pie she'd baked for him—apple pie.

There he was, striding through the darkness, outlined by the faint moon glow, more light than shadow. He pulled back the screen door and entered—her husband. He was the perfect image of everything good in a man, and she could not stop her heart from falling ever more in love with him.

When he saw her, he froze. He did not smile, but changed to granite before her very eyes. He let the door close with a hollow slap, and turned away from her. Something was wrong. Very wrong.

"I'm sorry, but I ate at Noelle's." he said, then went straight to his room.

Chapter Fifteen

She sat at the kitchen table, graced by lamplight. Washed and changed out of his work clothes, Aiden debated. Every instinct he had told him to keep his distance. And yet she was his wife now. She deserved more than that from him. Look at her, even at eight o'clock at night, working away with her head bent over her sewing, so intent that she didn't notice him standing in the doorway like a statue.

"Is that apple pie I smell?"

That got her attention. Her needle stilled in midstitch and her head whipped up. Instead of the censure he deserved, there was only a gentle look, more a question than anything. Those places within him began aching again—from the past, for the future…he didn't know.

"It sure is." She put her work aside and was already rising. Anxiety pinched the smooth skin around her eyes. "If you like it warm, it will take a few moments to heat. I just need to light the stove."

"Don't go to any trouble. I'll cut it, Joanna."

"I don't mind." She was already reaching up into the

cupboards for a plate and a cup, quick to please. "I have tea cooled, or I can fetch cold water from the well."

He hung his head. This wasn't what he wanted. He wanted a sensible, working type of marriage. Not one that made every piece of him hurt whenever he looked at her. He couldn't miss the pain he'd put on her face. He felt as if a cinch were drawing tight around his chest and he couldn't breathe. Like a man suffocating, panic set in. The need to protect himself from an endless pain.

His hand trembled as he took a knife from the drawer. He steeled himself, heart and soul, before he moved closer to her. He wanted to tell her that he didn't need anyone. That he didn't need her to slide a spatula beneath the wedge of pie he'd cut, and put it on a plate for him. That he didn't need her fresh baked dessert or her kindness or the veiled look on her face that told him she was hiding her heart.

He didn't need love. He didn't want love. It had only brought him devastation. He was still holding the shards of that life, unable to let go, unable to move on. Being near Joanna with the soft fragrance of baking clinging to her clothes, and her flower-scented soap, was tearing him apart. He wished he could forget the radiance he'd witnessed in her and what he'd seen of her heart. He wished he had something left inside him still able to care. He wished the twisting coil of turmoil within him would stop, simply stop, and leave him be.

He drew a ragged breath, willing himself to walk calmly to the table and set down the plate. It took all of his might not to notice as Joanna swept close with a cup of tea. He felt as if he were breaking apart as he sat down at the table.

"You worked a long time at your brother's." She lingered a moment too long.

He could feel the emptiness within him like a sore tooth. He grabbed up the fork, trying to pretend everything was as it should be. But he was only fooling himself. "Thad's fields weren't as hard hit as ours. That was a blessing, at least. Still, it took the better part of seven hours to clean them up."

"It's a hardship for him." She swept away, taking all the air in the room with her.

It was the only explanation he could come up with for why he felt as if he was gasping for breath. "It's his first crop. I helped him break sod this past spring. The first yield is never good. He wasn't expecting a solid crop until next year."

"But you were counting on the crop here, weren't you?" Her voice was resonant with understanding, her concern rich with layers. "If things get hard for you…"

He couldn't look at her, but he heard her silence and the weight of questions she did not ask. They stood between them as solidly as the table. He could feel them. He winced. "I hope that's not what you think of me. That I'm a fair-weather man. That if times get rough, I'll break my vows to you."

"No, that's not what I think. Not at all." Her words rang low and as sweet as the apple pie in front of him. Warmth crept into her voice, the kind that came with a deep caring. "I only meant that you weren't banking on having two extra horses to feed through the winter, and that's a cost to you. Now me and the children to feed and shelter, and that's a greater cost. If the crop isn't enough… Well, I'm already doing piecework for Cora Sims. I'm sure I could do more."

He squeezed his eyes shut. She had no notion of what she was doing to him with her generous compassion and willing heart. "Joanna, you do more than enough every day. We'll get by. I've got savings put aside. I had a good crop last year. You're not to worry."

"But with part of the wheat crop gone, I imagine we'll need to watch every penny."

"True."

"And my wages will help." She watched his reaction through her lashes. His jaw was granite, his gaze stony. "You don't think a woman ought to be concerned with making ends meet, is that it?"

"No, I was just thinking I'm not taking your wages." He cut into his pie with his fork, his voice flat. "I'm not a man who takes his wife's money. Now, before you start arguing—"

"How did you know I was going to argue?"

"You're a woman. And if there's one thing I've learned, a woman always has an opinion." His mouth crooked in the corners.

"Well, you are right about that, mister." She picked up her sewing and began stitching away. Poking the needle through the fabric gave her some satisfaction at least, as she could not accomplish as much with him as easily. "It's my opinion that I won't be a burden to you. I owe you, Aiden. More than you know."

"How did you come to that opinion?" His forehead creased as if he was puzzled. "You are a good wife, Joanna. You deserve all I can provide for you—more than I can do for you."

"You don't know what you're saying." She reached the end of the seam and knotted it swiftly. Her eyes were hot and she had to squint to see what she was doing. She tried hard not to think of those dark days of chaos and disappointment of her first marriage. Of trying so hard. "You appreciate everything I do. You compliment every meal I make. You see me, Aiden."

"It would be hard not to. All I have to do is open my eyes."

"You know what I mean." He could try to tempt her away from her feelings with that dry humor of his, but it wasn't going to work. Love bubbled like a wellspring in her soul, always running, always renewed.

She lowered her gaze, hoping that would hide any rogue feelings showing in her eyes. She bowed her head over her work, hoping the shadows would mask her. "You don't make me feel less than. I can't tell you what it means to me. Your kindness…"

She stopped there, willing her tongue to stop forming any more words that could give her away. She was in love with him. It would not be right to let him see that she had already broken a promise between them. She blinked hard and knotted the thread again and a third time, before weaving the end thread through the fabric.

"My kindness is the least of what you deserve, Jo-anna." He looked lost again. "You had heartbreak in your first marriage as surely as I did in mine. In little bits at a time. I can see how it was. One disappointment after another until there was nothing left but pieces of your dreams."

"Yes." She was not surprised that he could see this in her so clearly. Aiden always had that knack. She prayed he could not see her as clearly now. She wrapped her love for him up and hoped it was hidden deeply enough that he would never see. "We're a pair, aren't we?"

"Yep." He paused to stare out past the pool of light to the window, where night and shadows beckoned. "How do you do it?"

"Do what?"

"You've had heartache and hardship in your life, and yet you've never closed your heart. How have you done it?"

"I did not have your losses, Aiden."

"No, but love lost is the same in the end." His chest hurt something fierce. He set down his fork, feeling trapped, needing to feel the breeze on his face and the expanse of the sky blowing on by. She reached across the table and laid her hand on his. The shards that had once been his soul stirred.

"I should not have been here, waiting for you tonight." It wasn't understanding or sympathy in her words, but love. Quiet as dawn coming and as sure as first light, that's how she sounded.

Did she know she was so transparent? She deserved better than a man like him, barren of heart and grasping for any embers that might remain. He was too tangled up to pray. Too unsettled to feel his way to that calm place of God. Aiden passed his hand over his face, torn up inside, feeling like a rope unraveling shank by braided shank.

Footsteps crossed the porch behind him. Finn, was his first guess, but the heavy gait was wrong. Just wishful thinking, Aiden supposed, wanting his youngest brother to come back to his senses. Wanting to save him, maybe because he could not save himself.

A soft knock sounded on the door frame. He was already on his feet, heading toward the door. He didn't recognize the man's shadow on the back step until he came closer and saw the faint glint of a silver star. The sheriff. This had happened before.

"Clint." He yanked open the screen door. "Don't tell me this is about Finn. I'm not in the mood."

"You know that's why I'm here." The lawman swept off his hat. "Now, I can leave or I can tell you the truth. Which way do you want it?"

"What did he do this time?" Aiden tensed, as if he were bracing himself. "Tell me he's sleeping it off in a cell."

"I would, but that's not the whole truth. He's in big trouble this time, Aiden."

"What kind of trouble?"

"He was taking part in a robbery."

"I knew he was going to get into trouble again. How bad is it?"

"Bad. I'm holding him in jail until the judge comes to town. He was armed, Aiden. I regret having to tell you that someone got hurt."

"I was afraid something like this might happen." Aiden's wide shoulders slumped.

"You can see him tomorrow if you want. Thought I'd swing by Thad's place and let him and your mother know."

"That's good of you, Clint." Aiden wedged one shoulder against the door frame, as if bracing himself. "I appreciate you coming out all this way."

"That's all right. I'm sorry to have to bring you news like this." The sheriff took a step back into the darkness. "I know you've been trying to keep him on a better path."

"Nothing I've done has worked."

"Sometimes that's the way it is, and it's a shame, too. I'll be seeing you, Aiden."

"Thanks, Sheriff." He didn't move from the doorway. He stood stock-still, maybe too stunned by the news. Maybe too discouraged.

"I didn't mean to overhear." Joana was across the room without realizing it, drawn as if a rope were pulling her. "I'm sorry."

"I am, too." He sounded hollow, as if all the life had been sucked right out of him. "I was afraid he would get into worse trouble than before. He's not a bad boy, but he loses all sense when he's in the bottom of a bottle."

"This isn't your fault, Aiden."

"I made him leave. Without money. Without a place to live. I tried to do the right thing by him. To make him think about what he was doing."

"That was his choice." Her hand settled on his shoulder. She could feel the agony vibrating through him. "Likely he wouldn't have stopped no matter what you did."

"I should have done more. What, I don't know. Now I've lost him, too."

"I know you, Aiden. You did everything you could for him. You gave him a new start. I know, because you did the same thing for me. You gave him a chance to improve his life. Believe me, that's quite a gift to hand someone."

"He's going back to jail for a long time."

"That was his choice, too."

"I feel as if I failed him." Aiden sounded tortured. He moved away from her touch, slowly, as if breaking away hurt him, too, and strode into the darkness. There was no moonlight to illuminate him, just faint stardust. It gilded him in the velvet blackness of the night like a dream. His shoulders were wide, feet braced apart and head bowed as if in prayer.

She closed the screen door quietly. Should she follow him? Did he need comfort? Or would he want to be alone? She longed to go to him. She had to be careful not to give herself away, she thought as she padded down the steps. It wasn't easy to pull back her affection and lock it in her heart. She gave thanks for the night that hid her face as completely as it hid his.

"Aiden?" She ached to soothe him with the right words. To reach out and let her hand settle on his shoulder again, so he could feel that he wasn't alone. "You didn't fail him."

"It sure feels that way."

"I'm guessing that you haven't failed anyone in your whole life. You are so strong. In faith. Of heart. Of character."

She squeezed her eyes shut, willing back the love inside her. She could not let it show.

When she opened them again, he was facing her. He had moved as silently as the night, and he seemed a part of it. Lost and bruised, with only the faintest light to guide him.

"You're wrong, Joanna. I am not that man. You see someone else. Someone you wish to see. Not me."

"I see how much you are hurting. From this news of Finn. From what you've lost. From seeing me sitting in your kitchen, and that's my fault. I let you talk me into moving in when I should have stayed in the shanty."

"You misunderstand." He sounded as if he was suffocating. She could only see the faint outline of his forehead and nose. He was pure shadow. "I feel. Before you came, there was nothing, only hard work and making a living off the land and keeping my distance. You changed that."

"I didn't mean to."

"I know, but it happened just the same."

She worked at the thin gold band on her fourth finger, the one he had put there with a vow and promises he would not break. She didn't know what to say. Love beat stronger within her, and yet it was not strong enough. "I wanted to make your life better, Aiden. To make your burdens easier, the way you did for me and my children."

"I know that." His palms cradled her face, rough with calluses and tender with care.

She brought her hands up to his, holding on to his strength, taking in his sweet tenderness. He cared for her. That was more than she expected. More than she had dreamed. She breathed in the silence, and the night did not seem as bleak. The gleam of starshine seemed to linger like hope.

"I wish I were like you." His baritone voice was raw, as if speaking brought him pain. "But I cannot do this."

"Do what?" Was he talking about Finn again? she wondered. Or her presence in his house?

"I know, Joanna. I see how you look at me."

She squeezed her eyes shut. But it was too late. She had not hidden her love for him as well as she'd thought. Heat swept across her face and regret into her heart. She tugged what defenses she could around her and steeled her spine. Whatever he said next, she knew it was going to hurt. There was no other way it could be. "I know you can't love me, Aiden. I'm not asking for that. You have to know."

"I do." He grimaced, and what little she could see of him was tortured. "Don't think I don't want to. I wish I could. Prayer hasn't helped. I can't find my heart. Sometimes you lose too much of yourself and you can't get it back."

"I'm not asking you for anything." She had to stop him, because there was only one way this could end. She told herself she wasn't hurting. That he couldn't be rejecting her if he never loved her in the first place.

But hearing that he wished he could love her was worse than any loss. Any pain. She saw him for the first time, a man broken beyond repair, struggling for life the way a drowning man fights for air. He was going down and there was nothing she could do to stop him. Nothing but try to fix what she could. She did not want to lose him.

She drew in a ragged breath and gathered up the bits of her dignity. "Nothing between us has to change. Everything is the same, Aiden."

"It's not the same." He choked on the words. "I'll move out into the shanty."

"No, you don't need to do that."

"It's what I want." He stood firm. Resolute. "I won't

uproot the children again, and it makes no difference to me where I live. I'll move tonight."

"But it's l-late."

"It's only a mattress and my pillow. Not much to move."

"No, please I... I—"

"I'm sorry." Hearing the tremble in her voice was agony. He was cracking apart like a frozen river in spring, one sharp break after another. It was too much. It was more than he could take. "This isn't what I want. I wish—"

He couldn't finish that, not with words, not even in thought. The presence of her hands on his destroyed him. She was soft as moonlight and as comforting as prayer and her hands were small. How could she do so much with them? She was powerful enough to tug at the embers of his heart.

"You wish that you had never married me." Her voice was thin and raw.

No, that wasn't true. But when he tried to tell her, his throat closed up tight. He leaned forward an inch, longing for what he could not let himself have. She tipped her face up. The starlight dusted the curves of her face, revealing her loving heart. She shone like a polished pearl, lovely from the inside out, and he yearned for her tenderness the way stars longed for the night.

He cared deeply about her. He wanted to deny it, to lie to himself, to hide from the truth. But it was like life in his veins, like the beat coming back to his heart. He was drowning, without air to breathe or ground to plant his feet on. If he took her into his arms and let her settle her cheek against his chest and held her tight, he would find what was lost. Letting himself fall in love with her would be like walking in the light again.

Panic made him step back. His vulnerabilities were exposed and the depth of his soul found.

It took all his strength to let go of her. To do the right thing and protect them both. Life was too hard and love too uncertain.

"I'd best get settled." He left her standing there, graced by starshine and the rising moon, and holding his heart.

Chapter Sixteen

"That's a dear little dress you're making," Cora Sims commented days later, across the width of Noelle's comfortable parlor. "For your little girl?"

"Yes. From the fabric I bought at your store." Seated next to Noelle on the sofa, Joanna held up the calico frock. "I've made it a bit fancier than usual, with ruffles and satin ribbon trim."

"Adorable." Lanna Wolf, an old friend of Noelle's, put down the quilt patch she was sewing and leaned forward to admire the fine workmanship. "I love the backstitching you've done here. And the little embroidery work on the collar and cuffs."

"I'll have to have Ida remember this for when we start making baby clothes." Noelle paused, happiness lighting her lovely face as she waited expectantly for her hint to sink in.

"A baby? Really?" Matilda Worthington, Noelle's cousin, gasped on Joanna's other side. "That's wonderful news."

"Don't you tell your mother yet. I'm planning on letting her know in person. She is not fond of surprises." Noelle stopped to count her stitches with her fingertips.

"Thad must be beyond the moon," Lanna said. "Your first child. Joe and I are still waiting."

"It can come when you least expect it," Joanna found herself saying. Why there was a lump in her throat, she couldn't rightly say. "I had been married two years before I found out I would be having James. He was worth waiting for."

"I guess God knows when the time is right." Noelle sparkled, radiant with joy. "I'm thankful for this little one on the way. Speaking of which, I think I hear the patter of small footsteps."

Sure enough, James bolted into the doorway and skidded to a stop. Grass seed clung to his shirt and a grass stain was at his knee. Luckily, he wasn't wearing his new trousers. "Ma. Can me and Daisy have more pie?"

"Not right now." She secured her needle and folded up the tiny dress. "It's about time for us to head home. How about an extra big piece after supper?"

He looked around at the women watching him and squared up his chin. "Okay, Ma. I'll get Daisy's toys so we can go."

"Thank you, baby." The lump in her throat remained, stubbornly stuck in place. She leaned forward to slip her things inside her sewing basket as his footsteps padded away.

"Oh, he's such a dear." Cora watched him go with longing. It was clear to see she was not a spinster by choice, and that she wanted children. "You have such well-behaved little ones."

"They are good." Joanna secured the lid on her basket. "They are my greatest blessings."

"Aiden seems good to them." Cora folded up her work, too. "At my age, I keep hoping I might find a handsome widower with children. I think there's nothing that says more about a man than being a good father."

"We'll have to see if we can't find you one of those," Lanna said, and the conversation turned to which handsome widower in the county might be right for Cora.

Joanna lifted her basket and went to get her things in the corner by the front door. It was a beautiful sight to see the golden wheat fields out beyond the large windows. The air puffing in through the screens smelled like bread baking. Harvest time was coming. A few more days, and she would be busy cooking and baking enough to feed the men. A few days later, she had agreed to do the same, with Ida's help, in Noelle's kitchen.

Aiden. Whenever she thought of him she had to lock up the feelings in her heart. She was too busy to waste a minute crying for what was never meant to be. She was too vulnerable to really think about what she had done. She had tipped her hand, and Aiden had not only guessed her feelings, he hadn't spoken to her since, beyond a few thank-you's, and letting her know the date the threshers were coming. She put his meals in the empty shanty, not knowing how warm the food would be when he finally wandered in from his work. It was her fault that they were both miserable—all her fault.

She would do anything she could to wind back time. To work harder at keeping her feelings hidden. Or, better yet, she should have nipped them in the bud when she first realized she was falling for him. Now, she did not have his friendship or his presence in her life. She was alone all over again, and missed him terribly.

She knelt to unpack the preserves she'd brought, and began setting out enough jars for everyone.

Cora had come to fetch her reticule, but stopped at the colorful sight. "Look at what Joanna brought. The prettiest jams I've ever seen."

"And hopefully the tastiest, too." Joanna couldn't help being pleased. She had worked from dawn until dark over a hot stove. Canning was next. "The orchard is brimming with more than we could possibly use. If anyone wants fresh fruit, just let me know."

"I love peaches. Oh, and plums." Cora sighed. "I miss having my own trees, living in town as I do."

"Me, too." Lanna spoke up, joining them. "I'll bring dessert next week. If Joanna will let me drop by for a bucket of peaches."

"Sounds like a treat," Joanna agreed, unable to remember the last time she'd had this much happiness in her life. Although she was still getting to know these women, she had the feeling they would be good friends for life. She could see her little ones out front on the porch with Ida. James had his wooden mustangs and Daisy had her doll. Both children were well-fed and secure and happy.

The only thing wrong in her life was Aiden. She feared that was something that would never be right again.

Aiden forked fresh hay into the corral manger and watched the horses, tired from their fieldwork, amble over to get their supper. Over their sun-warmed backs, he could see Joanna coming toward the house from the shanty. It ripped him apart to watch her, but he could not seem to look away. No doubt she had delivered the evening meal, and her attention was riveted on the hillside between the houses where her children were playing.

He heard Thad come up behind him with the water bucket. "Why is she bringing our suppers to the shanty?"

Aiden winced, although he had been expecting the question. He set the pitchfork against the wall. "I told you this wasn't a real marriage. I gave Joanna the house, figured it was better for her and the kids, and I took the shanty."

"So you really are doing this? You're married to her but you're living apart from her." He upended the bucket into the water bin.

"That's right. Don't see as how it's any of your business." He tossed his brother a half grin. "Thanks for your help cleaning up, Thad. That storm left quite a mess."

Although, *he* was the one who'd felt like a mess that night, talking to Joanna. He flicked his gaze back to her. She was on the kitchen doorstep now, leaning down to speak softly to her son. The boy was looking at the barn and his face was squinted up, as if he was trying not to cry.

She had kept the children away from him; she probably thought he would be happy about that. He wasn't, but it was just as well. He blew out a sigh and kept to the shadows in the aisle. She soothed her hand over the boy's head. His nose was slightly pink from playing in the sun.

The boy needed a hat. Joanna ought to buy him one, and if there was a voice at the back of Aiden's mind saying that he could do it the next time he was in town, he ignored it. It was easier, sure, but sensible not to listen to that. The boy wanted a pa, that was plain to see. That could only spell trouble.

"I'm glad to help, you know that." Thad lowered the bucket, looking thoughtful. "I was going to head to town tomorrow and see Finn. You want to come?"

"I don't think he wants to see me." Aiden watched Joanna as she knelt to give her son a hug. It was a marvel how she radiated love. She was a vision in calico; somehow she was more beautiful to him every time he looked at her. And that tore at him, too.

Thad plodded closer. "I think you need to see him. And then there's the matter of getting him a lawyer."

"I don't see how we can afford to." Aiden braced himself against that pain, too. He'd let down too many people. "I don't see how we can afford not to."

"I talked to Noelle's friend Lanna. Her husband is a lawyer and he'll cut his fee for us. What do you think?"

"I can pay half if you can."

"We'll figure out a way." Thad led him down the aisle. "C'mon, I'm hungry enough to eat a bear."

"That's two of us, little brother." He hated that he wanted to drag his feet. Joanna was still in sight. She was lifting two five-gallon buckets, empty now, and swinging them as she walked. Thank heavens she was heading away from him. He wouldn't have to face her and remember the other night, when he had let her think that he regretted marrying her.

"Aiden, do you reckon she left us any pie?"

"There's a mighty good chance." There she was, about to round the far corner of the house. He drank in the sight of her, trying to harden his heart, fighting to keep from caring, but it came anyway. His feelings for her were sweet like spring. Two more steps, a swish of her pretty green skirt, and she was gone from his sight.

But the caring in his heart remained.

"Look at this place." Thad's voice brought him back to the moment.

They were standing in the shadow of the shanty. The amber prairie rolled out before them in a thousand shades of tan and yellow, but where did his eye go? Toward the far corner of the orchard that he could see. There was no sign of Joanna, but he knew she was there, picking fruit.

He ought to be out there helping her, but he couldn't make himself do it. So he followed his brother into the small house and went to wash his hands at the basin.

"I can't believe this is the same shanty." Thad glanced around as he passed Aiden the soap. "She put up new curtains for you and everything."

She had made such a difference here.

All he had to do was look around to see the spotless and polished stove, the gleaming counters and shelves, the gingham curtains, clean and pressed and fluttering in the breeze from the screened window. A cloth lay over the table, where supper for two was set out and covered and two place settings awaited them.

"Peach cobbler," Thad exclaimed as he lifted one of the tins. "It's my lucky day. Tell me again why you're not in love with that woman?"

Aiden winced, and rinsed his hands in the basin,

glad he could turn his back to his brother. He didn't want him to guess at the truth. He cleared his throat, wishing words alone were powerful enough to change his heart. "Love ought to be based on more than a well-baked dessert. But I don't want anything to do with love, anyway." He took the towel from the rack and ignored the subtle scent of sunshine and the soap Joanna used. "I'm not building my life on something that can be gone in a flash. It's foolish, plain and simple. It's not what life is about."

"I see."

It was the quiet way his brother said the words that made his lungs seize up. His hands fumbled as he hung the towel. "I'm glad you understand then."

"I do."

The way he said that made Aiden grimace. "You think I love her."

"Yep." Thad looked mighty sure of himself as he poured tea into the glasses that Joanna had left them. "I think she loves you back. Look at all she's done for you. This meal. She spent time on this. She put care into this. She could have spent half the effort and it would have been more than enough."

"She's a hard worker. It has nothing to do with me." He didn't believe it, but he wanted it to be the truth. More than anything. His hands shook as he pulled out the ladder-back chair at the table. There were comfortable cushions tied neatly to the chair seat and back. Joanna, again.

"You can say it all you want—" Thad stared as he settled across the table "—but that won't make it true. I know. I've been where you are. Letting yourself fall in love with a woman is a risk. There's no guarantee you won't get your heart broken in the end."

"You make too little of it." Pressure built in Aiden's chest, expanding against his ribs. He'd had enough of this talk. Instead of saying what he meant, he bowed his head for prayer. Since his throat was hurting, too, he growled, "You say the blessing."

"I'll say it when I'm good and ready, big brother." Thad looked to be in one of his stubborn moods. "You listen to me. You've got a mighty nice woman for a wife, and I think you're falling in love with her and it scares you to death."

"You don't think I haven't turned to my faith on this?" He leaned back in his chair, hurting, just hurting. Why wouldn't Thad leave it alone? "I've prayed for years on this. I've prayed until I've run out of prayers. I trust God knew what he was doing when he took Kate and my son from me. I don't know why, but everything God does for us is because he loves us. I accept that. But what I can't do is lay everything I am on the line again and lose what is most precious to me. I can't do it. I won't. I'm not strong enough."

There. He watched the realization dawn in his brother's expression, his brother who had always been someone he could count on, and he gave thanks, as he bowed his head, for Thad. "Are you going to say grace, or am I going to?"

"I'll say it." His brother bowed his head, beginning the prayer.

Aiden hardly heard it. What he heard was the rapid swish of his pulse in his ears and the truth in his heart.

* * *

The days had fallen into a rhythm, but although life was pleasant, Joanna couldn't say she was happy. Mornings were spent on chores around the house, and if she didn't work for Noelle or Cora, she squeezed in all the time she could working outside. Now, as she carefully twisted a peach from the branch of the reaching tree, she checked between the leaves for her little ones.

There was Daisy, sitting in a patch of small-faced sunflowers. She had a chain of them around her neck and was making what looked like a bracelet to go with it. James was not next to her. His wooden horses were there in the grass, but he was missing.

She laid the peach in the basket, slipped down the stepladder and scanned the orchard. Nothing. She didn't see him behind any of the trees or climbing in the branches. How had he scampered off? And why? He knew better. Then she saw Aiden talking to Thad in front of the barn, leading Clyde by the reins. The big draft horse was saddled and had his nose toward the ground, stretching out as if he was scenting something. Or somebody.

James. There he was, partly hidden by the dip of the rise, wandering close to the men and their horses. Thad's mustang gave a low nicker and turned, swishing his tail. Both horses watched the little boy hungrily, stretching out for the first fond caress.

She swept Daisy onto her hip and was already at the orchard gate when she saw Aiden focus in on the boy. With every step she took closer, she could more clearly see the strain on his face, the shadows in his eyes and the white lines around his tense mouth. Yet he was kind as he leaned down to speak to her son. James's shoulders slumped and he shook his head.

"...you oughtn't to run off on your ma like that." Aiden's low tones drifted toward her. "Here she comes. She's in a panic, if you ask me."

"I'm sorry, sir."

"You'd best tell that to her." Those words were kind, but she knew they cost him. All she had to do was look at how tight Aiden was holding himself to know.

She ached for him and for her son. Her soul felt near to cracking as she bundled the affection for him away, storing it down deep. With any luck, it would be deep enough not to show. She set Daisy on the ground. "I'm sorry, Aiden. He snuck off on me. Hello, Thad."

"Howdy, Joanna." He lifted his hat in greeting. If any man could stand next to Aiden and hold his own, it was Thad. They were clearly good men cut from the same cloth.

"I've got a crate of apples and peaches in the lean-to set aside for you. Maybe one of plums, if I can get to it." She took hold of her son's shoulder. "I'll have Aiden bring them in the wagon on Sunday."

"That's mighty kind of you." Thad mounted up. "We're going in to town to see Finn, although I reckon Aiden has probably already told you that."

No, he hadn't, but Joanna bit her lip. What Aiden chose to do with his time was surely not her concern. If it hurt that he hadn't turned to her and that he would not, she had to tuck that down deep inside, too. "I hope your visit goes well. I've been praying for Finn."

"That's gotta help." Thad tipped his hat to her before he wheeled his mustang around. "Come Sunday,

I'll let you have another ride on Sunny. What do you think about that, James?"

"That would sure be swell." The boy drew his shoulders up, hope vibrating through him.

"I get to, too," Daisy called out, holding out her handful of flowers. Clyde took a couple out of her hand as he walked by.

There was Aiden, towering far above them on the back of the giant horse. He sat rigidly straight, as controlled as a soldier, as remote as the farthest horizon. His mighty shoulders were braced, as if he were carrying a world of burdens on them. He did not look at Joanna as he passed by, but she could see the cords bunch in his neck and the muscles in his jaw clench tight.

If only she could forget his words. *Don't think I don't want to. I wish I could. Prayer hasn't helped. I can't find my heart. Sometimes you lose too much of yourself and you can't get it back.*

She watched him ride away into the sinking sun with regret weighing heavily upon her. Regret for rushing into marrying him. Regret for being a reminder of what he had lost. Regret for the love alive and committed in her heart, this time for a man who wanted to love her but never could.

"Ma, can you tie this up for me?" Daisy's innocent request broke into her thoughts.

Again, she tucked both her love and her hurt away, and knelt to twist the last flower into place around her daughter's little wrist, completing the chain.

"Ma?" James stood with his hands at his sides, watching Aiden disappear around the distant bend. "When I grow up, I want to ride a black horse, too."

James's admiration was sky-high for the man he wanted to be his pa. Another arrow straight to her heart. Joanna winced at the inner pain. Was this the way it was going to go? James pining quietly for a father, and Aiden always riding away? She was no different, she realized, wanting what could not be.

What could never be.

She took each child by the hand and headed back to the orchard. Whether she was happy or not, there was work waiting. She would have plenty of time to rest on snowy winter afternoons and think of her mistakes then—and of the man who would be sitting alone in his shanty, always separate from her.

From them.

Chapter Seventeen

The next morning the hurt on Joanna's face still troubled him. Maybe because it was difficult thinking of his little brother locked up behind steel bars. Finn had refused to see him. Or maybe because his failures weighed heavy on his soul. Either way, he didn't feel prepared for how she watched the ground instead of the world around her as she came out of the house in her Sunday best.

Her daughter hopped down the steps in two-footed jumps, her white-blond braids bouncing. The son saw him and took off at a run, eager to see the horses. Clyde gave a snort of welcome and stretched against the harness collar, reaching his neck as far as it would go.

"'Mornin', sir. Thank you kindly for the hat!" The boy skidded to a stop in front of Clyde, who was calm enough not to bat an eye. The gentle giant gave a low nicker and lipped the boy's hat brim affectionately.

Aiden nodded. It was the best he could do. He'd left the Stetson on the kitchen table late last night, knowing it would be found this morning. He held his heart firm and prayed that Joanna would hurry up so they could get this over with.

Heaven didn't seem to be listening today. Joanna was taking her sweet time, locking the door, checking the lock, grasping her daughter's hand. Every step she took toward the wagon seemed slower than the last. He shuffled his polished boots in the chalky dust, trying not to see the dread on her face or the little boy giggling softly as he petted the horses.

"Thank you for James's cowboy hat. He loves it." Her gaze was fixed on the wagon instead of on Aiden.

"Sure." That one word seemed to stick in his throat. Maybe because the bonnet she wore made her eyes bluer than wildflowers. Delicate curls fell down to frame her gentle face, making him remember the night they had stood not far from here, and how he had held her face in his hands, her sweetness in his soul.

He hadn't wanted to admit that then, but for some reason it was easier now when there was a vast distance between them. A distance so wide there was no way to cross it. They both knew it. Even if he risked everything within him by telling her how he felt, it wouldn't matter. He had hurt her, and now she watched at him with dismay.

"We'd best get on the road," he said, holding out his hand to help her up.

She didn't take it. With a little hitch to her chin, she swung her daughter into the back of the wagon. That smarted a bit. He told himself it was just as well. Taking her hand would only bring him closer to her. And being closer to her was the one place he could not be.

He waited until she was safely over the top rail before he climbed up onto the high seat.

"James," Joanna called out. "Leave the horses, honey, and climb up."

Something moved at the edge of Aiden's vision. Something pink. "Mister, do you know what?"

He stared into the girl's blue eyes—like Joanna's—and swallowed hard.

"I made all this." She patted the pink carnations wreathed around her neck. "Do you know what? I made you somethin', too."

To his surprise she stuck a flower in his shirt pocket.

"There." She gave it a pat, so innocent and pure hearted. "Did you know God made all the flowers?"

"Y-yep." The word scraped like a serrated knife. He swallowed hard. He couldn't feel a thing. He wouldn't let himself.

"Daisy, come sit down," Joanna said in that patient, gentle way of hers. "Sorry about that, Aiden."

"It's no trouble." Her nearness rubbed the edges of his heart raw. His throat worked and he gathered the reins. He could no longer make himself cold or steely enough not to feel. Longing whipped through his soul, regret though his heart. He released the brake. "You ready back there?"

"We're all seated." She sounded calm, as if he had never hurt her. As if they had never been anything more to one another than strangers.

He snapped the reins and the wagon lurched forward into the searing August sunlight. It was the brightness; surely that was the reason his eyes stung and why he found it hard to see.

* * *

"Why, look at you, children. You are simply charming." Ida knelt in the church aisle and welcomed the little ones with a grandmotherly hug, and then went on to tell Noelle how cute each child looked.

Joanna filled up with adoration. Ida was an absolute blessing. The older woman fondly praised Daisy's flowers and was delighted when the girl presented her with a carnation for her bonnet. Wearing the pink flower proudly, Ida hugged her again and complimented James's new hat. He put it on for a moment to show her, before taking it back off politely. Ida said he looked like a wrangler, and he happily settled next to her on the pew.

"I need to talk with Thad," Aiden said, a shadow at her back and nothing more, before striding off toward the far aisle.

Joanna caught her mother-in-law's curious gaze and shrugged. What could she say? She remembered the lovely lace Ida and Noelle had made for a wedding gift, stitching in all their hopes and prayers for Aiden. How did Joanna tell Ida that present was still wrapped up for safekeeping? That she and Aiden were like strangers again, and no amount of prayer, it seemed, would stop it?

She settled on the hard wooden bench, disheartened. There was Aiden standing at the back of the church, discussing something with his brother. He looked serious and so grim, his face a granite mask.

"How are you, dear?" Ida asked after the children were settled. "You look weary."

"It's a lot of work to keep up with the orchard. I suppose you know that, since it used to be yours."

"And glad I am that it's yours now. It was getting far too much for me to tend to at my age. I wouldn't mind lending a hand, if you would have me."

"And me," Noelle offered. "Although I'm not sure how much help I could be, but I'm excellent at moral support."

"You both are more than welcome." She had been alone for so long in the past, and now again in her marriage, that to have this friendly offer felt like a great treasure. Joanna hoped that she could offer them as much in the years to come. "How about after threshing day? I've been doing a fair amount to prepare for that, including enough baking for the both of us."

"You are a wonder, Joanna," Ida said as Daisy leaned against her for another snuggle. "And with all that is happening in your life, you get so much done. Now I have a question for you."

Uh-oh. She had a terrible feeling that her mother-in-law was going to ask about Aiden or their marriage. She sneaked a glance over her shoulder, and there he was, deep in conversation with Thad and another man.

"That's Joe Wolf," Ida told her. "He's a good lawyer, from what we hear. Now, how was Aiden after he came home from trying to see Finn?"

From trying to see Finn? What had happened? Had Finn refused to see Aiden? She knew that had to be hard for him; Aiden loved his family. "He said nothing to me about it."

"I suppose it was late by the time the day's work was done." Ida nodded. "I remember how it is. There's never enough daylight to get everything done in, and it seems the work doesn't end. He looks troubled. What's happened to Finn is a heartache for all of us. His lawyer says they are going to make some kind of a plea, so he will get less jail time. He wouldn't even see me when I tried to visit him."

While Noelle soothed Ida with comforting words, Joanna sat there silently, dismayed. She did not turn around. Aiden was hurting; she was hurting. What was the solution? She had once asked for God's guidance in helping Aiden, and she thought she'd been heard. She really had.

She stared down at the battered Bible clutched in her hands, the one that had been her ma's and her grandma's before that, and had been held through decades of prayers. As she stood for the opening hymn and then the opening prayer, no answers came to her. She had felt this way so many times, in need and feeling forgotten. Lost. When the sermon began, she took Daisy onto her lap. The little girl settled against her, a sweet weight in Joanna's arms and in her heart.

"Today's sermon will be from Psalm 71. *'But I will hope continually, and will yet praise thee more and more.'*"

Her soul stilled. How was that for an answer? Maybe she had forgotten to listen and to wait for Him—certainly God was worth waiting for. Humbled, she listened to the minister's words, realizing one thing. Faith, life and love were not easy. Sometimes you just had to hold on and—no matter what—believe.

She was still wearing her patched dresses, and it irked him no end. Aiden dumped a few cups of oats in the trough for Clyde and Dale. The old horses dug in, eager for their favorite treats. While they munched, he leaned to get a good look out Thad's stable door toward the front yard, where Joanna stood in the shade of the house talking with Ma and Noelle, a peach cobbler in hand. Faint snatches of conversation whipped by on the breeze, and he couldn't deny the way Joanna's gentle alto could bring him peace. Or how softer life was simply from being near her.

"How's the arrangement working out?" Thad asked wryly as he secured the lid on the grain barrel.

"Just fine, little brother. And keep in mind my marriage is none of your concern." He arched his brow, but judging by the grin on Thad's face, it didn't work.

"Let me know if you need help." Thad unhooked Sunny's lead from the wall. "I've got a fair bit of experience when it comes to marriage."

"Funny, as you've been married, what, four months?"

"I'm just offering, is all. Trying to be a good brother." He ambled past and clipped the lead on the mustang's halter. "Here come your stepchildren."

Aiden gulped. He'd done all he could not to think of them that way. They weren't his; they were Joanna's children. Sure enough, they were bounding across the grass. The little girl was in the lead, braids bobbing. The boy stayed with her, keeping watch over her. They had both changed out of their Sunday clothes, and as they pounded closer, Thad's wild mustangs broke into a run in the nearby field, startled by the sound and the motion.

The kids started talking. Thad answered, leading Sunny out into the yard. The mustang swished his tail and lowered his head politely to accept their eager strokes. He clearly wasn't one to mind basking in the glow of adoration. Aiden gathered his strength, took a deep sustaining breath and followed his brother out into the yard.

"Sir!" James ran right up to him with a grin just like his ma's and an earnestness that was hard not to like. "I got denim riding pants just like yours. Ma just finished 'em!"

So that's what Joanna had been doing late last night. He had noticed the parlor lights on past midnight. He had wondered if she had been unable to sleep, too. Watching the night skies had always soothed him. Maybe sewing did the same for her.

The boy seemed to expect some sort of approval, so Aiden gave him a nod. A small twitch of pain made it through his defenses. He shored himself up more as the little boy ran back to Sunny, but the days of not feeling anything were past. Emotions slammed into Aiden like a summer storm, crashing with a physical pain against his ribs, and deeper, against his soul.

Joanna. She was coming toward him like a song, lightly, breezily, carrying a tray with a pitcher and cups, her skirt rippling in the wind. Those patched skirts. He clenched his hands, fighting the pain and something worse.

He wanted to be angry about those dresses she wore, and about why she hadn't gotten new ones as he had told her to. A voice of reason somewhere in the back of his brain told him that maybe she was too sensible to go spending a bunch of money on dresses all at once. That would be just like her, he reckoned. But maybe she hadn't done it because she did not want to rely on him. Her stubborn independence made him grind his teeth.

He wanted her to be closer. He wanted her to keep away. He wasn't making a lick of sense and he knew it.

That irked him, too.

"I thought you all might be thirsty. It was a hot, dusty ride out here from town." She set the tray down on the top of the feed barrel and faced him. "Aiden?"

He was not strong enough to look at her. If he did, he felt he might come apart. All his defense seemed to be nothing against her loving presence. He cleared his throat and studied his boots. "Sounds good."

The kids clattered up to her, pressing close to her skirts. He did his best to shut out their happy sounds, telling Joanna how they were going to go riding. He heard James say, "I get to learn to ride by myself today! *He's* gonna teach me how to rein!"

"You mean, Aiden?" Joanna sounded confused. "No, honey, I think you misunderstood."

"Nah, I heard just fine."

Thad's promises, Aiden knew. Thad was trying to help, that was all. Aiden realized his mistake. He had been trying to stay back from the children, so hadn't been able to keep watch over what Thad was telling them.

He swallowed hard against something fluttering in him—panic. He felt trapped. Suffocating again, unable to get air. Then suddenly there was Joanna, offering him a cup of lemonade. She was like rain in a drought. Everything he wanted beat within him like a deadly thunderhead.

"Your ma said this was your favorite."

Her smile was likely to undo him, and yet he could not look away. Her hand against his was the greatest comfort and the deepest agony. He would have moved but he was rooted like an oak to the ground.

"Dinner won't be more than a few minutes." She was compassion and hope and love. It was all there in the brush of her fingers against his, before she slipped away. She gathered up the tray and the empty pitcher. "We'll be eating on the porch due to the heat. Don't be long."

His soul seemed to follow her, and there it was, the love he could no longer hold back, cracking like a lightning bolt against his spirit. He stood as if paralyzed, a man unable to think, and too afraid to feel.

"Aiden, you okay?" Thad asked.

Somehow he managed to nod. He glanced around, realized Thad held a cup, too, and took another sip of his lemonade. The little ones had already gulped theirs and were standing next to Sunny, who was trying to get at the sweet-smelling cups they held. The children's giggles lifted his heart.

"You don't look okay." Thad ambled closer. "Maybe it's the heat. You want to go sit in the shade for a spell?"

He shook his head, not trusting his voice. What he wanted to do was be alone and stay real still until this pain died down. Until the turmoil settled.

"Then if it's not the heat, it's got to be Joanna, right?"

His throat worked. How could he admit to that? It was folly, that's what it was, to let himself care about her. No—that wasn't the truth. He didn't just care about her. *Caring* was too miniscule of a word to describe what he felt for her. From the bottom of his scarred soul to the top of his battered heart, he loved her. What was he going to do about that? How was he going to stop it?

Thad was still there, concerned. "You told me once that you trusted God to know what He's doing. Maybe bringing Joanna and these kids to you is God's doing, too. Have you considered that?"

"I've been trying not to."

"Well, consider it. That's all I'm saying." Thad paused as the dinner bell clanged from the porch.

Aiden bowed his head, refusing to look up to see Joanna ringing that bell, refusing to note the sympathy on his brother's face.

"Sir?" The boy sidled up, peering at him from beneath the brim of his hat. Those big, need-filled eyes brimmed with too many questions, every one of which was too big for Aiden to answer now.

"What is it, kid?"

"I wanna be just like you when I grow up." Joanna's son looked as if he'd been gathering up hope the way his little sister picked flowers. "I'm gonna be a wheat rancher with lots of horses."

Aiden hung his head. There was nothing he could say to that, fighting as he was not to feel.

Thad saved him. "James? I figure we can tie Sunny to the porch rail, and after dinner is done, you can ride him. You wanna lead him to the house for me?"

"Do I!" James rushed up to take sole possession of the rope. "C'mon, Sunny. Come along with me."

Aiden was barely aware of feet scampering off and Thad's voice, calm and friendly with the children, moving farther away. All that he had been holding back broke apart like a winter's thaw. The keen rush of emotion that rolled through him nearly brought him to his knees. Perhaps this pain was life coming back to him. Whatever it was, it hurt. He drew in the hot air and let the sun bake him, trying to fight it. Trying not to be ripped apart.

There was Joanna on the front porch, waltzing down the steps with a carrot, a treat for Sunny. James and Daisy swirled around her skirts, excited by the horses and by the family surrounding them. Thad joked with James and then with his wife. Ma reached for Daisy's hand. Noelle leaned in to kiss Daisy's cheek. They were a family again.

Aiden had done everything he could to keep this from happening. He'd held back his feelings. He'd refused to care for Joanna and her kids. He'd stayed away from them. He'd barely talked to them. Hardly acknowledged them, and still, it happened just the same.

He clenched his fists, moving without realizing where he was going, only knowing he needed to get somewhere quiet and pray. He had to take this to the Lord because he was not strong enough to do it on his own. He was sure he would never be strong enough.

Chapter Eighteen

Oh, Aiden. Joanna caught a glimpse of him through Noelle's kitchen window as she grabbed the pan of rolls to carry outside. He stood far out in the sun-scorched bunchgrass beyond the mustang pasture, with his back to her. He gazed off at the river and the reaching prairie, hands behind his back, feet braced, looking like a solitary pillar of strength. Aloneness radiated off him like sunlight off the dry earth.

So much was pulling at him right now. According to Thad, Finn was seeing a judge next week, and it did not look good for him. It was a heartbreak for all the family, she knew, but especially for Aiden, who had fought so hard for his little brother, whom he loved. That was Aiden. He was faithfulness and loyalty. Those were a few reasons why she loved him so much, why she longed to go out to him and hold him until he no longer felt sore and alone.

If only she could. She tucked away her wishes and turned from the window. No matter what, she would not give up on him. She would not stop loving him. Love made a difference in this world, she firmly believed, and she would be Aiden's difference. She would wait and she would hope. Maybe all he needed was time. God had brought her here for a purpose—to love Aiden. She would not yield.

The breeze off the river was a pleasant relief after being in the hot house. Joanna pushed through the screen door, renewed at the sight of Daisy sitting next to Ida at the outdoor table. The little girl wiggled with happiness; it didn't look as if she could sit still.

"Ma!" Her grin was the widest ever. "Grandma Ida said we're gonna have ice cream!"

A rare treat. "We are?"

"Yes! To go with the cobbler we brought. I helped make it," she told her grandma, leaning toward her eagerly. "I sifted the flour and got to put the peaches in."

While Ida praised her as lavishly as any doting grandmother, Joanna slipped the pan of rolls onto the table and looked around. James's place was empty. Where was he?

"Joanna? Is that you?" Noelle was standing at the railing. "Thad went to look for James. He was right beside me on the bench when you went into the house. I felt him slip behind me, but he must have been moving fast. I called out to Thad, and he looked up just in time to see him dart around the corner of the house."

"He knows not to run off." Joanna fought down the panic. She tried not to immediately think of the long list of dangers to a small child on a working ranch—especially the wild mustangs. "I can't believe he's not right here. Noelle, will you watch Daisy?"

"Yes. Are you sure he didn't run off to the outhouse?"

"No." Thad's voice came from around the corner. "First place I checked. Then the barn." He strode into sight, worry and dust marking his face. "There's no sign of him in the corral. I'm going to check the mustangs' field next."

"He went to Aiden." Joanna was sure of it. She was already moving, hurrying around the wraparound deck to the back of the house. Panic beat with her footsteps, and she tried to stay clear and focused. She scanned the pastures and the stretch of field beyond, where Aiden was. No sign of a Stetson among the waving grass and wildflowers.

"James!" She hurried down the back steps. "James!"

No answer. She heard Thad and Ida calling out his name on the other side of the house.

She rushed through the fields, fighting panic, heading toward Aiden. Surely that's where James would go.

Maybe bringing Joanna and these kids to you is God's doing, too. If only he could get Thad's words out of his head. Aiden stared off at the river rushing below, churning, tumultuously, and realized that was just how he felt. As if he were in that dangerous current, being pulled under against his will. Life was like that river; a man had little control over it. He had to accept that the current was stronger, and let it take him where it would.

How do I do it, Lord? He truly had to know. Living hurt, and he couldn't remember the sky being so blue that it stung his eyes, or the sun a tangible heat on his skin. And the colors—they were everywhere, vibrant and shimmering. The thunder of the waterfall had never been louder, and a rainbow reaching from the cliff to the river below never brighter.

He was alive and whole and unable to trust. *Lord, how can I believe in love again?*

He couldn't; it was as simple as that. He could still feel the scars within him, wounds that could never heal. How could he take another chance on love? His entire being froze at the thought. Pain slammed through him. No, he could not lose like that again. He just couldn't. Love could be gone in a blink of an eye. Love was too risky. Love could take all a man was when it died. He did not want to risk like that again. He was simply not strong enough.

He hung his head, unable to believe, after all.

He jammed his hands in his pockets. He could not go back to the house, couldn't face the family he'd let come so close to his heart.

"Aiden!" Joanna's shout pierced his thoughts, high and shrill with panic. "Aiden!"

Instantly alert, he whipped around and there she was, racing through the field as fast as she could toward him. That's when he saw the mustangs running, too, and the stallion leading the pack, focused on something hidden in the grass. The top of a little Stetson. James.

Aiden was already moving. He climbed over the fence in one quick motion and hit the ground running. That stallion was closing in, ears laid back flat to his head. A sharp neigh of fury shattered the silence, but that animal's fury was nothing, nothing at all compared to Aiden's. All he could think about was James. There he was, just ahead, frozen in place, stiff with fear.

Aiden saw it in an instant: the stallion was going to

get there first. He was vaguely aware of Joanna's cries, of Thad shouting, but he knew they were all too far away to do anything. Aiden had to protect James. It was up to him. He changed direction, running toward the horse, pushing himself with all his might. His legs ate up the ground, but it didn't seem fast enough. The distance between them was closing, and there was James, standing stock-still and whimpering.

Aiden launched himself at the horse and hit it, shoulder to shoulder. Pain shot up his arm, but it was distant, nothing at all. His feet went out from under him and he hit the ground. Pain slammed into his ribs and side; must have been a hoof that struck him. The air was driven out of his lungs, leaving him gasping.

Time slowed down. He squinted up to see the stallion, knocked off stride, recover and rear up against the brilliant blue sky. Aiden didn't like seeing the underside of those hooves flailing in the air, because they were going to come down upon him. Sadness filled him, because he was not ready to leave this earth. But at least James was safe.

James. He could see the boy at the corner of his vision, standing with his jaw open, still frozen in fear. Regret filled Aiden at how he'd treated the lad, his stepson, and at the way he had spent his time here. But at least he'd accounted for something. James was unharmed, and he would stay that way. Thad was coming, and Joanna, too. That was a relief. As Aiden watched the horse rear above him, he felt at peace. At peace, because God had led him back to life. To what mattered most.

Something snaked across the blazing sky. A rope. Its noosed end sailed around the stallion's neck and pulled tight. Time snapped back, and Aiden heard the furious neigh, heard the rapid cadence of James's breathing and felt the pounding of footsteps beside him. The horse came crashing down, pulled a few feet away by Thad's strength. A shadow cut across the sun and fell over him like grace.

Joanna. His heart stopped when he saw at the stark concern on her face. His spirit stilled as she knelt over him, touching his cheek and then his chest with her fingertips.

"Aiden? Aiden, where are you hurt? I saw you go down, and I..." Tears pooled in her eyes, precious silvery tears just for him. "You've hurt yourself something bad, I can see it."

He gasped in air, but none of it seemed to reach his lungs. He couldn't rightly say she was wrong, but he didn't mind so much. Looking at her and drinking in her beauty and her goodness was enough to sustain him for this moment and for the rest of his life.

A tear plopped onto his chin. Her tear. His heart broke all over again with a great crash of love for her. It was a tide he could not hold back. A greatness he could not control. So he didn't even bother. God had put this love in his heart for a reason. It wasn't a matter of not being strong enough; all he had to do was trust God, come what may.

"I'm so mad at you for getting hurt." She sniffled and blinked hard, but those tears just kept coming, anyway.

He heard, loud and clear, what those tears said. "Sorry," he choked out.

"You should be." Fear, that's what he saw. And hurt. "Aiden, I know you don't want a real wife, but you are a real husband to me. I don't know if I could stand to lose you."

He'd put that hurt there. He winced and did his best to cowboy up. Loving someone with all you had was a frightening thing, but he was no longer afraid. He felt strong. Courageous. Because life was hard enough. Love didn't need to be, too.

"Thank you for this." She pressed a kiss to his cheek. "For saving my son."

Sweetness filled him right up. It sealed up every crack in his heart and every fissure in his soul. How about that? Air eked into his spasming lungs, and he hurt something fierce. But that was good, right? It let him know he was alive.

"No problem," he choked out, needing to correct her. "I saved *our* son."

"But…?" She shook her head, as if to tell him he was wrong, but then it must have struck her what he meant. Tears spilled from her eyes again, and the love in them, why, it was the loveliest sight he'd ever seen.

Another shadow fell across him. Little James, his face screwed up in heartache. He gave a sniff, fighting a sob.

Pain streaked through Aiden's chest as he lifted his arm to catch the boy's small hand in his. "Don't cry, little buddy. I'm gonna be all right."

"But you l-left."

"Aw, I wasn't going anywhere." It hurt to see what James needed—and what Aiden hadn't given him. He felt ashamed, and vowed on his life that he would move mountains for this child if he had to—for his child— to make this up to him. "I guess I was to teach you to rein this afternoon. We might have to postpone that for a bit."

James nodded, sniffling.

There. That was one thing made right. Now, for his biggest offense. That hurt worse than all the broken ribs in his chest. "Joanna, I love you."

"What?" She was gazing at him in shock, as if she were the one with the broken ribs. "What did you say?"

"I love you with all my heart and soul. I want you to know the whole truth I've been hiding from you and from myself. You are like the sun coming up in my life every day."

"I love you, too." He loved her. She could see the measure of it right there in his heart. Joy overwhelmed her. She had never hoped for so much. Aiden's love was a dream come true. She smiled through her tears. "But then you already know that."

"I do, but it never hurts to hear." He smiled back, and there it was, the zing of a deeper, emotional connection between them. She could feel it in the hitch of her soul and the brightening of her spirit. It was love, abundant and abiding and true.

"You are a great gift to my life, Joanna." Aiden struggled up onto his elbows.

She settled beside him, supporting him, taking him gently into her arms, this man she loved more than her life. Because he could not save his son, he had saved hers. What a treasure he was.

"I want a real marriage, Joanna. I want to cherish you the right way." He coughed a little, gasping in pain, but that didn't stop him. "I want to be the man you need in all ways. I won't let you down again. I promise you."

"You never let me down, and you never will."

"Then that's a yes?"

"Absolutely, beyond all doubt." It was in the happiness lighting her face and in the brush of her lips on his cheek.

Footsteps drummed on the earth. Thad was coming; he must have gotten the stallion secured. "You're looking a bit pale, big brother. I suppose I should go fetch the doc."

"Suppose so."

"Aiden?" It was Ma, bringing Noelle and little Daisy with her. Their little girl sidled up against Joanna's skirts. Ma was all business. "Let me take a look at that wound. I can put a poultice on that until the doctor gets here. Thad, let's get him in the house."

Aiden hardly noticed the pain. He was surrounded by family, the people he loved the most. He was in Joanna's arms, his love, his bride, his everything. Elation left him dizzy.

"Just a minute, Ma. There's one thing I've failed to do. Joanna, are you ready?" He pulled her gently to him and kissed her for real this time, tender and sweet. Their first kiss as man and wife.

Epilogue

November, three months later

These were Aiden's boots coming up behind her. Joanna let go of the scrub brush, leaned back on her heels at the foot of the stairs and swept her bangs out of her eyes. "I suppose you want something from our bedroom, don't you? Too bad. I'm afraid the floors are still wet."

"And you're not going to let me in with my boots?" He looked like a man who'd been working hard in the barn. Bits of hay and straw clung to his shirt and trousers, but that only seemed to make him more handsome. Perhaps it was because there were no more shadows. He was whole and alive and happy.

She couldn't resist teasing him, just a little. "Sorry. I'm not going to let you through. You'll just have to wait."

"Wait, huh? It might take a long time to dry. And it's not yet time for me to drive to town to pick up James and Daisy from school. I'm not sure what I ought to do with this free time."

She plopped the brush into the bucket of sudsy water and rose, wiping her hands on her apron. "You could go back outside and bring in more wood for our fires."

"I could, but it's turning awfully cold out there. It might snow."

"That's a handy excuse." She let her fingertips run up the placket of his flannel shirt, thinking of those ribs he had broken that were now good and truly healed. "Am I supposed to believe that a big man like you doesn't want to go outside in the cold?"

"That's right." His baritone dipped warm and low.

"Excuses, excuses, Mr. McKaslin." Her fingertips reached the top button on his shirt and she couldn't resist laying the flat of her hand there over the reliable beat of his heart. His devoted, faithful heart. "I can think of only one more chore that's left on my list and this is an important one."

"Is that so?" His hand covered hers, affection alight in his eyes. "You can trust me. I won't let you down."

"I know." Happiness filled her as she went up on tiptoe. "You could kiss your wife."

"My wife?" His right hand cradled the side of her face. "I love calling you that. Almost as much as I love kissing you."

"Lucky me." Joanna closed her eyes, breathless, waiting for the brush of his lips to hers.

His kiss was sheer perfection. It was pure sweetness and complete tenderness. It was like floating on clear blue sky without a storm in sight.

"So you only wanted one kiss?" he murmured against her lips.

"I suppose I could endure a second one."

"It will be tough, but I think I can, too." He brushed the tendrils out of her eyes. "I can endure anything as long as I am with you."

"Me, too." His lips claimed hers again, this time as reverent as a promise kept. As miraculous as grace. She gave thanks for this man's everlasting love. He loved her, honest and true, the way she loved him.

"I love you, Joanna, with all of my soul," he said, and kissed her forehead.

"As I love you." She was so happy, it was easy to see the future with her beloved. There would be more children filling this house one day, James graduating from school and taking over the ranch, and some day, far from now, Aiden would walk Daisy down the aisle. Joanna's dreams for her children were coming true.

But for her, there would always be Aiden, strong and true and loving. He was her shelter, her dream, her everything.

Lace curtains framed a snowy view at the parlor window directly behind them, a reminder of the power of love and faith. And of their great love.

"I have one more request." She stepped back to look into his eyes. "Take me to town with you."

"Sure. Let's go fetch our children home." He slipped his arm around her shoulder and they went off into the world together.

* * * * *

Ruth Axtell Morren wrote her first story—a spy thriller—when she was twelve, and knew she wanted to be a writer. There were many detours along the way. She studied comparative literature at Smith College, taught English in the Canary Islands and worked in international development in Miami, Florida, where she met her future husband. She has divided the intervening years between the Netherlands and the down east coast of Maine.

She gained her first recognition as a writer when her second manuscript was a finalist for the Romance Writers of America Golden Heart® Award in 1994. Ruth's second novel, *Wild Rose* (2004), was selected as a Booklist Top 10 Christian Novel in 2005.

Ruth loves hearing from readers. You can contact her through her website at ruthaxtell.com.

Books by Ruth Axtell Morren

Love Inspired Historical

Hearts in the Highlands
A Man Most Worthy
To Be a Mother
A Gentleman's Homecoming
Hometown Cinderella

Steeple Hill Single Title

Winter Is Past
Wild Rose
Lilac Spring
Dawn in My Heart
The Healing Season

Visit the Author Profile page
at Harlequin.com for more titles.

A MAN MOST WORTHY

Ruth Axtell Morren

He shall receive the blessing from the Lord, and righteousness from the God of his salvation.
—*Psalms* 24:5

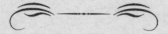

Chapter One

❦

Richmond, England, June 1875

The numbers wouldn't add up. Nick ran his ink-smudged finger up the neat column of figures and back down again.

A smothered giggle disrupted his concentration. With a frown, he glanced up from his desk, irritated that he'd have to begin adding for a third time.

He stared.

The most exquisite creature stood in the doorway to his small office, a finger to her lips. In her navy blue pleated skirt and sailor blouse, she appeared no more than sixteen.

Before he could do or say anything, she moved into his space, bringing with her a vitality the dusty nook had probably not seen in a decade.

Her eyes were wide, pleading, yet with a touch of mischief. "Shh!" she whispered. "Don't tell them I'm here."

He almost jumped out of his seat as she came around his desk and crouched behind it at his feet.

He drew his legs in, his eyes drawn to her slim, pale hands clasped over her knees. She lifted her head. "You won't give me away, will you?" Her sparkling deep blue eyes looked up at his in a conspiratorial smile. They must be what the poets called violet. Another part of his mind noticed the coppery shade of her hair. It was worn down, as befitted a schoolgirl, with a deep fringe across her wide forehead, and drawn away from her face with a wide blue bow in the back. Her hair was very straight but its toffee-colored tones glistened in the bit of light from his small lamp.

A noise at the door caused him to look up again. A youth and another young lady stood at the doorjamb, their faces peering doubtfully in.

The young gentleman ran a disdainful eye across the room. "You don't think she came in here, do you?"

The young lady, also pretty, but nothing compared to the one crouched at Nick's feet, put her hands on the hips of her similar schoolgirl outfit and took a slow turn about the cramped space, her slim nose wrinkled. "I daresay not. There's not space in here to hide a pin in!"

Nick couldn't help glancing down at the girl at his feet, and experienced once again a moment of shock at her loveliness as she glanced up at him, her finger to her lips.

"I say, you haven't seen a young lady run by here, have you, my good fellow?"

Nick immediately took umbrage to the young man's tone. Instead of replying, he picked up his pencil and pretended to go over his figures again.

The young man cleared his throat. "See here, I'm addressing you."

Without straightening from his work, Nick's gaze flickered up. "I beg your pardon?"

A look of annoyance crossed the young man's fine features. "Never mind. I shall look for myself. Come on, Lucy." He beckoned to the young lady standing at his side.

"Alice wouldn't hide in here," she said with a toss of her head. "Why are we wasting our time in this stuffy hole? There's nothing but dust and paper in here." As if to prove her point, she sneezed.

"You're right." With a sniff, the young gentleman backed out the door. The girl followed after him. Their voices faded down the corridor. "We shall find you, Alice. You can't hide from us!"

Silence descended once more in the office. Before Nick had a chance to move, the girl stood in one quick motion, smoothing down her skirt. "Thank you ever so much, Mr.—"

"Tennent," he said without thinking, pushing his chair back and standing.

She bobbed a quick curtsy then studied him a moment. He wondered what those stunning eyes saw. More than the other girl, no doubt, who had looked right past him as if he'd been no more than the blotter on his desk.

"You're Father's secretary?"

He nodded. So, this lovely creature was the offspring of Mr. Shepard.

She put a finger to her chin and tilted her head. "This is the first time he's brought his secretary out to Richmond, at least as far as I can recall." Her cheeks dimpled. "But then, I'm rarely home myself, so I wouldn't know."

He fingered the pencil he still held in his hand, trying to maintain a poise he was far from feeling. "I imagine your father wanted to have this project finished as quickly as possible. It demands much time and attention right now."

She cast a glance over the papers on his desk. "All Father's projects seem to require much time and attention." Was that irony in one so young? Her lashes, the same deep coppery tone as her hair, formed deep curves against the delicate, pale skin.

He frowned at her statement. "One doesn't rise to the importance of Mr. Shepard without a lot of time and effort."

Her eyes came up to study him. "You admire him."

"There is much to be admired." He lifted his chin a trifle defensively.

She ran a slim forefinger along the edge of the beat-up desk as she walked around it. He found he could breathe slightly easier when she'd moved a few feet away from him. "Most people do, don't they?" She glanced back at him, her finger still on the desk. "Admire him, I mean?"

"I imagine they do."

She nodded. "Is he a nice employer to you?"

He raised his eyebrows at her direct question, unaccustomed to someone asking him about his situation. "I have only been in his employ a fortnight, and it is not my place to comment on your father's treatment of his employees."

"Of course not. You were very cool to Victor."

Her statement threw him, until he realized she was

referring to the young gentleman just in the room. "A playmate of yours?"

"I've known them both since childhood."

"Does that make them your friends?"

She tilted her head and a slow smile spread across her face. "I...don't know. I'd never really thought about it."

As if the mention of them summoned them, he heard their voices once again from the end of the corridor.

"Now, I say, Alice, we've searched this place from top to bottom—"

She sighed and took a step toward the door. "I'd better leave you to your work before they barge in on you again. I do apologize for interrupting your work, Mr. Tennent. I'm sure it's important."

He shook his head, trying to dispel the wave of disappointment he felt at her departure. "No need to apologize." He looked down at his column of figures, reassuming a business-like tone. "Good day to you, Miss Shepard."

"It was a pleasure to make your acquaintance, Mr. Tennent."

She sounded like a society lady, the kind of women he only saw from a distance in London. Hearing Victor's voice closer, she flashed him a smile then spun on her heel and left the room, once again the young schoolgirl.

Victor and Lucy pounced on her as soon as they saw her. "Where in the world were you?"

Alice laughed, the sound coming out breathless and excited. "You sillies, I was behind you all the time." She'd moved far enough from the office door that they wouldn't suspect where she'd come from.

Victor turned away from her and marched in the direction he'd come from. "I say, this game is silly. I, for one, am too old to be playing at hide-and-seek."

Alice stifled a laugh. He only thought it was silly because he hadn't found her. "All right, what do you suggest we do?"

At the moment all she wanted to do was be alone somewhere and ponder the encounter she'd had with Papa's new secretary. *Miss Shepard.* The way he'd said it sounded so grown-up and ladylike. Everyone else called her Miss Alice. She would not be Miss Shepard for another year-and-a-half at her coming out.

In those few moments of conversation, she'd felt taken seriously by an adult. A young gentleman, at that. Her heartbeat quickened at the intensity of his gaze.

She went over his features in her mind. Dark, short-cropped hair over a high forehead, a thin face, a high-bridged nose. But most arresting were his deep-set eyes, their irises almost black, the eyebrows straight and dark above them before arching outward.

"Let's go riding." Victor's voice, always peremptory when he wanted something, brought her thoughts to a halt.

"It's too hot to go riding." Lucy sounded peevish.

She took the girl by the arm. "Come along, we can take a walk in the grove. It'll be cool in the shade."

Two weeks of holidays stretched out before her. How she'd hoped that she'd be able to see Father. But he was always off to London and she was forced to entertain unwanted guests. There'd be no peace now until she returned to school.

* * *

Alice stood on the grassy tennis court, her attention fixed on Victor, her racket held firmly in her hand. "Come on, put some spirit into your serve."

Just as she knew they would, her words brought a frown to his face. The next second, he slammed the rubber ball across the net.

But she was ready. The ball sailed out of her reach. With a laugh, she sprang towards it and then hit it dead-on with her racket. It went flying back, forcing Victor to sprint to connect with it. "I say, you're not playing the game as it should be played."

She laughed again. "I'm playing it the way I saw it played at Wimbledon last spring!"

"This is not a competition!"

When she sent it back again, she aimed it at his partner, Lucy. The girl didn't move from her position, merely raised her arm halfway in a vain attempt to reach the ball.

Alice blew her bangs off her forehead in frustration. "Lucy, it went right to you!"

Lucy made a face at her and let Victor fetch the ball. "You're not playing fairly, Alice. You know you mustn't make me reach for it."

What a bore it was to play with these three. She glanced over at her own partner, a neighbor's son, also home for the holidays. He was looking away from the court, leaning on his racket. Oh, to be paired with someone who showed a little spirit!

She lunged to the right, almost missing the ball Victor served back to her. Despite his indolence in the drawing room, once she taunted him, he was roused to make some effort. *Thunk!* Her racket connected with the ball and it went whizzing back to him.

A tall figure coming around the corner of the high yew hedge caught her attention.

She recognized the new secretary immediately. She hadn't seen him at all again yesterday, and wondered if he was forced to take his meals with the servants or all by himself in his little office off Father's library.

In the time it took for the ball to return over the net, Alice made up her mind. She knocked the ball at the wrong angle, so that it missed the net altogether and bounced sidelong into the shorter trimmed hedge on her side of the court.

"Alice! What are you doing?" Victor's voice was filled with disgust. With a shrug and shamefaced smile his way, she skipped toward the hedge. She stooped to retrieve the ball where it had landed in the soil beneath the hedge and stood in time to meet the young secretary coming along the path.

"Hello, Mr. Tennent."

He looked different in the bright sun. Hatless, his short ebony curls gleamed. His face was slim, the cheekbones rather prominent, but his eyes were as dark and intense as the day before.

They widened slightly as if surprised that she'd remembered his name. "Hello, Miss Shepard."

She thought of him confined to that tiny office. "Would you like to join in the match?" With his tall, lean build, he would probably prove a swift player.

His gaze flickered over the court then returned to her. "No, thank you." His tone sounded more formal than yesterday.

"We're having ever so much fun."

He looked away from her. "I have no time for sports."

She fingered the edge of her racket, refusing to give up so easily. "I should think playing a hard game of tennis would help you in your work."

A slight crease formed between his dark brows. "I fail to see how swinging at a ball on a grassy lawn would aid me in figuring the financial assets of a company."

"Exercising your body will keep your mind sharp."

Amusement began to dislodge the severity of his expression. She leaned forward, pressing home her point. "It's been scientifically proven. You are breathing more deeply of oxygen, for one thing. More than in that airless cubbyhole my father has you closeted in."

Before he could say anything, Victor shouted from the court, "Are you going to join the game or remain talking to a clerk all day?" Laughter from the others drifted over to them.

She turned back to the court, ashamed of her friends in that moment. She remembered the secretary's question of the day before. These "friends" were mere acquaintances, offspring of her parents' friends, forced on her during the holidays to keep her company.

Mr. Tennent's face remained expressionless. "If you'll excuse me—"

"Wait." She stopped, casting about for another way to lengthen their exchange, not quite sure why. "Why don't you join me for a game tomorrow—" her mind ran on, thinking of possibilities "—before breakfast, before you begin working."

He looked away from her. "I know nothing of the game." The words came out stiffly as if forced out of him.

She laughed, relieved. For a moment she'd thought perhaps it was her company he didn't want. "That's all right. I can teach you."

His eyes widened slightly before resuming their formality. "I have no time for games. Good morning." Before she could draw breath to argue, he hurried off.

She looked at his receding back, frowning at the rebuff.

"Come on, Alice, or you shall have to forfeit the game."

With a sigh of frustration, she hurried back to her place, prepared to meet Victor's serve.

Lucy gave a disbelieving laugh across the court. "Goodness, Alice, are you so bored you're forced to seek out your father's employees?"

"Why shouldn't I be nice to Father's employees? Maybe he'll prove a better tennis player than all of you!" More determined than ever to get the serious young man out on the tennis court, she whacked the ball that came flying toward her.

Nick shook his head over the report. The mining company had already had one shaft collapse in the last year. Another was hardly producing. If he were a partner, he'd recommend to Mr. Shepard that he sell his shares of the company.

He gathered up the papers and prepared to go to the larger office adjoining his "airless cubbyhole," as the young Miss Shepard had put it. He paused, considering once again the girl's invitation to a game of tennis. To lessons, no less! He told himself once again, as he had all the rest of the afternoon, that it was nonsense. No matter that no one of her class had ever bothered to notice someone as lowly as a clerk, let alone issue such a friendly invitation....

The girl was no more than fifteen if she was a day. She was his employer's daughter. He had no business daydreaming of her, lovely creature or not.

He stopped at Mr. Shepard's door, hearing a female voice. Nick paused, his hand on the knob, his breath held.

"But Papa, why can't you go rowing with us? The day is glorious and we shall have such a grand time on the water."

"You know I must return to town tomorrow, and I have work this afternoon. Now, you have your friends here you must amuse." Shepard's voice was firm.

"You're forever working. It's a holiday."

Something in the plaintive feminine tones caught at Nick's heart, and he eased open the door a crack.

Miss Shepard stood with her back to him, in a maroon dress with a large bow at the back where the ruffled material was gathered. Its mid-calf length and her long hair worn down with a matching ribbon told him more clearly than anything else that she was still a schoolgirl.

"You'll just have to content yourself with seeing me at dinner this evening." Mr. Shepard stood and indicated the meeting was over.

"Very well, Father." She turned around, her chest heaving in a sigh.

What kind of a man could ignore such a tender request? The next instant he remembered his own cold refusal of her invitation to play tennis the day before. But that had been different. He was here to work and not to amuse himself. Still, the image of himself as a hard-hearted brute like the girl's father persisted as he waited behind the door.

What he'd seen of his employer thus far—a man who expected a lot and was all business—qualities Nick admired—took on a different perspective when seen from his personal life. Something about the glimpse of Miss Shepard's forlorn face as she dragged her feet toward the exit, elicited a response he'd never thought he'd feel for someone of her pampered station. There were enough people in real want not to waste his sympathy on a spoiled little rich girl.

When the door clicked shut behind her, Nick waited a few more seconds before clearing his throat and entering the library from the side door to his office. His footfalls made no sound on the thick Turkish carpet as he advanced toward the large mahogany desk planted in the middle of the room as if to proclaim its owner firmly in control of the space.

Nick cleared his throat again.

"Yes, what is it?" Mr. Shepard didn't look up, and a trace of impatience underlined the clipped words. He was a man in his fifties, his hair still thick but with threads of gray fading the burnished coppery mane. It occurred to Nick that Shepard must have had his daughter late in life.

"I have the information you requested on Rafferty, Limited."

Shepard adjusted the spectacles on the bridge of his nose and thrust out his hand. "Well, bring it here."

Nick handed him the sheaf of papers, hoping his employer would notice the careful analysis he'd made of the mining company. But with a wave of his hand, Shepard dismissed Nick. Nick's years clerking at a bank had inured him to being treated in such a manner. Clerks were usually ignored until someone needed something pressing and then barked at to produce it immediately.

But he'd looked forward to just a hint that Mr. Shepard had noticed all his extra effort.

Nick returned to his office, unable to help comparing his own footsteps with those of the girl who'd been just as summarily dismissed.

This was a mistake. Nick knew it, yet found he could do nothing to change his course of action.

Setting his alarm clock for an hour earlier than usual, he rose with a sense of foreboding that he was about to make a fool of himself. After washing and shaving, he stood a moment looking at his sparse wardrobe of black suits appropriate to a clerk. What did one wear to a game of lawn tennis?

Finally, he donned a clean white shirt and waistcoat and one of his two black frock coats, calling himself a number of names as he buttoned up the front. He looked like he should be heading to a counting house instead of outdoors. The young men he'd observed the other day had worn light-colored trousers and loose jackets.

Nick did own a straw boater—more appropriate in the country than the top hats he usually wore.

Setting it on his head, he headed out the door, not bothering to go by the dining room to see if breakfast had been laid out yet. This household was not one to rise early, he'd observed in his few days' residence.

He walked past the garden beds, deciding he'd see if Miss Shepard was there and return at once if she wasn't. If he saw anyone else, he'd pretend he was out for an early morning stroll. Surely the girl hadn't meant the invitation seriously. He imagined her sleeping form. Of course she didn't remember a casually issued invitation. Yet, she'd remembered his name. That fact still amazed him.

The grass was damp with dew. The toes of his polished shoes were already wet before he'd gone halfway across the lawn.

He recalled Miss Shepard's words about exercise being good for his mental acuity and couldn't help smiling. What did she know about real toil? He'd been up at the crack of dawn since he'd been able to walk, toddling out after his brothers and mother to the mill.

A riot of birdsong hailed him from the great boughs of the trees on the vast property. He realized he'd never been in such a pleasant setting. Childhood was a memory of dismal, gray surroundings and of hunger and barrenness. Since coming to London, he'd lived in a different sort of gray, from sunup to sundown in a treeless environment, going from his dingy room, downing a quick breakfast in the drab dining room crowded with half-a-dozen other young clerks, and rushing to catch the steamer across the gray Thames to the grim city of finance.

He passed the last flowerbed and looked over the hedge at the carefully clipped, emerald green lawn with its chalked lines marking out an oblong.

He stopped short at the sight of Miss Shepard holding a racket in one hand. Her head was lifted up, a hand shading her eyes from the early morning sun. He followed her line of vision and saw a bird in flight. His gaze returned to her. Her long hair fell down her shoulders like melted caramel to the small of her back. For all the loveliness of her silhouette, something about it conveyed loneliness. His gut tightened as he recalled the sound of longing in her voice toward her father.

She must have seen him out of the corner of her eye because she dropped her hand and ran over to him.

"You came!" She stopped about a foot from him, her smile wide. In that instant, all his doubts evaporated like the dew in the warm morning sun. He didn't doubt the welcome on her face; she was too young to have learned to mask her feelings.

He found himself caught once again by her beauty. She had the most exquisite features, delicate and perfectly formed like a porcelain doll's—pink-tinted cheeks, a perfect little nose, lips a deeper pink than her cheeks, her teeth white and even. Her heart-shaped face was framed by those silky locks of hair.

Then he looked down at the damp grass, remembering his ignorance of the game. "Yes."

"Have you really never played tennis before?"

Did she think the average person indulged in tennis? How little she knew of life. His eyes met hers again, expecting to see triumph, but only simple interest was visible in those blue depths. "No."

"Very well, let's get started. I imagine you haven't much time."

"You imagine correctly." What was he doing here? He should be finishing breakfast and going to his desk.

"I brought an extra racket, in case you decided to come." She slanted him a friendly smile as she spoke, leading the way to the edge of the court.

She picked up a racket from a white wrought iron chair and a wire basket full of rubber balls. "You take this side of the net. Stand in the middle since we're playing singles, and I'll go on the other. I shall serve to you and you try to hit the ball back to me. Just follow my motions."

Still amazed that she wanted to teach him, he took the racket from her and gripped it in his hand. It didn't weigh much, its handle made of wood and wrapped in leather at the base.

She hit the ball with an underhanded swing and it came over the high net toward him. He didn't even have to move to reach it. He swung with all his might and with a sense of triumph connected with the ball. Instead of going back over the net where he expected it to, it flew up toward the sky and landed back on his side of the net, skittering away in a series of small bounces.

His face flamed at her laughter.

"You needn't hit it quite so hard to return it across the net," she said in a kind tone. "Also, a lot depends on the angle of your racket when you hit the ball. Let's try again, shall we?" She stooped and grabbed another ball from her basket.

He gripped the racket, determined to hit the ball over the net this time. He controlled his swing, barely tapping the racket against the ball and sent it dribbling into the net.

"That's better," she said, no hint of laughter in her voice. "Let's try another."

She continued sending balls his way. He missed as many as he managed to hit, but she continued encouraging him with every one.

Then he began to catch on and managed to send more balls back to her. Gradually he gained confidence because Miss Shepard was so patient and encouraging. He enjoyed watching her vitality as she ran across the court, so unlike the passive stance of the other women he'd glimpsed on the court at other times in the day. Perhaps it was because she was still a girl. She had not yet assumed the airs of a young lady just come out. Even the perspiration making her face shine appealed to him.

In some ways she reminded him of the girls of his boyhood. In their ragged frocks and bare feet, there was no room for stiffness and formality. They ran and skipped about, unfettered by social constraints or petticoats and high-buttoned shoes.

She continued sending balls his way a while longer. He was beginning to think it a tame sport when a ball went flying over the net so fast it made a whooshing sound as it cut through the air. He had to sprint to connect with it. He just made it and sent it back over.

She laughed as she went running for it. "This is the way I prefer to play!" Again, it came hard at him, and he had to jump to the side to reach it. He missed it.

"I see." He retrieved the ball and returned to his place. He swung hard at it and again, the ball went too high.

"I'm over here, you know!" Laugher bubbled in her voice.

He winced in embarrassment at his overconfidence.

Before he could run after the ball, she had gone for it. This time she resumed her gentler game. "I think we need to practice a bit more before you're up to my speed." The words were said to him in a friendly manner but he took them as a challenge, vowing to find a way to master this game.

Beads of sweat rolled down his temples as the sun grew warmer in the sky. At that moment, she picked up the ball and strolled to his side of the court. "You really need proper tennis garments. You must be sweltering in your suit. Why don't you take off your coat?"

He mopped his brow, thinking how unpolished he must look compared to the suave young men she'd played with yesterday. Instead of removing his coat, he snapped open his watch. "I really must go. I need to get to work."

She nodded, though her down-tilted face and puckered lips expressed disappointment. Then she brightened. "Have you breakfasted?"

He shook his head.

"I haven't either. Come, you must be as hungry and thirsty as I am." Before he could refuse, she was walking off the court. "Leave the racket here. I'm sure someone will be out to play later. Hurry, I'm famished!" She waited for him to catch up to her and the two walked back to the house.

Her next words surprised him. "Are you from London?"

He wasn't used to anyone taking a personal interest in him. "No. I grew up in Birmingham."

She tilted her head. "That's funny. You haven't any accent that I can tell."

"That's because my mother was—" He bit his tongue, he'd almost said "a lady." He hesitated. "From Kent."

She smiled. "Not far from here?"

"A bit. She was born in Whitstable."

"Ah, by the sea."

He found her blue eyes fixed on him as if waiting for more information. "She was a governess before she married my father." He looked away. "He was a miner."

"Oh." The single note was filled with wonder. "However did they meet?"

"She was working with a family up there and had left them." Refusing the master's advances, he added mentally. "She had begun a small school for the miner's children."

"And she met your father!" Her eyes gleamed in excitement. "Oh! Love at first sight, I bet it was."

He looked straight ahead of him, amused and irritated at the same time by her romantic schoolgirl notions. "He died when a mine shaft collapsed, leaving my mother to raise four sons. He was a widower, when they met. His two boys were at the school. Then my brother and I came along."

"How sad," she said softly. "My mother died giving birth to me."

He looked sharply at her. Her tone was almost casual. "I'm sorry," he said finally, feeling the inadequacy of the words.

"Oh, it's all right. It happened so long ago. Tell me what happened after your father died."

He took up the thread of his own history, his mind still on her motherless condition. "My mother moved us into town, where she found work in a mill."

Miss Shepard was silent for only a moment. No doubt she'd lost interest by now. "And when did you come to London?"

He smiled at her persistence. No one from her station had ever asked him about his origins. "When I was fifteen, my mother gave me five pounds she had saved and bought me a rail ticket to London. I found work at a bank. I was good with numbers, you see. Numbers and letters. She'd made sure we all received learning."

"And now you've become my father's private secretary?"

He nodded.

"That's good. Poor old Simpson is becoming forgetful, I've heard. He's been with Father forever!"

They reached the house and he held the door open for her then followed her into the breakfast room. He still hadn't gotten accustomed to the fact that there were separate rooms for breakfasting and dining—and that most in the household took their breakfast in bed.

He stopped short at the threshold of the breakfast room at the sight of his employer. Mr. Shepard was seated squarely behind *The Times* and Nick debated a few seconds what to do. Retreat? Go forward as if accompanying the man's daughter were the most natural thing in the world?

Before he could decide, Miss Shepard breezed in ahead of him. "Good morning, Father. You've beaten us down to breakfast." She leaned over and kissed him on the cheek.

"What are you doing about so early?" He glanced over his paper, then lowered it further when he caught sight of Nick. Nick greeted him, hesitating at the doorway. The man gave a mere nod in acknowledgment and turned his attention back to his young daughter.

"I was just practicing tennis. Look whom I found." She turned to Nick. "He hasn't breakfasted either, so I brought him along. What will you have, Mr. Tennent?" Before her father could say anything, she moved to the sideboard and began lifting lids. "There's scrambled eggs, kedgeree, bacon…"

Mr. Shepard grunted and turned back to his paper.

Nick followed to the serving dishes and took up a plate. The girl had succeeded in distracting her father from any mention of tennis lessons. He pondered her adroit maneuver as he helped himself to the wide array of food. His own boarding house fare usually consisted of lumpy porridge and a weak cup of tea.

Concentrating on his food, Nick listened to Miss Shepard chattering away to her father. He answered in monosyllables, with an occasional "What's that you say?" thrown in, but he never lowered his paper more than a fraction.

Nick marveled at how Shepard could have produced such a lovely creature—and not realize what a treasure he had. Poor motherless child. He knew she had a much older brother. Nick had seen him a few times at the firm—Mr. Geoffrey Shepard, a pompous man in his late twenties.

Miss Shepard leaned forward, setting down her knife and fork. "Did you hear me, Papa?"

"What's that you say?"

"I said we are planning an excursion to Richmond Park. Can you not come?"

"I return to London this afternoon. Take Miss Bellows with you."

Nick knew he referred to a companion of sorts he'd briefly met in the servants' quarters. His gaze rested in sympathy on Miss Shepard's crestfallen features. He turned with a start to find Mr. Shepard focused on him, his gray-blue eyes sharp and piercing. "I'll need those figures on Henderson, Ltd. before I go."

"Yes, sir." Nick drained the last of his tea and stood. "I'll get to it right away."

Miss Shepard smiled at him. "So long, Mr. Tennent. Perhaps I shall see you tomorrow?" Her eyes told him she was referring to the tennis court.

"Perhaps. Good morning, Miss Shepard." With a bow, he left the room.

Of course, he couldn't join her again tomorrow. It was sheer folly...

Chapter Two

Awake since the sky had begun to lighten, Alice let out a massive sigh of relief when she saw Mr. Tennent walking across the lawn toward the court.

Not until that moment did she realize how disappointed she would have been if he hadn't shown up. She'd prayed hard last night that he wouldn't be discouraged after only one lesson.

She fingered the head of her racket as she watched his long stride. His serious air made Victor and the other boys of her acquaintance seem just that—boys! Biting her lip, she glanced down at her calf-length plaid skirt and sailor top. How she wished she were one year older and wore ankle-length dresses like a lady. Did Mr. Tennent see her as just a schoolgirl? She cringed, remembering the silly game of hide-and-seek she'd been playing the day she'd burst in on him.

She smiled as he approached her. "Good morning."

He nodded, his dark eyes meeting hers, their formality lessening as he gave her a slight smile. "Good morning, Miss Shepard."

She tilted her head. "Ready to have another go?"

"If you've the patience and fortitude."

Her smile widened in relief. She handed him the extra racket. "You did very well for your first time. Come, I'll serve first."

"Very well." He shed his coat this time and laid it carefully on a wrought iron chair by the side of the court.

She began gently, giving him a chance to review what she'd taught him the day before. They played for about twenty minutes before taking a break.

"I brought some water for us," she said, leading him to the yew hedge where she had stashed two stone flasks. "It should still be cold."

"Thank you." He took the one she handed him then waited until she had uncapped hers and brought it to her lips before following suit. "How did I do today? Any improvement?" he asked, lowering the flask.

"Oh, a vast amount. You're a natural athlete."

He made a sound of disbelief.

"You don't believe me? It's the truth. I can tell. You're nothing like most of the boys on the court who try and act as if they knew something." She studied his face, hoping she was convincing him not to give up, but the steady way he regarded her was hard to read.

Mr. Tennent wiped his brow with his handkerchief, pushing back his dark curls.

Hoping to draw out more about his fascinating past, she said, "Tell me more about your mother."

He looked away from her, and she bit her lip, afraid she had offended him. Her governess had always said she was too direct.

But he answered with no sign of displeasure. "She had to take us into the mill with her when we were young, and put us to work as soon as we could wind a thread around a bobbin."

"She must have been a brave woman to raise four boys all alone." His tale had haunted her last night. It had sounded so unbearably romantic.

He pocketed his handkerchief. He was standing in his vest and shirtsleeves. Even in his typical clerk's attire, he stood out. There was something distinguished about him. "No matter how tired she was," he continued in a quiet tone, "she always gave us a lesson after dinner in the evenings before we went to bed. She had saved a few schoolbooks and one or two storybooks from her teaching days. Those and the Bible formed our only amusement at home."

She pictured the cozy scene, a mother with her four boys surrounding her on a settee, or with her arms around them on a wide bed flanked by soft pillows. "It must have been nice to have a mother read to you at night."

"Didn't anyone ever read to you at bedtime?"

She blushed beneath his close scrutiny. "My nurse told me stories when I was very young, and then Miss Duffy, my governess, read to me when I was a little older."

"I'm sorry you didn't have a mother to read to you at bedtime," he said softly.

His tone was so gentle it was as if he had known how lonely her childhood had been. Afraid he'd pity her, she set down her water bottle and picked up her racket. "Come on, let's get back to our game before you have to work."

He followed her out to the court. This time, she hit the ball a little harder and enjoyed watching him run to meet it. She, too, was forced to run across the court when he returned it equally forcefully. Laughing from sheer joy at the physical exertion, she swung at the ball and watched it clear the net.

By the time they finished their lesson, they were both red in the face, but never had she had more fun on the court.

"What about tomorrow morning?" she asked him, hoping she didn't sound too eager.

"It depends on your father. I might be called back to London."

Her shoulders slumped in disappointment. "Of course." Trust Father to ruin her fun. "Do you think he'll bring you back out again?"

"I have no way of knowing."

"Well, if you should come back, I challenge you to a match."

He nodded slowly, his deep set eyes looking into hers. "You're on."

As soon as he had a free moment back in London, Nick inquired of one of the clerks in the firm and found out where he could get tennis lessons. It meant money he could ill afford, and having to go across town to Regent's Park, but he was determined the next time he faced Alice Shepard across the court, he would no longer be a clumsy novice.

He hadn't been able to get the young girl out of his mind since he'd returned to the city, no matter how many times he'd told himself he was being silly to keep thinking about her.

But her smiling face wouldn't leave his thoughts despite the effort he put into studying his employer's files and tallying columns of numbers.

He'd never been in love. No young woman had yet caused him to veer from his single-minded focus on the path to success.

The feelings Miss Shepard elicited in him were a puzzle to him, not least because he didn't know how to classify them. She was too young for it to be love, he felt. But if it wasn't love, it certainly was a sort of obsession, which he'd have to eradicate sooner or later. He could ill spare time for such dangerous complications.

In the meantime, however, at a safe distance in London, he preferred to postpone the moment and content himself with daydreaming about her as he rode the early morning ferry to work, as he walked the distance to the office, as he made the return journey in the evening.

And every evening, after work and a light supper, he stood across the net from his new instructor, imagining Miss Shepard in his place. He'd spent part of his last salary on a lightweight pair of twill trousers and a linen jacket, vowing to look as dapper as any young gentleman when they next met.

Back and forth went the ball, the instructor calling out advice as he sent it across the net to Nick. Nick grew to enjoy the thrill of competition. He found it as thrilling as predicting the direction of the price of a company's stock.

He remembered Miss Shepard's words. *You're a natural athlete.* Did it mean she'd actually looked past his shabby frock coat and seen something more than just her father's secretary? He'd never thought of himself as athletic, even though until coming to London, he'd spent any spare moment outside when he wasn't working in the noisy, dusty environment of the mill. But that was playing in the street with boys his age, with no sports equipment. A ball was a rotten cabbage, a cricket bat a broken chair leg. But even those had been few and far between as any piece of wood was quickly consumed in the stove, and extra food was rarely to be found.

Nick had no idea when and if he'd be going back to the Shepards' country house, but he'd be prepared just in case, even if it cost him a fortnight's wages.

He wanted to match Miss Shepard's skill and show her he was a worthy opponent.

Each morning he joined the hundreds of anonymous young men clad in black frock coats and top hats hurrying down Fleet Street to their offices. He pulled open the brass-handled door, glancing a moment at the understated plaque to the right: Shepard & Steward, Ltd., Investments.

Some day it would read Shepard, Steward, Tennent, & Partners.

He hurried down the corridor to his office, nodding his head to the various clerks he passed. "'Morning, Harold. 'Morning, Stanley." Rushed syllables as everyone hurried to his place in the maze of corridors and cubicles.

He entered the quieter sanctuary upstairs in the rear, the executive offices of the full partners. His own desk, situated in a small corner of an office he shared with the senior secretary, was neat, the way he'd left it the evening before.

Nick sat down and opened the file he'd been studying the previous day, glad for the momentary solitude. Mr. Shepard would expect a report by noon on the assets of the small factory, which manufactured iron fastenings.

"Shepard wants you."

He looked up to find Mr. Simpson, the other secretary, walking to his own desk, the larger of the two in the room. The old man guarded his boss from all he considered intruders, including Nick.

Nick stood now and grabbed up his pad and pencil. "Yes, sir."

The man stood by the doorway, as if to make sure Nick obeyed the summons. His bristly gray eyebrows drew together in their customary frown as Nick passed him with a curt nod.

Dark walnut wainscoting covered the walls of Mr. Shepard's private office. Oil landscapes in heavy wooden frames lined the space above. Some day he would have an office like this one.

Shepard stood at a window overlooking the busy street below, his hands clasped loosely behind them. He turned only slightly at the soft sound of the door closing.

"Ah, Tennent, have a seat. I need you to take a letter."

"Yes, sir." Nick crossed the deep blue Turkish carpet and sat in the leather armchair facing the wide desk.

Mr. Shepard twirled his reading glasses in his hands. "This is to the Denbigh Coke Company, Denbighshire, Wales.

"Gentlemen— After a careful review of your firm, it is with regret that we inform you that we must decline the opportunity to offer you the venture capital you requested to expand your colliery. Although your firm's net profits for the preceding year showed…"

Nick's pencil hurried across the paper, his mind unable to suppress the satisfaction at Shepard's decision. It mirrored the one Nick would have made in his place.

Mr. Shepard's peremptory tone interrupted his thoughts. "Read it back to me."

"Yes, sir." He began at the top.

"Very good. I'll sign it as soon as you have it ready. Make sure it goes in today's post."

Nick stood.

"I will be heading back out to Richmond this weekend. I have various projects that need catching up on. I trust you will be free to accompany me?"

Unable to help a spurt of excitement at the announcement, Nick's fingers tightened on his pencil. It was quickly doused as he realized his employer would keep him too busy to allow him any free time for recreation. "Yes, sir."

"Very good."

Nick reached the door.

"Bring enough to stay a week."

Nick turned slowly. A week in Richmond? His heart started to thump. "Yes, sir."

An entire week in the same house as Miss Shepard.

This time he couldn't contain his excitement. He even began to whistle as he made his way back down the dark corridor.

Alice returned from church at noon on Sunday.

She stopped short in the doorway, her hands flying to her cheeks as at the sight of the tall young man emerging from her father's library. "Mr. Tennent!"

To her further surprise, he smiled, looking as glad to see her as she felt to see him.

"When did you arrive?"

"Early this morning," he said. "Your father was going to come Friday evening but was delayed with other engagements."

She moistened her lip, trying to appear collected. "I—I've just come from church."

"I see."

An awkward silence ensued. Then her eyes widened in sudden horror. "Have you been working?"

He colored. "I was just going to read up on some documents."

"On the Sabbath?" She couldn't help the shock in her voice.

He looked away as if ashamed. "Yes."

She frowned. "Father doesn't forbid you from attending services, does he?"

"No, of course not. I... I've already been to services."

"You have? I didn't see you."

"That's because I attended chapel."

"Chapel?" Her eyes widened in further shock as she understood his meaning. "You're Methodist?"

His dark eyes seemed to hold a touch of defiance. "My mother was Church of England, but she attended chapel with my father."

"Oh!" She wondered at the thought of a lady leaving her church for the lowly Methodist chapel for the sake of her husband. She thought of something. "Our cook, Mrs. Clayworth, attends chapel."

"Does she?"

She bit her lip, afraid she'd offended him. Did he think she equated him with their cook? Actually, she'd always been curious about those attending this other sort of church. All she'd ever heard of Methodists was disdainful. The only one she knew, the cook, was firmly decided in her faith. "Maybe I can go with you some time?"

He drew back a fraction as if surprised. "Perhaps." There was no encouragement in the reserved tone.

She shifted on her feet, wondering if he was still interested in playing tennis. Then she remembered she had a prior commitment. "A party of us is going riding this afternoon. Would you like to join us?"

He fingered a corner of the sheaf of papers he held in his hands. "I—I was just looking over some correspondence your father has given me." He cleared his throat. "He's away this afternoon."

She smiled in relief. "Perfect. Join us at the stables after lunch. We're riding to Richmond Park. It's awfully nice there. There's a wonderful view of the Thames from the top." When he didn't say anything, she suddenly understood his hesitation. "Oh, if it's about proper clothing, you can borrow a habit of my brother's. He's a little stockier than you, but he has outfits in his wardrobe from when he was younger. I'll ask the butler to take something out for you." When he continued to hesitate, she tilted her head. "What is it?"

Again came the defiant lift of his chin. "I've never ridden before."

"Never?"

A faint smile tinged his lips. "Perhaps I've been atop a donkey once or twice when I was a boy."

"Well, it's not so very different. You can have Maud. She's a gentle mount."

He glanced away. "I'd only slow your party down."

"Nonsense. It's not as if we're racing. It's to be a leisurely ride to Richmond Park and back. You'll have a grand time, you'll see, Mr. Tennent. I'll meet you at the stables at three. You mustn't work all day."

Before he could refuse her, she hurried down the corridor, calling behind her, "I'll see you at three!"

She'd go down to the stables and make sure a groom had Maud saddled and waiting.

Father would certainly not approve of a Methodist in their riding party. That was worse than Low Church! For once, Alice was thankful her father was away.

A grand time, indeed. Nick frowned at the pale horse beneath him. With a groom's help he'd managed to mount the beast—nag, he amended, glancing down as he remembered young Victor's derisive snort when he'd seen the horse being led out—without disgracing himself.

Miss Shepard walked up to Nick's mare and patted

her neck. "Hello, there, Maud. Aren't you glad you're not being left behind today?" She smiled up at Nick. "She was my first horse after I'd graduated from a pony. Father bought her for me. She's a trustworthy soul."

At the wistful note Nick forgot his discomfort of being atop a horse. He attempted a smile but before he could say anything, he stiffened as the groom bent down to adjust his stirrups. Nick held his tall boots tightly against the horse's flanks. At least the animal seemed as gentle as Miss Shepard promised. It hadn't moved since being brought out of the stables.

"Good for the glue factory," Victor muttered with a snide look in Nick's direction, before moving off to his own mount. Nick was tempted to box the young fellow's ears, but the eager look on Miss Shepard's face stopped him.

But how was he was to maintain his balance once the creature started moving? There was no pommel on the saddle, just a smooth leather seat. Nick's knuckles were white on the reins.

Thankfully, the horse was relatively small in stature. Not like the great beast that Victor rode. The young gentleman certainly looked elegant seated atop the deep brown horse, holding the reins and riding crop loosely, looking as if he and mount had been born for each other.

Miss Shepard stood back from his horse and looked Nick up and down. "You need to sit farther back in the saddle and loosen your hold a bit. Remember, it's not about gripping the saddle, but about balancing on your horse. She'll carry you."

Before he knew what she was about, she moved down

to his boots and took hold of one of his ankles, causing him to jerk back in surprise. "Easy there," she murmured. "Keep your feet bent slightly out, not gripping the horse's flank. That's right." She adjusted the position of his foot to illustrate her point. "Yes, like so."

She gave him a few more pointers, all the while touching his legs and boots to demonstrate. Unfortunately, with each movement, he grew more tense, his breathing more erratic.

She looked up at him, her blue eyes earnest, and took his hand in hers. He realized how unaware she must be of what her touch was doing to him. It only proved how young she was. "Now, hold your hands about that far apart, not closer. Don't let the reins touch the horse's neck." She ran her hands up his arm, adjusting its angle. The more she spoke, the more afraid he became of moving lest he lose the correct position; the mare would undoubtedly know and take advantage.

As if reading his thoughts, Miss Shepard smiled up at him. "You'll get the feel of it after a while."

Victor maneuvered his horse alongside them. "Are we going or not?"

"Just a minute." Miss Shepard's usually polite tone held a trace of asperity.

"If I'd known you were going to give a riding lesson, I would have opted out of this excursion."

"Well, you may still do so."

With a sneer, Victor wheeled his horse about, causing the mare under Nick to shift. Nick couldn't help splaying his hands on the saddle beneath him, ruining all Miss Shepard's careful positioning.

Instead of scolding him, she immediately went to the mare's bridle. "There, Maud, Mr. Tennent meant nothing by that. You must be patient a moment longer." She didn't even turn when Victor spoke to the other young lady in a loud voice.

"Come along, Lucy. They can catch up when he finally figures out how to get his horse to move." With a snide laugh, he urged his horse forward, Lucy following behind.

Nick gritted his teeth. How he'd love the chance to show Victor a thing or two. "Perhaps this is not the right time for me to go riding."

"Nonsense, Mr. Tennant. Victor just likes to show off. You mustn't mind him. Now, let's see, where were we?"

"How to get her to move."

Miss Shepard smiled. "Right, just a very gentle contact with the horse's mouth." She explained some more and showed him how to bring the mare to a halt. Not until he had done so a few times was she satisfied.

"Very good."

Before he could take any satisfaction in this small success, Miss Shepard went to her own mount, a beautiful bay mare. A groom was immediately at her side but she gave him no chance to assist her. She placed a foot in the stirrup and swung herself up in one deft move. He watched her graceful figure in a blue riding habit. She seemed perfectly at ease on her horse.

At least he needn't be ashamed of his own appearance. The riding habit he'd borrowed—a tweed jacket, tan-colored jodhpurs, and tall boots—fit as if made for him. Even the snobby Victor had given him a keen look.

Miss Shepard turned her horse about. "Ready?"

He nodded. She conveyed the message to her horse, and with a second's hesitation, Nick gave his own horse the command. The other riders were nowhere to be seen as they clip-clopped out of the stable yard.

Thankfully, his horse followed the other as they walked down the long, tree-lined drive that led away from the house.

Miss Shepard turned briefly to him. "We're going to go away from the river and head uphill. The way is easy, only a gentle rise."

Soon, they spotted the other riders farther up ahead. Nick was too busy concentrating on staying on his horse to attempt any further conversation as they rode down the lane. Before he knew it, they'd left the village behind and were among tree-studded meadows.

The tension in him began to ease as he realized his mare would keep her steady, sedate pace, and he allowed himself to enjoy the countryside. For as far as he could remember, he'd lived in the city, between its stone and brick, dirty, choking heat in summer and thick, sulfurous fog in winter.

The ride proceeded smoothly from there. Miss Shepard stayed at his side, instructing him now and again as to the proper handling of the horse.

"She pretty much knows what to do on her own. You are just her guide, to nudge her gently now and again."

Victor rode back to them at a trot, and tried to engage Miss Shepard in conversation, but when she only answered his mocking comments in monosyllables, he rode off again, muttering about having slowed down the whole group.

Soon they could see the Thames far below them, edged in lush green foliage, small wooded islands visible here and there along its snaking course.

They continued climbing along terraced walkways. "We'll go into the park through Sheen Gate," she said. "I'm sure that's the route Victor took." A short while later they entered Richmond Park and spotted Victor and Lucy ahead. Miss Shepard quickened her horse's pace a little, and Nick gave his own reins a slight tug to raise the horse's head, as indicated by Miss Shepard, and tightened his knees the least bit. The horse obeyed and followed after the other one at an increased gait.

His initial fear of falling wearing off, Nick relished the faster pace. They soon caught up to the other riders.

Miss Shepard guided her horse abreast of Victor's. "Let's stop at Bishop's Pond and rest a moment."

"Had enough already?" His words were directed to Miss Shepard but he swung his gaze back toward Nick.

"No, but neither are we in any rush." Without waiting for Victor's answer, she slowed again until she was just ahead of Nick. She twisted in her saddle to him. "It's a pretty spot."

They arrived at the willow-edged pond and dismounted. Nick had another moment of uncertainty, wondering if his horse would stand still while he got down. He held the reins in one hand and swung one leg over the back of the animal. With a breath of relief, he found himself with his two feet firmly planted on solid ground.

Miss Shepard walked her horse toward him. "Let's lead them to the pond. I'm sure they're thirsty." She petted Maud's withers. "Aren't you, dearie, after that long ride in the sun?"

The others had already left their horses at the water's edge and were walking about the shaded glen.

Miss Shepard showed him how to remove the horse's bit before letting them drink.

She knelt beside the water's edge and removed her gloves. Taking a handkerchief out of her jacket pocket, she plunged it in the water. Squeezing out the excess water, she used it to wipe her forehead and cheeks. "Ah, that feels refreshing." She grinned up at him, her rosy cheeks damp.

Without thinking, he pulled out his dry handkerchief and handed it to her, finding that around her he merely reacted instead of deliberating before an action. He envied her impulsive behavior, though she was young, not yet out of the schoolroom. His eyes traveled over her, her contours already those of a woman.

"Oh, thank you." She took the handkerchief from him and wiped her face dry before jumping back to her feet. Refolding his handkerchief, she gave it back to him. He took it without a word. Bending down to the water, he wet it and did what she had done, squeezing it out and using it to mop his own damp forehead. The water felt cold and helped to ease the heat he felt in his face, heat that was due to more than the sun.

She took the wet handkerchief from him. "Here, we'll spread our hankies out on this rock and they'll be dry by the time we leave. Come, I want to show you my favorite spot."

"What about the others?" He gestured to Lucy and

Victor. Lucy sat on a boulder, fanning herself with her hat. Victor was throwing stones into the pond, causing a plopping sound with each one.

Miss Shepard shrugged. "He's trying to scare the frogs."

He also seemed to be ignoring Miss Shepard, for which Nick was thankful.

"Come on!" Miss Shepard urged. "We shan't be long."

They walked along the pond's edge and bent down under some willows trailing their long fronds into the water. It was about ten degrees cooler in the shade.

"Isn't it like a cave here?" The shadow and sunlight speckled her face, and he felt as if they could have been under the water, in another world.

He stared at her. Words seemed to get trapped in his throat. What was happening to him that he couldn't form a coherent sentence?

She squatted down by the water's edge again, this time resting her folded hands and chin on her knees. "How do you like working for my father?"

He stood beside her, observing the shadowy light on the crown of her hair. She'd tossed her hat on the ground beside her. Her hair was twisted in a loose knot at the nape of her neck, making her look older than—

"How old are you?" he asked sharply.

She jutted her fine chin out a notch. "I shall be seventeen next month."

"Sixteen then." His heart plummeted at the discovery of how young she truly was.

"Almost seventeen."

He couldn't help smiling at her insistence.

"How old are *you?*"

Her direct question startled him. "Twenty-three." His lips twitched. "Last March. Eons older than you."

She closed one eye and tilted her head upwards. "Six years, that's not so much. But you do seem old."

He drew his brows together at her appraisal. "How so?"

"You're so very serious." She nodded toward the other end of the pond. "Take Victor. He's not so much younger than you. He's nineteen, but he seems like a boy compared to you."

"I've had to grow up a lot faster than Victor."

"Were you always so serious?"

He mulled over the question. "I've never thought about whether or not I was serious."

"You can't always have been serious." There was a glint in her dark blue eyes.

"Perhaps I was born serious."

She laughed. "You *do* have a sense of humor."

"Alice!" Victor's annoyed shout came through the trees.

With a loud sigh, she stood and shook out her pleated riding skirt. "I suppose we should walk the horses."

"Yes." He picked up her hat and handed it to her.

"Thank you." Her quick smile was grateful and friendly.

She probably had no idea what it did to him, making all his years of rigid self-control slip away.

She was still a child, he reminded himself as he held the feathery willow strands aside for her to walk through.

Victor stalked toward them, his hands in his pockets, his features sulky. "Are you ready yet? There's nothing here."

Lucy came up behind him. "Where shall we go?"

"Let's ride up to Oliver's Mount so we can get a good vista of the river." Without waiting for an assent, Miss Shepard headed for the horses, which stood quietly grazing on a sunny patch of grass.

Victor hung back and gave Nick a look. "I say, old fellow, you were a sport to take that sway-backed old nag." His lips turned upward at one corner. "You looked quite a sight on her. Your legs were practically dragging on the ground." His voice lowered. "You know, Alice likes to put first-timers on old Maud. Sort of her secret joke, you know. But I think you've passed the test." He winked. "Why don't you turn the tables on her and try my mount? Show her what stuff you're made of. She's quite a horsewoman, as you've seen. She'd admire you to no end if she saw you on a real horse." With a last wink, he walked away from Nick and joined Lucy, leaning down to help her mount.

Nick considered the youth's offer. He was tempted to accept. How much different could the other horse be? He'd seemed to behave well during their ride over.

Shaking his head, he scolded himself for being a silly fool. He was too old to fall for some masculine gauntlet thrown down before him to impress a young girl.

With a sigh, Nick gathered up Maud's reins. Just as he was about to put his foot into the stirrup, Victor led his horse up. "Well, what'd you say, old boy, have a go?" His gray eyes held an unmistakable challenge.

Ignoring the voice of reason, Nick exchanged reins with him, telling himself if he maintained a sedate pace, everything would be all right. Victor had been right about one thing, he had made a ridiculous picture on that mare, as he now observed Victor sitting atop her.

"What are you doing?" Alice drew alongside of him on her horse.

Victor smiled disarmingly. "Oh, nothing to turn a hair about. I just offered the fellow a decent mount."

Nick wondered if the boy even knew his name.

He managed to get himself astride by himself, although this horse was considerably higher. He drew a deep breath as the horse snorted and shook his head.

Miss Shepard's eyebrows were drawn together in a frown. "Are you sure you're ready to ride Duke?"

He managed to pat the horse's neck to show his ease, but that only caused the horse to paw the ground as if sensing Nick's own nervousness.

Before Miss Shepard had a chance to voice any more objections, Victor started to move away from the pond. Duke immediately began following the other horse, and Nick had no choice but to concentrate on maintaining his balance. Victor got Maud to go at a much faster clip.

"Victor, slow down." Miss Shepard's admonition was in vain. Duke kept a good clip, determined to follow the lead horse. Nick tried to slow the horse, but that only seemed to make the horse more determined.

They reached a wide open field. Victor slowed and waited for Nick's mount to catch up to him. "How does a real horse feel beneath you?" His smile held something nasty in it.

"Fine." Nick sat erect, trying to remember all Miss Shepard's directives. The horse shifted restively beneath him.

"Well, let's try for a little canter, shall we?" Without waiting for Nick's response, he gave a smart swat with his riding crop to Duke's rump.

The horse responded to the whip with lightning speed. If he hadn't already been gripping hard, Nick would have flown off. Instead, everything became a blur as he flattened himself against the horse and squeezed his thighs against its sides.

He heard Miss Shepard's alarmed shout. "Victor, what are you doing? Mr. Tennent, just keep your balance—" The rest of her words were lost in the wind.

How in all that was holy was he supposed to stop a galloping horse?

His lips stiff with fear, his throat paralyzed, Nick hung on. The ground flew by in a dizzying mass of green, every sound drowned out by the thundering hooves against the earth. If the horse tripped on a tussock, Nick would be done for.

Why had he accepted the stupid challenge? To prove himself to some naïve young girl?

He had no more time for rational thought. All he could do was pray that he'd keep his seat. He grabbed a hunk of mane with each hand, his knees the only thing keeping him atop the beast's great heaving body.

A hedgerow faced them. Would the horse clear it? As he braced for the jump, the horse suddenly veered to the side.

"Drop your stirrups!" He heard Miss Shepard's scream and just in the nick of time, he let his boots slip from the irons. A split second later, he felt his hands wrenched from the mane, his body thrust from the saddle and he was sailing through the air, headlong across the hedge.

Chapter Three

Alice reined in her horse and stared in horror as Mr. Tennent went flying over the hedgerow and landed with a thud against the earth.

The next second she was off her horse, running to him. "Lucy, my horse," she shouted over her shoulder, "Victor, go after Duke!"

She tore through the holly bushes, unmindful of their sharp leaves and knelt by Mr. Tennent. He'd landed on his side and now with a groan rolled over onto his back, one arm clutching his ribcage.

"Are you all right, Mr. Tennent? Where does it hurt?" She smoothed back the hair from his forehead. The far side of his face was scraped along the cheekbone.

He began to sit up, his face contorted. She pushed him gently down again. "Lie still."

"It's my shoulder and side." His voice was laced with pain.

She glanced up as Victor's shadow loomed over them. He didn't have his horse.

"Where's Duke?"

"Long gone." He kicked the ground in disgust, hardly sparing Mr. Tennent a glance. "He'll come back as soon as he's run off his high spirits."

She glared at him. "How could you give him Duke to ride?" With a shake of her head, she turned away from Victor, pressing her lips together to keep from saying more. He'd hear about his irresponsible behavior later, she promised herself. "We need to get Mr. Tennent back. He's hurt." She leaned over him and drew in her breath at his ashen face. "Do you think, if we helped you mount, you could ride back atop Maud? We'll take her reins. It's just too far for you to walk if you've broken something."

"Yes…all right." With a grimace, he began to sit up, still clutching his arm. Quickly, she put her arm around his shoulders to help him. "Victor, get on his other side. Let's see if you can stand, Mr. Tennent."

Lucy stood behind the hedge, holding two of the horses, her face frightened. "Is he all right?"

Alice made a quick decision. "Lucy, ride back and have them summon Dr. Baird. Quickly!"

The girl did as she was told and hurried off.

Alice turned back to Victor. "I'll have Mr. Tennent ride in back of me. Help him mount once I'm in the saddle."

"But Alice—"

Without waiting for Victor to finish his sentence, she led her horse through a break in the hedgerow and brought him to stand near the two men. At least Victor had helped Mr. Tennent up. Alice swung up onto her horse then looked down at Victor. "All right, see if he can mount behind me."

Victor bent down and cradled his hands for a foot-hold for the other man. With a sharp intake of breath, Mr. Tennent attempted to lift himself onto the back of her saddle. Alice twisted around to see if she could help pull him up, but he was managing to swing his leg over the horse's rump. His stifled groans made her wince, but finally he settled on behind her.

"Just hold on to me with your good arm." Without asking his leave, she grasped it from behind her and brought it around her waist. "I'll get us home as quickly as possible without jostling you more than necessary, I promise. Are you all right, sir?"

"I'll make it."

Without a word to Victor, Alice picked her way around the hedgerow and back down the path.

Mr. Tennent said nothing more on the ride home, but she could hear his intake of breath each time his body was jarred. *It's all my fault,* she thought, not knowing which was worse, taking a first-time rider on such an ambitious jaunt or not stopping Victor. Obviously he'd challenged poor Mr. Tennent to mount the gelding.

"We're almost there, Mr. Tennent," she said, trying to keep her voice cheery. "See, there's the rooftop already visible over the treetops." At last they were going up the long drive. A couple of stable hands were waiting for them as soon as she pulled the horse to a stop in front of a house. At least Lucy had alerted them.

"Help him down gently. He may have broken something."

"Yes, miss." John, an able-bodied stable hand raised his arms to help Mr. Tennent down. "Have no worry, we'll get you down. What happened?"

"He took a spill and landed on his side. One arm is injured."

Once on the ground, Mr. Tennent remained hunched over, cradling his arm.

Alice swung down from her horse and handed the reins to the other groom. She turned immediately to Mr. Tennent and gasped at the sight of his pale face. "John, help him inside. I hope the doctor has been summoned."

"Yes, miss. Miss Lucy told us to have him fetched."

"Good. Come, Mr. Tennent, let's get you where you can lie down." She walked on his other side, a hand on his elbow.

The servants stood gawking when they entered the house, lifting up a murmur as Alice led him to the nearest sofa. A maid brought a throw and the housekeeper piled pillows behind Mr. Tennent. Although he thanked the servants and didn't complain, she could see he was in great pain.

As if sensing her distress, he looked up at her, one corner of his lips lifting. "Don't worry, I'll be fine."

She drew near, kneeling beside the sofa. "Oh, Mr. Tennent, I'm so sorry this had to happen."

He shook his head briefly and reached out his good hand to her. "Don't upset yourself. It wasn't your fault," he said.

Finally Dr. Baird arrived. The elderly doctor set down his bag and looked Mr. Tennent up and down through his spectacles. "Well, young man, what have you been up to?"

"Falling off horses," he said through a grimace, as he began to swing his legs off the sofa.

"There now, hold still before you do yourself more

harm." The doctor helped him sit up and motioned to one of the servants. "Get his coat off." Mr. Tennent flinched as the arm of his coat was gently slipped off. Alice bit her lip, cringing with each jar and jostle of his shoulder.

The doctor took Mr. Tennent's chin in his hand and tilted it upward. "Scraped yourself good there, I see. Bring me some soap and water and be quick about it," he told a servant, then proceeded to poke and prod Mr. Tennent's shoulder. "Humph. Hurt, does it? And there?"

After a few more hmms and humphs, he straightened and peered over his spectacles. "Good news. It looks like your shoulder isn't dislocated. Just a fractured clavicle." At the question in the other man's eyes, he cleared his throat. "Your collarbone is broken. You'll have to bear up a bit longer while I set it. Now, where else does it hurt?"

Mr. Tennent indicated his side with his hand.

He had the servant remove his vest then palpated some more through his shirt. "Your ribs don't appear broken, but I'll have to do a more thorough examination." He turned to the others in the room. "Why don't you leave us alone, so the young gentleman doesn't feel he might disgrace himself before the ladies." He turned to the housekeeper. "Mrs. Thorpe, a glass of water. I'll give him something for the pain afterwards."

The woman nodded her head. "Yes, sir."

Alice left the room reluctantly.

After what seemed like ages, she was allowed back into the side parlor. Mr. Tennent, his shirt draped over his shoulders, had a sling around one arm and a wide layer of white bandaging across a good part of his chest.

A square white gauze covered part of one cheek. He gave her a crooked smile.

She sat down beside him on the sofa. "Oh, Mr. Tennent, how is it? Are your ribs broken, too? Is it very painful?"

"A few bruised ribs, but I'll live."

"I'm so terribly sorry to have brought this about."

He frowned at her. "You have nothing to be sorry about. You didn't do anything but help me. I was the one who behaved foolishly," he said, turning away in disgust.

"Oh, no! It was I who should have stopped Victor."

"It was stupid to take his offer."

"Mr. Tennent, did you happen to notice what startled the horse so? The next thing we knew Duke was off at a gallop. Did something spook him?"

He eyed her a moment. "You didn't see anything?"

She shook her head. "No, Lucy and I were in front of you. Tell me—"

Before she could finish her thought, she noticed Mr. Tennent looking past her.

"What's going on here?"

She jumped at the sound of her father's voice. He strode across the room and planted himself in front of Mr. Tennent, who stood immediately.

Alice joined him. "Oh, Papa, poor Mr. Tennent has had an accident. He was thrown by Duke."

Her father looked his secretary up and down.

Alice touched his good arm. "You must sit down, Mr. Tennent. You've had an awful accident."

Her father motioned for him to take his seat. The

younger man hesitated but at her father's impatient gesture, he finally complied.

"Mr. Tennent hadn't been riding before, and Victor challenged him to ride Duke—"

Her father's heavy brows drew together. "What the dickens did you mean going riding if you've never sat a horse?"

Alice interposed herself between her father and his employee. "Father! Didn't you hear me? It's my fault. I invited him to come along with us. It's Sunday, after all, and I knew he wasn't working. I had him ride Maud. You know Maud is the gentlest creature alive, but Victor played a very mean trick on Mr. Tennent—"

"Quiet, Alice, and let Mr. Tennent explain himself. I'm sure he doesn't want to hide behind a schoolgirl's skirts."

She stopped, feeling herself color with shame. A schoolgirl's skirts! He made it sound as if Mr. Tennent was some sort of coward and that she was—why, not even a young lady but a little girl!

Flushed with embarrassment, she moved away without a word. Surely, her father wouldn't hold her defense of Mr. Tennent against the poor man. She chanced a glance at him and bit her lip at the set look on his face. Once again, he stood. His face was awfully pale, and she was afraid he might pass out. "Papa, Dr. Baird said—"

Her father flicked his hand once again. "Leave us, Alice."

There was no use arguing with her father when he took that tone. With an audible sigh, she stepped back from the two men. Giving Mr. Tennent a last look of sympathy, she dragged her feet to the door, hoping she'd catch something of their conversation, but neither man said anything.

"Close the door, Alice."

"Yes, sir." Once she'd exited the room and closed the door softly behind her, she put her ear to the door. At first, there was only silence, then came the low sounds of masculine voices, but she could distinguish nothing.

At least there were no shouts on her father's side, but she knew from experience that her father never raised his voice. His low tones could be as scathing as another man's roar.

Nick waited, squaring his shoulders and trying not to wince at the pain the movement caused him. Would he lose his job over his own stupidity?

The older man gazed at him a moment, an unreadable expression in his eyes.

"I brought you here to work, not to take a medical convalescence." The dry words, expressing no anger, were all the more quelling for their subtle sarcasm.

"I assure you, Mr. Shepard, this will in no way hinder my job. I can still work." He moved his hand to prove his point. Unfortunately, he couldn't keep back the spasm at the sudden jolt of pain that shot through his collarbone.

Mr. Shepard grunted, clearly not impressed with his stoicism. "Well, take your rest today and we'll see about tomorrow. If you're not fit to do any work, I'll have to send for another clerk."

Before Nick could think of a suitable reply, Mr. Shepard wheeled about and headed for the door.

As soon as he was alone, Nick collapsed back onto

the settee, letting his head fall onto his good hand. What had he done? Risked the best position of his life to go gallivanting about on a horse? A silent, bitter laugh escaped his lips.

A soft clearing of throat caused him to start up again, sending another stab of pain along his collarbone. Miss Shepard stood just inside the doorway. She looked so pathetically sorry, he wished he could comfort her. She'd been wonderful, taking charge and bringing him home.

He straightened despite the pain in his ribs. "It's all right."

She ventured farther into the room until she stood by the settee once again. "Was Father very hard on you?"

He managed a smile. "No. He told me to rest today."

Relief flooded her pretty face. "Oh, yes, you should. Why don't I help you up to your room?"

She was still thinking of his comfort. He hadn't felt so taken care of since he'd been a toddler. "That's all right, I'll manage."

"At least let me ring for a servant to help you up the stairs. You're on the top floor, aren't you?"

He didn't relish the thought of all those flights of stairs to the attic. Nor the stifling heat once he got up there. "Very well."

She hurried to the bell pull. Instead of leaving him alone, she pulled up a chair and waited with him. With her hands folded in her lap, her normally rosy cheeks pale, she looked like a young schoolgirl called before the schoolmistress. He contrasted it to her self-possession right after his fall. She'd even assumed all responsibility before her father.

"I should have listened to you," he said with a forced smile.

"It's all right. I bet Victor made it sound like you'd be a coward if you didn't mount Duke."

He shook his head in self-contempt. "But I'm old enough to know better than to accept a schoolboy's challenge."

She tossed back her bangs. "Oh, I know how Victor is."

He remembered her hand stroking his forehead, her small hand grasping his and bringing his arm around her waist.

"I hope this unfortunate experience won't put you off horseback riding forever."

Her remark was so ludicrous under the circumstances, he had to laugh, then winced at the pain in his side. "Let us hope not."

"Oh, I'm sorry to make you laugh."

He shook away her apology.

"What I meant was that, someday, when all this is behind you, I hope you'll get back on a horse again. That's the only way to overcome any bad memories of a fall. When I was first thrown—"

"*You* were thrown?"

"Oh, yes, everyone is thrown at least once, especially when first learning."

Before she could continue, a young male servant entered the room. She stood. "Oh, Davy, please help Mr. Tennent up to his room and have something cool brought up to him to drink. Help him in any way he needs."

"Yes, miss." The young servant took Nick by his

good arm and smiled. "Just tell me, sir, whatever it is you want."

The two made their way slowly up the stairs. All Nick wanted to do was collapse on his bed. The region around his collarbone and his whole right side pained him terribly, despite the powder the doctor had given him. He'd been partially truthful to Mr. Shepard about his ability to continue working. He flexed his fingers now, ignoring the pain the movement caused up in his collarbone. At least his fingers weren't broken, too. He prayed that by tomorrow the pain would have diminished enough for him to be able to write.

He tried to forget the doctor's words about avoiding using that hand and arm. "The bone will take about twelve weeks to heal. The pain will diminish gradually. Don't use your hand if it gives you any pain. Little by little you'll be able to do things again. If it hurts, desist activity."

Twelve weeks. The words were like a death knell. Would Mr. Shepard be that patient with him? Would he still have a job after his bones had knit back together?

When she didn't see Mr. Tennent at breakfast, Alice went to look for him, wondering how he had fared the night.

She spotted the servant coming down the stairs. "There you are, Davy. Did you go up to Mr. Tennent yet?"

The servant stopped halfway down. "Yes, Miss Alice. I brought him up a breakfast tray."

She smiled in relief. "Oh, thank you for remembering him. How was he?"

"He looked better than yesterday, but he's in a heap of pain." He shook his head. "Nasty thing, broken bones. I know, when I dislocated my shoulder once, it hurt something awful and took weeks to mend."

She drew in her breath, feeling Mr. Tennent's pain afresh. "Did yours heal completely?"

He swiveled one arm around and grinned. "Yes, miss, right as can be. But it laid me up some weeks, believe me."

"Well, thank you for being so attentive to Mr. Tennent."

"Think nothing of it." He frowned. "He insisted on getting up and dressed." He added hastily, "I helped him, o' course. I'll check on him again around lunchtime."

"Very well, thank you, Davy."

Alice turned toward the library, knowing she would have to insist Father send Victor away immediately. He hadn't shown the least remorse, even going so far as to claim it was Mr. Tennent's fault for not being competent with a horse.

Unfortunately, Father hadn't wanted to discuss the matter further with her last evening at dinner. Well, he'd have to listen to her this morning, she decided, as she turned and headed in the direction of his office.

Alice left her father's office feeling worse than ever. He'd told her she had behaved irresponsibly, taking a man who knew nothing of horses riding up to the park. He hadn't even agreed that Victor should be sent away.

Feeling at loose ends, she reached Mr. Tennent's

small office. Maybe she could tidy it up for him while he was laid up.

His door was ajar. She pushed it open and gasped. "Mr. Tennent, what in the world are you doing in here?"

Her father's secretary glanced up from the papers spread out before him on the desk. "Good morning, Miss Shepard. I'm doing precisely what it appears I'm doing."

The words held no reproach, but were uttered as a simple statement of fact. She was glad to see Davy had placed a fresh gauze bandage over his cheekbone. The white sling around his arm and neck contrasted sharply with his black coat and accentuated the paleness of his face.

She frowned, noticing how he was attempting to write with his left hand. If he hadn't looked so pitiable, she would have found the sight amusing. Not waiting for permission, she entered the cramped office and planted herself in front of his cluttered desk. "It looks to me as if you are *trying* to work."

He set down his pencil. "Your conclusion is correct."

"You suffered a bad fall yesterday and broke a bone and bruised some ribs. You are supposed to be resting. Surely, Father doesn't expect you to be writing!"

He ran his left hand through his short sable curls. "See here, Miss Shepard, I truly appreciate your concern." The trace of impatience in his voice softened. "Thank you for sending Davy up to me yesterday and again this morning. However, as much as I like being waited on hand and foot, the reality of my situation is that your father is paying me to carry out certain functions within a given time and if I prove incapable of doing so, I cannot fault him for finding a replacement."

He took a deep breath as if gearing up for what he was going to say next, and she couldn't help catching the grimace the gesture caused him. "This is the best job I've had in my career. If I lose the opportunity given to me, I may not get another. I do not plan to end my life as a clerk."

She walked around the desk until she was standing close to him, his words both touching and intriguing her. "How do you plan to end your life, Mr. Tennent?" she asked softly.

He lifted his chin a notch. "Owning a company of my own like your father, so I can make a difference in the world."

Make a difference in the world. No one had ever spoken to her like this before. As if what one accomplished mattered in the world.

"What kind of difference would you make in the world, Mr. Tennent?" she asked softly.

Instead of waving away her question as if she were too young or too ignorant to understand, he seemed to ponder it. He rolled his pencil in his good hand. The lamplight gleamed against the rich color of his hair.

"I would use my wealth to help those in need. Build schools, provide good housing, clean water, hospitals…" He glanced up at her. "Do you know what it's like to have a gnawing pain in your belly because you have nothing to eat?"

She shook her head, mute.

"Do you know what it's like not to have a dwelling to come home to at night after a long day's work? There are many people who do, Miss Shepard." He drew in a breath, then stopped, the pain evident. "That is why I want to become a very wealthy man, so I can do my bit to help alleviate the want of others."

The words thrilled her to the marrow. Suddenly, she felt as if she understood her own undefined yearnings and dissatisfaction. To have such a noble purpose in life!

"I hope you realize your dream, Mr. Tennent."

A few seconds passed between them in silence. Then he gave a short laugh. "I may be farther away from it than ever if I don't get this work done."

The two of them surveyed the papers on his desk.

Before he had a chance to stop her, she took the pencil from his loosened hold and the paper he'd been writing on. "Very well, Mr. Tennent, you dictate and I shall be your fingers."

She glanced around, spotted a chair, and dragged it over.

"I—you can't very well—this involves mathematics—"

She stuck out her chin. "Mr. Tennent, I am not ignorant of mathematics. In a year, I shall finish my schooling and I'll have you know I get outstanding marks in mathematics. Now, what were you calculating when I walked in?"

With a resigned sigh, he turned back to his papers. "Very well, but only because it seems I have very little choice at the moment. Just stop any time you are tired of amusing yourself."

Did he think she was simply seeking to entertain herself? She would just have to show him.

An hour later, after making steady progress, she sat

back with a satisfied sigh. "I say, what you've taught me about stocks and shares is a lot more useful than what they teach us at Miss Higgins's Academy. I never knew Father was involved in so many enterprises."

Mr. Tennent adjusted his weight on the wooden chair, carefully cradling his injured arm.

"Does it hurt you much today?"

He touched the area just under his collarbone. "Some. It's still a bit swollen here."

She looked down. "I tried to convince Father to send Victor away, but he refused."

"You didn't have to do that." He sounded displeased.

"I explained how Victor tricked you into mounting Duke." She moistened her lips together, recalling the most unpleasant part of the interview. "He also knows the responsibility I bear. He agrees I was foolish and impetuous as always..." Her voice trailed off. By now she ought to be accustomed to her father's dry tone, which never failed to erode her confidence when pointing out her faults to her.

"You were in no way to blame." His tone gentled. "It was gracious of you to invite me for an outing. You cautioned me about riding your friend's horse. It was silly pride on my part, so I deserve what I got."

She reached out and touched his hand. "He's not *my* friend—not anymore. As a skilled horseman, Victor was the most responsible. He should have known better. You could have been killed."

His glance went to her hand and she felt herself coloring. Quickly, she removed it and sat with her hands clasped in her lap.

"He is, isn't he?"

She frowned. "He's what?"

"A skilled horseman."

She made a face. "Oh, that. Well, yes, naturally."

"Naturally." He mimicked the word. "I suppose he has been riding since he was five."

She giggled. "Oh, probably since he was four."

His dark eyes lit with humor. "His parents probably sat him atop a horse before he could walk."

"Oh, no, before he began to crawl!"

They both ended up laughing.

"Alice, what are you doing here?" Her father stood in the doorway to the library.

She jumped up from her chair. "I am acting as—" she gave a little bow "—Mr. Tennent's secretary."

Her father pursed his lips, his eyes going from her to Mr. Tennent and back again, making her feel as if she'd done something wrong. "That is not amusing."

"Of course it isn't. Mr. Tennent is injured, and I feel partially responsible. As such, it is only right that I assist him while his injury heals."

"Mr. Shepard—" Mr. Tennent stood rigid, and her heart went out to him, having to work for her father.

Her father advanced into the small room, cutting him off. "So, you are unable to write?"

"I—" He cleared his throat and began again. "In a few days, perhaps—"

Did Father inspire such fear in all his employees? "Dr. Baird gave clear instructions that Mr. Tennent is to do nothing to put undue pressure on his collarbone for a few weeks. He mustn't bend his arm in a way that will aggravate the bone."

Her father had turned his attention back to her halfway through her speech. "In that case, I shall have to summon Mr. Simpson."

She gave a disbelieving laugh at the mention of Father's old secretary. "Mr. Simpson is getting forgetful, you said so yourself. We are making splendid progress." She took up the papers she'd completed and handed them to him.

He took them without a word and examined them.

Mr. Tennent cleared his throat. "Mr. Shepard, I assure you, in a few days, I'm sure I can manage on my own."

Her father handed the papers back to his secretary. "Very well. In the meantime I have to return to London. I shall determine things upon my return." He turned to her. "I don't want you making a nuisance of yourself here."

"I shan't be a nuisance."

"Nevertheless, I prefer you not spend your time here, Alice."

She pressed her lips together, knowing it was useless to argue with her father and knowing just as certainly that this was one command she was going to disobey.

Chapter Four

The next few days were like a little bit of heaven to Nick. Despite the pain in his collarbone and ribs, coupled with the inconvenience of wearing a sling, he had never enjoyed such a time in his life. He felt as if he was living an interlude where all the best things were combined: work he enjoyed with a helper he was coming to admire more and more each day, carried out in the most agreeable surroundings he'd ever known in his life.

Her father's prohibition notwithstanding, Miss Shepard appeared in Nick's little office every morning promptly at half-past eight and didn't move from her chair until he gave in and let her help him with any writing he needed done.

He realized now, looking at her bent head, that working had never been so lighthearted. For despite making progress on the reports he had to write, the hours seemed to fly by and many moments were spent in laughter as Miss Shepard found something amusing in what they were doing or reading.

He eased the kinks out of his neck then stopped short

at the shot of pain to his collarbone. Dr. Baird had not exaggerated when he'd warned Nick it would take some weeks before he was fully healed.

"Are you all right?"

He looked over to find Miss Shepard's eyes on him. "Yes, I'm all right." He'd also never had anyone as solicitous as she, seeming to anticipate his every need and be aware of every twinge of discomfort he experienced.

She laid her pencil and pad on her lap. "You should take a rest. You've been bent over this desk since early morning."

There was still a lot to do before her father returned. Mr. Shepard hadn't said how long he'd be away, yet Nick expected him at any moment. "You're the one who should take a break. You are on holiday. Why don't you go outside and play a game of tennis. You haven't played since I had my fall, have you?" His tone came out sharper than he'd intended, but he thought once again about Mr. Shepard and what he'd say if he came back and found his daughter holed up in this office.

She shrugged. "No. But I prefer being in here helping you. Besides, there is no one to play with."

"What about Victor?" He'd seen the boy hang about the corridor the first few days, looking daggers at him at the sight of Alice sitting beside him.

Her eyes lit up in hilarity. "He finally packed his bags and had the pony cart hitched up to take him to the train station this morning."

"Where is your young lady friend?"

"Lucy? Oh, she had to go home, too. Her family was going hiking in Scotland." Her voice sounded wistful, and he realized once again how lonely this wealthy girl's life was. The only mother figure she seemed to have was a middle-aged companion who preferred spending time with the housekeeper.

Nick stood. "Well, it's time we both had a break. It's almost lunchtime anyway." Usually he'd had a tray brought to the office but he decided to do something differently today.

Miss Shepard stood immediately, a smile breaking out on her face. Nick steeled himself against that smile, reminding himself his life had no relation to hers. She clasped her hands in front of her. "What shall we do?"

He hadn't got as far as thinking of that part. "What would you like to do?"

She tilted her head a fraction and thought a moment, a slim finger against her chin. Then she looked at him, a sparkle in her eyes. "Have you ever played chess?"

He smiled in relief. Finally, there was something he did know how to do. "Yes."

If she was surprised, she didn't show it. She turned to leave the room. "Well, come along then."

She led him to a wide veranda with latticed railing in the back of the house. "It's too nice a day to be inside." She sat on the floor and brought out a polished wooden box and a folded game board from a shelf under the low table and began to set out the ivory pieces.

He remained standing, watching her array the carved chessmen in rows at either side of the checked board. "My mother taught me to play chess."

"My governess taught me. She said it was a good game of strategy…and patience." She smiled as she added the last.

"Were you in need of those qualities?"

She shrugged. "All I knew then was that if I learned how to play chess, perhaps I could play with Father. But he had little inclination for games that last so long."

Before he could comment on that statement, she waved him to the low couch facing the board. "Have a seat, Mr. Tennent." She gave him a sly smile under her tawny brows. "This should be an easy win for someone good at mathematics. I shall even let you be white, since you are the guest."

He sat down across from her and soon they were immersed in the game and even forgot about lunch.

He found he enjoyed pitting his skill against hers. Just as with tennis, she didn't make things easy for him, and he appreciated that. Whenever she captured one of his pieces, she'd give him a small smile of triumph.

They played in silence for quite some time, when Miss Shepard raised her eyes to him. "Mr. Tennent?" There was no amusement in them now. "What was your house like growing up?"

Surprised at her question, he answered flatly, "Small and dingy with the smell of boiled cabbage. It was always damp. And cold in the winter. My brothers and I would huddle together under a blanket."

She leaned her chin on her fist. "Were you the youngest?"

He shook his head. "The second to youngest."

To his bemusement, she continued questioning him about his family, and he found himself telling her about his brothers—from Jim, working in the mill, and Thomas the postal clerk, to young Alfie, with his dream of opening his own shop.

"So, you are the only bachelor among them?"

"Yes," he said in a guarded tone.

She tilted her head a fraction, a gesture that never failed to enchant him. "Why haven't you married? You are certainly old enough."

He shrugged. "Up to now, I haven't had either the desire or the opportunity, I suppose. And although I am certainly old enough, I'm not *that* old."

She frowned. "But all your other brothers found the time."

"I have put all my energy into my work." To help his brothers continue their education and support his mother. "It takes money to set up a household."

"Does it take so much money to support a wife?"

"It certainly takes money to raise children."

"Do all your brothers have children?"

"The oldest two do."

She smiled. "So you are an uncle at least."

"Yes."

"Are they all still in Birmingham?"

"Yes."

"And your mother?"

He nodded.

"Do you see them often?"

He looked down. "No."

"That's a pity." She sighed.

"A clerk has few holidays."

She sighed again.

He focused once more on the board between them.

"I'm almost a woman now."

He raised startled eyes to her. Where had that thought come from?

Her violet eyes stared guilelessly into his. He kept

his voice neutral, for fear of what she might read in it. "You have a few years yet."

With another sigh, she lowered her gaze to the chess pieces.

Nick followed suit, determined to keep his thoughts on the game. He waited for her to move, his heartbeat thudding between his ears. What had she meant by that remark? He mustn't forget himself around her, he cautioned himself, as he found himself doing countless times each day in her company.

"Checkmate." Amusement laced her tone.

His glance jerked up. "What?" He followed her slim fingers, which held the queen she'd just moved. "How is that possible?"

"See?" She gestured over the board. "If you move your king here, my knight will knock him off. If you move your king in the only other square, my other knight will get him."

He studied the only two possible moves available to his king, his brow knit. How had she done that?

She sat back with a satisfied sigh. "Maybe if someone had been paying closer attention to his game, he wouldn't have left himself open for attack."

He looked across to her laughing eyes. "Maybe if someone felt more comfortable with her skills, she wouldn't have to rely on distracting me with idle talk to win the game."

"I won fairly and squarely. If you allow yourself to be so easily distracted, I can't be held responsible for your loss. Now, if you'll excuse me, my queen shall take your king to her castle and lock him in her tower." She lifted both his king and her queen off the board in one swoop.

Without thinking, he seized her hand in midair. "My king will call out his legions of knights to rescue him—"

She giggled, pulling her hand away but he held it fast. "If you want your king back, you shall have to pay the ransom," she said with a thrust of her chin, her laughing blue eyes glinting with challenge.

He tightened his hold on her hand imperceptibly. "And what do you demand for the release of my king?"

"A kiss."

Her gaze held his as securely as his hand held hers. Somewhere he heard a bird twitter on the lawn and far-off footsteps in the corridor, but he was helpless to look away.

Like a spectator in a drama, he watched himself inch forward until her face was inches from his, and he breathed in the sweet flowery scent of her downy skin. Shutting off the warnings in his head, he closed the gap between them, touching his lips to hers.

He leaned his elbows against the table, ignoring the pain the movement caused. Miss Shepard pressed her lips inexpertly against his.

"Sweet Alice," he breathed against her, taking a gulp of air before sealing her lips once again with his. This time they parted beneath his.

He didn't know how much time had elapsed—a few seconds or an eternity—when the clearing of a masculine throat penetrated the fog of his mind. Miss Shepard and he broke apart simultaneously.

"Father!" She jumped up from the floor, her hand going to her mouth.

Nick bumped his arm against the table and stifled the cry of pain as he struggled to his feet.

He stood up as Mr. Shepard advanced into the room.

His employer's dark gaze traveled from one to the other. He gestured to Nick. "I didn't realize I was paying you a salary to amuse yourself with my daughter."

Heat flooded Nick's face, and he swallowed, unable to defend his conduct in any way.

"Father, Mr. Shepard isn't—"

Mr. Shepard flicked his fingers in her direction. "Alice, leave us, please."

"But Father—"

"Alice." His tone was that hard, unyielding one Nick recognized from the office.

"Yes, Father." She lowered her head and walked back into the house.

Mr. Shepard waited a few moments until they no longer heard his daughter's footsteps. "I want you out of here. Now. You can collect any outstanding wages at the office."

The worst had come to pass. Nick stared at him. "But—you don't—" He cleared his throat, hating the tremor his voice betrayed.

The man eyed him as if he were a lower form of life. "I don't want to hear any explanations from a man who presumes to rob my daughter of her innocence. Understood?"

He nodded.

Shepard turned away and began walking out the way he'd come. At the entrance he paused. "You can request the pony cart to take you to the station. Do not make any attempt to see my daughter or to address her in any way." His heavy eyebrows bristled at him. "Is that understood?"

Nick swallowed. "Yes, sir."

In the echo of the closing door, Nick looked down at the toppled chess pieces. Slowly, he began picking them up with his left hand and setting them back into their box. He replaced the lid, his heart thudding all the while.

Numbness invaded his thoughts as well as his heart.

He had no idea where he would go or what he would do.

His future was finished.

He returned to London on the afternoon train as soon as he'd packed his small bag. He'd been forced to ask for Davy's help and had to fight the sense of shame that he was being run off the property. Davy chatted away as if nothing out of the ordinary had occurred. He probably assumed it was natural for Nick to return to London after his week of convalescing.

A part of Nick kept hoping for one last glimpse of Miss Shepard before he left the house but she was nowhere to be seen. She'd probably been sent to her room. How were young ladies of her class punished for stealing a kiss from an unsuitable young man?

He leaned against the high-backed seat in the train, his growling stomach reminding him it had been several hours since breakfast. He gazed out at the landscape, his mind going over Mr. Shepard's words. He had no justification for what he'd done. How to explain to a man that he'd found his young daughter irresistible, that in all the years of his youth, he'd never done such a thing, until he'd met her—a girl on the brink of womanhood, more special, more beautiful, like no other girl he'd ever met?

On arriving in the city, he stopped that same afternoon at the office and collected his wages. He stared down at the measly pile of coins. They were his only protection from the streets until he was well enough to seek another job.

Suddenly, a spurt of rage replaced the numbness. After all these years, he would not return to the pool of anonymous clerks from which he'd used every ounce of toil and ingenuity to rise above. Because of one moment of foolishness, would he be condemned to the ranks of slavery the rest of his life?

Pure, blind rage filled his veins and brought a pounding to his temples. He clenched his hands, ignoring the pain that shot through his collar. He thought of his oldest brother, breathing in the dust-laden air in the cotton mill, of Tom, who was trying to support his young brood on the hundred pounds he made a year as a shipping clerk, of Alfie, who dreamed of owning his own shop one day.

How was he going to help each one get ahead? His mother counted on him. When she'd given him all she had to come to London, she'd told him, "The Lord has blessed you with a fine mind, Nicholas. It's up to you to use it and make your way in the world to help your brothers."

And now none of that would materialize. All because of one moment of insanity with a young girl way above his reach.

He banged the door of Shepard & Steward behind

him, ignoring the call of one of the clerks. He didn't stop until he reached the street. Then he kept walking, thrusting himself through the crowded sidewalk.

"See there, watch where you're going!" A red-faced hansom cab driver waved his whip at him.

Nick stopped just in the nick of time at the edge of the curb.

He didn't know where he was going, he only knew he had to walk somewhere—anywhere—until this knot of rage loosened from his windpipe. It was strangling him.

He continued walking, unmindful of how many blocks he'd gone. His collarbone ached with the swinging movement of his arm. His ribs throbbed with each stride.

He was in no shape to seek another job now. Not until the sling was off. But he would not return to clerking in a bank. Soon, his wages would run out. He'd have to find something before then.

His steps slowed as he reached the river and stood gazing outward.

He pictured Miss Shepard's face, the way she'd met his kiss with innocent ardor. He shook the image away. She was only a girl. Best to forget the sentiments she'd awakened in him.

But he couldn't prevent the bitterness that threatened to swallow him up at the notion that she could never be his. He was tired of Britain and the ceiling it imposed over his head. No matter how much he worked, he'd never be good enough to set his sights on anyone like Miss Shepard. It was vain to think that some day, if he earned enough money, he could ever win the approval of her father.

He tried to pray, knowing the Lord advocated humility and forgiveness. But he felt no inclination now to humble himself and accept the consequences of his rash act.

Was it so wrong to fall in love with a girl like Miss Shepard?

And for a few moments he allowed himself to dream of what it would have been like to be able to work to attain her. He could have risen in her father's firm to the position of a junior partner. And then he would have dared to offer for her. He would have worked hard for her. He wouldn't have begrudged her anything.

But it was never to be. He'd never find a comparable position as he'd had at Shepard and Steward, not now, when Shepard would likely give him a bad reference or none at all.

It was time for a drastic change in his life.

He looked at the ships downriver and he felt the answer. Was the Lord telling him to leave England? Did his future lie across the ocean where so many had gone before him to make their fortunes?

The idea took hold. He'd take his last wages and book passage to America.

He'd work as hard as it took. By the grace of God, he'd make it and then—

Then he'd return and claim Miss Alice Shepard's heart.

Confined to her room for the rest of the day, Alice spent the time on her knees, alternately pleading for leniency for Mr. Tennent and reveling in the memory of her first kiss.

What had come over her to ask him to kiss her? Her cheeks heated at her brazenness. But she was not sorry she'd done it. She remembered the look in his dark eyes: shock and then wonder and then he'd leaned toward her and she'd been astounded to know that he felt the same as she did.

Oh, the second his lips had touched hers, she'd felt herself falling off a precipice, a delightful precipice from where there was no return.

Why had Father walked in at that moment? He'd ruined everything. She hadn't been able to hear anything through the door and had had to run up to her room, afraid he'd see her in the corridor when he left the veranda.

She looked in vain out her window, but it faced the back of the house, and she had no idea what could have happened to Mr. Tennent.

Nicholas. She whispered the name to herself, liking the sound of such a fine name, watching the glass cloud up under her lips. *Nicholas Tennent. Alice Shepard Tennent. Mrs. Nicholas Tennent.* Her heart thrilled at each variation.

Her father would have to allow them to marry now, since he'd caught them kissing. No matter that she wasn't quite seventeen. She was willing to wait however long Father required. Surely, by the time she was eighteen she would be old enough to be Nicholas's wife. She'd prove how able she was!

At dinner, her father summoned her downstairs to his office.

"I've sent Tennent away," he said with no preamble.

"Away? Where, Father?"

"It doesn't matter." His tone was its usual even one, with no emotion, simply matter-of-fact as if he were discussing his latest business acquisition.

She took a step forward on the thick carpet. "But Father, I love him. You can't just send him away."

"You have behaved disgracefully today. I cannot have my only daughter carrying on with every man in my employ as if she were some hoyden."

"Father! I was not carrying on! I love Mr. Tennent and am going to marry him!"

He looked her up and down. "Has Tennent actually had the temerity to propose to you?"

She tossed her head. "You didn't exactly give him the opportunity."

"You'd better get any notions of marriage out of your head. There will be no proposal. Tennent has left my employ. It's clear you cannot be trusted to carry on like a well-behaved young lady under your own roof, so I will have you spend your future holidays with your Uncle Sylvester and Aunt Hermione." He raked a hand through his hair and gave a weary sigh. "I should have done so long ago…since your mother died."

She fell back. Her father sounded as if he were giving up on her for good. What had she done so wrong, but fall in love?

In the coming days, no matter how much she cried and pleaded with him, her father remained unmoved. As she watched her trunk being packed, she waited for rescue from Mr. Tennent. Somehow, he must be able to get word to her, so she could tell him that she was being sent away.

She had no idea how to reach him, and her father had Miss Bellows, her companion, watch her like a hawk now.

She spent the final days of her holiday far from home with her strict aunt and uncle and their unpleasant offspring. They treated her like a person in disgrace.

Of her father she heard nothing. By the time she returned to school, her tears had dried up. Life held no joy and each day was a drudgery to be gotten through.

The hope she had of hearing from Mr. Tennant grew slimmer and slimmer over the year until it finally disappeared altogether, leaving only a hollowness in her heart.

Chapter Five

July 1890

Nick allowed his valet to put the final touches to his cravat and turned from the glass. "Thank you, Williams." He turned to the room's other occupant. "Well, will I pass muster?"

"The picture of a young millionaire." Lord Asquith, a good-looking gentleman in his mid-thirties, lounged against the settee in Nick's hotel suite.

Nick raised an eyebrow. "Young?"

The baron rose with an easy grace, his evening suit looking as natural on him as if he'd been born in it. "Of course. What are you? Thirty-five, thiry-six?"

He grimaced. "Thirty-eight last March." Where had the last decade of his life gone?

"Just as I said, young, rich, powerful, just returned from America, and—" he lifted an eyebrow significantly "—unattached. The society mamas will latch on to you like a swarm of hungry locusts. Come along, I know just the place to take you this evening."

Nick picked up his white kid gloves from the table. "What did you have in mind? I hope nothing like last night when I was subjected to about as much boredom as a man should be required to endure for an evening."

Asquith chuckled. "Oh, no, nothing like. I do apologize. I know Lady Petersham is insufferably stuffy, but she has connections. If she accepts you into her circle, then everyone will follow suit."

"Who said I wanted to be accepted?" Nick closed the door to the hotel suite at the Savoy and the two headed down the corridor.

Asquith just shook his head as if the question were not even worth an argument. Upon his arrival back in England, Nick had been introduced to Asquith by a business associate. The young baron had taken a liking to Nick and decided he needed to be "introduced" to London society.

They rode down the lift to the spacious marble lobby of the newly opened hotel. At the front doors, the porter bowed and held one open. "Do you require a cab this evening, sirs?"

Asquith gave a brief nod.

While they waited under the porte-cochère, Nick glanced down the busy street. Gaslights cast their glow over the dark sheen of cabs and private carriages. Pedestrians hurried down the Strand. It was a city as choked with traffic as when he'd left it fifteen years ago.

"As I was saying, you'll have a very different experience this evening at Mrs. Alice Lennox's gala."

Alice. Nick cast a quick glance at Asquith, but then gave a mental shake. The name was common enough.

The truth was he'd been thinking of the person the

name conjured up ever since he'd decided to return to London. It had been too many years, he'd told himself every time he thought of her. Too late to do anything about something that never really had a chance to begin.

Nick hardly heard Asquith's words as he pictured the lively face of a girl he'd known for such a brief time, but whose equal he hadn't met since.

"…a most elegant woman, charming, beautiful and eminently worthy. I tell you, her virtues are innumerable."

Nick pulled his thoughts back with an effort. "Who can find a virtuous woman? For her price is far above rubies…"

Asquith quirked an eyebrow at him. "What's that you say?"

"It's something my mother would oft quote me."

"Well, your mother would doubtless approve of Mrs. Lennox. A modern day saint, if there ever was one."

Nick slapped his gloves against the palm of his hand. "I have yet to find one who couldn't be bought off with a fine pair of rubies."

"You are a cynic when it comes to women."

"Merely a realist." He'd discovered that to his misfortune once he'd achieved financial success, and time had not proved him wrong as his wealth grew.

"Ah, but you haven't met Mrs. Lennox."

A hansom cab pulled up at the curb and the two got in.

Nick glanced at Asquith as the porter closed the folding doors in front of their legs. "Where are we headed?"

Asquith opened the trap door behind them and spoke to the driver. "Clarendon's." Then he settled back in the snug seat and rested his hands atop the ivory head of his walking stick. "You know the hotel on Albemarle, don't you?

"I know *of* it, though I've never been in it."

"Now, where were we?"

"A paragon among women," Nick replied dryly.

"Ah yes, Mrs. Lennox. You said yourself you were looking to make a donation to a worthy charity. Well, Mrs. Lennox is your answer."

Nick glanced sidelong at Asquith, his curiosity aroused. "How's that?"

"She runs a housing charity."

Housing was an area of definite interest to him. "Tell me more."

"She is forever fighting with the building companies for decent housing for the working classes. Tonight she is hosting a ball for the charity, as a matter of fact. It has a long name to it. The Society for the Betterment of the something or other." Asquith tapped his fingers against his walking stick. "It'll add to your stature if you donate to a cause such as hers. She's loved by society and working man alike, not to mention the fact that she's a goddess among women."

Nick pictured some imposing matron as cold and quelling as a London fog. Certainly not the girl he'd dreamed of for too many years before relinquishing the cause as a hopeless youthful fantasy. God had blessed him immeasurably in his business pursuits. It was enough.

They were driving through the most fashionable streets of the West End. He peered through the hansom window at the streetlamps and quaint facades of the men's clubs along St. James's.

"Have you joined any clubs yet?"

He looked at the young lord in surprise, not having considered such a prospect. "As I recall, those require membership by invitation."

Asquith shrugged. "I can put your name up at a few of mine. Filled with doddering old bores for the most part. Still, you'll want to join one or two. They're quiet places where you can read the papers and get a hot meal when you tire of hotel fare."

Nick shook his head, glancing back out at the passing street, unable to accustom himself to his new stature in London. When he'd left, he hadn't enough in his pocket to buy provisions for his sea journey, and now he was negotiating to buy entire companies.

They entered a quiet tree-lined square before being stalled amidst several coaches. "We can get out here or we'll be sitting in our cab all night. Mrs. Lennox's balls are renowned. Come on."

Nick followed Asquith out of the cab. On the next block, a crowd congregated under the portico of the large hotel. Ladies in long dark silk capes and upswept hair ascended the red-carpeted steps on the arms of gentlemen in black evening attire. Music wafted from the open doorways into the street.

Asquith nodded to several people on his way in but didn't stop for anyone. "The invitation says it's in the grand ballroom." Nick followed him up the curving marble staircase at the rear of the lobby.

The strains of music grew louder as they approached the room on the floor above. Asquith presented his invitation to a doorman and they entered the long ball-room studded with marble columns and crowned by crystal chandeliers.

They stood a moment at the edge of the sea of well-dressed people. Although he'd attended several society events in San Francisco, Nick had never grown used to them. London society was a different kettle of fish altogether. He'd never learned the subtleties of family names and histories. His gaze traveled over old and young faces. All looked as if they were part of an ex-clusive club to which only they knew the language.

His senses were assaulted by perfumes and po-mades overlaid with cigarette smoke. The chandelier light glinted off the jewels in women's hair and around their throats.

With a tap at his elbow, Asquith began to weave through the crowd. Nick followed in his wake, his suit brushing against a palette of colorful gowns, taffetas and crepes, lace ruffles and wide puffed sleeves.

He had little chance to observe anyone in detail as Asquith strolled from group to group as if greet-ing guests in his own drawing room. "Good evening, Lord Dellamere… Good evening Mrs. Stanton… Yes, a lovely evening… I saw him at the club earlier…"

Amidst his casual exchanges, he turned to Nick. "Come on, let's find the bar."

The marble-topped bar in an adjoining room was three-deep in black-coated gentlemen and wreathed in smoke.

"Just a soda water for me, thanks."

Lord Asquith gave him a second look before nod-ding. "Very well."

Nick took the time to let his gaze wander back through the wide doors into the ballroom. Not one familiar face, but he hadn't expected to see any acquaintance. He'd certainly not moved in these circles when he'd left.

"Here you go, soda water."

He took the thick tumbler from Asquith. "Thanks." He'd never cared for spirits much. His mother had been a strict teetotaler and during all those years of fighting to succeed, he'd considered it just another dangerous habit and needless expense when every penny counted. Now that he could afford to be liberal, he had no taste for the stuff.

Asquith lifted his champagne coupe in a salute. "Welcome back to the beau monde." They sipped their respective drinks in silence.

An orchestra was playing a waltz and the ballroom filled with dancing couples. The thrum of voices swirled around him like a swollen river, its noise undulating in volume but never lowering enough to make the words distinguishable from one another.

"Where do so many people come from?" Nick mused.

"I told you Mrs. Lennox's galas are coveted events."

Asquith surveyed the room over the rim of his glass. "Quite a good turn-out. The Society's coffers should be filled. Ah, there she is." With the stem of his glass he indicated a cluster of people coming through the ballroom doors. "The queen of the event. Surrounded as usual by her court."

Nick focused on the group of well-dressed ladies and gentlemen. They did indeed appear to be surrounding one individual but he couldn't see her through the mass.

Asquith took him gently by the elbow and urged him forward. "Time for introductions."

Nick had to fight the urge to hang back. Would this grand lady look down her nose at him, seeing beyond the evening clothes to the former clerk, the son of a miner?

With a greeting here and a pleasantry there, Asquith made his way to his target. Before reaching it, the group abruptly parted, and Nick saw her.

Standing about ten feet from her, he came face-to-face with the girl of his dreams.

The years fell away, and he was back in Richmond, a twenty-three-year-old clerk with nothing to recommend him but his ambition, and Miss Alice Shepard was exacting a kiss from him.

He stared at her, hardly believing the reality. She hadn't changed. As beautiful as on that long ago summer, and yet completely transformed. For the woman in the emerald green evening gown that hugged her small waist before flaring out at her hips in a fall of cascading lace was no longer a sixteen-year-old schoolgirl but an exquisitely fashionable lady as foreign to him as he must appear to her.

He'd both dreaded and longed for this moment. Torn between the desire to go in search of her once he returned and a greater fear that he'd wake to the grim reality of finding her another's, he'd been paralyzed into inaction.

At that instant her eyes met his.

Like a dream, he read the question in her eyes give way to uncertainty. He knew the instant she recognized him. She left the company around her and directed her footsteps toward him. Would she indeed remember him? He swallowed, finding his throat tight. His heart drummed in his chest and his breathing became erratic.

Nicholas Tennent. Alice could scarcely believe her eyes. Was her memory playing tricks on her? Surely the distinguished gentleman looking so intently at her was not the same man she'd given her childish heart to so long ago?

She didn't have to search her memory for his name. How many times had she repeated it to herself and written it down in her diary, making long scrolls under his name and hers in her schoolgirl script?

Nicholas Tennent. The name evoked pain and longing. For a second she thought she would faint. All the old wounds of anguish and abandonment threatened to erupt.

No. She clamped down on those old emotions. She had come a long way from the girl she'd been. The wounds were long since healed over and the scars practically faded.

The thoughts and questions tumbled through her mind in chaotic jumble. What was Nicholas Tennent doing here after all these years? Where had he been all this time? Surely not in London? Wouldn't they have run into each other at some point?

Leaving her companions in mid-conversation, she began walking toward him. She no longer recollected how long it had been since her heartbreak. Her glance skimmed over his features. His hair was as dark as she remembered, combed away from his high forehead, his bearing straight, still slim but his shoulders broader.

Did he remember her at all? He must, the way he was looking at her. His dark eyes hadn't moved from her face.

They reached each other and she held out her hands, hesitating only an instant before she spoke. "Mr. Tennent, is it truly you?"

"Miss Shepard." He bowed, taking both her hands in his.

"Mrs. Lennox, now. She is the lady I have been telling you about." Lord Asquith's amused drawl came from the side.

Alice drew her gaze with difficulty away from Mr. Tennent's bowed head to see Asquith swirling his champagne glass around. "Telling him about…?"

"The newly arrived Nicholas Tennent, who has come all the way across the Atlantic to attend one of your galas."

Her eyes turned back to Mr. Tennent unable to absorb what Asquith was telling her. "America?"

"Yes." His dark scrutiny was unnerving. "You are Mrs. Lennox now?"

She nodded.

Lord Asquith drew her attention away again. "May I infer from this that you two are old acquaintances?"

Mr. Tennent answered before she had a chance to collect her thoughts. "I worked for her father for a short time."

Indeed her thoughts felt scattered in a thousand different directions. All her years of social poise slipped away at the keen way Mr. Tennent was regarding her. Her hands still felt the pressure of his hands on hers although he'd let them go immediately.

Lord Asquith rocked back on his heels. "You worked for old Shepard? When was this?"

"A long time ago."

"I must hear more." He turned to her. "Come, Alice, if the man is going to be close-lipped, you must give me the particulars."

Before she could think how to answer, Mr. Tennent turned to her. "Would you care to dance?"

"I beg your pardon?" She couldn't seem to stop staring at him. In the few seconds in his company, she felt like the girl she used to be.

"I merely asked you for this waltz." His voice, by contrast, sounded smooth and composed.

When had he undergone such a transformation? Realizing he was awaiting her reply, she nodded, hardly knowing what she was saying. "All right."

He handed Asquith his glass and offered her his arm. As he led her toward the ballroom, he leaned closer to her. "I thought it the best way to escape Lord Asquith's curiosity."

"Oh, I see." His proximity was making her dizzy. It was just the shock, she told herself, like seeing someone one had thought long dead.

Only years of training enabled her to follow the waltz that was just commencing. She kept her eyes fixed on Mr. Tennent's even as her thoughts wondered where he had learned to dance so effortlessly. Had he known when she'd met him? She remembered how he hadn't ever ridden, or played tennis. Long suppressed memories tumbled into her head, sitting beside him at the desk, working and laughing over any silly thing that struck her, all ending the day of that fateful kiss.

"What are you thinking? You seem far away."

"I was thinking about Richmond."

His dark eyes looked into hers as if he, too, were remembering that day. But then he answered and she only detected amusement in his tone. "You doubtless remember an awkward young clerk. As I recall you said I was too serious."

It seems he didn't recall their kiss at all. Taking her cue from him, she put aside the memory and strove for a light, cordial tone. "I remember the serious, but I don't recall awkward. My memory is of a young man of great intelligence and ambition with a very strong sense of purpose."

He looked slightly taken aback with her description and she found herself blushing. "I didn't think you'd remember me at all," he said quietly.

She frowned in puzzlement. "Why shouldn't I remember you?" She wanted to add that she'd never forgotten him, but realized how foolish that would sound.

"It's been a long time."

Slowly, she nodded. His face had matured. Gone was the thin, pale, slightly long visage. In its place was a darker, more rugged complexion, as if he'd spent much time in the outdoors. "I'm surprised you remember me at all," she said with a laugh that sounded nervous to her ears. "An awkward young girl, pestering you as you tried to carry out your secretarial duties."

Amusement crinkled the corners of his eyes. "Let me assure you my memory is of a beautiful young girl poised on the verge of womanhood."

She could feel the warmth steal into her cheeks and

felt shaken by her reaction. It couldn't be, not after so many years. She'd been married and known real love.

As if reading her thoughts, he said, "There have been a few changes since that time. You are married."

She looked away. "*Was*. My husband...passed away four years ago." Dear, sweet Julian. How she still missed him.

"I'm sorry," was all he said, his tone betraying little.

Her gaze traveled back to his face and she found him still watching her. "There's something different about you."

She caught a hint of humor in his eyes. "Perhaps the cut of my suit? Savile Row's finest."

She remembered the dark, stiff suits he wore on the tennis court and almost laughed. Then she shook her head, hardly giving his black cutaway coat and snowy white shirt a glance except to note how handsomely he filled them out. "No, it's not that." She tilted her head a fraction. "There's a self-assurance I don't remember."

"The suit—and enough money in the bank to buy out half the people in this room." His glance went beyond her and skimmed the ballroom.

The words gave her pause. They had a harsh ring to them. "Have you achieved your dream?"

His gaze returned to hers. "You remember?"

She nodded her head. "Of course I do."

The music came to an end and the two stood there as other couples walked by them. With an inquiring lift of an eyebrow, he took her arm and led her to the edge of the dance floor.

"Things didn't quite turn out the way I expected," he said.

She wasn't sure what he was referring to but suddenly she needed to know. "What happened the day Father found us?"

If she'd thought he'd forgotten their kiss, she'd been mistaken. He stared at her. "You don't know?"

"No. Father never told me anything but that he'd sent you away."

"I was sacked immediately—deservedly so."

She drew in her breath. "I didn't know. The only thing I knew for certain was that you'd disappeared. I'm sorry you lost your job over me."

"Don't be. As it turns out, it was the best thing that could have ever happened to me."

The abrupt tone cut her to the quick. What had been her banishment had meant freedom for him.

"You've prospered in America."

"I left London determined to seek my fortune across the Atlantic."

"And have you?"

He shrugged. "America has treated me well."

Something in her felt saddened at the man standing before her. He was no longer the earnest young secretary but a hardened, self-assured businessman. The kind of man she'd vowed never to give her heart to.

She didn't catch what he was saying. "I'm sorry?"

"I said, was your father very angry with you that day?"

She looked down at her clasped hands. "As it happens, he sent me away, too."

"He sent you away?"

At his sharp tone, she lifted her head. "Yes, to some relatives in Scotland. I spent the holidays with them from then on."

"I didn't know." He cleared his throat, the first sign of hesitation since she'd been in his company. "Did they treat you well?"

"They were tolerable." She smiled, not wanting to dwell on the unpleasant things of the past. "Father concluded he could do no more with his wayward daughter. They kept an eagle eye on me for the next year or so, until he finally allowed me to come back to London when I finished school."

He was staring at her. "I'm truly sorry. I should have behaved more honorably."

She felt herself redden again. "You did nothing wrong."

After a moment, he said, "You were married."

"Yes. I met my husband shortly after I returned to London. We were married after my twenty-first birthday." Without her father's approval, she added silently. "Julian—my husband—was ill when we met but he recovered for a while. But then the consumption recurred. But he left me with a great gift."

Before he could ask her anything about that, she said in a determinedly bright tone. "So, you've been in America. Is that the reason I haven't seen you in a London ballroom until tonight?"

He nodded slowly, as if still puzzling over what she had told him.

"How long have you been away from England?"

"Since I last saw you."

"But that's been—"

"Fifteen years."

"Has it really been that long?" she whispered, not

sure which stunned her more, the fact of how much time had passed, or that he remembered.

He nodded, his dark eyes studying her.

They were interrupted by one of the trustees of the housing charity. "Mrs. Lennox, may I have a word with you?"

Alice looked at Mr. Tennent, torn between wanting to continue speaking with him and wondering if it were not better to let the past remain where it was. "I'm sorry, Mr. Tennent. If you will excuse me?"

He bowed over her hand. "Thank you for the dance, Miss—Mrs. Lennox."

She smiled. "The pleasure was mine." Against her better judgment, she asked, "Are you in London for long?"

"That depends."

His gaze held hers, and she found herself saying, "If you are free tomorrow, I will be home in the afternoon."

He nodded. "What time?"

"Two o'clock? Number fifteen, Park Lane."

"I'll be there."

Nick watched Miss Shepard—Mrs. Lennox, he reminded himself—finding it difficult to reconcile his image of a carefree girl with this elegant lady. Soon, she was surrounded with other guests, and if he thought he'd have another opportunity to approach her, he saw it was a vain wish. Better to wait until the morrow when he could find out more about what had happened to her since that fateful day of their kiss.

A widow. What kind of man had she married?

A thousand questions swirled in through his mind.

Seeing Lord Asquith heading his way, and reluctant to answer even the most general interrogation about his acquaintance with Miss Shepa—Mrs. Lennox, Nick turned and weaved through the crowded room until able to exit without being seen.

Although the evening was young, he headed back to his hotel suite. His mind was too full of memories and questions to be able to concentrate on anything else. Not even work would distract him tonight.

Chapter Six

Nick arrived promptly the next day at Mrs. Lennox's address. He paid his cab fare and proceeded through the black wrought-iron gates up the walkway to the colonnaded façade of the Park Lane mansion. Similar imposing structures lined the wide, tree-lined avenue. Once, he'd aspired to such a London address. Now, he glanced indifferently at them, his thoughts fixed on the coming visit.

He'd found it hard to sleep when he'd arrived back from the gala. For so many years he'd worked toward this moment until as the months turned into years and his goal nowhere in sight, he'd realized what a pipe dream it was and gradually he'd abandoned it.

And now, he'd seen her again, when he was the man he'd dreamed of becoming and she was free.

The moment had found him unprepared.

Why hadn't he come back sooner? The question had plagued him all night, and he'd not been able to come up with a satisfactory answer.

He adjusted his silk tie and rang the bell, feeling as nervous as a boy on his first courtship.

He thought again of what she'd told him of her being sent away. Shepard had proved more hard-hearted than he could have ever imagined. If he'd known she'd be sent away, would he have left like that? But what could he have done? A penniless clerk with no job prospects would make a poor knight to a sixteen-year-old damsel in distress.

No. He'd had to make his fortune to be worthy of courting Miss Shepard. And that had taken him many more years than he'd foreseen.

But was he fifteen years too late?

He smoothed his hair back and gave his tie one final adjustment just as a maid opened the door.

As soon as Nick gave his name, the servant stood to one side. "Yes, Mrs. Lennox told me to expect you. Come this way, please."

He was led to a drawing room at the rear of the house where no street noises penetrated. "I will inform madam that you are here."

"Thank you." Left alone, Nick glanced about the well-appointed room. Oil landscapes filled the walls in gilt frames, dark velvet couches graced two sides of the room. Everything exuded refined taste. He walked over Oriental carpets to peer through the long windows facing the back. Precisely clipped yew hedges formed geometrical shapes within the walls of the wide garden. Bright flowers bobbed their heads within the green borders.

A slight noise behind him caused him to turn away from the view and look back into the room.

He saw no one. His eyes traveled slowly over the furnishings, the book spines on a floor-to-ceiling shelf, a piano at one end of the room, a set of nested tables, a chintz-covered armchair and a carved trunk before backtracking.

He heard it again, a low sniffle. He walked toward a desk, glad for the thick carpet which muffled his footsteps.

He peered under the desk.

A young boy, his large dark eyes looking up at him through a mop of dark bangs, sat crouched within the small space meant for a person's legs. He clutched a furry stuffed animal to his breast.

Nick smiled tentatively. "Hello."

The boy didn't reply to the soft greeting. Could he be Mrs. Lennox's son? The thought jolted him.

Of course. It would be natural for her to have children. Nick straightened and took a step back. "I'm not sure how comfortable it is down there. I know when I was a lad, I liked to find odd nooks and crannies. You can pretend to be in a cave, hiding away from a band of pirates, or perhaps you're in your tent, bivouacked with your troops, planning tomorrow's battle."

The boy continued staring at him.

Nick leaned against the back of a couch, and put his hands in his trouser pockets, pretending to be at ease. "What is your friend's name?"

The child looked from Nick to the stuffed animal in his hands. It appeared to be a rabbit from the long floppy ears hanging off the sides of its head. But at Nick's scrutiny, the boy took the animal and hid it behind his back.

Before Nick could think how to reassure him that he was not going to take the thing away from him, Mrs. Lennox entered the room.

"Good afternoon, Mr. Tennent. I'm so glad you could come today. I was almost doubting that it was really you at the gala yesterday evening." She advanced toward him with a welcoming smile.

She seemed more relaxed than she had last evening. But just as beautiful. She wore a high-necked blue gown with long sleeves which were gathered at the shoulders. Her hair was done up but in the sunlight filtering through the sheer curtains, he detected once again the coppery highlights he remembered so well.

He took her hand in his, feeling its soft warmth. Reluctantly, he let it go. "I know exactly what you mean." To fill the silence, he looked back towards the desk.

She followed his gaze. Immediately seeing the boy, she bent down and held out her hand. "Austen, my dear, what are you doing down there? Have you said hello to Mr. Tennent? He is an old friend of Mama's."

So, it *was* her son. He drew in a breath, still having difficulty reconciling the young girl he'd known with the mother of a boy already in short pants and sailor collar.

The little boy took his mother's hand and slowly let her lead him out of his hiding place. When he stood, Nick saw that he was older than he'd supposed. Perhaps six or seven instead of four or five.

Mrs. Lennox turned to Nick with a smile. "Let me present you to my son, Austen Lennox. Say, 'how do you do, Mr. Tennent.'"

The little boy held out his free hand, his large brown eyes gazing up at him through black lashes. Nick took the small hand in his, closing his hand around it. As soon as the handshake was over, the little hand disappeared into the pocket of the boy's short pants.

She turned to Nick again. "It's such a lovely day, would you like to sit out on the terrace?"

He agreed and followed her to a brick terrace overlooking the garden he had seen from the window. Mrs. Lennox ordered coffee to be brought out to them.

Austen stood behind his mother's skirts, and she bent over him, her hand on his head. Her hands were exactly as he remembered them, pale and slim. She wore only a thin gold band on her ring finger. "Would you like to stay with Mama and Mr. Tennent, or would you like to go up to Nanny Grove?"

"Nanny Grove," he whispered. She straightened and smiled at Nick. "Austen is going up to his room and wants to bid you goodbye." With a little nudge from her, he stepped forward and held out his hand.

Nick felt a pang, transported back to his own childhood for an instant. He used to be afraid of large strangers at that age. He stooped down before the boy and took his hand with a smile. The thin little wrist stuck out from his navy blue shirt. "It was nice to have met you, Austen. I hope we'll see each other again."

The boy only nodded. Nick released his hand and took a step away from him, imagining his height might intimidate the boy.

"I'll be up to see you soon and we'll go to the park later, all right?" his mother whispered, bending over Austen again.

Nick moved off to stand at the edge of the brick terrace, unsure what to say. It wasn't often he was unsure of himself these days.

How to begin with a woman he had only briefly known so many years ago? A woman who had impressed him to the extent that no other lady had succeeded in displacing her memory?

This elegant lady was no longer the vivacious girl he remembered. Would the two of them have anything to talk about? This Alice Lennox seemed remote, with none of the young Miss Shepard's impulsiveness or enthusiasm. Yet something in her slim straight shoulders affected him in a way that made him feel as vulnerable as he hadn't since he'd left his native shores for America so long ago.

Had that young girl's spirit been irrevocably suppressed? Was there any hope of resurrecting it? What had come to take its place?

He turned around when he heard Austen's departure. The two watched him for a moment.

With a sigh, Mrs. Lennox motioned to a cushioned wicker settee. "Please, have a seat, Mr. Tennent."

He took the place beside her as a maid set down the coffee tray. Mrs. Lennox poured dark Turkish coffee from the long-handled copper pot into two tiny porcelain cups. He took the one offered him. "Thank you." He waited until she had sat back and had taken a sip from her cup before he spoke. "Your boy is quiet."

She colored and looked away, as if the remark were aimed at herself. "Yes, Austen is rather bashful. He... well, he was only three when he lost his father, and I don't know how much it has affected his behavior." She ran her finger along the rim of her cup.

Nick was suddenly transported back to the afternoon he'd first met her in his tiny office. She'd walked along the edge of his desk, running her slim finger along its edge. Little had he realized then how the young girl would turn his life upside down.

He blinked away the sudden image. "I beg your pardon, what did you say?"

"I was saying that Austen was a happy baby, but it seems he has become more timid with each passing year. He's also a bit frail. Like his father. I worry about him. I know I shouldn't. I trust in God's mercy." She sighed.

"I don't know too much about children," he said, seeking of a way to reassure her, "but I imagine a lot of children are naturally shy at his age. How old is he?"

She smiled and he felt he'd said the right thing. "He's seven."

He cleared his throat. "How is your father?"

"He passed away last year. I moved back here to be with him four years ago when I was widowed. This was Father's London home."

The news stunned him. He'd always thought of Shepard as being in London the day he returned successful. "I'm sorry."

She sighed. "But I still have my brother. Do you remember him?"

"Yes, I met him a few times."

"He runs Father's firm now."

He nodded, hard pressed to imagine the man he remembered running anything. Perhaps he'd matured.

An awkward silence followed. "You never married again?"

"Oh, no." She looked as shocked as if he'd asked her if she'd committed a crime.

"Most women do. You've been widowed how long?"

"Four years. But I loved my husband."

He felt a twinge of envy for the man who had inspired that kind of love and loyalty.

"Besides, I have Austen. And my work."

The wicker creaked as he sat back against the settee, feeling he'd offended her with his blunt remark. "Your work?"

She smiled sheepishly. "Actually, you were the one to inspire me in this direction."

He paused in the act of sipping his coffee. "Me? How so?"

"You were the first one to ever cause me to question my privileged station in life. You challenged me to look around me at how other people lived."

His lip curled up at the corner. "I was a rather priggish, unyielding sort back then, as I recall."

She smiled. "Not at all." She looked past him, sobering. "Later, when I met my husband, he helped me see even more how we must help our fellow man."

Nick's pleasure at having inspired her in any way evaporated as he listened to her wax on about her husband's role in her life. He'd taken her off to live in a small vicarage and given away anything they had to the needy in their parish. To hear her tell it, Julian Lennox had been a saint among men.

After several moments of listening to an extended

eulogy about the poor curate's selfless life among his parishioners, Nick concluded the man had been a weak individual who had caused Miss Shepard to be cut off from her parents' wealth.

Mrs. Lennox took a sip of her coffee, her eyes sad. "I think it broke his health eventually, but he wouldn't have been happy any other way. Since Julian's passing," she went on, "I returned to London and with a few other dedicated women have formed a society to help those working families who have no decent place to live. When I was widowed, I realized my own plight. With few resources, I would have been hard-pressed to find a wholesome place for Austen and myself."

He frowned. "With few resources? But your father?"

She looked down at her half-empty cup in her lap. "My father disinherited me when I married Julian."

Nick's frown deepened. "And yet you returned to him?"

"Yes. He was willing to accept his grandson, and I had few options.

"Since my father passed on, my brother, Geoff, allows me the use of this house." She sat up and smoothed her skirt. "But that's more about me than I meant to bore you with. What brought you to London after so many years?"

"My mother's funeral."

He heard her soft intake of breath and he met her gaze, which was full of sympathy. "I'm so sorry."

He stared down at the dregs of his coffee and without planning to, found himself saying, "I always meant to come back sooner." Her own story of nursing her consumptive husband only made him feel the inadequacy of the monetary assistance he'd rendered his mother.

"Was she ill very long?" she asked gently.

"No, not with the last illness." Why hadn't he come back sooner, he'd asked himself continually since the day he'd received the cable of her death.

"She had been sick often?"

"Off and on through the years." He gave a humorless laugh. "Poverty and lack are what ultimately killed her."

"Again, I'm so sorry."

He set his cup down on the table. "She worked long and hard over a lifetime until she was worn out. I helped her once I began earning wages, but I always meant to come back earlier. Alas, I was too late."

"I'm sure she knew your heart."

Their eyes met and he read genuine sorrow in hers. "Your loss was worse."

Her eyelashes flickered down. "I miss Julian. It was very difficult at first, but at least I know where he is. He had the assurance of the resurrection and of his Savior's love. He died peacefully at the vicarage, with those he loved around him."

They sat quietly some minutes. Nick thought about how blessed the departed man had been with such a woman's love. He'd known no such love in all his years abroad. Ever, really.

She offered him more coffee and he gave a brief nod.

"I also came to London for business."

"I see." She stirred her cup and set the tiny spoon down on the saucer. "Tell me all about America," she said, sitting up straighter. "Is it as big as one hears? Why did you decide to emigrate? Oh, I know, you probably had heard that fortunes are made over there practically overnight, but it seems so brave to set out by yourself. I want to hear all about it."

As her questions tumbled forth, Nick recognized the young girl of fifteen years ago. He wasn't sure if she was just making an effort to distract him from his grief, or if she was genuinely interested, but he decided to indulge her.

He took a sip of coffee. "After I left your father's firm, I didn't even wait until I was fully healed but booked passage aboard a steamer bound for New York harbor." Shaking his head, he continued. "I traveled steerage, a way I would never recommend to anyone."

"Was it very bad?"

"Overcrowded conditions in the airless hold of a ship, through calm waters and stormy. What was most disagreeable, I think, was the lack of fresh air. The food wasn't the worst I've eaten, and the company comprised all kinds of people, mainly families hoping for a new start, or men going on ahead and hoping to send for their families as soon as they'd saved for their passage."

She leaned forward, her chin in her hand, fascinated with his description.

"The trip lasted ten days, and whenever the skies were clear, I took my blanket up on the deck and slept under the stars."

"Oh, I should love to do that! You weren't afraid of rolling off the side?"

He smiled at her little understanding of a steamship. "I found a nice little sheltered spot under a smokestack. Anyway, it was my first and last experience traveling steerage. I'm happy to say this time around I was able to travel first class."

"And what did you do once you arrived in New York? Did you know anyone?"

"Not a soul." He could laugh about it now. Arriving with no money in his pocket and no acquaintances had been a different matter. "I went along with some of the single men I'd traveled with. There was a sort of network of immigrants. These men knew of others who'd gone before them; some had family members. I found a room in a boarding house, full of Irishmen, Scotsmen, Russians, Swedes and Norwegians and soon found work on a construction site."

Her eyes widened. "A construction site? Not as a secretary?"

"No. I had only my old bank references—" He stopped, realizing too late where that might lead. "Anyway, I didn't want to start over as a clerk, I'd spent too many years toiling in that department. So, I used my meager muscles this time instead of my brains."

She looked down. "My father didn't give you a reference when you left his employ?"

He shrugged. "He found me kissing his daughter, as you may recall. He was in his rights to send me packing with nothing."

They looked at each other steadily. "It was my fault you were dismissed."

"No." The word came swift and sharp. He rubbed a hand across his jaw, looking away from her at last. Did she regret it? "If not for his dismissal, I would never have gone to America and found the opportunities I did there."

"How did you go from a laborer to the owner of your own firm?"

Again, he smiled. "It didn't happen overnight. I spent some months at construction work, until deciding to head west. I heard from many that California was the place to be if one wanted to get ahead. I hopped a freight car from New York and was on my way."

"Oh, what an adventure! I wish Austen could hear you. How long did that trip take?"

"Quite a long while because I didn't go directly to California. I stopped several times in between, picked up a little work here and there—harvesting fruit in orchards, working as a farmhand for a bit on the great farms in the Middle West, ending up on a ranch in the West for a while." He smiled ruefully. "I was determined to get over my fear of horses after that fall."

She laughed. "I'm so glad! I was afraid you'd never want to get on another horse again."

"I not only did, but learned to ride a Western saddle. Even learned to lasso a steer."

"A real cowboy." She shook her head. "Austen would love to hear your stories," she repeated.

Did this mean she wanted to see him again? "Perhaps I can share them with him."

But she only nodded and said, "Perhaps."

Nick continued telling her the highlights of his adventures, playing up the amusing incidents and downplaying the months and years of deprivations and hardships before he'd had his first break.

She sighed as if satisfied with a well-told tale. "So you ended up in San Francisco."

"Yes, I found work in a dry goods store, unpacking cases, stocking shelves. Soon, I was working as a clerk, keeping track of inventory." His lips curled upward. "So, after all that time, I ended up doing what I had tried to avoid."

"What was that?"

"I'd vowed never to go back to clerking."

"Ah, but this time, it seems it was not in vain."

"No. It still took a few years, but gradually I worked my way up until I was manager of the store, and when the owner decided to branch out, he put me in charge of another store. Soon, I was overseeing a whole district. I saved every penny until I was able to invest my money. I borrowed some and went into a partnership with another fellow and we bought our own store.

"After a few years, having paid off the debt and making a profit, I began to buy other things—railroad stock, tea from China, government bonds…"

She drew in her breath. "You've been to the Far East?"

"I've made a few crossings."

"Goodness. My own life seems very dull in comparison."

He looked downward. "I've learned something about such a life. If one doesn't have someone to share one's success with, it is a lonely journey."

"You never married?"

He shook his head slowly, once again debating how much to tell her. "I had little time when I was working toward success until recently." He shrugged, his tone taking on a cynical edge. "I quickly discovered that when one has money, it's very easy to attract a woman's attention. Unfortunately, one cannot easily trust the authenticity of any avowals of love and fidelity given to a wealthy man."

He drained the last of his coffee and set the cup down, knowing he should go. "I am grateful for all I have been given. That is one of the reasons I wanted to see you again. Lord Asquith had already been telling me about your charity, and I wanted to look into it. Besides opening a branch of my firm here in London, I've returned to England because I wanted to donate something to a worthy cause."

"Oh, that's wonderful, Mr. Tennent." Her face took on an animation he remembered. "Would you like to visit our charity and see something of the work we do?"

He nodded. Any reason for seeing her again would be a good one. "Yes, very much so." He paused for only a second before saying, "Would tomorrow morning be too soon for you?"

She blinked as if surprised, but then agreed.

They discussed a time then he stood. He'd also learned not to overstay his welcome. "Thank you for the coffee and conversation."

Nick left the Shepard mansion, deciding to walk back to his hotel. He needed the time to sort through all the impressions he'd received in the last hour in Mrs. Lennox's company.

The impression that superseded all the others was that the girl he remembered was still there beneath the elegant society lady. Her eyes had sparkled with enthusiasm at his tales of his adventures in America's West.

As a man of thirty-eight, he found himself as fascinated by this woman as he had been at twenty-three by the girl on the verge of seventeen.

Where would this fascination lead him?

His pace quickened at the anticipation of seeing her as soon as tomorrow. He wasn't a man to spare any effort once he set his course.

Would Alice Lennox see anything in him worthy of her time and attention after all these years? After knowing the love of a truly worthy man like her late husband?

Chapter Seven

The next morning after spending some time with Austen in the nursery, Alice went to the small office of the Housing Society she oversaw. She was deep in budget matters, when her assistant popped her head in. "There's a gentleman here to see you." She handed Alice a card.

Alice took it from her. *Nicholas Tennent. President. Tennent & Co.*

The card was on high quality paper and the letters printed with understated elegance. She set down the card, trying to ignore the sudden flutter of nerves. Since issuing her invitation yesterday, she'd been of two minds about this meeting. "Send him in, please."

Mr. Tennent entered and once again Alice marveled at how distinguished he looked. She couldn't help a sense of proprietary pride that she had known all along that he'd make his mark in the world. She stood and held out her hand. "I'm so glad you could stop by today. I know you must be very busy."

His hand enveloped hers and gave it a quick, firm

shake. His dark eyes appraised her. She had the sense that he missed very little.

"Please, won't you have a seat?"

"Actually, I'd be more interested in seeing your facility and looking at some of the projects you've undertaken."

"Of course." She could see he wasn't a man to waste time. "Come then, I'll give you a quick tour and then perhaps we could look at a group of houses we have constructed in Bethnal Green."

"I look forward to it." The two exited her office and she led him down the corridor. "When did you first move into these quarters?"

"About two years ago. When I first came back to London, I was a bit at sea. Austen, of course, was very young, and I spent most of my time with him. But he had his nurse, and I found I had too much time on my hands. It…made things worse." She didn't like to recall those lonely weeks, feeling so out of place in her parents' old home. She sighed, brushing away the memories. "I had been very active with my husband in his parish, so little by little, I began informing myself of the situation here in London. This is a much bigger place, so at times the situation of the needy can seem overwhelming. That's when I decided to focus on one area where I might be able to help.

"I met a woman—Macey Endicott—who was very involved with the housing question. She is a remarkable woman. I hope you will meet her. She is on the Society's board of trustees. It was she who encouraged me to use my influence in society—" she gave a disbelieving laugh "—whatever little influence I had left, to help raise awareness of the situation."

He raised an eyebrow as if in surprise. "Little influence? What I saw the night of the gala showed me a lady of great influence."

She shook her head. "Four years ago, I would say I had very little. I had been away from London society for many years."

His eyes remained on her. "But you seem to have overcome that drawback."

"Perhaps. If so, it was due in great part to Miss Endicott. She is quite a champion of women and their rights." She shook her head with a smile. "She is quite respected, being wealthy in her own right, and by virtue of her many publications on such subjects as the reform of women's education and women's suffrage."

Alice watched him as he listened carefully, asking questions from time to time. She showed him the rest of their small quarters. He appeared interested in every detail.

When they stood outside on the curb, he hailed a hansom for them. "I notice there were only women in your office. Is that deliberate?"

She nodded, surprised that he'd noticed. "In a sense. You see, there are very few options for a woman who finds herself either widowed or single with no means of her own. A woman depends wholly on her parents or on a husband to support her, but you'd be surprised at the number of women who have neither alternative.

"I wanted to be able to offer some type of employment for women in this situation. Some of these women have children and it becomes even more challenging for them to find decent care for them. That is why you'll frequently find a child or two playing quietly by his mother's desk."

"My mother would have benefited from women such as you."

A hansom pulled up at Mr. Tennent's summons.

He handed her up into the cab and then came up to sit beside her. There was little room on the seat and her skirt brushed against his trouser legs. She made a show of adjusting her gown in the small space, suddenly conscious of his nearness, and attempted to continue her discourse. "One of my dreams is to offer a facility here under our roof as a nursery. Perhaps rent the floor above us for such a venture." She turned and slid open the hatch in the back and gave the driver instructions.

Mr. Tennent raised an eyebrow. "Shoreditch?"

When she turned from the hatch, she found his face very close to hers. She moved back a fraction then chided herself for her sensitivity. "I wanted to show you some of the housing that has been built over the years for the working classes and compare it with what we've done. The area around Spitalfields and Shoreditch has grown enormously and there is a terrible lack of adequate housing. It's also a railroad terminus which results in very mixed neighborhoods from lower middle class to very lower class."

The cab turned sharply at a corner and she was thrown against Mr. Tennent. Before she could right herself, he reached up a hand to steady her. "Tha—thank you." She adjusted her hat to conceal her confusion. What was wrong with her?

"It's quite all right." She could feel his glance on

her but his words revealed nothing out of the ordinary. "Would it cost so much?"

She'd lost the thread of their conversation. "To what?"

"To fix up a room for your female employees' children."

"Oh. Yes, it would. That would mean fewer funds available for our building projects. Presently, almost all donations we receive are used to help people with their housing. That need is most pressing of all." She shifted into her corner seat in preparation for another turn. "Tell me how it is in America. Are there such frightful conditions among the working classes?"

He described the cities he had seen. She listened, studying his three-quarter profile, finding herself remembering how drawn she'd been to him so many years ago. The strong lines had matured into the face of a very striking gentleman. His jaw was cleanly shaven. He hadn't really changed much over the years, but there was a cragginess to the lean contours of his face. The slight diffidence she remembered was gone but in its place was a subtle irony. It reminded her of her father, and she recoiled from the thought.

"Overcrowding exists in many workmen's neighborhoods but there is much industry and mobility." He glanced beyond her at the passing streets. "London has certainly grown since I was last here. Not that it wasn't a busy place then."

"Yes, it has seen unprecedented growth. No other city comes close, even your New York City."

"New York is a remarkable city."

"I should like to see it some day."

His dark eyes turned to her. "Perhaps you will."

Why did she feel there was more to his words than his light tone implied? She shook aside her fanciful notion. "I doubt it…at least not any time in the near future."

"You sound so very certain."

She folded her gloved hands on her lap. "I have my work here. And Austen is young still."

"When you were a girl, you struck me as someone who would seek the kind of adventure found in travel."

Her smile was bittersweet. "Yes, I was full of dreams."

"Haven't any of them been fulfilled?"

Was it whimsy or gravity she read in his tone—or irony? "Not in the way I had foreseen," she answered carefully.

"What *had* you foreseen?"

How could she answer that? That she'd foreseen a future with him? "A place to belong," she finally said, looking past him. So many years of yearning for what she'd never found in her home.

When he said nothing, she risked a glance at him. A furrow had formed between his brows. "Didn't you find that?"

"Oh, yes. But not where I had imagined." She took a deep breath. "It took a very humble, patient man to show me that it was only to be found in the Lord, that He loved me no matter how unlovable I might consider myself."

Before she could discover if he had understood what she meant, they arrived at their destination. Mr. Tennent descended the cab and turned to give her his hand. She stepped onto the broken pavement, still feeling the firmness of his hand after he'd let go and turned to the driver.

He paid the man and instructed him to wait for them then turned to survey the neighborhood. In the distance they could hear the rumble of trains.

They walked along a street lined with small shops. "We're not far from the Great Eastern Goods Station."

"This area looks fairly prosperous." He sniffed the air, which had a yeasty smell to it.

"There's a large brewery a few blocks to the east of us." She led him down Commercial Street. "There are quite some shops and warehouses along here due to the railroad station." As they continued farther, the storefronts and buildings became more varied. "You'll see how things begin to deteriorate the more distant from the station."

She turned down a narrow side street. Here, the buildings were clearly more dingy, many in a state of disrepair. Children of all ages ran and played in the streets, despite the traffic of wagons and drays. The scent of brewer's yeast grew stronger.

She indicated a row of two-story brick buildings. "The London Building Society put up this row of dwellings, but already the tenants have complained of countless problems. Partitions separating the individual dwellings are less than a full brick length, which leads to noise traveling through, not to mention the more serious problem of water leakage. Shoddy bricks are used, hollow ones which are cheaper, of course, but also ones that crumble easily over time."

She stopped in front of one dwelling, where rubbish was piled in the front. "No foundation has been laid, or worse, the existing gravel is hauled away and sold, and rubbish is used to fill the holes. You can imagine what happens over time."

"The building begins to sink."

"Yes. Many of these buildings were put up ten or twenty years ago when there was such a clamor for housing, and speculators bought up the land and quickly put up dwellings. It's only now that the problems are manifesting." She pointed to a roofline. "See how it sags? Too few scantlings in the rafters."

He smiled. "You seem as knowledgeable as a builder."

"I've learned over time. Our Society has put up some buildings in the last few years, and I wanted to be sure they would be sturdy and well-ventilated. We'll go there next, so you can compare the difference."

They turned a corner and the area became grimmer. Here, the houses were much older, their brick exteriors dilapidated. Several idlers lounged on the broken front stoops. Windows were boarded up. Piles of refuse filled the narrow, muddy street. Mr. Tennent stopped at the sight of a group of dirty-faced men standing nearby. "Perhaps we should turn back."

She hesitated. "Yes, I just wanted to show you how quickly the neighborhoods degenerate. Here, you see men who are habitually unemployed. The only activity is drinking." As she took a step back, she noticed one of the men eyeing her.

Before she could take another step back, he sauntered over to her. "Wot are the toff doin' in our neighborhood, I'd like to know?" He spat, just missing their feet by inches. His grimy shirt was pulled half out of his trousers and his vest was missing buttons. He carried a half-empty gin bottle in one hand.

Mr. Tennent took her lightly by the elbow and began to back away.

The man was quicker than he looked. He circled around them. "My, aren't we the fancies."

In a few seconds they found themselves surrounded by a group of ill-featured men. The acrid smell of sweat mingled with the pasty smell of yeast.

Mr. Tennent stopped and eyed them. "We didn't mean to intrude on your private turf, gentlemen," he said politely.

The man snapped his suspenders back and guffawed. "*Our* turf." He turned to the others. "How d'ye like that, eh? *Our* turf? That's wot hit is, awright." He swaggered up and took hold of one of Mr. Tennent's lapels. "I like the feel o' this coat. Feels pretty foine to me, hit does."

Alice began to pray silently. She eyed the rest of the men nervously.

Before she could decide what to do, the man flipped out a knife from his belt. Alice jerked back.

He brandished the knife before Mr. Tennent's face. "I think I'll have this coat." He brought the knife up to his jawline.

A soft cry escaped her lips. The sound distracted the man and he turned to her. "Foine lady we 'ave 'ere."

She shrank back and experienced an instant's reassurance as Mr. Tennent's hold on her arm tightened. Her fear returned as she realized how impossibly outnumbered he was.

The man's unshaven jaw came to within inches of hers, his foul breath fanning across her face.

She prayed even more.

Nick judged the distance between himself, the knife, and the malodorous fellow threatening Mrs. Lennox.

He pressed her elbow an instant to reassure her then moved a step. "Leave the lady alone, or aren't you man enough to face me?" he said, infusing his look and tone with scorn.

The man's attention swung immediately back to him, his stubbly cheeks deepening in color and his broken-toothed leer fading. "Why you—" The knife swung out, but Nick was ready for him. In a deft movement, he grabbed the man's bony wrist.

As he'd calculated, his hold wasn't as firm as it had appeared, the alcohol probably giving the man more confidence than warranted. Nick easily pulled his arm up and over, spinning him around and bending him double. The knife and bottle fell to the muddy ground. "Pick up the knife, Alice." Keeping his tone quiet but commanding, he held the man's arm up at a painful angle. Half-starved wretch. Nick had met many like him in his early days on the road.

With a push strong enough to put him out of commission until they left the area but not enough to seriously hurt him, Nick shoved him to the ground and kept a foot between his shoulder blades. He turned to Alice, relieved to find she had done as he'd asked. She held the knife as if it were a snake. He took it from her by the blade then brandished it slowly to the ring of men. "Anyone else care to have a go?"

They all backed away from him a few steps.

"We meant no disrespect entering your neighborhood. This lady runs a charity to build decent housing for men like you and their families."

The men began mumbling denials that they'd meant no harm and bowed to Mrs. Lennox.

One of the men shuffled his feet, not quite meeting Nick's eyes. "Charlie there was just sportin' wif you."

"Well, we'll call it even then." With his free hand, Nick dug into his pocket and fished out some coins, all the while keeping the knife pointed up. "Here, if anyone is in need of a hot meal." Was it a hopeless wish that they wouldn't spend it at the nearest tavern? But he couldn't leave them with nothing. He knew what it was like to be hungry.

They grouped around him eagerly and he made sure that each one got something. With a hand to the brim of his hat, he finally backed away from them, taking Mrs. Lennox firmly by the elbow.

When they arrived on Commercial Street with its busy traffic, he stopped and turned to her, only now allowing the tension to drain from him. "Are you all right?"

She brought a shaky hand to her cheek and gave a jerky laugh. "The question is, are you?"

Amazed that she could think of him, he glanced at the knife he still held upside down by the haft. "Remember, I'm armed now." He looked around him but seeing nowhere to dispose of the knife, he stuck it in his belt, under his coat. "I'll get rid of this when we're far from here."

"Yes, please do." Her voice sounded shaky.

He tipped her chin up with a fingertip, permitting

himself to study her face more closely. "Let me take you somewhere for a cup of tea."

Her eyes met his. "No… I'm quite…all right. Let me recover a moment." She took a step back and he let her go immediately, wondering if he had overstepped his bounds. "Do you think the hansom is still waiting for us?"

"Yes, I'm sure of it. Come, if you're up to walking a block further. We should get away from here, at any rate."

"Oh, yes." She immediately began to move. He hurried to catch up with her and put his hand on her elbow once again. She felt fragile beneath his light grip. He thanked God that they'd escaped the ugly situation. If anything had happened to her—

It was only then he recollected he'd called her Alice. Would she remember? Would she be offended?

She turned to him with a rueful smile. "I do apologize for bringing you here. It was not my intention to put your life in danger. You must think us far more uncivilized than Americans if as soon as you arrive you are threatened by a bunch of drunk idlers."

"It wasn't your fault." He frowned at her. "I'm more concerned that you should ever come to parts like this on your own."

"We usually come in groups. And I don't make it a habit of going into the worst neighborhoods, but as you can see, sometimes it's only a matter of turning down one street corner."

His brow knit, thinking of her exposed to such dangers in the course of her work.

"I'm still marveling at how quickly you disabled that man."

He was more amazed at how quickly she'd discounted the risk to herself. "It wasn't so difficult. He was drunk, as well as emaciated by hunger. His grip was actually feeble. Any able man could have disarmed him."

"Still, he had the knife, and he was surrounded by so many."

"I've met more than my share of poor unfortunates consumed by drink and hopelessness. I've learned it's often the ringleader one must disable and the rest prove harmless."

She gave a disbelieving laugh. "Have you been in many such situations before?"

"Some. But the same tactics often hold true in business."

They arrived at the hansom and he helped her up. As they rode away from the area, she turned to him. "You called me Alice back there."

She had noted it. He tried to read her expression. "I'm sorry. I suppose I wasn't thinking clearly at that moment."

"There's nothing to apologize for." She looked down at her lap. "In a way it seems we've known each other for a very long time, although in truth, we've barely had a chance to become acquainted."

He felt a spurt of hope. "Perhaps we shall have an opportunity now."

She smiled, the sweet, angelic, beautiful smile he remembered. "I feel we could be friends again," she said slowly.

She had said "friend." Did that mean there was hope of nothing more? He cleared his throat, hesitating. "Would you mind very much if I called you Alice…and you called me Nicholas—or Nick?" He waited, hardly realizing he held his breath.

"No." Her voice was whispery soft. "I'd like that."

"Very well… Alice."

The shy look in her eyes made her look seventeen again. "Pleased to renew the friendship, Nicholas."

He liked the sound of his name on her lips, even as he yearned for their friendship to deepen into something more. Had he waited too long? He found it a miracle—a godsend—that she was free after so many years. He didn't even care at the moment that her heart had been given to an idealistic young curate, if only there was the possibility of a future with her.

She was a woman like no other, and he was determined in that moment to make her his own.

"If you still have time, I'd like to show you some of the terrace houses we've built."

He blinked, disconcerted that her train of thought had taken a completely different turn "I thought after our run-in, we could go someplace for a cup of tea."

She chuckled. "Oh, I'm quite recovered now, thank you. Do you have time for one more visit, this time as far as Bethnal Green?"

She sounded so hopeful he didn't have the heart to turn her down. In truth, he had many pressing things to do at his office that morning, but at the moment, all he wanted was to prolong his time at this woman's side.

"Yes, of course. That is why I came, after all." Not the whole truth, but that could wait. He already felt the years slip away and much territory regained since he'd first met her. At her answering smile, he sat back, content for the moment to steal glances at her soft profile while the hansom bumped along.

Alice. Even her name mouthed in silence was nectar, and he savored the syllables on his tongue.

Alice took Nicholas—even pronouncing the syllables to herself caused a blush to steal over her—to the working class suburb just to the northeast of London. She waved to a line of two-story row houses along one side of a quiet street.

"Our society was responsible for this construction. They are four-room dwellings as you can see, with plenty of windows for ventilation." They walked down the paved sidewalk as she pointed out the features. "We used the latest construction methods, including plenty of running water and toilets—radical fixtures according to many, but why should the poor live with things the rest of us are taking for granted?"

She waited for his reaction, but he said nothing, appearing to study the plain facades.

"You see they are well-kept."

He nodded. "No rubbish in the streets." Children played on the pavement. A few stopped their game to stare at them.

Alice walked up to the door of one dwelling and rang the bell. "Let me see if Mrs. Brown is at home. Then perhaps you can see the inside of one of these."

A red-cheeked woman in her twenties, holding a baby in her arms, answered the door. A smile broke out on her face at the sight of Alice. "Oh, Mrs. Lennox, what a pleasure."

"Hello, Mrs. Brown. I have brought an old friend from America. I wanted to show him some of the houses the Society has built. Would you mind very much showing us your home?"

The woman moved inside. "Oh, not at all, madam. Come right in. Would you like a cup o' tea?"

"No, thank you, we don't want to trouble you."

The woman led them from a small front parlor to the kitchen at the rear of the house, where a toddler sat playing on the floor. She showed them a narrow back garden where a scullery was located. Then they climbed a staircase to the upper floor and ducked their heads into two small bedrooms, one facing the street, one facing the back.

Nicholas turned to Mrs. Brown as they walked back down the stairs. "How many children do you have living here with you?"

"Four, sir." She smiled proudly. "The two oldest be at school now. They'll be along shortly."

He nodded.

Alice smiled and held her hand out to the woman. "Well, thank you ever so much, Mrs. Brown." She tweaked the baby's cheek. "How big she's grown since the last time I saw her."

Mrs. Brown beamed. "Yes, that she 'as."

"How is your husband?"

"Oh, Jerry's ever so well. He found work at the railroad just up the road."

"Well, let me know if you need anything."

Nicholas shook her hand at the door. "Thank you for showing us your home."

"That's quite all right. We be ever so grateful to Mrs. Lennox for 'avin' put such a good roof over our 'eads."

They walked back down the steps. Alice chanced a glance at Nicholas's profile. He appeared deep in thought. So long accustomed to thinking of him as Mr. Tennent, his first name made her feel like a schoolgirl again, as if she were breaking the rules somehow.

"You can see the difference, can you not? Although both neighborhoods hold families earning very low wages, anywhere from eighteen shillings a week to twenty or twenty-one. And that is when they can find work. Mr. Brown, for example, was unemployed when I first met Mrs. Brown."

"How did you meet her?"

"I was working at a mission run by Miss Endicott, the lady I mentioned to you earlier. They offer food and temporary shelter to unemployed people."

He glanced at her. "This woman seems to have had a profound influence on you."

She tilted her head. "In a sense. I believe, more, that she offered me an outlet to make myself useful after I was widowed and had come back to London to live. Julian was my true inspiration."

He said nothing.

"He had a servant's heart. He wasn't afraid to go into any quarter where there was a soul in need." She sighed, feeling the familiar sense of unworthiness whenever she thought of him. "It was probably on such a mission of mercy that he contracted the tuberculosis that eventually killed him."

"You are carrying on his work."

It was a statement not a question, she realized. She pondered it as they made their way down the sidewalk past the row of terrace houses. "In a sense. Being his helpmate opened my eyes to the futility of my father's way of life."

He raised his eyebrows in question.

"Living to make a profit."

"You find that futile?"

"It's all Father ever cared about." She smiled sadly. "He suffered a heart attack a year ago and his work was over. There was nothing of it he could take with him. Julian's life, on the other hand, had a sense of eternal purpose."

"But your work would not go forward without the help of those whose purpose is to make a profit."

She pursed her lips. "I suppose you are right. But I'm glad I am not of their ranks."

He helped her back into the hansom and once he'd seated himself beside her, asked, "Where to now?"

Afraid she'd taken up too much of his time already, she laughed. "I imagine you have had enough of London neighborhoods. You can drop me off at the Society. Thank you for coming with me this morning." Once again his rescue filled her heart with relief and admiration. He had certainly come a long way from the secretary whom she'd taught tennis and horseback riding. The tables had somehow been reversed, and it was she who now felt in his debt.

"It was my pleasure. It was most informative. I was serious about making a donation. That's one of the reasons I've come back to London."

She looked down at her clasped hands, remembering his bravery. "You were very kind to those men back there. It was generous of you to give them something." She felt a deep sense of relief that he was not, after all, cut from the same mold as her father.

"It doesn't mean I believe in simply giving a handout. It's not the answer."

She nodded thoughtfully. "It depends on the individual case. In this case, it was generous of you, all the same."

When they reached her building, he accompanied her to the door. "Are you sure I can't take you somewhere for a cup of tea?"

She held out her hand with a smile. "Thank you, but no. There are things I need to do, and I've taken too much of your time already. I truly am grateful that you came with me today. Perhaps you can visit us again some time."

"I should like that, Alice." The words were spoken quietly, but the way he was looking at her made her think he meant more than merely a visit to the charity.

She inclined her head a fraction, wondering whether to leave the invitation open-ended or make it specific.

"You used to do that."

She smiled. "What?"

"Tilt your head like that. Like a wood nymph deciding if it wants to flicker its golden wings and flitter away."

She laughed, delighting in the fanciful imagery. "I never suspected you of being poetic."

"I'm not. It is only you who brings me to any flights of fancy."

Now, the look was unmistakable. She glanced away and tried to keep her tone light. "I'm surprised you remember such a detail about me."

"I remember a lot of things."

"Do you still play tennis?" she asked to change the course of the conversation.

"I do."

Her eyes widened.

"You find that surprising?"

"I suppose I imagined you too busy with your business to leave you any time for trivial pursuits."

"I have been. But I found the time to continue with the game. Don't forget, you were the one to challenge me to look beyond the world of finance." He grinned, erasing the years between them. "I wanted to be able to hold my own with you on the tennis court and on the chess board." He looked sheepish. "Did you know I even paid for extra tennis lessons when I returned to London?"

Her eyes widened. "You did? And I never knew…" She laughed aloud, feeling lighthearted all of a sudden.

He joined in her laughter.

Then she said on the spur of the moment, "Would you like to come back out to Richmond on a weekend? We could have a match. Or, a re-match, should I say?" Her smile faded. "I'm sorry. Perhaps that place holds unpleasant memories for you."

"Not at all. Why should it?"

"Because of your riding accident…and my father."

"No, I have no bad memories of Richmond." His voice was quiet, his gaze warm.

"I'm glad. Let me know when you'd like to come out."

"Would this weekend be too soon?"

It was too soon. Once again, apprehension filled her. Things were moving too quickly. But she found herself saying, "Not at all. The weather is too hot to stay in London anyway. We can take the train out. I like to get out of the city for Austen's sake."

"You said he was frail."

She looked away and nodded.

"Very well. This weekend then."

"We can ride out Friday evening if you'd like," she told him. "I generally take the five o'clock train out of Victoria. I shall invite Miss Endicott as well. I'd love for you to meet her."

"Very well. I'll meet you at the station." Once again, the look in his brown eyes said more. But she chose to ignore it as the fancy of a sixteen-year-old girl who no longer existed.

Chapter Eight

Nick walked back to his office with a buoyant step. He'd had a remarkably good morning in the company of Alice.

His steps slowed, remembering their brush with danger in that rundown quarter. He didn't like to think of her involved in such hazardous work. He wondered over this new friend of hers—Miss Endicott—who seemed to hold such influence over her.

These questions revolving in his mind, he arrived at his new London headquarters. He'd arranged to have it purchased through his London agent before he'd even stepped foot back on his native soil. The imposing gray granite office building was a suitable testimony to his years of toil. It overlooked the Bank of England and the Stock Exchange in the heart of the financial district. His gaze traveled farther down Threadneedle Street. Only a few blocks away was the office of Shepard and Steward, where he'd been forced to leave so dishonorably fifteen years earlier.

A pity, he could no longer show Mr. Shepard what

he'd lost in dismissing him. His ire rose anew at the thought of her father disinheriting Alice. How could a man with so special a daughter be so cold-hearted? And what of her brother? Hadn't he defended his sister's share of the business?

He turned slowly, glancing to the east, remembering again the encounter with the derelict man. Beyond the wealth represented by this financial district lay neighborhoods filled with men who'd been broken by adversity. Had the Lord sent him back to his homeland to do something with his wealth to help these men and women? Together with Alice to mitigate the circumstances of their lives?

Not one given to romantic notions, he believed in the blessings that came to those who worked hard. Nevertheless, he recognized his good fortune was also due to God's grace. Having achieved far above what he'd set out to, he wanted to put his money to good use in education and decent housing for those who were laboring the way his mother had.

His office's shiny brass plate winked at him: Tennent & Company, Ltd. He entered the building and let the door shut behind him, muting the traffic sounds and sunshine.

"Good afternoon, Mr. Tennent." Clerks greeted him as he walked past them and headed for the lift to his private office at the top.

His secretary, a young man who reminded him of himself so long ago, jumped up from his desk as soon as Nick entered the outer office. "Good afternoon, Mr. Tennent." He handed him a stack of papers. "I have the letters for you to sign. Mr. Paige stopped by and desires to make an appointment about the impending purchase of Bailey and Company."

Nick took the stack and began glancing through it. "Yes, arrange something for Thursday morning or afternoon. I may be leaving early on Friday."

"Yes, sir. Another appointment?"

"What?" He glanced up. "No, just leaving early for the weekend."

The clerk stared at him.

"What's the matter?"

"Oh, nothing, sir. I—just—you've never left early before. You're usually here later than most of us."

"Well, that is about to change." He carried the letters to his desk and picked up a fountain pen and began to sign the letters. He handed them back to the young man. "I want you to do something for me."

"Yes, sir." His secretary waited, the letters in his hand.

"I want you to find out everything you can about the firm Shepard & Steward, Ltd. Investments. I believe that is still the name of it. At least the name of Shepard will appear in it as the principal partner. Understood?"

The younger man gave a quick nod. "Very good, sir. I'll get on that right away."

"Assets, liabilities, the members of their board, you know the things I expect."

"Yes, sir."

"Dig deep. I want to know what they've invested in over the years."

The young man grinned, enjoying the painstaking work of investigation as much as seeing the accumulation of profits. Nick had chosen well.

When the secretary had closed the door softly behind him, Nick sat down at his desk chair and swiveled it around to stare through the slatted window blinds. The afternoon sun cast several buildings including the Bank of England in shadow. Beyond it rose the dome of St. Paul's Cathedral.

Nick's thoughts strayed from the sight to the things Alice had told him—or not told him—but which he'd observed in the few hours he'd been in her company.

He stroked a finger against his lips. The dangerous encounter today had had one benefit. It had allowed him to take a step closer to Alice—she'd accepted his friendship. Yet, for all her gratitude, he sensed a reserve in her that went deeper than that natural to a lady toward a gentleman of scant acquaintance. Her strange words came back to him, stunning him as much now as they had when she'd uttered them. "No matter how unlovable I might feel." How could such a beautiful, accomplished woman with every material advantage feel unlovable? He would have given her his whole heart if he could have. Instead, a poor young clergyman had been the one privileged to show her love.

Dear God, why? He didn't miss the irony. He'd left, thinking himself too poor to offer Alice anything; yet, she'd chosen a man probably more destitute…almost as if rejecting everything her father's world stood for.

Alice had forsaken all wealth to follow her heart. Nick had never known that kind of love, except for his mother's to his father.

Would Alice hold his wealth against him now?

By early Friday evening, however, Nick reclined in a tub of steaming water and smiled to himself, like a man replete after a full banquet. Perhaps he oughtn't to have felt this way, but he couldn't help himself.

He'd enjoyed the train ride from London in the company of Alice and her son. Any trepidation he'd had over the militant Miss Endicott had quickly dissolved upon meeting the lady. She'd proved an elegant, charming woman in her fifties who was clearly fond of Alice.

After some debate over suitable gifts, Nick had brought Austen a boy's adventure book and Miss Endicott a box of chocolates. Undecided between a bouquet of flowers or a luxurious box of chocolate bonbons for Alice, he'd finally settled on a book for her as well.

"It's the latest Sherlock Holmes tale," he said as she removed the brown paper wrapping in the train compartment.

"The Sign of the Four." She read the title on the cover and smiled at him across the seat. "Thank you. I enjoyed the first Holmes mystery and I'm sure I shall this one, too."

Austen sat close to his mother in the corner of the compartment during the ride, clutching his raggedy stuffed rabbit closely to his side.

As soon as they arrived at the Richmond house— looking little changed from fifteen years ago—they had separated to their rooms until dinnertime. Nick was shown to a spacious bedroom on the first floor. The masculine-furnished room with its four-poster mahogany bed was quite a contrast from his cramped, hot room under the eaves during his first stay in the house.

Now, soaking in the hot, scented water of the tub, he devised a strategy to follow over the coming two days the way he did when approaching the purchase of a company.

During the train ride, he'd questioned Alice some more about her years away from London. She'd spoken little about the time immediately following his departure, but had been quite effusive about her years at the parsonage. In retrospect, Nick decided he had one sole advantage over the late curate. Nick was alive. No lifeless memory could compete in the long run with a living, breathing person.

His spirits lifted as he thought of the coming weekend. He emerged from the tub and donned the evening clothes laid out by his valet.

He adjusted the gold cuff links in his starched white shirt as his valet tied his black bow tie. After helping him on with the jacket, the man gave his lapels a final smoothing down then stood back, giving Nick a full-length view of himself in the cheval glass.

Nick eyed himself critically. The black swallowtail coat and matching waistcoat fitted him well. His white shirt collar stood up stiffly around his neck. Would he pass muster before Alice? She who had grown up among the well-dressed?

Thanking his valet and giving him the evening off, Nick made his way downstairs. No one else was about as yet, so he wandered onto the terrace.

The evening air was a few degrees cooler than the heat of London. Nick glanced about him. The low table and comfortable sofa were still out here, in the same place they'd been when he and Alice had played that fateful game of chess. He could still remember the feel of her soft lips against his.

He sighed and went to lean his elbows on the wood balustrade. The tinkle of a fountain in the garden made a pleasant sound.

His thoughts drifted back to Alice. How would she view him now? Would she accept him fully into her circle? She had turned into the beautiful woman he'd envisioned. A wonderful mother as well. Unlike many women of her class who relegated their offspring to their nanny, she had seemed to enjoy her child's company.

He debated how soon he could express his feelings to Alice. Would she be ready to accept his suit? Would she ever be over her husband?

He had learned over the years to be patient, to bide his time. He knew how to keep his eyes on a company for many a year until the time came to approach the owner and make an offer that couldn't be refused. He also knew there were times when one had to be more aggressive and make a preemptive strike, buying out a company that in future could be unwelcome competition.

However, neither way seemed clear with Alice Lennox.

"May I join you out here, or do you prefer a few moments of solitude?"

Nick turned at the soft tones of Miss Endicott. Not Alice.

Hiding his disappointment, he gestured to the older lady. It wouldn't do to alienate Alice's friend and mentor. "Not at all. Please do."

Miss Endicott was a tall, slim woman, fashionably dressed in a soft gray evening dress. Her still-dark hair was coiled at the nape of her neck.

She stopped at the latticed balustrade and looked out at the quiet evening. "Refreshing after London, isn't it?"

"Yes."

They stood a few moments listening to the tinkle of cascading water and the chirp of crickets around them.

"Whenever I'm here, I wonder why I continue to live in London." A trace of humor underlay her quiet words.

"Why do you?"

"That is where my present interests lie."

He glanced sidelong at her. "You've influenced Mrs. Lennox in the direction of her interests as well."

"The Housing Society, you mean?" She considered. "Yes, perhaps to an extent, but she was already helping the needy long before. When she came back to London, after she was widowed, I suppose I thought it would help her to overcome her grief."

Had Alice been so grief-stricken at the loss of her husband? "Did you ever meet her husband?"

"No. I didn't know Alice until she returned to London four years ago." She looked down at her hands resting on the balustrade as if debating. "Alice seemed quite lost after Julian passed away, even though they both knew his death was imminent. He'd been ill off and on almost from the day she met him. But I think she kept denying it, even when he knew very well he wouldn't last long."

She gave a deep sigh before continuing. "When I first met her, she seemed a little like a child who doesn't understand why she's found herself alone again."

He looked sharply at her. "Again?"

Miss Endicott pursed her lips, musing. "I sometimes

think of Alice as a little girl looking for a loved one…
who's never quite been there for her."

Nick thought of Alice's lack of a mother and absent
father. "She never found it at home."

There was understanding in her eyes. "No."

But hadn't she found it with Lennox? The thought
was a bitter pill.

They remained silent a few more minutes. Then the
older woman looked at him. "You know, you're the first
gentleman Alice has invited out here to Richmond."

"Am I?" The calm words belied the impact of her
words. He cleared his throat. "Was Julian—I mean, Mr.
Lennox—never here?"

She gave a small laugh. "Oh, no. Mr. Shepard did not
approve of an impoverished curate for his only daughter." She leaned her back against the balustrade and
eyed him. "You must be very special."

He made a noncommittal sound, feeling once again
that he had no advantage over the penniless cleric.

"It takes a great deal of drive to have succeeded in
owning your own firm when you started out as a clerk."

He shrugged, unable to deny her appraisal or willing to accept any undue merit for his success. From
what she'd said already, his wealth would be viewed as
a liability in Alice's eyes. "A lot of work and the good
sense to know when to take the opportunities God has
given me are all the credit I can claim."

She nodded her head. "No false modesty. I like that."

"I have never learned the complexity of what passes
for conversation in polite circles."

She laughed. "Nor have I. I like a person who knows
his own mind and isn't afraid to speak it." She paused.

"It almost makes me hazard to ask you what your intentions are toward Alice."

The two stared at one another in the gathering dusk.

He considered. If anyone's blessing were necessary, he calculated it would be this woman's. Before giving himself time to draw back, he gambled on forthrightness. "Alice is the only woman who has ever meant anything to me. I want to marry her."

She blinked. "I see. You don't mince words."

"You said you appreciated directness." He looked away from her and toward the fountain. "The fact that I know what I want doesn't mean I don't acknowledge certain—hurdles."

"Julian."

The name reverberated in Nick's mind like a thousand ripples pushing him away from his goal. "Mrs. Lennox seems to have loved her late husband very much."

"Yes."

He glanced sidelong at Miss Endicott. The tone wasn't wholly affirming.

"There is love, and there is—" Again, she hesitated.

"Worship?"

She turned her eyes on him, as if assessing him. "I didn't know Alice then. I can only conclude from what I've heard from her that she feels a deep gratitude to him."

The words arrested his attention. "What do you mean, exactly?"

"I gather from Alice herself—the little she speaks of her past before Julian—that she was very unhappy growing up. And then her father sent her away. I don't know the reason, but it seems almost as if she was banished." She shook her head, "At a time when most girls are planning their coming out."

Nick's hold on the balustrade had tightened at the mention of her exile. Would this be one more thing to come between Alice and himself?

"Alice was very young and impressionable when she met Julian. And lonely. She had never really known a father's love. When she met Julian, I don't know how much was love and how much was a desire to be loved." She gazed onto the gardens as if looking into the past. "Whereas her father was a man consumed by his drive for money, Julian had no interest in material gain, not for himself at least, only to help those in need." She sighed. "Julian was about as far as she could go from her father's world."

Her words confirmed what Nick had already feared.

She turned back to him, her voice becoming brisk. "I don't know how much Alice has told you about me. I believe in the rights of women."

He smiled slightly. "Alice mentioned a few things…"

"I just say this in order to tell you that I've done my utmost since her widowhood to encourage Alice to be her own person. She never really had a chance to explore who she was since she left home. That is one reason I've persuaded her to take charge of this charitable work. It gives her something of her own."

"I see." The picture Miss Endicott painted for him gave him much to think about. Her next words surprised him even more.

"I would hate to see her give that up in a second marriage."

He met her look squarely. "I have no interest in clipping her wings."

She nodded. "Only a person strong enough in his own identity can allow another the freedom to fulfill hers. Just don't go too fast with her, that's what I suppose I meant to say when I came out here."

Before he could think of how to reply, they both heard a sound at the opened French doors.

Alice stood silhouetted against the lamplight within. He drew in his breath at how lovely she looked. She had changed out of her travel outfit into a deep blue evening gown. Nick allowed his gaze to travel over her slim figure. Her hair was drawn up high atop her head, with soft wisps framing her nape and temples.

"Am I interrupting something?"

Miss Endicott chuckled. "Not at all. Come and join us, my dear."

She took a few steps onto the terrace. "Dinner will be served in a little bit." She turned to Nick with a smile. "I've left Austen with Nanny Grove. Thanks to you, his head is filled with thoughts of pirates and mutiny on the high seas and buried treasure. I hope they don't keep him awake too long."

Miss Endicott moved toward the door.

Alice reached out an arm. "Oh, please don't leave on my account, Macey."

"I'm going to fetch my shawl. I'll peek in on Austen." She glanced at Nick with a friendly look. "It was lovely chatting with you."

He bowed. "The pleasure was mutual."

After Macey left, Alice turned to Nick, feeling unaccountably shy. It was almost as if it was the first time she'd really been alone with him since the evening they'd met. Maybe it was the fact of the semi-darkness or that they were both dressed in evening clothes. There was enchantment in the twilight air.

His handsome elegance took her breath away. She turned away abruptly, determined to bring her thoughts under control. "It was so nice that you could come today, Nicholas." It still felt oddly intimate to be pronouncing his Christian name aloud.

"Thank you for inviting me."

Casting about for something to say, she motioned to the gardens. "Shall we walk a bit before dinner is announced? I can show you some of the grounds, though—" she gave a jerky laugh "—not much has changed since you were last here."

He fell into step beside her. "I had little chance to see the grounds when I came with your father."

She wondered what his memory of those few days was, but didn't ask, afraid to resurrect her own feelings of that time. "There is one new thing. Father decided a few years back to dig a pond. He wanted to stock it with fish, but I think only the goldfish survived. Would you like to see it?"

"Lead the way."

Their footsteps crunched over the small pebbles of the path. Soon they reached the willow-lined pond and Alice led him off the path onto the grassy perimeter of the pond. "I remember the summer Father hired a crew of workers to dig the pond and landscape the area around it." She sighed. "A pity he hardly enjoyed it once it was stocked with fish."

The plop of a frog from the edge into the water broke

the stillness. They stopped as if by mutual consent. Nick turned to her. "Do you still have the tennis court?"

She smiled at him, relieved at the safe topic. "Oh, yes. I hope you are ready for that rematch."

His white teeth flashed in the gathering dusk. "Name the time and place."

"Tomorrow mid-morning?"

"I'll be ready." He stood so close she caught a whiff of his cologne, a sharp, fresh scent.

She took a step back. "Shall we return?"

"If you'd like."

She walked by him. He stood perfectly still until she had passed him, then followed silently in her wake.

She was relieved he didn't do anything to detain her. She compared his gentlemanly conduct with that of many of the gentlemen of her acquaintance, who were only too eager to "befriend" a lonely widow. She had grown adept at foiling all advances.

The thought of someone taking Julian's place had always filled her with repugnance. No one could be what he had been to her. Why then did she feel like the girl of sixteen drawn to her father's employee, an intense young man so wholly unlike Julian?

Nick walked outside again in the early morning before breakfast. He'd had trouble falling asleep the evening before, his thoughts troubled over Miss Endicott's words for a long time. He found it hard to reconcile the picture she painted of Alice with the poised and self-assured woman he'd seen thus far. What tormented him the most was what Miss Endicott had said about Alice's banishment. Had she had to pay an unreasonably high price for their innocent kiss?

Had he left her all alone to face her father's wrath?

Nick wanted to ask her what had happened when he'd left, but had already sensed a constraint in her since the evening they'd met again.

Without consciously thinking about it, he strolled along the same path Alice had led him the evening before and found himself back at the pond.

The early morning rays shot through the feathery willow fronds. Ripples in the dark surface attested to the presence of fish. He approached the edge of the water.

A sudden voice halted him.

"Now, you mustn't be afraid. Only babies are afraid."

Nick peered through the low branches of the willow tree to see Austen squatted by the edge of the pond. He had his stuffed animal in one hand and a toy sailboat in the other. He placed the boat into the water and then set the floppy rabbit atop it.

The animal wouldn't stay on and the boy fumbled to get it balanced on the narrow surface. "That's all right, Moppet, I've got you. No, you can't get off yet. Just a few minutes."

He let go and pushed the boat away from him. "There you go, Moppet, I told you you'd be all right. It's not so frightening anymore, is it?"

At that moment, the boat dipped a fraction to leeward and the rabbit plopped into the water. The boy gasped and reached his arm out. "Hold on, Moppet, I'll come for you."

But the rabbit drifted away, a few inches beyond Austen's reach.

Nick ducked under the willow boughs and reached his side. With a glance around, he spotted a broken stick. "Not to worry, we'll fish him out." He maneuvered the animal, which was beginning to sink, alongside the edge of the pond.

Austen immediately scooped up the soggy creature.

"A few hours in the sunshine and he'll be none the worse for wear," Nick said in reply to the boy's troubled look.

"Th—thank you," he whispered.

"Nothing to thank me for." Nick kept his tone casual, afraid the boy would run off. "Watch you don't let Moppet drip on you. Would you like me to carry him for you?"

The boy shook his head but heeded Nick's warning and held the animal farther out from his body.

Nick hunted around for a way to keep the conversation going. He was curious about Alice's son. "It's early to be out. Were you thinking of pirate ships this morning?"

Austen nodded.

Nick indicated the sailboat. "That would make a good pirate ship if you hoisted a skull and crossbones flag on it." He took the string up from the ground before the boat drifted off. As the boy watched him, he paid out more line until the boat was in the middle of the pond. "There's not enough of a breeze here, it's too sheltered by the trees. What we could do after breakfast, perhaps, is take her down by the river. Would you like that?"

The boy nodded, more vigorously this time.

"How about some breakfast first then?"

Austen stood up. Nick brought the sailboat back into shore and lifted it out of the water. "Come along then. You put Moppet out to dry on the terrace and maybe he'll be ready to go with us after breakfast."

Austen skipped ahead of him. Nick watched the light blue sailor suit disappear around a bend and felt a pang. He could have had a son like that. Where had the years gone? All he'd known was work. He'd allowed little to sidetrack him from his goal. Well, he'd reached his goal and found it wasn't enough.

Macey served herself to some sausage from the sideboard and set down the silver tongs. "I like your gentleman."

Alice looked up from the array of breakfast dishes. "I beg your pardon?"

Her friend filled her plate with eggs and broiled tomatoes before replying. "I said I approve of your Mr. Tennent. He strikes me as a man who knows what he wants."

Alice felt an immediate dislike of Macey's description. It made Nick sound too much like her father. "Mr. Tennent isn't mine. I'm sure he'd be the first to tell you that. We met very briefly years ago, and I was so glad to see him again, to see that he'd achieved what he'd set out to do. I always felt badly that Father had been such a difficult employer."

Macey chuckled. "Excuse me, my dear, I didn't mean to imply that you had any but friendly interest in Mr. Tennent."

Even as Alice searched the older lady's expression for irony, she continued. "I was very impressed with him. I had a nice conversation with him before dinner, and of course, during. It was a very pleasant evening all in all." Macey shook her head. "It is hard to picture him from his humble origins."

"Yes, I'm still overwhelmed by what he has become. He told me once that his mother was a governess, so I'm sure she gave him a good foundation in learning and manners."

"Ah, that would explain it." Her friend seated herself at the table. "May I pour you a cup of tea?"

"Yes, please." Alice finished serving herself and joined Macey. "He wasn't with Father's firm very long." She looked down, fingering her knife. She'd never told the other woman about her friendship with Nicholas. "Father wasn't very fair to him when he had a riding accident." At the look of inquiry on the other woman's face, she nodded toward the window. "It happened right here at Richmond. It was really my fault." She proceeded to recount the horseback riding incident to her.

"Goodness, my dear, it certainly wasn't your fault. You behaved very responsibly. Victor should have been horsewhipped for instigating such a thing."

"I agree." She shook her head bitterly. "Father wouldn't even send him away. Instead, he ended up firing Mr. Tennent when he couldn't perform his work." That wasn't the whole truth but she couldn't talk about the rest. It was too private and too painful a memory.

Macey set down her fork and knife and pondered. "The last time I saw Victor, he was at the Goodwins' house party right before the Derby. He was showing off his new wife as if she'd been one of the fillies."

"Yes, he's married now and has two children. He's been my solicitor since Julian passed away. Geoffrey recommended him to me, though my insignificant affairs are hardly worth his trouble."

Alice stirred her tea then blinked at the sight of Nicholas and Austen entering the room together, her son actually smiling up at the man. It gave her a pang. Julian should have been walking into breakfast with his son. She strove to keep her tone cheerful for Austen's sake. "Good morning, you two. Where have you been?"

"Mr. Tennent is going to take me to the river to help me sail my boat after breakfast." With those words, Austen walked over to the sideboard and began surveying the food, as if he'd said the most normal thing in the world.

With a quick look at Nicholas, Alice rose and handed her son a plate. "Is that so?"

Nicholas came over to them and picked up a plate of his own. "I met Austen at the pond this morning. Unfortunately, there was no breeze for him to sail his boat."

She drew her brows together. "Austen, dear, I've told you you mustn't go to the pond by yourself."

Austen hung his head. "I forgot, Mama."

Not wanting to scold him in front of others, she spooned some eggs onto his plate. "Well, I'm glad Mr. Tennent found you." She turned to Nicholas, grateful that he'd been there. "Thank you for taking care of my son. He doesn't realize how dangerous a large body of water can be."

"Doesn't he know how to swim?" he said in an off-hand tone as he helped himself to the array of food.

She felt a prickle of defensiveness at the question. "No, he's only seven." She lifted her chin a notch. "I never learned myself."

"I'm amazed. You were so accomplished at all sorts of sports."

"I spent all my time away at school and there was no appropriate place. The river's current here is too swift."

"Of course. I didn't learn until I was an adult." Nicholas turned to Austen and winked. "Would you like to learn to swim? There's nothing more fun than swimming, not even sailing."

Austen stared up at Nicholas and slowly nodded his head. Alice noted how similar their shade of deep brown hair was and she felt a catch in her throat. Neither Julian's nor her hair color was as deep a brown. Austen had inherited his paternal grandmother's dark, rich sable shade.

"Good. This is the right time of year." He continued serving himself. "I remember how sumptuous your breakfast fare seemed to me the last time I came out here."

The words distracted her from the notion of how Nicholas proposed to teach Austen to swim. "Did it really?"

"Oh, yes, I'd never seen anything like it."

Macey offered Nicholas tea or coffee.

"Coffee, thank you. A custom I got used to in America."

Alice listened to them chatting, still surprised at how well her friend and Nicholas were getting along. She encouraged Austen to eat. At the moment he seemed too interested in listening to Nicholas. It was the first time she'd seen him interested in anyone besides herself and his nanny. She wondered how this man had succeeded in enthralling both her son and friend in such a short time. Macey was very particular in her acquaintances, shunning most of Alice's set, and Austen… Alice frowned, not liking to dwell on her son's shyness, which seemed extreme at times.

As they were finishing up their breakfast, Nicholas turned to her. "Do you think we could postpone our tennis match until after our sailing expedition?"

She smiled with an effort, realizing it was good for Austen to have a male friend. "Of course. Where are you two planning to go?"

"To the river. We can go to the boat landing."

Alice forced herself to relax. She knew she tended to be overly protective of Austen but he was all she had left. "There's a strong current at the river. Are you sure that's a good idea?"

"Oh, don't worry, I'll keep a close eye on Austen."

She felt torn. "It's just that I know how little boys are. You need to watch them all the time."

"Why don't you come along with us, then?"

She smiled gratefully. He seemed to understand. "Yes, I should like that."

"I promised Austen we'd go right after breakfast. Is that all right?"

"Yes. Why don't we meet at the front of the house in ten minutes?"

Nick handed the line to Austen. "Hold on tight, if you let her go, she might end up all the way in London."

The little boy looked at him with alarm and Nick couldn't stop from reaching out and ruffling his dark hair. With the exception of the darker shade, it was as straight and silky as his mother's.

"Don't worry, if that should happen, we'd send out a search party." He winked across Austen's head to Alice, who stood beside her son. She was looking particularly fetching in her wide hat with a gauzy yellow ribbon fluttering in the light breeze. She wore a light muslin dress in a matching shade of yellow and held a frilly parasol in one hand. "I assume you have some sort of launch here we can use on the river."

She motioned to the pair of flat-bottom boats tied up at the side of the landing. "Yes, these punts are ours."

"You see there? No cause to worry." He steadied Austen's hand on the line. "All right, bring her in a little. See that boat coming downstream? We don't want her to run into it."

A party of summer residents was rowing toward them, their laughter floating over the water.

Alice's hand came onto her son's shoulder. "I see the steamer coming. You must move back."

Nick turned in the direction she was indicating. The large steamship bringing passengers from London was churning the water far downstream. "It's coming on the other side. I think we'll be all right here."

"I don't know, it creates quite a wake as it passes," Alice murmured, worry in her tone.

"We'll move back then." Nick squatted down and helped Austen bring in his boat.

The noise of the paddlewheel grew. When the steamship passed by them, Nick waved and Austen followed suit. The young boy laughed when the passengers crowded along the deck waved back. Nick turned to him in surprise. It was the first time the boy had behaved so spontaneously.

"They don't know us! Why are they waving?"

"People like to wave at strangers when they pass them from a train or ship. Haven't you ever waved at people from a train window?"

He shook his head.

"Well, then next time you can do it."

When the steamer had passed and the water became quiet again, Austen let his sailboat back down into the water.

"Watch it, Austen," his mother cautioned as he bent far over the landing. "Don't lean so far out."

"It's all right, I've got him." Nick was crouched beside the boy.

Alice smiled at him ruefully. "I'm sorry. I just worry."

"It's natural, I suppose," Nick said.

"Do you think Moppet will be dry when we get back?"

Nick squeezed Austen's shoulder gently. "I don't know. He may need all afternoon after the dunking he took."

"Do you think we could put him on the boat next time?"

"I think we could tie him on. That way he'll be sure to stay on. He might get a little damp from the spray, but he can always dry off again in the sun."

Austen nodded and continued his focus on his sailboat.

Nick found himself enjoying the time as much as the boy. It had been eons since he'd played. He remembered sailing a boat fashioned out of old newspapers. Austen's was an expensive wooden boat, detailed down to the view inside the cabin of the pilot's seat. But the experience was the same, he realized. Pretending to be commanding a sailboat over the seas.

He glanced up at Alice, who was watching them. As their eyes met, he smiled. She returned the smile but then quickly glanced back at her son.

Nick reminded himself to go slowly with her. Like a butterfly ready to take flight, she seemed as unreachable as she had fifteen years ago.

Chapter Nine

Nick cut quite a dashing figure on the court. No longer the shabbily-garbed secretary, now he looked equally at home on the court in his light-colored flannels and white shirt as on the dance floor in his evening clothes.

Alice gripped her tennis racket in two hands, ready to sprint to either side of the lawn. The ball flew over the net, and she ran backward to the end of the court and reached it just in time to send it back. It forced Nicholas to sprint toward the net in time to volley it back.

The game had begun gently but soon heated up. Alice marveled at what a competent—and competitive—player Nicholas had become since his first lesson so many years ago. She was hard pressed to keep up with his powerful serve and was already panting with the effort of running back and forth across the grassy court in her long skirt.

Again the ball sped across the net, in a low, powerful thrust. She returned it with a backhand swing and watched in satisfaction at the nice low arc she'd achieved. Nick's racket connected with it and it bounced back. Alice rushed across the court.

She swung her racket, but wasn't in time to hit the ball. Nick's friendly voice came across the court. "Good try."

She shrugged and smiled. "I'm not defeated yet." She picked up the rubber ball and returned to the far end of the court. Swinging her arm overhand, she called out, "Thirty-forty," and sent the ball across the court.

It was a good serve. She watched as the ball skimmed just over the net to the other side of the court. Nicholas slammed it back across and once again Alice dashed to the net to volley it back.

Back and forth it went until she missed it again.

"Game," he called out.

She wiped her forehead with a hanky from her skirt pocket and approached the net. The two shook hands. "You've come a long way since that first game."

His grip was firm and warm and he returned her smile. "That first teacher of mine was very patient. I never forgot her words of advice."

She wrinkled her brow. "What words were those?"

"That exercising my body would aid my mind."

She laughed, surprised and gratified that he should remember the words of a schoolgirl. "Well, I am glad I told you something useful at any rate."

His smile faded. "You told me a lot of things I remember."

She felt her face flush and patted her handkerchief over her cheeks. "Would you like something cool to drink?"

"Yes, I could use something refreshing."

They walked off the court and took seats on the wrought-iron chairs under the shade of a tree. His white shirt was unbuttoned at the collar, exposing his tanned throat, and his sleeves rolled up. He looked more at ease than she'd ever seen him, like a man comfortable with himself. She poured them each a glass of cold lemonade which had been brought out to them.

He patted his own forehead with a handkerchief. His dark hair was damp against the edges of his skin. "Thank you," he said taking the glass she gave him.

She took a sip from her glass and gave a nervous sounding laugh. "I must say that you gentlemen have the advantage over us ladies in playing the game. You can run all you want over the court and not fear stumbling. We, on the other hand, have the encumbrance of our skirts."

"It's amazing you can run across the court at all. At least you are not so heavily clad as many women."

"Yes, I wear my skirt above the ankle." She found herself wondering how many women he had played tennis with. "Do you play tennis often in America?"

"Not as often as I'd like."

"Is there a club where you play?"

"Yes."

"Are there many members?"

"Yes, it's a popular club."

"Do many women play tennis in America?" There, she'd asked as directly as she could. It shouldn't have mattered, but it did.

"Oh, yes, women are very sporty in America. They've taken up tennis with a will even though the game is much newer there than here."

"Do they play well?"

He regarded her over the rim of his glass before setting it back down, and she wondered how transparent she was being. "As I said, their progress is hampered in large part by the heavy clothing they wear. I don't know how more don't expire of heat prostration. I rarely play mixed doubles, preferring to play with a few of my male acquaintances who are very competitive at the game." He glanced away. "It helps keep me on my toes."

She smiled, feeling more comfortable. "I noticed your—ahem—competitive streak."

His gaze flickered back to hers. "I admit, when I play I play to win. I don't see much point in it otherwise."

Her smile deepened. "There is the benefit of exercise."

"I know, yet what makes the game exciting for me is to win." He shrugged, looking away again, as if uncomfortable. "It may be a failing of mine to want to win. I don't play with those I consider inferior to me. It would give me no pleasure to beat someone who wasn't a worthy opponent. That's why there are only a few I bother to play with."

She laughed nervously. "If I'd known that, I wouldn't have been so bold to play against you."

His brown eyes met hers immediately. "That was different."

She cocked her head to one side. "How so?"

"You are a woman, for one thing, and well…you first introduced me to the game." His lips curled up at one end. "Besides, you are a formidable player, despite your long skirts."

"I don't know whether to be insulted or flattered."

She removed her straw hat with the narrow round brim and fanned herself. "I must confess, I have made some concessions in my attire. Besides, my shorter skirt I—" she lowered her voice "—I refuse to wear a corset to play. But it's a deep, dark secret, for if anyone should know, I would be excluded from any respectable tennis club, including Wimbledon."

She could feel her skin coloring under his scrutiny but his tone was light when he replied. "Well, you may rest assured I shan't let it be known."

His steady gaze hadn't left her face and she wondered why she'd told him such a thing. Just like fifteen years before when she'd dared him to kiss her, he brought out something uninhibited in her. "Sometimes, I feel as if we had seen each other only yesterday."

"You at least haven't changed outwardly."

She found herself blushing again. "Thank you, sir. I know it is mere flattery, but a lady of my age appreciates such remarks all the same."

His dark eyes remained serious. "I only spoke the truth. You appear as young as you did at—what was it you told me so emphatically? 'Almost seventeen'?"

She laughed. "I was desperate to grow up back then."

They sat in companionable silence, sipping their drinks. She felt at more peace than she usually did in London. "I want to thank you for taking time with Austen."

"You needn't thank me for something that gives me pleasure."

"Not everyone—especially a man busy with his affairs—would take the time with a young boy, especially one as shy as Austen."

"Perhaps he just hasn't had the opportunity to be brought out of his shell."

She rubbed the sweat beads on her glass, feeling on guard once again. "His childhood must seem very different from yours."

He emptied his glass in one long swallow, during which Alice found her gaze riveted to the strong contours of his neck. He set his glass down. "It is, yet those differences are more superficial than anything." A faint smile crossed his lips. "Boys will be boys."

"Do you—" it was hard for her to formulate the thought "—think he is too...timid?"

He seemed to be evaluating her question and she was grateful for that, unlike her brother and other well-meaning gentlemen, who were quick to point out all they thought was wrong with Austen.

Just as Nick had years earlier, he seemed to take her concerns seriously. "He is timid, but then lots of boys are at that age. He just needs to gain confidence in himself and his abilities. In the right atmosphere, surrounded by the right people, he'll do that, in his own time and way."

She poured him another glass of lemonade, as she pondered his words. "Do you think he's surrounded by the right people? I'm afraid sometimes I want to shield him too much." She set the pitcher down, afraid to meet his gaze as she said the last.

"You're his mother, that's your prerogative. I think any boy would be privileged to have you as a mother."

Her eyes locked with his. There was something unmistakably tender in both his look and tone.

He cleared his throat. "I wanted to ask your permission, actually, about something concerning Austen."

"Yes?" Wariness tinged her voice and she had to force herself to relax.

"I was thinking of taking him on a treasure hunt. You know, since you were reading him the book about pirates."

She smiled in relief. "Oh, yes! What precisely would you do?"

"Well, I could draw up a map, using the property around here and its landmarks. We could make a morning or afternoon of it. I'd bury a little chest somewhere."

"Oh, it sounds delightful. Perhaps we can walk into town after lunch and look for a chest and some treasure."

"Yes, I thought about that." He grinned ruefully. "I'll probably have to go by myself, however, since you need to stay and distract Austen."

She smiled. "Of course. I'd been meaning to ask you if you'd like to accompany me to church tomorrow morning."

He didn't hesitate. "Of course."

"Would you like to go the chapel you attended before?"

His glass stopped halfway to his mouth. "Have you ever been there?"

She shook her head. "No, but I remember how I wanted to visit with you. We never had the opportunity."

"No, we never did." He continued regarding her and she looked away, remembering the end of that day.

He set the glass back down with a clink. "We can go tomorrow if you still wish to. I don't mind accompanying you to your church. I attended a number of different churches in America and found that God's presence in them had more to do with me than with the different buildings I was in."

She stared at this man who had made such an impression in a few short days so long ago and now again was amazing her with his insights. How many things he must have done since she'd last seen him. He made her feel as if she'd done very few brave things in her life, except for marrying Julian. How had she ever broken away from convention?

Nick watched Austen's face from the moment he entered the breakfast room the next morning, wanting to see when the boy noticed the map set beside his plate.

Alice looked up from her place at the table. "Good morning, darling."

"Good morning, Mama." The little boy glanced from his mother to Nick. "Good morning, Mr. Tennent."

"Good morning, Austen. How did you sleep?"

Nick had to strain to hear his low tone as the boy looked down. "Fine, sir."

"Anymore dreams of pirates?"

The boy's dark eyes came up. "No, sir."

"Pity." Nick said nothing more, but picked up his knife and fork.

The little boy carried his stuffed rabbit with him to his chair. First he set down the animal to one side, then as he moved to push his chair out, his gaze stopped at the roll of paper held with a string.

Nick's gaze darted to Alice. She, too, was watching her son. As if sensing his focus, she looked at him, and he winked at her. She gave him a barely discernable smile, and the two went back to pretending they were in the middle of their breakfast.

"What time should we leave the house?" he asked Alice.

"I was told the service begins at half-past nine. We should be all right if we leave at a quarter past. The chapel is a short walk from here in Richmond."

Austen had taken up the worn looking paper, unfurled it and untied the string. He was studying the map intently now. When he looked at his mother, a frown marred his brow. "What's this?"

"What's what, dearie?" His mother looked up from her plate.

He waved the paper. "This. It looks like a—map."

Alice reached out her hand. "Let me see it, Austen dear."

The boy brought the paper over to his mother.

She held it in her two hands and studied it, her coppery brown head bent over it, close to Austen's deep brown locks. "Hmm. It looks to me like—" she paused dramatically "—a treasure map."

Austen's eyes widened. "A treasure map!"

A sense of pleasure pervaded Nick at the thought that he had brought about the boy's wonder. The feeling left him bemused. He was used to dealing with business transactions in the hundreds of thousands of dollars, yet he was as anxious as a schoolboy to see how Austen would react. Is this what fatherhood was like?

Alice met Nick's gaze. "Why don't you take a look, Nicholas, and see if my guess is correct?"

"Certainly." He took the paper, which he had creased

repeatedly to make it appear soft and worn looking, and spread it out on the table. He'd spent part of last evening with pen and ink drawing a detailed plan of the grounds around the house after having spent most of the afternoon looking for a good hiding place for the chest he'd purchased. After poring over it for a few minutes, he looked back up at Austen and then at Alice. "I think your mother is right."

Austen's dark eyes grew rounder. Then his mouth split open in a wide grin. "A treasure map! Do you really think so?"

He nodded. "It certainly appears to be. See the black X here?" He pointed with his forefinger. "I would say pirates usually mark the location of their treasure in that fashion, wouldn't you say so?" He looked to Alice.

"Oh, yes, I have heard it so. In fact, in all the pirate stories I've ever read, it's been that way. X marks the spot."

The boy's head was bent over the paper. "And look, this is our pond."

He followed Austen's forefinger. "Yes, you're right. The willow trees are surrounding it."

"Do you think this is our house?" His little finger pointed at another object.

"Well, it certainly looks like this house."

Now Austen looked from one adult to the other. "This map means there's a treasure buried near our house!"

Austen's large brown eyes stared up at him, enthralled by something it had taken Nick a moment to think of and only a few hours to put into place. He could see Austen wanted to ask him something but held back.

He decided to make it easier for him. "Would you like us to go on a treasure hunt together?"

Austen turned to his mother and at her nod he turned his eyes back to Nick and nodded his head. "Yes, please." The words came out in a whisper.

"But first we must go to church," Alice told him.

"But we can go immediately after church," Nick said with a wink.

Austen gave him a big-toothed smile, revealing one adult tooth that had grown in and another which was only halfway in. "All right."

"Now, come and finish your breakfast," said Alice. "We don't want to be late."

Nick rolled the map back up and handed it to Austen. "Here you go, you might want to study it a bit more while you eat breakfast."

He took the map and continued looking at it as he walked slowly back to his place.

Nick sipped his coffee, content to watch Austen flatten the map under his mug of milk and his napkin ring.

"Austen, dear, finish your porridge."

The boy obediently took a spoonful, his eyes still fixed on the map. Nick smiled, unexpectedly looking forward to the afternoon's treasure hunt.

Nick enjoyed the service at the chapel. He was gratified that Alice had suggested going to his church.

He glanced at Alice over Austen, who walked between them. The three of them could have been a family. Maybe, soon they would be. He found himself wondering if Alice would ever want more children of her own.

"When can we go on the treasure hunt, Mr. Tennent?" Austen looked up at him under the brim of his straw hat.

Alice answered for him. "Right after lunch, sweetheart."

"Are we going to eat right away?"

She smiled. "Yes, I imagine so. Church has a way of making people hungry."

As they approached the iron gates at the bottom of the drive, Nick noticed a carriage pulled up in front of the brick mansion. Alice's footsteps slowed. "That looks like my brother's carriage. He and his wife sometimes come here for the weekend although I didn't expect them on a Sunday."

She quickened her step slightly and walked up the gravel drive.

Nick wasn't sure how he felt about seeing more of Alice's family. He'd seen Geoffrey only a handful of times at her father's office, but had never been formally introduced. He doubted the man remembered him.

When they entered the house, they heard voices immediately, coming from the rear.

"It sounds like they're on the terrace. Come, Austen, let's say hello to Uncle Geoffrey and Aunt Wilma." Alice took the boy's hand when he seemed to hang back.

Two couples stood on the wide porch, drinks in hand, talking and laughing. Nick recognized Geoffrey Shepard immediately, although the man had grown stouter and his light brown hair was gray at the sideburns. Nick stopped abruptly in the doorway when his eyes fell on the other man.

Victor.

The man stood as cool and self-assured as he had fifteen years ago when he'd played such a dirty trick on Nick.

Nick wasn't sure what he was feeling at the sight of the man who'd ultimately precipitated the course of action that had taken Nick away from England and across the Atlantic for so many years.

Victor's attention had gone from Alice to himself, the careless smiling fading, replaced with an insolent look which appraised Nick from top to bottom.

Alice leaned up and gave her brother a kiss on the cheek. "Geoff! I didn't expect to see you here this weekend."

"Hello, Allie." Her brother returned the quick embrace in a perfunctory manner. "That's because I didn't expect to be here, but Wilma was complaining of the heat and we decided to head out for the day."

One of the ladies sauntered closer. "And then Vic and I decided to tag along and make it a party. But we didn't know you had guests of your own." Her dark eyes swept over Nick and came back up to look boldly into his eyes.

"Oh." Alice's voice slowed as she contemplated the two of them. "I suppose we had the same idea." She turned back to her brother, her voice assuming its customary poise. "Geoffrey, I don't know if you remember Mr. Nicholas Tennent. He used to work in Father's firm."

Shepard lifted his prominent chin a notch and scrutinized Nick. "No, can't say that I do." He took a step forward and held out his hand. "Geoffrey Shepard, pleased to meet you. In what capacity did you work?"

Nick returned his look with a level stare. "I was your father's secretary for a few weeks."

The man paused for a fraction before releasing Nick's hand. "I see." As he turned away from him, he pursed his full lips. "Tennent, Tennent, the name sounds vaguely familiar."

Victor chuckled, approaching them. "You've probably heard my story of how Tennent here thought he could ride and took your old horse Duke out. Turns out it was the first time he'd ever sat on a saddle!"

The group erupted in laughter. Nick clenched a hand, restraining his inclination to wipe the smug smile off Victor's clean-shaven face. His glance flickered to Alice to see if she, too, remembered the account that way. Her eyes met his and he saw with relief that she was the only other one who had not joined in the laughter. Instead her blue eyes looked pained—and seemed to be entreating him.

He turned back to Victor Carlisle. His erstwhile rival was no longer a youth but had matured into a good-looking man in his mid-thirties, by Nick's calculation. His black hair was raked back from a high forehead and his gray-blue eyes challenged Nick to dispute the account.

"You were the one?" Shepard's tone held amazed disbelief. "Well, I never… At any rate, it looks like you survived." He took a sip of his drink. "Actually, I don't believe that's where I heard your name. You haven't any connection to Tennent & Company, do you? A distant family member?"

"I own the firm."

Shepard drew his thick eyebrows together, eyeing him sharply. "You don't say." He shook his head. "Funny I've never run into you before."

Alice stepped next to Nick. "That is because Mr. Tennent has been residing in America He's only recently returned."

"That explains it. I've heard a few things about your company."

"All naughty, I hope." The lady who had been watching Nick the whole time moved a step closer and smiled at him.

"This is Victor's wife, Cordelia," said Alice quietly.

Nick shook hands with her. Victor's wife held his hand a moment longer than was polite and gave him a coy smile. "You must tell me more about that horse ride." She glanced at her husband who was refilling his glass. "I'm sure there's more to the story than Vic is telling us."

He removed his hand from hers. "It happened so long ago, I hardly remember the particulars."

Alice touched him lightly on the elbow. "And this is Geoffrey's wife, Wilma." He turned with relief to the nondescript, prematurely stout woman with a haughty expression in her light blue eyes.

Mrs. Carlisle sidled back up to him. "If you've been with Alice, I assume you've been to church and must be parched. What will you have to drink?" She waved her glass in front of him. "Some champagne as the rest of us are drinking?"

"Thank you, no. I believe I'll wait for lunch."

Alice smiled at them, although her manner seemed unnaturally subdued. "We were just going in to luncheon. We have some plans for the afternoon." She looked toward Austen and smiled.

"Hello there, Austen." Victor went over to him and patted him on the head. "Cat got your tongue?"

The boy moved his head away from Victor's hand.

Alice put an arm around her son and propelled him toward Shepard. "Say hello to your uncle and aunt."

Austen did as his mother instructed, holding out his hand like a little gentleman.

Miss Endicott arrived just then and the company moved into the dining room. Nick noticed that Alice allowed Austen to remain with them at the table.

The group exhibited the high spirits due to drink and hardly included Nick in the conversation. Miss Endicott sat beside him and addressed him from time to time, but he found he preferred to observe Alice in this milieu. He'd made it a habit over the years to assess the terrain before making a move. It usually worked as well in business as in the social arena.

By the time luncheon was over, however, he'd drawn his conclusions. They were no different than most of what passed for society in San Francisco. Wealthy husbands bored with their own wives' society and wives who enjoyed spending their husbands' money and whose conversation consisted of empty-headed gossip and the planning of amusements.

He'd also had enough of observing Victor singling Alice out, while his wife kept Nick in her sights.

Austen had spent most of the luncheon hour playing with his food. Nick felt sorry for the boy and as soon as they had risen, he walked over to him. "All ready for the hunt?"

The boy nodded vigorously and went to tug on his mother's hand.

"Just a moment, sweetling."

Victor, noticing, asked with a smile, "Where do you want your mama to take you?"

The little boy looked down at his feet. "Some place."

"You must speak up, little fellow, if you want to be heard." His taunting chuckle gave Nick another desire to slug him.

Alice came to the boy's rescue. "Oh, it's just a little outing the three of us had planned."

Victor forgot the boy as he turned to Alice. "Oh, what a shame. I really was hoping to see you this afternoon."

"Oh?"

All mockery left his features and he said in a serious tone. "I needed to talk to you about something."

"Oh, what?"

"Well, it's private. As your solicitor."

She frowned. "Can't it wait until tomorrow? I can come by your office in the morning."

Nick strained to hear their words. What did Vic need to talk to her about?

He shook his head. "I'm afraid I'm all tied up tomorrow."

Her glance went from Austen to Nick and back to Victor as if helpless to know what to do. "In that case…" She turned to Austen. "Perhaps you can wait a moment, darling. Mama must see Mr. Carlisle for a few minutes."

Nick had had enough. Couldn't she see the man was deliberately putting her in a bind? "Why don't I take Austen along with me this afternoon? You go on with your business and Austen and I will have our adventure."

She bit her lip, again looking at her son. "I so wanted to go with you."

Nick cleared his throat. "It's all right. Come along, Austen. We'll have a grand time."

He was rewarded by Austen's wide smile.

Nick glanced at Alice. "We'll be fine."

She looked torn. "If you're sure…"

He held out his hand to Austen. "We'd best be going. We don't want anyone else to find it, do we?"

At the boy's look of alarm, he added, "You still have the map?"

The boy patted the side pocket of his sailor shirt and nodded.

"Good. You never know who might want to steal it. Come along."

Austen put his warm hand in Nick's. He enfolded it in his own, feeling the vulnerability in the small fingers that wrapped themselves around his. "We'll be back later this afternoon."

"Very well."

He tried to give her a reassuring smile, but he was feeling none too happy himself. The afternoon he'd planned with such care and thought had just been altered in the space of a few seconds. His mouth firmed in a grim line. By the same man who'd interfered with his life in such a malicious way fifteen years ago.

Taking hold of the boy's hand, he said, "Come along, treasure awaits." With more confidence in his tone than he felt, he left the house.

Once on the back lawn, he turned to Austen. "Let

me see the map." He unfurled it and pretended to study it. "See, this is where we are. Now, if I'm reading this correctly, we must head south from this point…"

He had no great confidence in himself to entertain a shy, seven-year-old boy for the time it would take to find the buried treasure. He'd deliberately made the hunt challenging, even going off the property, because he'd wanted this to be a whole afternoon outing for the three of them. Well, it was not to be. He'd have to swallow his disappointment and hope for a quiet evening with Alice when he returned. By then her brother and his guests should have tired of the country.

A burst of laughter from the dining room threw that hope to the wind.

Chapter Ten

Alice turned around when she heard footsteps, but it was only a servant coming to light the lamps in the drawing room. Where could Nick and Austen be?

"I'm sure they'll be along soon."

She turned on the sofa to Macey's soft tone beside her. "I know." She had thought Nick would be gone an hour, two at most, and then come marching triumphantly back with Austen holding a treasure in his hands.

But it had been—she glanced at the glass-domed clock on mantelpiece—five hours. What kind of treasure hunt had Nicholas devised for a seven-year-old that lasted this long? What could he have been thinking? Of course, he didn't have children of his own and might well forget that Austen would need to come home and have his supper on time. She tapped her foot and tried to contain her worry.

She pictured Austen exhausted, hungry, wanting his mother...

"They've no doubt forgotten the time."

She tried to smile at Macey but instead felt resentment grow within her. What kind of responsible adult forgot about the time when he was with a child—someone else's child at that?

"I say, Alice, how did you pick up with Father's secretary after all these years?" Geoff came over to sit beside her on the other side of the sofa, a champagne glass in hand. "I can scarcely remember the chap, but I hear he's making some noise in the city these days."

She turned her attention to him, glad for anything to distract her. "I met him at the gala I hosted last week. You were there."

"Yes, Wilma and I stopped in for a few minutes but I don't recall seeing Tennent. What was he doing there? Is he also taking the London social scene by storm the way he is the financial world?"

She glanced at her brother in surprise. "What do you mean?"

At that moment Victor and his wife came in, dressed for dinner.

Her brother swirled the bubbly golden liquid around in his wide, shallow glass. "I hear he's buying up companies right and left. What brought him to the gala?"

"He was interested in the charity work the Society is doing."

Geoff nodded and took a sip of his drink. "That would figure."

Before she could ask what he meant with the remark, Victor, helping himself to a glass of champagne from a tray, wandered over. "Discussing the prodigal returned?" He shook his head then regarded his glass as if pondering. "No, that wouldn't be quite accurate.

The penniless made good?" Snide laughter followed. "Careful, Alice, I would watch my step with that one."

She started at the sound of footsteps at the door, but it was only the servant again, this time to wind the clock. As he turned to leave the room, she signaled to him. "Excuse me, William, but has Mr. Tennent returned with Austen?"

"No, madam, not to my knowledge."

"Please let me know as soon as they do."

Victor glanced down at her, a knowing smile on his lips. "Getting worried, are you?"

She looked down and arranged the folds of her skirt to avoid his interrogation. "Not at all. It's just, well, it is almost dinner time."

Geoff grunted at her side. "I know that look of yours. You fuss overmuch over Austen. The best thing for the little chap is to be sent off to school. It'll make a man of him."

She sighed. "Please, Geoff, I've told you before—"

"And I've told you before that if you don't send him off to school soon, he'll become a milk-sop holding on to your skirts until he's twenty-one. The little fellow hardly lets you out of his sight when you're in the room and he's scared of his own shadow. I've never heard him speak above a whisper."

Victor flopped down on a nearby armchair. "If you haven't persuaded her yet to let go of the apron strings, you're not going to do it this evening." He stretched his legs out before him and took a sip of his glass.

She pressed her lips together, still annoyed with him for delaying her on a silly matter that could have easily waited until they had returned to London. By the time she'd left the library, Nick and Austen had been long gone.

Mirroring her thoughts, Victor said, "I do think they should have been back by now. I wonder where Tennent has absconded with your son…" He glanced sidelong at her. "What do you know of this fellow, anyway? Appeared out of the blue from America and seems to have made himself cozy with you almost immediately."

Alice sat up. "Victor! How dare you say such a thing!"

He tilted his glass toward her. "For someone who worries about her only son so much, you were awfully willing to allow him to go off all afternoon with a stranger."

She felt her cheeks burn. "And whose fault is it that I was unable to accompany them?"

Geoff patted her hand. "Come now. It's too late now, though I do think Vic has a point." He shook his head. "One hears things in the city, don't we, Vic?"

Alice looked from Victor to her brother. Geoff didn't tend to blow things out of proportion. "Tell me what you heard."

Geoff pursed his lips as if deciding how much to say. It annoyed her that he still treated her like a baby sister when she was a full-grown woman of thirty-one. "He's said to be a Yankee shark." At her look of confusion, he added, "Swallows up companies right and left." He nodded at Victor. "He'll confirm it."

Victor set his glass down on the table in front of them and folded his hands in his solicitor's manner, all mockery wiped off his face. "In the few months he's been in the city, he's begun to wield a lot of clout. I represent companies. As soon as any show a sign of weakness, it's as if these investment companies are on the lookout. They come in and make an offer. They buy up shares and before he knows it, the owner has no more control." He gave a contemptuous laugh. "Next he'll be marrying a duchess or countess like any Yankee tuft hunter."

Geoff sniffed. "He may have been born a Brit but he's as crass as any American. And far more cunning. I wouldn't have anything to do with him if I were you."

Alice folded her hands in her lap, revealing nothing of the disquiet the words caused her. "I'm sure you're exaggerating."

He shrugged. "Ask anyone. They'll tell you Tennent & Company gets wealthy on the misfortune of others."

Geoff snorted into his glass. "The worst part is how he throws his money around to charities, like a typical Yankee, putting on that front of humanity when all along he is nothing but a greedy capitalist."

Her hands tightened. It couldn't be. Nicholas seemed too fine a man to stoop to such things.

A childish voice came wafting through the opened doors to the terrace. "Do you think it had been there very long?"

Forgetting all else, she jumped to her feet, hearing Austen's childish voice, followed by Nicholas's lower reply. Hurrying to the door, she saw them stepping onto the terrace.

Her son carried a wooden treasure chest against his chest. Alice rushed outside and knelt in front of him, her arms reaching out. "My darling, wherever have you been?" With an effort she kept her voice calm.

Austen held up the chest, a large grin splitting his

face. Nicholas's hand rested lightly on his head. "Look what I found, Mama!" He looked up at Nicholas. "Didn't I find it all by myself, Mr. Tennent?"

Nicholas winked at Austen before turning to Alice with a smile, which she found she couldn't return at that moment. "You certainly did," he replied to Austen, his eyes still on Alice. Didn't he know the anguish he'd put her through?

"Look what's inside, Mama." Austen stepped away from her and knelt on the floor before the wooden chest. He dug into his pocket and pulled out a large key. "We had to find the key first. It was buried under a tree." He stuck the key in the lock and lifted the lid. Inside lay a pile of jewels—glass and paste that Nick had procured at a shop in the village the day before. "Aren't they beautiful?" He smiled proudly at her.

She touched a strand of pearls. "Yes, dear, they are beautiful. But, dear, you were gone so long." She smoothed back the hair from this forehead and picked a dried leaf from his hair. "Goodness, look at you. Your face is smudged with dirt and—" Her glance traveled down the length of him.

His short pants were streaked with dried mud, his stockings had fallen, showing red scratches on his thin legs. "Where on earth have you been?"

Nicholas cleared his throat. "We ran into some rough country, eh, Austen?"

She frowned up at him. "Indeed? Wherever did you two go?"

"Mama, we went up to Richmond Park, we had to go through a forest, and we had to ford a stream, and then we had to climb a tree. There was another clue there—"

Nicholas had taken him off the property! Alice stood and took Austen by a hand, keeping her voice steady with an effort. "You can tell me all about it, but let's get you upstairs and cleaned up. Nanny Grove will be frightened when she gets a look at you."

For the first time, Austen hung back from her outstretched hand. "But, Mama, I want to stay with Mr. Tennent."

Nick touched him on the shoulder. "Run along with your mama. I'll come up and say good night to you if you'd like." He lifted an inquiring brow toward Alice. "Perhaps read you a story?"

She turned away from him without answering. Austen beamed up at him. "Yes, I should like that very much. May he, Mama?"

"We'll see." She tugged on his hand once more. "But we'll have no story tonight if you don't wash up and have supper first."

She walked back into the house, not sparing Nick a parting glance. Her brother's words came back to her. How much did she really know about Nicholas? How could she be so gullible to think he'd be the same man she'd met fifteen years ago? She'd scarcely known him then, and yet she'd built her dreams on him.

She was no longer that lovesick girl. Her fingers tightened on Austen's hand. Her son was too precious to her to trust to anyone but herself.

Austen walked alongside Alice, carrying his treasure chest under his arm. At the door of the drawing room, she couldn't help one last look back. She regretted the impulse when she saw Cordelia sauntering up to Nicholas, two glasses in her hand.

Cordelia was known for her flirtations. Was Nicholas a womanizer as well? Was that why he hadn't ever married? Alice turned away from the sight, feeling sick inside.

"Mama, you should have seen where the treasure was buried. It was under some tall reeds. We had to dig with our hands and bits of sticks and stones."

She lifted the hand tucked into hers. "Goodness, your nails are filthy." She frowned. "Didn't you get hungry all day? You missed teatime."

"Oh, Mr. Tennent brought along some biscuits. He had them tied up in a handkerchief—the way real explorers carried their food, he told me—and a flask of water. Did you know in the desert they look for 'oases'? Those are places where's there's a little lake and usually date palms. He said that's what we'd snack on if we'd been in the desert—"

In the moments that followed, she heard "Mr. Tennent said this" and "Mr. Tennent did that" countless times as Austen continued telling her about their afternoon together. Alice listened, injecting the appropriate sounds of wonder at intervals as she helped him strip off his clothes and sponge the dirt from his body. Moments passed before she realized the anguish in her heart. She never remembered her little boy showing such enthusiasm for life. And she hadn't been there for his most exciting day.

Why did it have to be a near-stranger who'd enjoyed it and not his own father? Why hadn't she ever thought to plan such an outing for her son herself?

Austen stuck his head through the neck of his nightshirt and poked his hands through the sleeves. "Mr. Tennent told me ever so many stories of when he was a boy. Did you know he had a little brother and they did everything together?"

"Yes, I knew…" She remembered the day she'd asked him all about his family. The day she'd demanded a kiss from him. Shame filled her now at her brazen behavior.

She combed back her son's damp hair, disquiet filling her at how in only one afternoon, this man had succeeded in winning over her son so completely. Would Nicholas Tennent succeed in displacing Austen's father from her son's tenuous memory?

Austen crouched down and retrieved his treasure chest. "I wish I had a little brother like that."

"Darling, it's a bit dirty. I don't think you should take it with you to bed."

He brought it to his table instead. Alice had dismissed Nanny Grove after she'd brought up his supper tray, preferring to do things herself this evening. "Now, come eat up your porridge and drink your milk."

He bent his head and said grace then picked up his spoon. "Mr. Tennent's mama used to give him a cold potato she'd baked for him the night before, and he'd put it in his pocket the next morning to take with him to the mill." Austen's dark brown eyes stared up into hers. "When he was seven, he had to go out to work." His tone was solemn.

"Did he indeed?" How much had he resembled her little boy at that age? She realized with a pang that in coloring—even in slimness—Nicholas could have looked a lot like Austen at his age. She searched for similarities in her son to his father. But his face resembled her own more from his little pointed chin to his slim nose.

"He'd eat his potato on the way to the mill. That's where he worked. There were big machines there that made loud noises. He said at first they scared him. They were always moving the way he imagined the octopuses in the ocean would move about in the stories his mother read to him. Only on Sundays were they still."

Touched by the stories, she had to resist the urge to soften toward Nicholas. "Now, eat your supper."

He took a sip of milk. "His mama used to read him bedtime stories at night just like you do, Mama, and he heard all about jungle explorers. She didn't have many books, though, but he said she remembered ever so many stories and would tell them out of her head. He says he thinks she made lots of them up. Did you ever make up stories?"

She glanced at the row of beautiful books that ranged her son's bookshelf. "No, I guess I don't need to."

"We caught a frog at the pond today."

"Goodness, you seem to have done a lot of things today." She looked back down at the trousers. "I shall have to mend these."

His gaze followed hers. "That happened when I slid down the tree. Mr. Tennent said we had to go and have a lookout, to make sure none of the pirates were following us.

"He showed me how to catch the frog. We had to sit ever so quietly for the longest time at the edge of the pond. I got tired sitting there, but then a frog came hopping to sit on a rock near us, and Mr. Tennent swung his hands out like this—"

"Careful with your glass—"

She caught his glass before it went over. Austen resumed demonstrating, cupping his hands around a make-believe frog. "He held him like so and showed him to me. I wanted to bring him home."

"Where is the frog now?" She glanced at the treasure box nervously.

"Mr. Tennent made me let it go after a bit. But I got to hold it." He sighed and took another sip. "I wanted to show it to you, but Mr. Tennent said the frog probably had his own family to go home to."

"Yes, indeed." Grateful at least for that, Alice sat back. "All finished?"

"Almost." He was quiet, and she was glad to see he ate with relish. Most nights he picked at his food. She wondered what he was thinking—reliving his adventures with Nicholas? She felt more disappointed than ever that she had not been along—even a little jealous, she had to admit. But she couldn't ignore the fun her son had had in a man's company.

How could she reconcile the two images of Nicholas Tennent she'd received this evening?

Her experience with her father had seared her for life against men whose sole ambition was to gain wealth. She sighed, focusing on her young son once again. "Would you like to go away to school, like your cousins?"

He stared at her, his bowl tilted toward him, before

shaking his head. "Mr. Tennent never went away to school. But he did go to Sunday school every Sunday."

She stood. "All right, let's brush your teeth and you can pick out a storybook."

"I thought you said Mr. Tennent could tell me a story tonight?"

She bit her lip. "Very well. But he needs to eat his dinner, too."

"Can he come up afterward and say good night to me?"

"Very well." She tucked her son into bed and bent down to kiss his forehead. "And perhaps he can tell you a short story out of his head, the way his mama used to tell him."

He smiled up at her. "I should like that."

She pulled over a stool and picked up his book. "If you don't mind your mama's storytelling, I shall read a little bit from the book Mr. Tennent gave you and then go down to my guests."

Satisfied with the arrangement, he settled back against the pillows and waited for her to begin.

Nick was aware the moment Alice reentered the drawing room. After changing for dinner he'd rejoined the company on the porch and waited for her, wondering if he had imagined the displeasure in her expression and tone when he'd returned so late with Austen. He needed to explain how time had gotten away from them.

"Well, here is our hostess at last," murmured Cordelia, who hadn't moved from his side since he'd reentered. "Playing at nanny again, Alice, darling?"

Alice glanced her way, her eyes skimming past Nick's.

As usual, Alice looked beautiful in a pale green gown of shimmering satin. She shook her head at the servant's tray and ignored Mrs. Carlisle's remark. "I'm sorry I'm late. Shall we go into dinner?"

Miss Endicott rose from the settee. "Yes, dear, we were just waiting for you." She turned to Nick. "Come, Mr. Tennent, would you like to escort an old lady to the table?"

Disappointed not to be able to escort Alice, he offered Miss Endicott his arm with good grace. "I shall be honored to do so, although I must take exception to your calling yourself an old woman. You are nowhere near that."

She chuckled as they walked toward the dining room. "Thank you. My, I haven't seen Austen looking so happy since I've known him."

Noticing Alice's sharp glance, he shrugged off the remark. "I just took him to do the kinds of things little boys like to do."

She smiled. "You both looked a little the worse for wear when you came in. I hope you had as enjoyable a day as Austen seems to."

His lips crooked upward. "Indeed I did. I haven't had the chance to be a little boy myself in many years."

He watched Alice lead the way into the dining room and then stand in the background as the guests seated themselves. Assuming she would sit at the foot of the table, he made his way there, but instead, Mrs. Shepard took the hostess's chair, her husband at the head.

Having no idea where Alice would sit, he was forced

to seat Miss Endicott first, where she indicated, and then take the place beside her. Mrs. Carlisle promptly took the seat on his other side. Alice took a seat too far removed for comfortable conversation and he wondered if it had been deliberate. Why was she acting so reserved? His jaw tightened with annoyance when Victor sat down beside her.

Dinner proved long and tedious with Shepard dominating the conversation and Mrs. Carlisle addressing almost all her remarks in low asides to Nick. The only one genuinely friendly to him was Miss Endicott. To her credit, Alice did not seem on the same friendly terms with Victor as he with her. She spoke little and ate little. Only once or twice did he catch her looking at him, but instead of smiling, she quickly averted her gaze.

What had gone so wrong?

When at last they all retired to the drawing room, he didn't know how to speak with Alice alone. If he singled her out, all eyes would be on them. He didn't care what any of them thought, but how would Alice feel? This was her world, and once before he'd made the mistake of underestimating it.

The two couples lit cigarettes and the room was soon filled with smoke. Miss Endicott sat down to the piano and began to play softly.

Nick turned with relief when Alice came up to him but his joy was quickly tempered by her serious look. "If you wouldn't mind going up to see Austen, I told him you would tell him a bedtime story. One of those you know out of your head."

He narrowed his eyes at her. Was there a tinge of

sarcasm in the last words? Her tone sounded too polite. "Of course not. I'll go now."

"He might have already fallen asleep. He was quite exhausted. If he is, please don't wake him."

Although she seemed to be avoiding his gaze, he waited until she was forced to look up. "You can trust me. I won't disturb him." He made his tone deliberately gentle. She gave him a quick look before nodding her thanks and moving away from him.

With a sense of relief at leaving the tense atmosphere of the drawing room, he walked up to the little boy's room. He truly had enjoyed himself this afternoon, and only wished Alice had been a part of it. He'd wanted to tell her that if she'd given him the chance.

Austen was already half-asleep and he remembered his promise to Alice, but at the sight of him, the little boy sat up. "I thought you'd never be done with dinner."

He took the stool beside the bed. "It was a rather long meal. Now, lie down. You need to get your sleep if you want to have more adventures."

Austen settled back down under his covers. "Will you tell me another story about when you were a boy?" he said through a yawn.

"All right. Let me think." He rested his chin on his fist, pretending to ponder. "Ah, here's one. When I was—"

"Did you know my father?" Austen's brown eyes looked at him solemnly.

Nick's thoughts stilled. "No, I didn't, but I have heard that he was a very fine gentleman."

Austen sighed. "I don't remember Papa. I have a little picture of him. I'll show you tomorrow if you like."

"Yes, I should like that. I'm sure he was a father you could be proud of. I don't remember my father too well, either, but I know he was a fine man, too."

The little boy folded his hands atop the bedcovers, his thin wrists jutting out from his striped nightshirt. "What do you remember best about him?"

Nick thought back. Ever since receiving news of his mother's passing, he had thought a lot about his youth and childhood. "I remember someone dark-haired, like myself, and smelling kind of funny, like the coal that always covered his clothes. He worked down in the coal mine, you see. And then I remember the smell of soap, once he'd washed up and came to kiss me good night, just like your Mama does with you every night."

Austen picked at his bedcovers. "I don't remember my papa at all."

The forlorn tone touched him. He reached over and covered the little hands with one of his own. "You were very young when he passed away. It's all right. He remembers you. That's what's important."

Austen turned one of his hands around and took hold of Nick's. Nick enfolded it in his own, feeling an odd spurt of emotion at the trusting gesture. The boy's large brown eyes met his. "Do you think so?"

He nodded. "Absolutely. And you have your mama to tell you all about him, so you won't forget the kind of man he was, even though you don't remember the details yourself."

Austen nodded and smiled. "What story are you going to tell me?"

Nick sat back although he didn't let the boy's hand go. "Let me see…where was I…" He pursed his lips, as if searching his memory, before beginning again. "This one is about a man who rode the rails. That means he'd hop on a freight car and go wherever he wished…"

He hadn't even gotten halfway through the story when Austen's breathing slowed and his hold on Nick's hand loosened. Nick fell silent and waited another minute to see if the boy would awaken.

Assured that he slept peacefully, Nick slowly pulled his hand away. He got up from the stool and yawned, wishing for a moment he didn't have to go back downstairs.

But he wanted to see Alice. That thought alone propelled him back to the drawing room.

The murmur of voices reached him before he entered the room. Miss Endicott had stopped playing and sat in an armchair reading. The others lounged on the sofas and chairs. After a pause when he stepped in, the low talk resumed. Cigarette smoke hung in the lamplight like thin cotton strands, its acrid smell reminding Nick of the gin mills in the lower quarters of San Francisco. His gaze roamed over the room, narrowing when he saw Alice on the couch with Victor sitting too close beside her. She looked up as soon as he entered. He half-expected her to avert her gaze, but instead she straightened and rose, excusing herself from Victor.

She reached him before he'd taken more than a few steps into the room. "How is Austen?"

He blinked at her lack of greeting. "I expect off somewhere dreaming of pirates and freight cars and—"

"Frogs," she finished for him.

Was that the beginnings of a smile at the corner of her lips?

"Yes, likely frogs figure in there somewhere."

"I wanted to thank you for spending the afternoon with him." She knotted her hands, looking down, her tone low. "I just worried when you weren't back after a couple of hours. I'm sorry if I overreacted."

His hurt at her earlier coldness dissipated at her halting words. He wanted to reach out and take her hand, but didn't dare with the company around them. "I'm sorry we were gone so long. The time flew by and he didn't seem tired. If I'd seen his energy flagging, I would have brought him back immediately, I hope you believe that." He smiled. "Even if it'd meant carrying him."

She seemed to search his face but didn't return his smile. "I appreciate that."

"What are you two up to with your private murmurings in the corner?" Victor sauntered over to them and draped an arm around Alice's shoulders.

A look of annoyance skimmed her features, and in a deft movement, she sidestepped his embrace. "I'm just asking about Austen."

"You'll never let the boy grow to a man the way you coddle him."

Her face flushed.

Nick eyed Victor. "I found him like any boy of his age."

Victor's insolent gaze swept over him. He sported one of the thin mustaches beginning to be seen on young men both in England and America who fancied themselves swells. "How many seven-year-old boys are you acquainted with?"

Nick's ire rose. "I have nephews." Whom he'd only just seen at his mother's funeral.

"As the father of two boys, I think I speak with more expertise than a bachelor."

Alice put a restraining hand on his arm. "Please, Victor. I think I know my son better than anyone." She then took a step away from them. "I believe I shall retire for the evening. Good night, everyone." She gave him a fleeting look. "Good night, Nick. Thank you for taking care of Austen."

"Good night, Alice." He'd hardly gotten the words out of his mouth when she was gone, almost as if she were running away from him.

He hesitated a moment in the room, but not liking the stifling smell of cigarette smoke, and seeing Mrs. Carlisle eye him, he bowed to Victor. "If you'll excuse me."

He wandered back out to the porch and from there onto the lawn. Tomorrow they'd be leaving this country house, and he didn't know what precisely had gone wrong. He hoped he'd have a chance to talk to Alice, but knew from the trip coming down that the train compartment would afford little privacy with Austen, Miss Endicott and the nursemaid along.

Well, he consoled himself, he still had the endowment to her charity. Perhaps in London he could make another appointment with her at the Society to discuss the gift.

"It was stuffy in there, wasn't it?"

He swirled around at the husky female voice. Mrs. Carlisle stood at the edge of the verandah, silhouetted against the light from the drawing room. Unlike Alice's more modest gown, Mrs. Carlisle's silk sheath had a low v-neck, leaving most of her shoulders and upper arms bare.

He knew her type well. Bored and needing attention. As he debated how to decline her advances, she sauntered down the steps onto the yard where he stood.

"A lot of hot air."

She chuckled, a low-throated sound and looked up at him, knowing undoubtedly how it showed her creamy neck to advantage.

"I was on the point of retiring," he said.

"What a pity. The evening is young." She eyed him. "You don't like my husband, do you?"

"Let's just say I had a brief acquaintance with him in his youth."

"How droll. Sometimes he seems to be still in his adolescence."

Nick took a step away from her. "Well, if you will excuse me, Mrs. Carlisle—"

"I shouldn't hold out much hope for Alice, if I were you."

Her words stopped him. "No?"

"I pity the man who fancies himself in love with her. She is the kind of woman who appears weak and will always have some poor gentleman in tow, but her heart will never be his."

He stood silent, unwilling to hear the words, but powerless to move away.

"She'll always hold up Julian as a standard, and the poor man will never live up to the dead paragon." She gave a bitter laugh. "The living can never compete with an ideal."

The words, so like his own thoughts, chilled him. He merely inclined his head. "Good night, Mrs. Carlisle."

Her throaty laugh followed him. "Good night, Mr. Tennent, and sweet dreams."

Chapter Eleven

Alice reread the note in the masculine scrawl:

Alice,
Thank you for the weekend in Richmond. It was
most enjoyable to me, not least for the time spent
in your delightful son's company.
I hope that I can see both of you again.
The reason for the present is to make an appoint-
ment to further discuss an endowment to the So-
ciety. I could come to your office or residence,
or you can come to my office. I leave it up to you
whatever is most convenient to you.
I remain, as ever, your servant,
Nicholas Tennent

Her glance strayed to the bottom of the note where he'd written his address on Threadneedle Street. His business no doubt. Or, *businesses*. She remembered Geoff's and Victor's remarks and tried to push them away as merely masculine envy.

She turned over the envelope that lay on the desk. The Savoy Hotel was embossed on the back flap. The image of the hotel as his residence conjured up a transient with no permanent home.

Did Nicholas plan to remain in London or was he here only temporarily? How little she still knew of him.

Her son had done little but talk of Nicholas since their return. Was she jealous of Nicholas's success with Austen? The ugly thought lodged in her mind and she couldn't brush it aside so easily. Was she such a terrible mother to begrudge her only son some masculine companionship?

She'd always been protective of Austen, but now she realized how difficult it was for her to trust her only child to someone else. Julian would gently admonish her to trust their son to the Lord's care. Tears welled in her eyes, blurring the note before her. Despite her trust in other areas, she felt little able to relinquish control in this area. Austen was all she had left. All that was truly hers.

She wiped at her eyes and picked up the note from Nicholas once more. When she'd first seen the envelope in her stack of mail, she'd felt a spurt of anticipation. Now, her confusion returned. And if she were honest with herself, did it not include disappointment as well?

He'd written that he hoped to see *both of them again*. When Nicholas had bid them goodbye at Victoria Station the day before, he'd taken her hand in his and thanked her for the weekend. Then he'd stooped by Austen and shaken his hand.

She'd watched, touched by their exchange. Nicholas

treated him like a miniature adult. He'd promised her son they would be seeing each other again.

Yet, here in the note he expressed only an intention to see her regarding a charitable donation. What did she want? Staring out her rain-spattered window, she chided herself. It was she who had pushed away any friendly overtures on Nicholas's part.

Shaking aside her own foolishness, she focused on the latter part of the note. The only reasonable thing to do was reply to his request and meet with him to discuss the particulars of the charitable donation.

"Mama."

She turned with a smile to her son. "What is it, Austen? Why aren't you with Miss Grove?"

"I told her I left Moppet down here and had to get him."

"Of course. Then you'd better hurry up to your lessons. If you finish early, we can go to the park together."

"Is Mr. Tennent coming, too?"

She turned away from him, feeling sudden guilt. Had she driven her son's only friend away? Or, had Nicholas's interest in the boy already waned? "No, dear."

"Why not?"

"Mr. Tennent is a busy man. I imagine he is at his office working right now."

"When is he coming to visit? He said he'd see me soon."

"I don't know exactly when. We've only been home one day." She glanced down at the note. Should she say anything to her son about the note? Or would that be raising his hopes unfairly?

Austen located his stuffed rabbit behind a sofa cushion and came to lean against her. "Mama, will you write to Mr. Tennent and ask him to visit us? Tell him we could take my sailboat to the Basin."

She put her arm around his shoulders. "You and I can take it with us today. We don't need Mr. Tennent for that."

"But I should like it if he came with us."

She touched the strands of hair that had fallen against his forehead. "You don't want to be with just your mama?"

"I should like it better if he came with us," he repeated stoutly, unaware how the words cut her. Why did Julian have to die and leave Austen fatherless? There had been no confusion in her life then.

"Very well, we shall see what we can do. I'm sure you'll see Mr. Tennent very soon. Now, run along and finish your lessons." She kissed his forehead and gave him a little shove.

"All right, Mama." He ran off, but at the door he paused. "Don't forget to write to Mr. Tennent."

"I won't."

When he left, she sighed and turned back to her desk. After rereading Nicholas's letter, she picked up her pen and let it hover over her stationery a second more, debating her opening. Before she could decide, she heard the front door ring. Her heart began to pound. Could it be Mr. Tennent? Of course not, she scolded herself for acting like a silly schoolgirl.

At the soft knock on the parlor door, she twisted around in her chair. "Yes?"

The maid poked her head in. "It's Mr. Carlisle, madam."

Victor. She dismissed the slight annoyance at his

unannounced visit so soon after seeing him the day before. He was her solicitor after all—at Geoff's insistence. "Show him in."

Victor strolled in, presenting his usual dandified appearance in a black broadcloth coat and finely checked trousers. "Hello there, Alice."

She stood and smoothed her gown. "Hello, Victor, what brings you by today?"

He leaned down and planted a kiss on her cheek and she had to brace herself against flinching. His cheek smelled of bay rum, a scent she'd never cared for. Ever since he'd become her solicitor, he'd become excessively attentive.

She'd spoken to Geoffrey about it, but her brother had pooh-poohed her concerns. "He's like a brother to you! It's nothing but a little harmless flirtation. Don't be such a prude, Allie."

Victor glanced down at her desk, and she had to refrain from moving in front of it to prevent him from seeing the note from Nicholas. "I was in the neighborhood and thought I'd stop by and see how you made it back."

"How thoughtful of you." She deliberately moved away from her escritoire and took a seat in an armchair, motioning for him to do the same. He sat down on the adjoining sofa and smoothed his brightly colored four-in-hand tie. "Been corresponding with that chap Tennent? You seemed a bit tight with him for such a short acquaintance."

Deciding silence was the best defense, she sat straight, her hands folded in her lap.

Victor leaned back against the velvet upholstery and seemed to study the ceiling. "Curious how he sud-

denly popped back into London after all these years."
He shook his head and chuckled. "From lowly clerk
to head of a company. Only in America does one see
such things."

"I think it shows his talent and energy."

He lowered his face to gaze at her sidelong. "Or ruthless ambition."

Alice swallowed, wanting to refute the allegation.
Instead, she asked through stiff lips. "What do you
mean?"

"A man with nothing doesn't get to where he is without some cold-blooded maneuvers. I've heard he buys
out any company that shows the least weakness, fires
all the principals—'restructuring' he calls it—then in-
corporates it into his vast enterprise of Tennent & Company." He shook his head. "One can't help admiring his
tactics, in a Neronian sort of way."

"I don't know how you can compare him to a ruthless Roman emperor, Victor. Just because he has made
something of himself. I think it's admirable."

Victor let out a skeptical sniff. "Making something
of himself is one thing. To go from a penniless young
man to one who throws his wealth around—"

She gave a laugh, which came out sounding sharper
than she'd intended. "Oh, come, you're exaggerating.
These things happen all the time in America."

"Poor Allie, you've lived a sheltered life in the north
with your curate. A man who puts up at the Savoy, in-
stalls himself in an office building in the heart of the
city, drives in a newly purchased coach, and buys up
companies as if they are weekly groceries doesn't strike

me as an innocent lamb. Even in America business is a ruthless affair."

"If you've come to criticize Nicholas, you needn't bother—"

"Ah-ha. So it's like that, is it?" He sat up, eyeing her with his customary cynical amusement.

She blinked. "Like what?"

"Nicholas," he mimicked. "Be careful, sweet Alice. You've been alone some time now and are vulnerable. Be careful you don't give your heart to someone whose heart is as hard as granite."

She stood up and walked away from him. "You are fancying things which are not there. I merely admire Mr. Tennent if he has made something of himself, and wished to make him feel welcome since his return." She fingered the lace on her collar, keeping her back to Victor.

"Of course, dear, if that's what you say. Anyway, I came by today to tell you that Cordelia and I wanted to have you over for dinner some evening this week."

"I don't know..." She hated those evenings, filled with a lot of worldly society couples whose interests were so far removed from her own. At the same time, she knew how valuable such connections were to the charity. It was her duty to continue to make these people aware of those less fortunate than themselves. "Let me look in my engagement book." She crossed back to her desk. "Which evening were you thinking of?"

He came to stand behind her, so close she had no space to move away. "I'm not sure which evening Cordelia has in mind. Let me have her confirm with you."

"Oh, very well." She stifled her annoyance that he

didn't have a definite date in mind. Had he only come by to criticize Nicholas?

"There's one other thing."

She glanced at him, then quickly away when she found his face inches from hers. "Yes?"

"Your portfolio has taken a plunge lately. Bit of a recession on the market, you know. I'm afraid your income will be going down this quarter."

"Oh." She chewed her lip. Why did it always seem Victor took pleasure in being the bearer of bad tidings where her finances were concerned? "Well, it only means I shall have to be more careful of my expenditures."

"Yes." His hand came up to her face.

She jerked her head back. "What are you doing?"

"Just brushing away a stray lock." He tucked the supposed strand of hair behind her ear, while she stood rigid. Despite that they had known each other as children, she was tired of the liberties he took. Lately, he was going too far.

She took a deliberate step back. "Well, if that is all, Victor, I have some things to attend to."

"As do I, as do I." Before she knew what he was about, he leaned in again and planted a soft kiss on her cheek.

She flinched, and his low chuckle vibrated against her skin. "My, you are getting jumpy these days. Sure it's not that Tennent making you so nervous?"

With a wave, he moved away from her. "I'll see myself out. Cordelia will be in touch." He sauntered away from her before she could think of a retort.

After he'd left, she took up Nicholas's note once again and reread it. Then she picked up her pen.

Dear Mr. Tennent, Why not "Nicholas," she asked herself? She decided she was letting herself go too quickly. There had been no one since Julian and there wouldn't be.

She needed time to get a proper perspective on her newfound friendship with Nicholas Tennent.

I received your kind letter. There was no need of thanks. Both Austen and I enjoyed our weekend in Richmond and we thank you for your company.

If you would like to discuss a donation to the Society, why don't you visit here at my residence later in the week? I suggest Thursday or Friday afternoon—

She deliberately set the date as far to the end of the week, and in the latter part of the day, denying herself the pleasure of seeing him sooner. With distance, her own feelings would have a chance to settle. And give Austen's memory of his weekend adventures with Mr. Tennent an opportunity to fade as well.

You may let me know the date and time conve-nient to you by return post.
In the meantime, I remain, sincerely, your ser-vant,
Alice Lennox

There, that was sufficiently businesslike without being unfriendly. She perused it one more time and before giving herself a chance to question or reword it, she quickly folded it and put it into an envelope. It would go out in the afternoon post. Or, perhaps tomorrow morning's was better. She didn't want to appear too eager. This was strictly about business.

Yes, tomorrow's post was soon enough. He'd receive it by mid-morning and still have plenty of time to decide on seeing them by week's end.

Nick frowned as his eyes skimmed down the contents of the brief note, beginning with "Mr. Tennent." His disappointment deepened as he read "Thursday or Friday."

He'd waited until late Monday afternoon, expecting an immediate response to his note to her. It was not until almost noon Tuesday that he'd received her reply, and now she was postponing a meeting until the end of the week.

Wasn't she interested in a donation for her charity?

Or was it that she didn't want to see *him?* He considered the various possibilities. Perhaps she didn't want him to see her son?

Their ride back in the train from Richmond had been pleasant enough. As he'd foreseen, there had been no time for any meaningful conversation. Austen had taken up most of his attention, but the more the boy had chattered away with him, the more Nick had sensed Alice's withdrawal. Could she possibly resent the boy's attention?

He couldn't fathom it and wanted to talk to her about it. But, he looked down at the note again; it seemed he would have little chance until Thursday or Friday. At least she wanted him to come to her house. He'd see Austen again. Funny how much he'd missed the little fellow.

He'd leave the entire afternoon free to spend with him. If Alice allowed him to.

He sighed and picked up his pen. He would request a meeting on Thursday at half-past two. That should still qualify as afternoon and not interfere with the lunch hour.

Alice paced the front parlor from a quarter past two onward. She stopped in front of the mirror hanging over the mantelpiece and adjusted the ruffled collar of her gown for the third time.

She tucked a stray strand of hair into her coiffure.

"Mama, I think I see him."

She jumped at the sound of Austen's voice. Her son had stood at the bow window for the last half hour. He craned his neck through the foliage of the potted plants, peering into the street below. One small hand held back the gauze outer curtain.

"Austen, please get away from the window." She couldn't help going over and glancing over his head.

He sighed. "No, it's not him. I thought it was him." The gentleman with the bowler hat and dark suit walked briskly by, swinging his walking stick back and forth over the pavement.

"Now, come away from the window."

"Yes, Mama." He let the curtain fall and walked beside her, dragging Moppet in one hand.

"Come, let's read a storybook while we wait for Mr. Tennent. Now, remember, he is here to see Mama on business, so after greeting him and speaking a few minutes, you must excuse yourself. When he is ready to leave, I shall summon you again and you may say goodbye to him."

His solemn eyes looked into hers as he settled beside her on the sofa. "Yes, Mama," he said with a sigh.

Since their return to London, nothing she'd tried to engage Austen in could compete with his memories of the treasure hunt.

She picked up the edition of *Coral Island,* which she had hoped would assuage his desire for adventure. "Now, remember, when we last left Jack and Peterkin, their ship had been wrecked. Let's see what happens when they awake."

He settled beside her, putting a thumb into his mouth. She frowned at the habit he'd almost given up until this week. "The ship struck at the very tail of the island," she read.

"Mama, you have to speak like a pirate when you read it."

She looked down at Austen's serious gaze and smiled. "Very well."

But just as she turned back to the story, they both heard the doorbell ring.

Austen immediately scrambled off the sofa. "I know that's Mr. Tennent. Mama, may I go out and greet him?"

She was about to impress upon him that one awaited one's guests to be announced, but at the sight of his eager face, she didn't have the heart. "Very well."

She closed the book slowly as he ran off. Then she stood and smoothed her skirt, deafened to all sound but the hammering of her heart.

* * *

Nick was giving his name to the maid when a door opened to the side of the corridor and then Austen was running toward him. "Mr. Tennent!" The boy suddenly stopped short and hesitated, as if unsure at the last moment how he would be greeted. Nick smiled at him, feeling happier than he'd have imagined a moment ago at seeing the young boy, and squatted down.

Before he knew how it had come about, his arms were around the young boy, and Austen's arms were about his neck.

"I didn't think you'd ever be back," he said against Nick's collar.

Nick squeezed him a second before sitting back. "Of course I would. I told you I would." He stood slowly and handed Austen the package he'd brought.

The boy's eyes grew round. "Is this for me?"

He nodded.

Austen just stood staring at it.

"Well, why don't you open it?"

The boy pulled at the string, then growing bolder, tore through the brown wrapping. He took out the navy blue captain's hat with the gold anchor insignia at the front.

"Put it on and see if it fits."

With wonder in his eyes, he set it on his head.

"Well? How does it feel?"

Austen's mouth curled into a smile. "Just right. Is this a real captain's hat?"

"It is. If we're going to go sailing together, you've got to look the part."

"Are we really going to go sailing?"

"Certainly." He coughed softly. "That is, if your mother gives you permission."

"Let's ask her now."

"Wait a minute. I have something for her, too." He picked up the parcel he'd set down and took Austen by the hand. "Tell me what you've been up to since you returned to London." With a glance at the maid, he crossed the threshold.

Austen tugged on his hand. "Mama is waiting for you in here."

The maid shut the door behind him with a nod, and Nick allowed Austen to lead the way. She was waiting for him? That perhaps boded for good.

Alice stood by the sofa when he entered, her glance going from Austen to him and back again.

Nick advanced into the room, letting go of Austen's hand when he reached Alice. He handed her the bouquet of roses he'd brought. "Hello, Alice." Would she address him as Mr. Tennent?

"Oh, goodness, what's this?"

He gave a nervous laugh. "Well, I hope their scent gives them away."

She carefully drew aside the paper and gave a small gasp.

He cleared his throat. "I hope you like pink."

"Oh, yes, indeed, I do." She bent over the dozen pink roses and breathed in deeply. "They smell wonderful." Her eyes lifted and she smiled. "Thank you."

He felt the tension in him easing at her shy smile.

"Let me ring for someone to put them in water. Please, have a seat."

Nick took a seat on the chintz sofa, listening to Austen show off his new cap to his mother.

Alice came back and took a seat in a nearby chair. She turned to her son, who'd come to sit beside Nick. "Austen, darling, Mama must talk with Mr. Tennent for a little bit. You may come back in a few moments and have your own visit."

Nick bent and touched him on the shoulder. "Do as your mother says. Perhaps—" he spared her a brief glance "—we can do something together afterward."

She pressed her lips together, as if the idea didn't please her. Was she still holding the treasure hunt against him? They were silent as Austen dragged himself off the sofa and walked slowly to the door.

When it closed, Nick turned back to Alice. She sat with her hands folded primly on her lap. Before he could say anything, she said, "Mr. Tennent, thank you for coming."

He felt a stab of disappointment—mingled with irritation—at the formal name and tone. Hadn't they just enjoyed a weekend of getting reacquainted? "What happened to 'Nicholas'?"

She averted her gaze. "I thought since we were meeting to discuss—uh—business, it was more business-like."

He quirked an eyebrow. "Business? Since when is charity business?"

She met his eyes once more. "Isn't it for you?" There was something in her tone.

"No." When she didn't reply, he said, "Thank you for—" he paused imperceptibly "—agreeing to see me."

She looked down, so he was sure the inflection was

not lost on her. "Well, yes, you said you wished to discuss a donation to the Society."

He leaned forward. "Yes. I had in mind a donation to be able to build a row of terrace houses such as you showed me last week."

She pursed her lips. "That would be a substantial cost."

"I understand. It would only be an initial donation. I would like to see several such dwellings constructed in time."

"I don't know what to say."

He smiled slightly. "You could ask how much the initial donation would entail."

"Very well. How much did you have in mind?"

"One hundred thousand pounds."

Her mouth fell open, as if she'd never heard of such a sum. "I beg your pardon."

He repeated the sum.

Her eyes began to light up, realizing he was serious. Before Nick could feel the pleasure of the giver, the light faded. "You must be very wealthy to be able to afford so large a donation."

"The Lord has prospered me in my time away from England."

"Has he?"

He drew his eyebrows together at her tone. "You sound doubtful."

"They say you are…aggressive in your business dealings."

"I see." What had she heard? Rising, he walked toward the window. "When one is successful in business, one makes enemies. One gets used to slander."

She rose as well. "Is that all they are—rumors?"

He swung around to her. "Who have you been listening to?"

She made a vague gesture. "Businessmen."

His jaw hardened, not liking the fact that she was so quick to doubt him. "Let me guess. Victor or your brother?"

"I trust Geoffrey's judgment."

His jaw hardened. So they were back to that. Her family against him. "Are you interested in the donation or not?"

"I shall have to discuss it with my board of trustees."

His annoyance grew. "Then I shall let you get on with it." He took out his pocket watch and snapped it open. "If you will permit me some time with Austen, I think we've concluded our business."

She drew back and he had a moment's remorse at the hurt look in her eyes. "I shall call for him."

While she went to the bell pull, he turned away from her again and waited by the bow window, his hands clasped behind his back. Perhaps he'd been too hasty in his anger. But if she doubted him so quickly, what hope was there for them? And by that brother of hers, who'd probably rejoiced when she'd been disinherited. He shook his head in disgust.

The two waited in uneasy silence until the maid came.

"Please send Austen to me."

"Yes, madam."

When Nick felt the tension couldn't increase anymore in the room, the door finally opened and Austen walked in, his sailboat already in his arms. "Hello, Austen. That didn't take too long, now, did it?" His tone was gentle and friendly. No one would suspect he had a hard lump of anger in his chest.

He grinned. "No, sir." Ignoring his mother, he walked over to Nick.

"Now, what would you like to do this afternoon?"

"May we go sailing?"

Nick's glance went immediately to Alice. "If it's all right with your mother."

She twisted her hands together, clearly on the spot. Well, he felt no pity for her this afternoon. "Why don't you do something here at home, darling?"

Austen looked down and didn't say anything.

"I don't mind taking him to sail his boat. Where do you usually go sailing, Austen?"

Nick's quick words drew a smile from the boy. "The Round Pond."

His mother frowned. "But that's all the way in Kensington."

"We can go in my coach," put in Nick quickly. "It's parked right outside."

Her gaze went from his neutral one to her son's, visibly torn. Nick hid his impatience and waited. If anyone was going to disappoint this boy, it wouldn't be he.

"Please, Mama, mayn't I go with Mr. Tennent?"

She drew in a deep breath. "Very well, but don't be too long."

Nick exhaled in relief. "We shan't," he promised with a small smile as a peace offering. "Come along, let's be off."

At the door, he patted Austen on the shoulder. "Wait for me at the front door."

As soon as Austen had left, Nicholas turned to Alice, wanting to reassure her. "Thank you for trusting Austen to my care."

She pressed her lips together, and he suddenly realized she was near tears. "He's all I have." she whispered.

The words tore at his heart, and he almost entreated her to go along with them. Instead, he reached his hand out and patted her awkwardly on the shoulder. "I won't let him out of my sight."

She nodded wordlessly.

"We'll be back soon. I shall await your committee's decision."

Nick put his disquiet aside and concentrated on helping Austen up into the landau. The little boy scrambled onto the seat at the front and bounced up and down on the red leather upholstery a few times. "Oh, I can look all around me."

Both sides of the top had been folded down for the fine weather. Nick smiled up at him before addressing the coachman. "Take us through the park to the Round Pond."

The coachman tipped his top hat at him. "Yes, sir."

Nick climbed into the carriage and sat facing Austen. "Tell me what you've been up to since you returned from Richmond."

The boy's smile disappeared and shrugged. "Nothing much. Mama has engaged a governess to give me lessons and Nanny Grove takes me for a walk every day." Austen's gaze didn't stay fixed on him but roamed over the parkland as they entered Hyde Park through Stanhope Gate and rode under an alley of plane trees.

As the boy chattered on, Nick allowed his thoughts to return to Alice. She seemed deeply distressed about allowing her son in his company. What had her brother been telling her about him? Nick intended to get to the bottom of it. His frown deepened, not liking the things his secretary had begun discovering about her father's company.

"Do you think there'll be enough wind to sail my boat?"

He forced his attention to the boy in front of him. "If not, we'll go another day and today make do with towing her along by her string."

"May we really go again another day?"

"Of course, why shouldn't we?"

The little boy shrugged and looked out the side. "I don't know. I've been asking Mama since we arrived home when you were going to visit."

His deep sigh stirred Nick. Why hadn't Alice replied sooner? He'd contacted her the day they'd returned. He remembered his own yearnings as a boy, how little they were ever satisfied until he'd become resigned to be content with his lot in life.

But why would Alice not want to indulge her son, when clearly the boy was lonely and in need of some male companionship?

His concern grew, and he had to strive to keep his tone light whenever he spoke.

Alice attempted to catch up on her correspondence while Austen was away. She usually reserved this time for Austen, and now found the time weighing heavily on her hands.

At the sound of carriage wheels, she rose from her desk and looked out the window, but it was only a passing coach. She forced herself to sit back down and pick up her pen again, determined not to behave the way she had over the treasure hunt.

Austen was in good hands, she repeated to herself. Nicholas, whatever he might be in business, seemed to genuinely care for her son. Her eyes drifted to the large bouquet of roses in the corner of her desk. She touched a soft petal, moved by the thoughtfulness of his gifts to both her and Austen.

Letting her pen drop, she bowed her head. *Dear Lord, Forgive me for this worry. Help me to be unselfish toward my son.* She thought of Julian and his gentle example of selfless love. He'd taught her to put her trust in God above all. She'd thought she'd succeeded as they lived always on the edge of poverty and had had to face death constantly with Julian's illness.

It was only now that Austen's affections were straying beyond the safe boundaries of his home that she was beginning to see how much she clung to him.

Forgive me, Lord. Grant me your grace. Show me who Nicholas Tennent really is. Is he the ruthless tycoon they tell me he is? Is he the best example for my Austen?

About an hour later, as soon as she heard a coach pull up in front of the house, she rushed to the window, careful to keep behind its lacy veil. She watched the two descend, Nick helping Austen down, then holding his hand and carrying his sailboat in the other. Austen chattered up the whole walk to the front door, exhibiting more animation than he did at home.

She couldn't see them when they entered under the

portico. The dim sound of the door penetrated to the parlor, and she held her breath, wondering if Nicholas would ask to see her. What would she say? Part of her wanted to run out into the hallway and see him again, part of her wanted to remain hidden.

But no one came. A few minutes later, she saw him return to his coach. Only then did her breathing return to normal. With a sigh, she turned to go to Austen, feeling more lonely than she had for a long time.

Chapter Twelve

Alice spent the next week immersing herself in her work. After receiving a formal letter from Nicholas's firm about the intended donation, she truly began to believe it.

Overwhelmed with what the Housing Society would be able to accomplish with such a sum, she wanted to do something to show her appreciation to him. She decided to plan a special dinner with the entire board of trustees. Nicholas would be given a chance to address them and outline the vision he had for the donation, and they in turn could honor him with a special plaque.

Perhaps they could name the first terraces after Nicholas? On a burst of inspiration, she jotted down the various ideas she had.

Keeping herself busy with work helped assuage the disappointment she felt at not having seen Nicholas on a personal level. He'd been to see Austen three times, usually taking him to sail his boat, but always when she was at her office.

She bit the end of her pen. Nicholas knew where her

office was located, so if he had wanted to see her, he certainly could have done so. He even had a legitimate pretext with the pending donation.

It was for the best, she told herself, looking back down at her notes. Wasn't it what she'd wanted? Simple friendship and nothing else. She should be thankful things had resolved themselves so satisfactorily. Austen was happy and thriving. And she had peace.

"Hello, are you busy?"

Alice started up at Macey's voice. Her friend stood at the door of her office. "Oh, hello, come in. I'm never too busy to see you."

Macey entered the room, pulling off her gloves and smiling broadly. "I mustn't stay long. I've too much to do, but I wanted to say goodbye before I left."

She looked at her friend in bewilderment. "Left? Where are you off to? What about the dinner I'm organizing?"

Macey sat down opposite her and undid the ribbons of her bonnet. "Oh, I shall be back in time for that. It isn't for at least a fortnight, isn't it? Tell me how the plans are coming."

Alice brought her up to date, still disconcerted that she wouldn't have her friend's help in organizing it.

"But you've got everything pretty much settled," Macey said in reply to this. "It's just a matter of ordering things and securing the ballroom."

"Where are you going, anyway?"

Macey removed her bonnet and smoothed down her hair. "Didn't I tell you last week? I'm sure I meant to. I'm off to catch the steamer to Le Havre. I'm taking a holiday in Deauville."

"Deauville! Goodness, Macey, when did you decide to go to Deauville?"

"A few weeks ago. Elizabeth Wilcox raved about it when she came back."

Alice made an effort to inject some enthusiasm in her tone while she tried to suppress her dismay. "Well, it sounds lovely. When are you off?" Macey always left London in the summer, but it was usually not far from the city, where Alice could visit on the weekends.

"Tomorrow, my dear. I'm sure I must have told you."

Alice stared at her. "Tomorrow?" Why did she feel suddenly abandoned? She shook her head with a wan smile. "I don't remember. It must have slipped my mind, what with going out to Richmond last week and planning this and all..." Her voice dribbled off as she glanced back down at the papers on her desk.

Macey placed her bonnet on the seat beside her. "How is Mr. Tennent, by the way? I've been meaning to ask about him. Have you seen him since we came back from Richmond?"

"Yes, once. He stopped by when he first broached me about the donation."

Macey frowned. "Only once?"

Alice shuffled her papers around. "Yes. But he has taken Austen out a few times—close to home," she added. "I know he is a very busy man."

"Taken Austen out, but not you?"

Alice's gaze shot up. "I beg your pardon?"

"I know he is a busy man, but I shouldn't think he was too busy to stop by and see you." Macey folded her hands in her lap.

Alice made a point of arranging her papers in a pile. "Oh, well, I'm busy, too."

"I liked him."

"You did?" Why did Alice have the urge to burst into tears and tell her friend all about her wayward heart?

The older woman looked at her in surprise. "Yes, why? Don't you?"

"Yes, of course. I mean," she added, not meeting her friend's gaze, "you are usually so critical of men. Why are you championing Nicholas Tennent?"

Macey sat back. "There's something forthright about him. He appears a strong, yet not overbearing, person. I don't get the impression with him that he would be afraid of a woman who knew her own mind." She nodded, warming to her view. "A woman could form a true partnership with a man like that."

Alice stared at the older woman. She'd never heard her talk like that of any man.

When she said nothing, Macey asked gently, "Has something happened between you two?"

"Oh, no," she said quickly, too quickly. "Why should it have?"

"Then what is it?"

"Nicholas and I are...only acquaintances," she began.

"But I thought you two had known each other years ago."

Alice studied the neat words on the stationery before her. "Yes." That magical period of hardly more than a week. "It was so long ago. He was with Father's firm for a very short time. Until Father dismissed him."

"Oh, that's too bad. He struck me as someone who would have been an asset to the company."

"It was all my fault."

Her friend gave a small gasp then she leaned forward. "I'm sure you did nothing so terrible."

Alice had never told anyone about that day. Only her father had known. Long minutes passed before she was able to speak. "I fancied myself in love with him."

"Oh, my dear…"

Alice swallowed. "I was a foolish young girl looking for attention. Mr. Tennent seemed to notice me. For the first time, someone was genuinely seeing who I was." She held up a hand before her friend could say a word. "Don't misunderstand. He did nothing wrong, nothing improper. It was I who pestered him." She pressed her lips together, finding it difficult to tell the rest. "It was I who threw myself at him, until one day—" her voice lowered to a mere whisper "—I demanded a kiss from him." Her face flamed with the recollection. After a few seconds, she continued. "Father caught us."

"Oh, no!"

"He immediately dismissed Nich—Mr. Tennent." She shook her head, still grieved by that act. "The poor man was completely innocent. He was out of a job, with no references, just because of my silly schoolgirl behavior. That's why he was forced to emigrate. Father sent me away to live with relatives." She said softly, "I never saw him again, until the other evening."

"Your father could be quite harsh."

When Alice made no comment, Macey reached across the desk and patted her hand. "What an awful thing you both went through. Young love can be very painful. But that's all in the past. Your Mr. Tennent has returned and you've been able to renew the acquaintance. It sounds like a storybook."

Alice put a hand up to her mouth to stifle her emotions.

"What is it, Alice?" Her friend's low tone was filled with concern.

Unable to sit still, Alice got up and walked to the window overlooking the street. "I don't know." She hugged her arms to herself, wishing she could understand what she was feeling.

Macey came up behind her and touched her on the elbow. "Did he say something to you—or Austen?"

She shook her head. "No…no, it's just me. I don't know what I'm saying. Don't mind me," she said with a nervous laugh. "I'm just tired and confused," she added under her breath.

"Don't be afraid of your emotions, my dear."

Alice pressed her lips together, trying to regain her composure. After a moment, she said, "I have never sought anyone since Julian. I loved him. I can't…" She shook her head, unable to say anything more.

Macey put her arm around her. "There, my dear, don't fret. Your heart won't be betraying your late husband if you still feel something for Mr. Tennent."

"But I don't know what kind of man he is!" She didn't voice her greatest fear. What if he was a man just like her father?

Her friend patted her arm and stepped away. "Well, perhaps you need to take the time to find out."

Alice turned slowly to look at her. "What do you mean?"

"I mean just that. Get to know him."

She swallowed back a bitter laugh. How was she to do that when he wasn't even around? He was too busy with his business concerns. "It's for the best if we leave whatever was in the past, in the past," she finished with more firmness than she felt inside.

Alice turned back to her desk. "Come, I'll ring for some tea. Tell me more about Deauville before you leave. I envy your being able to just take off at a moment's notice."

"Well, why don't you come with me?"

Alice laughed as she went toward the corridor. "Yes, I'll just run away from all my responsibilities for a few days and not tell a soul where I am—"

"I'm serious, Alice. Take some time off for a proper holiday and come along with me. You know I'll pay all your expenses. You don't have to worry about a thing. It will do you the world of good."

Alice shook her head at her friend. "You know I can't go anywhere right now. What about the dinner I'm organizing?"

Macey took her seat once again. "You have a good staff here. They can carry out your instructions, we'll be back in plenty of time for the finishing touches. If you need, I can put off my trip another day or so to give you time to get your things together."

Alice walked slowly back to her own seat after requesting the tea. "Are you serious? You know how busy I am. I couldn't possibly just leave for more than a few days."

"Yes, you can."

"What about Austen?"

"What about him? Take him along. Children love the

seaside. Think of it. A sandy beach and plenty of sunshine and fresh air, just what he needs." Macey nodded at her for emphasis. "And you, too. You look tired, my dear. If you continue as you've been, you'll work yourself to exhaustion and then where will your son be?"

"Hush, Macey. Don't say such things, even in jest."

Her friend's tone softened. "There now, Alice, I'm not trying to frighten you. I just want you to get away from things here for a little bit and take some time to enjoy yourself. The time alone with Austen will do you good. What do you say?"

Get away from things here for a little bit. Alice focused on those words and, suddenly, the plan sounded all too agreeable. If she left London, she wouldn't have to think about Nicholas Tennent. Wouldn't have to wonder why she was missing those dark eyes looking into hers, demanding something from her which she was afraid to respond to.

Nick paused in the letter he was dictating to his secretary and stared out the window. Would Alice be in her office at this time of day? It had been over a week since he'd last seen her. He'd kept away from her deliberately, sensing she needed time. He'd also needed the time to get over his anger.

The anger had long since dissipated. He'd thought by keeping away longer, he'd hear from her, if only on the subject of the donation.

But all he'd received was silence. Any communication about the donation had been from the treasurer of the society.

His strategy clearly had not worked. He gave a derisive snort. Was she really glad to be rid of his presence? Perhaps she'd believed even more slander from her brother or that sly Victor.

A soft cough interrupted him. He glanced at his secretary, who sat with pencil poised over his pad. "I'm sorry?"

"You were saying?"

"Oh, yes, where was I?"

The young man looked at his notes. "The share price of Henderson Limited fell two points yesterday."

"Yes." He cleared his throat and continued. He needed to stop dwelling on Alice and concentrate on his business concerns.

Two sentences later, he snapped open his pocket watch. Perhaps he could stop by to discuss the housing project. He knew she was planning a dinner where he would present his ideas to the board of trustees.

Four o'clock. Was it too late?

He turned abruptly to his secretary. "Excuse me, we'll have to finish this tomorrow. I'm going out."

The man blinked at him. "Oh. Very well, Mr. Tennent. Do you want me to continue when you return?"

"No, I probably won't be back at the office until late." With some final instructions, he bid the man goodbye and left the office.

A young woman sat at the front desk of the Housing Society.

Nick presented her with his card. "Is Mrs. Lennox in?"

She looked at him in surprise. "No, sir. She's away."

He eyed her more closely. "Away?"

"On holiday, sir."

"To Richmond?" She'd probably left early for the weekend, he thought, stifling the sense of disappointment he felt that this time he'd not been asked along.

"Oh, no, sir. She's gone to France."

He stared at her. She might as well have said to China.

"Is there some message you'd care to leave for her when she comes back?"

Nick collected his thoughts. "Er, no. That is, can you tell me how long she will be away?"

"A fortnight, sir."

Another tremor jolted him. "Do you know where she went exactly?"

"I'm not at liberty to say, sir. I'm sure her family can inform you if you are a friend of theirs."

Nick replaced his hat on his head. He was no friend of the Shepard family, that was certain. It looked like someone was trying to separate them again. "Thank you. Good day to you."

"Good day, sir."

When he returned to his office, his secretary hadn't yet left.

"You're back, sir?"

Nick sighed heavily. Another long evening behind his desk awaited him. Although he'd told himself it was time to make some changes in his life, he found he had no heart to go to concerts or to the theater by himself.

"I'm glad you returned, sir." His secretary laid an envelope on his desk. "This came by the late afternoon post."

"Thank you." He didn't recognize the neat script on the front. "Why don't you get on home?"

"You don't wish to finish your letter?"

He shook his head knowing he'd not be able to concentrate on figures now.

"Very well, sir, good night."

After he'd left, Nick looked at the envelope more closely. It was postmarked *Deauville*. His pulse quickened. Could Alice have written him? But it wasn't her writing. He turned the letter over. On the flyleaf was written M. Endicott.

He picked up his letter opener, more puzzled than ever, and slit the envelope open. Could something have happened to Alice?

Dear Mr. Tennent,

Greetings, or should I say "bonjour," from the coast of Normandy. At the last minute, I invited Alice and Austen to accompany me on my annual holiday. The outing has really done wonders for both of them. The weather has been wonderful and this lovely resort village is perfectly charming.

I am writing to suggest that if you can spare a few days from your business—or if you can perhaps find some business to do in France—that you come to Deauville. I recommend the Grand Hotel. It is very pleasant.

I look forward to your arrival.
A bientôt!
Macey Endicott

Nicholas reread the letter two more times before it began to sink in. Alice's friend was on his side.

He stuffed the hotel stationery back into its envelope and stood. Glancing at the wall clock, he saw it was only five o'clock. But he mustn't waste any time. He had a lot to do before catching a boat across the Channel.

"Mama, may I go back on the beach after tea?"

Alice looked at her son across the wide wicker table on the hotel veranda. "It's a little late in the day. Perhaps tomorrow."

Austen was distracted by the waiter who set down a platter of pastries and teacakes in the middle of their table.

"Oh, don't those look delicious," Macey said. "Which one would you like?"

Austen examined them carefully, his brow scrunched up in indecision.

Alice smiled then allowed her gaze to wander beyond their table to the ocean view on her right. She hugged her teacup in her hands. Macey had been right to urge her to take this holiday. In the few days she'd been here, she already felt a calming of her spirit.

The excitement of the journey across the English Channel and their location by the sea had also distracted Austen enough so that he hadn't mentioned Nicholas more than a few times. As for herself, she'd managed to push him to the recesses of her mind, at least during the daylight hours.

Nicholas. As she said the name to herself, she suddenly saw him walk out onto the terrace from the hotel lobby.

She blinked. Was she dreaming? How could she suddenly be thinking a name and conjure up the person in question? She lowered her cup, barely aware when it hit the saucer.

He was surveying the hotel guests on the veranda. In a few seconds he'd see them. Her heart sped up. She wasn't ready to face him. At the same instant she felt a burst of elation and longing so acute, it laughed to scorn all her illusion of having forgotten him. What was he doing here?

His eyes met hers and she had to clench her hands together to keep from springing up from the table and running toward him.

He made his way across the other tables to them.

Then he stood before her. "Hello, Alice." He gave her a brief nod, before turning to Macey, breaking into a smile. "Miss Endicott." His smile widened as he came to Austen. "Hello, Austen, fancy seeing you here."

Austen jumped up from his chair, almost sending it toppling backwards. "Mr. Tennent! How jolly to see you here. I've been bathing. Can we go into the ocean together? Mama won't let me go beyond the very edge."

Nick glanced briefly at her before turning his attention back to Austen. "I should like that very much."

Macey extended her hand to Nicholas. "I'm so glad you could come. Please, sit down."

Nicholas glanced back at Alice, as if asking her permission. "Yes, yes, of course, please sit down. What are you doing here? Did you know we were here?"

As he pulled out the chair, Macey touched her hand, drawing her attention away from Nicholas. "Mr. Tennent is here because I invited him here."

Alice stared at her friend. "What?"

"I thought it would be nice if Mr. Tennent joined us here at the hotel for a few days, so I wrote to him."

Nicholas cleared his throat. "I was so glad to receive Miss Endicott's note and decided to combine a short holiday with business. I have been meaning to cross the Channel to look at a few firms I've had my eye on."

"I see." She nodded, understanding. Of course, business had brought him. "Well, I wish you success then."

"I came principally to enjoy a holiday, if you don't find my presence an intrusion to your own."

"N-no, of course not." She looked away from his keen observation.

Macey signaled the waiter for more tea and an extra place. Alice was able to compose her thoughts somewhat as Nicholas turned his attention to Austen.

She sighed, listening to Austen's chatter. Nicholas was remarkably patient with him. It was hard for her to believe the picture of him as a ruthless business executive. Her father had never exhibited the kind of attentiveness Nicholas was showing her son.

Was it all a front? Would it endure after Nicholas obtained what he wanted?

What did he want? Did she want to know?

The question left her full of expectancy and fear.

Mid-morning the following day, Alice emerged from a beach hut and stood a moment, shading her eyes from the bright sun, as she searched for Austen and Nicholas along the crowded seashore.

The Normandy beach was a wide, flat expanse of sand, the sparkling water lapping softly at its edge.

Shouts of children came to her from the water's edge and she strained to hear her son's voice.

She squinted at the two figures far out in the water, and she felt a momentary rise of panic. Austen had never ventured so far out. Her worry eased only slightly when she saw Nicholas standing right beside him. Her son was splashing around, clearly showing him he could swim.

Alice and Macey had only been on the female beach up to now. But today, with Nicholas's appearance, they had chosen the mixed beach so that he could teach Austen to swim. Alice had been reluctant at first until Nicholas had convinced her that there was less danger in the water if he knew how to swim.

Alice smoothed down the hip-length skirt of her dark blue wool serge bathing costume, hesitating to join Nicholas and Austen out in the water. Here in France, she'd noticed the beaches were less formal than across the Channel. Even some of the newer bathing costumes of the women had shocked her at first with their bloomerless skirts above the knee.

Still, she felt self-conscious appearing before Nicholas in the outfit. It was short-sleeved, with narrow bloomers beneath the skirt. Dark blue hose and espadrilles laced around her ankle and calf completed the suit.

Finally, seeing no help for it, she began walking over the hot sand, skirting the holiday goers. Family groups sat together on canvas chairs on the sand, and dozens of children played along the water's edge. Others, fully dressed, wandered through the crowds.

She reached the edge of the water and allowed the

506 A Man Most Worthy

mild surf to sweep over her toes, cringing a bit as the cold water seeped into her shoes.

"There she is!" Austen waved both arms at her. "Mama!"

She ventured farther in, allowing the water to swirl about her ankles.

Nick and Austen begun running toward her, their legs kicking up the water. She hugged her arms to her chest as the water splashed her. "Stay away from me! You're getting me wet!" she scolded in mock anger.

As their intent became clear, she screamed, "Oh, no, you don't!" Before she could back away far enough, they grabbed her hands and pulled her into the water.

She cried out at the shock of cold water. "No!" It was useless to struggle against their firm tugging. Her feet stumbled in the wet sand but Nicholas's strong grip didn't let her fall.

"Oh, it's too cold!" The next second, Nicholas lifted her from behind and threw her into the water. She was plunged in up over her head and screamed as she went in.

She came out, spluttering and dripping, determined to exact her revenge. "How dare you throw me in!" Laughter mingled with outrage in her voice.

"You'll soon warm up." Nick laughed, but before he could say another word, she lunged toward him, toppling him backwards. "Hey!" he went under, his legs pulled out from under him.

He easily fought free of her grasp and came up from the water, shaking the water from his hair. Austen laughed with glee. "You both went under!"

Nicholas began walking toward her again, a glint

in his eye. "Does she realize the penalty she must now pay?" The words brought back a flash from that day over the chess board and its dire consequences. A part of her thrilled as it had then when she'd ventured such a daring challenge.

Seeing his intention, she backed away, shaking her head. "No, you don't! Now we're even."

Austen began clapping his hands. "Mama, you've got to swim away!"

But before she could make another move, Nick lunged for her and, grabbing her by the waist and plunging her under. Alice struggled to loosen herself but he only tightened his hold around her. She grabbed him by the arms and attempted to push herself upward and him down, but he moved his arms around her, bringing her against his chest. Although she kicked her feet, he held her fast.

He rose, bringing her head out of the water but not loosening his hold.

Austen came up beside them. "Mama, Mr. Tennent has caught you!"

Alice's hands were flattened against his chest. He gazed down at her and chuckled. She felt the sound resonate against her palms.

"Yes!" she managed breathlessly. Before drawing away from him, she looked up into his eyes and found herself captured by the look in his eyes. It both frightened and exhilarated her as nothing had since that long ago day above the chess board. She felt as daring as the girl she'd been then. If they'd been alone, she would have reached up on her toes and kissed him.

"Mama, he won't let you go!"

Suddenly she became aware of their scandalous position. She pushed herself out of his embrace and was almost surprised—and a little disappointed—when he let her go immediately. He turned abruptly to Austen and pulled him out of the water by the armpits and splashed him back down again. "And now I've got you!"

Austen shouted with laughter. Nicholas repeated the dunking. As if hiding herself, Alice crouched down in the water up to her neck and watched them. Nicholas stood waist-high in the water, and she couldn't help noticing his muscular upper arms and shoulders through the short-sleeved suit whose dark wool material clung to his skin. When he glanced her way, she turned quickly toward the beach.

Her eyes scanned the crowds until she spotted Macey holding her bright blue parasol.

Alice whirled around when Nick approached her from behind. "Oh—!" She gave a nervous laugh. "I was afraid you'd try to drown me again."

"Drown you? What are you talking about?"

"I'm not lowering my guard around you and Austen again."

He smiled, standing tall above her. "All right, let me see your stroke."

She adjusted her oiled silk bathing cap. "I told you, I'm a very poor swimmer."

He frowned. "How is that, growing up in Richmond?"

She averted her gaze, feeling self-conscious under his scrutiny. "Well, the river has too strong a current, and there was nowhere else appropriate. Remember, I grew up in London."

His next words took her by surprise. "I can teach you the basics."

"Oh, I'm too old—"

"Nonsense, I didn't learn until I was out west in the States."

His dark brown eyes held a teasing light. "Think of it as recompense. There's finally something I can teach you."

A flutter began in her stomach at the thought of his holding her the way she'd seen him hold Austen.

"Mr. Tennent is going to teach Mama to swim!" chanted Austen, jumping up and down in the water. The ocean reached his upper chest, and Alice admonished him to be careful.

"He'll be all right." Nicholas turned to Austen. "Show your mother what you can do already."

Austen promptly flopped onto his back and floated on the surface, the soft swells carrying him. "See, Mama, I can float!"

"My goodness. That's wonderful."

She turned to Nicholas with a smile. "So quickly!"

"Now, it's your turn."

"Oh, I don't think—" she said, backing away.

He stepped toward her. She backed away some more, but that only brought her into deeper water.

Before she knew what he intended, he bent to lift her. She yelped and circled his neck with her arms, afraid he was going to dunk her into the water again.

"Relax," he murmured, holding her above the water

and cradling her body against his chest. "I won't let you go. I'm just teaching you to float."

"All right," she stuttered, letting go of his neck.

"We'll go where it's shallower. Come along, Austen."

Austen splashed along beside them.

Nicholas began to ease her into the water. She couldn't help grabbing one of his arms, feeling the rock-hard biceps beneath her fingers. She bit her lip to keep from crying out.

"Don't worry, I've got you. Besides, the water is only about three feet deep here."

She glanced up at his amused tone. "Just don't let me go, yet."

"I won't, I promise." His eyes met hers and she felt for a few seconds that the threat of drowning didn't presently come from the water beneath her. As if unaware of the sensations he was awaking in her, he drew his glance from hers and said in a calm voice, "Your body will naturally float, if you let yourself relax."

She marveled how anyone could sound so normal when her whole body had gone rigid from the feel of his arms under her and his body so close to hers.

"You must relax." His tone became soothing.

She tried breathing deeply, looking beyond him at the puffy white clouds overhead.

"Put your head back and stretch your arms out." As he spoke, he pushed her torso upward, so she felt as if her head were going to sink into the water. She resisted at first but then as the soft swell of the water beneath her bore her up and down, she began to marvel at the ride atop the gentle waves.

He was soon able to let go and she gave a little laugh. "It feels wonderful, just floating."

"Mr. Tennent, let's build a sandcastle!"

She started at the sound of her son's voice, she'd felt so tranquil.

"Very well, let's ask your mother." Nicholas's dark eyes loomed over hers again, his head blocking the sun. "Are you game?"

"All right." She smiled into his gaze, wondering at the feelings this man was reawakening in her. She felt like an adolescent once again.

"Come on!" shouted Austen.

They followed Austen out of the surf and chose a location near the water's edge, where the sand was hard-packed and wet.

She retrieved her straw hat from beside their beach chairs, trading her beach cap for it, and went to kneel beside her son, who was already busy digging in the wet sand with his two hands. "You know, when the tide comes in, the castle will disappear."

Nick looked up from where he was beginning to heap up sand into a mound. "That's all right. The tide is going out now, so it'll be hours before that happens."

They worked together for a good while, the shouts of other children on the beach floating around them.

Soon, a small crowd of children had gathered round. Some began to build their own castles nearby, chattering in French as their sturdy hands heaped up the sand.

Alice was decorating crenellated walls with seashells. She glanced over at Nick, whose head was bent near her son's, both concentrated on their side of the now sprawling edifice.

She felt a pang at the sight of the two dark-haired heads, one whose straight hair flopped over his brow, the other, whose crisp waves glinted in the sun.

It gave her a good feeling to see her son so active and normal. She paused over the word, realizing how worried she'd been about him since Julian's death, and her own move back to London. How would Julian view the scene?

He had been such a gentle man. She was sure he would be happy that his son had someone he could look up to. But could he? Once again, her brother's and Victor's warnings came back to her.

She pushed their ugly words aside. Her thoughts returned to what she'd felt earlier held against Nicholas's chest. How different from what she'd known with Julian. She pressed her lips together, resisting a comparison. Julian had been so good to her. He'd offered love and solace to a lonely, unloved young woman. But he'd been sick much of their married life. She'd never undergone a sense of wanting to abandon all moorings to an unknown, unfettered experience as she had in Nicholas's arms. It frightened her. It meant a letting go of all that was safe and calm.

She glanced over at Nicholas now, remembering he was the one who had first kindled these yearnings in her so long ago. He looked up at that second, and her cheeks grew warm. He lifted his brows in inquiry but she shook her head and bent over her work in the sand once more.

Why had Nicholas come to them now and why was he being so kind? What did he want from this friendship? The questions she'd thought to escape by leaving

London resurged and she saw only danger ahead with a man who'd awakened her once before and was doing so again. Once before her heart had known devastating heartbreak because of this man.

Could she trust it to him again?

Chapter Thirteen

Nick stood in waist-deep water, watching Austen flail his thin arms in the water, creating more splashing than movement but little by little, his small body began mobilizing away from him.

Alice clapped her hands. "Very good. You'll be a champion swimmer soon."

Nick came up beside her. "Are you ready for your lesson?"

She took a deep breath before plunging into the water and beginning the breaststroke he'd been teaching her.

"That's right, bend your knees and kick hard. Very good, bring your face up with each stroke." He kept his tone impersonal, although each day it was becoming more and more difficult to keep his distance. She swam a bit farther, keeping parallel to the beach as he'd taught her. When she finally stopped and stood to look back from where she'd started, she asked, "How did I do?"

"You're a remarkably quick learner. Come, swim back now."

While she complied, he glanced down at Austen who

was tugging on his arm. "Look at me dive!" The boy held his nose and ducked under the water, no longer afraid of submerging his head completely.

When Alice stood next to him again in the water, she said, "I'm going to sit with Macey a while."

He glanced at her wet bathing costume, steeling his features to betray nothing of what he felt inside at the revealing silhouette. "We'll be out soon," he told her.

"We're going to build another sandcastle," Austen added.

Nick watched Alice leave, wondering if he had scared her away. He'd tried his best in the preceding days to be nothing more than an attentive friend to her and an uncle figure to her son. Since his arrival, they had regained much of the friendliness they'd first enjoyed in Richmond, but he still sensed a reticence in her that he hadn't been able to break through.

Later that evening after dinner, he waited on the veranda, hoping she would come down after bidding Austen goodnight. They'd spent most evenings with Miss Endicott and in the company of some of the other guests, sometimes crossing the bridge to the neighboring town of Trouville or strolling down the long lit pier between the two towns.

He breathed a sigh of relief when he saw Alice entering the verandah by herself this evening. He turned to her from his view of the ocean when she came to stand beside him by the railings. "Where's Miss Endicott?"

"She decided to stay upstairs tonight. She asked me to give you her excuses."

Was his ally helping his cause along this evening? "Is she feeling unwell?"

Alice shook her head. "I think she merely wanted a quiet evening to herself."

Before Alice could suggest anything with the other guests, Nick said, "Would you like to walk along the beach?"

Instead of replying immediately, she stood a moment, gazing out at the black sea. To avoid a refusal, he said, "We can see the remains of today's sandcastle."

She smiled. "I imagine the tide has washed it away."

The steady rhythm of the waves beckoned them. The murmur of other holiday guests came over the verandah, but the beach was wide and empty.

They descended the shallow wooden steps onto the grassy sand dunes. Before leaving the steps, she halted. "Let me take off my shoes so we can walk on the sand better."

He held out his hand and she put hers in it while she bent to remove her heeled slippers. Holding them by the straps, she straightened. "Thank you."

"Ready?"

"Yes."

"Come." He offered his hand again and after a second's hesitation, she put hers in it.

The dune grasses shifted in the breeze. A lacy cloud drifted over the half-moon overhead.

He enjoyed the feel of her soft hand in his, realizing he'd never allowed himself this kind of companionship with a woman.

They walked in silence until they neared the spot where they had built a sandcastle earlier. The water now swirled around it. What had been sharp edges before were only shapeless mounds.

"So much work," she murmured, taking care not to step too close to the encroaching waves.

"Yes, like everything in life."

She glanced at him, as if surprised. "Do you see your own work that way?"

"In a sense. I hope it will outlast me, but I know I have only a season to accomplish what I wish."

"You have no one to leave it to?"

His dark eyes surveyed her over the sandcastle and he shrugged. "I have my brothers and their offspring, but I've provided well for them over the years."

She disengaged her hand from his and hugged her light cashmere shawl closer.

"Cold?"

She shook her head. "My wrap is sufficient." After a few minutes, she asked, "Why haven't you ever married?"

He gave a deep sigh, breathing in the sharp, salt-laden night air, having known this question would eventually come. He paused, deciding how to answer. She was waiting attentively.

"When I met you, you were too young." He didn't flinch from the surprised look in her eyes. "I had nothing to offer you, even if your age had not been an issue. Your father would never have countenanced anything between us."

He gave an embarrassed laugh. "I don't know if you'll believe me when I tell you that when I sailed for America, I had every intention of working hard until I had enough to come back and declare myself to you."

"I never knew," she said softly, her gaze roaming over his features as if seeing them for the first time.

He shook his head. "I was confident I would make a fortune virtually overnight. It didn't work out that way. The years went by and fortune seemed to elude me despite my efforts. I realized after a while that it had been a vain notion to think I could come back to England and win you. After several years had passed, I imagined you married with children."

She looked down at the sand at her feet.

He shoved a hand through his hair, finding the next part the most difficult. "Five years ago, I decided it was time for me to marry and settle down, begin to build a dynasty and all that rot." Again, he gave a shame-faced laugh.

"I had had no time for romantic entanglements up to then. All my time and resources had gone into building up my company. But then I felt I had reached the place where I could begin to enjoy the fruits of my success. I began to look around me at what San Francisco society had to offer."

"You met someone?" came her soft voice.

"Yes." When she said nothing more, he continued. "I fancied myself in love. I should have known what she fancied was my pocketbook."

"No—"

He looked up at the swiftly spoken word.

"How can someone have treated you so shabbily." She sounded angry.

"Do you really think all women are as selfless as you?" he asked gently, touched by her obvious outrage.

"But, you have so many other assets than material wealth. I'm sure there were many women who would look beyond that."

"Do you think so?"

"I'm sure of it."

"You are as kind as you always were."

"I'm sorry if she hurt you."

He gave another cynical laugh. "I think if anything was hurt, it was my pride. I know now I was not really in love with her, if the state of my emotions are anything to be judged after I found her giving herself freely to another man."

Her sharp intake of breath caused him another bitter smile. "I don't know how anyone could be so cruel."

He ran a hand through his hair, looking away. "She was young, and I cannot say I blame her now for not falling in love with someone more interested in his work than in her."

"You cared more for your work?"

He chanced a cautious glance at her, gauging her tone. "At that time, yes."

He wanted to take her hand again, but she stepped away from him. "Shall we continue?"

"If you'd like," he said, sensing her withdrawal.

He led her beyond the high water mark to where the sand was dry and still warm from the day's sun. They passed another couple strolling along arm-in-arm. They had walked about a quarter of a mile when he halted again to gaze out at the dark ocean and listen to the sound of waves. The surf had risen a little and small white caps were visible in the moonlight.

She stooped to pick up a piece of driftwood and tossed it into the waves. It disappeared in the dark. "I wonder if I'll find it washed up tomorrow."

"Like me after fifteen years."

She glanced up at him and smiled. "I'm glad you decided to return after so long."

Her softly spoken words encouraged him. "When you tilt your head like that, you look just like the sixteen-year-old you used to be."

She gave a nervous laugh. "I'm far from that girl."

"I want to kiss you."

Her gaze shot upward at the abrupt statement.

She swallowed. "Perhaps that's not a good idea."

He lifted a tendril of hair that had blown across her cheek. "Why not?"

She looked away. "I'm not that girl you knew, nor are you the man I knew." She ended in a tone so low he had to bend to catch the words.

He stroked her cheek with the back of his hand. With one step she'd be in his arms, but he sensed she was as skittish as the strands of hair tossed about her face.

"Perhaps who we are now is better," he murmured, his fingers continuing their caress. Her skin was velvety soft.

"I don't know." Her voice was breathless although she tilted her head back a fraction, as if seeking his caresses. "You scare me sometimes."

"Scare you?" He narrowed his eyes at her, her words throwing him. "How do you mean?"

"You seem so sure of yourself, of what you want." Were those tears glinting in her eyes?

"I've never forgotten you, Alice," he murmured, his voice growing husky as he came to the end of the words, "and I've wanted you for a very long time." His gaze roamed over her, seeking some sign that she wanted him as much as he wanted her.

Not allowing her a chance to move away, he circled the nape of her neck with his hand and drew her closer. "Kiss me, Alice," he whispered against her, his lips hovering just over hers.

And then he touched them with his own.

He kissed her slowly, savoring the moment. He dug his fingers into her hair, bringing it tumbling from its loose knot. It was as silky as he'd always imagined.

Alice gasped as his mouth came down and covered hers. His lips felt warm and soft against hers. Had he truly wanted her all this time? Her body and spirit thrilled at the thought. As she leaned closer to him, her arms inched upward, her hands clutching his lapels.

He kissed her thoroughly and she got the sense he knew exactly what he was doing. The way she imagined he did everything.

She couldn't help responding. Giving herself as she'd never done before, she felt like a bud that had only begun to open before its development had been arrested. Her petals unfurled at last, stretching out towards the sunshine.

Moments later they broke apart slightly. She felt dizzy with the sensations swirling through her and was glad of his hands on her back. She murmured against his shirt front. "You must have kissed a lot of women."

"I've had little practice."

She looked up at the words to find a frown creasing his brow. He loosened his hold enough to peer into her face. "I've just dreamed of this one for a very long time."

His answer stunned her. He couldn't mean he'd thought of kissing her for so many years.

She gave a nervous laugh. "I hope I didn't disappoint you, then."

He brought a finger up to touch her cheek. "No, you didn't disappoint. On the contrary. You've made me want you more."

The answer frightened and thrilled her. Yet, he spoke only of wanting her. "Does this mean that you are pursuing me the way you do a business enterprise?" Although she spoke the words lightly, she searched his eyes, fearing the truth.

"Is that what you think?"

"I don't know what to think."

With a sigh he let her go and stood a few feet away from her, looking out at the ocean. Had her answer displeased him?

He took up a piece of driftwood of his own and threw it into the surf. "I've learned over the years to go after what I want. Sometimes it takes me years before I get what I want, I'll admit." He turned to her again, and she stepped back, his words chilling her more than the breeze.

She drew the shawl tighter around her. "Do you always know what you want?"

"Generally speaking."

"Do you always get what you want?"

His mouth twisted. "As you have heard, no." After a moment he spoke. "What do *you* want, Alice?"

"I don't know," her answer was almost lost on the sound of the surf.

"Are you sure about that?"

She struggled to discern the meaning of his words. Did he think she was playing a game with him?

Before she could find a suitable reply, he said, "What are you so afraid of?"

How could she tell him it was the feelings he awakened in her that she feared most of all?

Abruptly, he turned away. "Come, you're getting cold. I'll take you back before you get a chill." His voice sounded almost harsh.

Had she disappointed him so much with her response? Would he again go without a word, leaving her unfulfilled, yearning…brokenhearted?

He began walking back toward the hotel—a distant glimmer in the dark, not bothering to offer his hand or arm this time.

She followed silently after him, unsure whether she felt anger or disappointment.

Nick plodded through the sand, her accusation still smarting. Did she truly think he was as cold-blooded as to equate her to a business? He'd told her he'd never forgotten her and dreamed of their kiss—had that meant nothing to her?

The kiss he'd dreamed of for so many years had finally materialized. Manna in the desert, elixir to a dying man, the taste of her lips lingered in his memory—and made him wish for more.

He'd restrained himself, unsure if she'd welcome his kiss. But she'd given herself to him in a way that had emboldened him to hope that perhaps she could someday give him her heart.

Chancing a glance in her direction, he could read nothing from her expression in the dark. Unlike the young girl who'd kissed him inexpertly so many years ago, Alice was now a widow, someone who'd known the love of a man—a most worthy one from all reports. Was she comparing his kiss to her late husband's—a man who'd had the advantage of enjoying years with the woman he loved?

He dug his hands into his pockets, swallowing the bitterness that rose in him and threatened to spoil the recent intoxication of Alice's embrace. Clamping down on his emotions, he quickened his step, when all he wanted was to stop and grab Alice once again and crush her to himself until his kisses obliterated her late husband's.

By the time they reached the hotel and he put a hand to her arm to help her up the steps, he had no idea how to proceed.

He knew very well Alice was not like a business— although he'd faced plenty of complicated situations in the latter, situations requiring careful proceedings and lots of finesse. But his fiasco in San Francisco had taught him how little he understood women.

He was a different man now, and Alice was a completely different quantity from the young woman who'd jilted him. At the moment he had no idea how to read her. In the light spilling out from the wide doors of the hotel, she looked coolly elegant and not like a woman whom he'd so recently ravaged with his kisses.

"Thank you for the walk," she said in the well-bred tones of a lady being returned from a concert. "It was lovely."

Lovely? The moment he'd waited for for fifteen years relegated to a description one used to describe blanc-mange or a bouquet of flowers?

She looked away from him. "I think I'll retire now."

He nodded. "Let me walk you to your room."

"Very well."

They walked silently up the stairs. At her door, she held out her hand, not meeting his gaze anymore. He took her hand in his. At the last moment, he found he didn't have the control necessary to merely shake her hand and leave. Tentatively, feeling as unsure as a schoolboy, he leaned down and kissed her on the cheek.

He felt her stiffen a fraction. Feeling rebuffed, he bowed his head. "Good night. Sleep well."

Was he destined to destroy whatever he reached for in the emotional realm? Was he the man Alice thought he was—nothing but an avaricious, ambitious, ruthless business tycoon?

How could he convince her otherwise?

Alice stood a long time at the narrow balcony in her room, staring out at the sea, hearing the relentless swish of waves, in and out. The sound mirrored her feelings, which swung from exhilaration at the remembrance of Nick's kiss to the doubts and fears rising to displace it.

She remembered the last time in her life she had allowed herself to feel like this. Only Nicholas had ever touched the deepest places in her.

But she'd paid a high price for reaching for what she'd wanted without weighing the consequences.

Banished from home, she had had to endure the strict atmosphere of her austere aunt and uncle and endure the taunts of their offspring. She hadn't been allowed to return to London until her twenty-first birthday.

That had been a turning point for her. A large party had been planned, of course, at a hotel ballroom. At the last moment, her father had absented himself. It had been the loneliest day of her life—swarmed by acquaintances and few loved ones.

Acquaintances. It had been Nick who'd first taught her the difference between them and real friends.

That day, Alice had realized her father would never change. She would always be waiting for him to come home, and something more important would always keep him away or give him only enough time to come in and leave before she'd have a chance to do something to capture his attention.

A week later she'd met Julian. He was a young divinity student visiting a relative in Richmond. She'd met him at church one morning. He'd called on her the next day.

His dreams of his own church and helping the poor in his community had inspired her. During the six weeks he'd been at his relatives recuperating from an illness, she'd grown to admire the young man.

But she'd never felt with him what she'd experienced with Nicholas.

Her mind went over that summer before her seventeenth birthday when she'd first met Nick. He'd fascinated her then as he did now. His strength of mind, strength of purpose, his ability to focus on her and make her feel like the most special creature on earth.

But he'd disappeared and crushed her youthful heart.

Why hadn't he ever written to her? Not even a note to tell her he could no longer see her? Day after day she'd waited for a line, one word from him. She would have run away with him then.

But she'd heard nothing. Her world had been ripped

apart by him. She'd even gone back a few days later to Richmond Park where they'd ridden and found their two handkerchiefs still lying on the rock, stiff and dry.

She still had them folded away in a drawer.

And now?

Did Nicholas love her? He had said nothing of love. Only want. Did he want her as a possession, like owning a business? She'd vowed long ago never to marry a man like her father.

She gripped the iron railing under her hands, knowing she should go in but knowing she would only toss and turn in bed. She had loved Julian, she was sure of it, but the tumult she felt around Nicholas threw what she'd felt for Julian in doubt. It reawakened all her girlhood longings.

She put her head in her hands, hating the direction of her thoughts. Why did her love for Julian now seem so pallid in contrast to what Nicholas stirred in her?

But she'd been a good wife! She'd supported her husband in his work and nursed him through his illnesses and been with him at the end. Nothing else could compare to that.

Why did Nicholas have to reenter her life now and confuse her so? And what of Austen? Would he think so little of his mother if he thought his father was being replaced? She thought of how good Nick was with Austen. Her son was finally emerging from his shell and behaving like a normal, active seven-year-old. Would Nicholas cause him to forget his father?

Would Nicholas always be there for Austen?

Her son had already lost one father. She would not let him lose two.

* * *

The next morning, Nick was down early, having woken at dawn and watched the sun rise over the Normandy coast. He entered the dining room, impatient for his first sight of Alice to see how she would greet him. Would she repudiate him? Ignore what had happened between them? Ask him to leave?

He heard Austen's cheerful voice soon after he had sat down. The boy came over to his table, followed by his nanny.

"Can we see if my sandcastle is still there this morning?" was his first question as he took his place.

Nick nodded to Miss Grove and pulled a chair out for her. "I'm afraid I checked on it last night, and it didn't survive the tide." At the look of chagrin on the boy's face, he added, "We'll build another one."

"After breakfast?" He lifted his chin as his nanny tied the napkin around his neck.

Nick smiled and sat back down. "I thought we might visit the hippodrome. Have you ever seen horses race each other around a track?"

Austen shook his head.

"It can be quite exciting." He signaled a waiter over and ordered breakfast for the boy. His French was rudimentary—taught to him by his mother when he was a boy. He turned to Miss Grove, who had a better command of the language. "I'm afraid you'd better order your own."

She smiled and turned to the waiter.

At that moment, he saw Alice and her friend enter the dining room together. They spotted him and made their way to the table.

He stood before they reached it and waited for them.

He nodded to Miss Endicott and turned immediately to Alice.

"Good morning," he said, trying to read her expression.

She lifted her blue eyes to him, the corners of her mouth lifting in what seemed to him a tentative smile. Was she, too, unsure how to proceed? It gave him hope. It meant she was not rejecting his suit out of hand.

His own smile grew and he pulled out a chair for her.

"Thank you," she murmured.

She looked so fetching today in a white gown all ruched up the front, with big blue bows matching the deep color of her eyes going up the length of it.

He turned reluctantly away from her and to Miss Endicott.

"Thank you," she replied when he'd pulled out a chair for her as well. "It's a fine morning, is it not?"

He made an attempt to join in the casual pleasantries as they ordered their breakfast and he mentioned his idea for visiting the famous hippodrome. They seconded the idea enthusiastically.

"Perhaps we can take a ride around the countryside afterwards," suggested Miss Endicott. "I've heard there are some lovely chateaux and apple orchards to be seen."

They continued planning their day as they ate.

When they broke up after breakfast, planning to meet again in a short while, Nick arranged for a trip back to Le Havre to follow up with a company which looked promising. He could work some this evening to catch up.

He didn't have a chance to talk alone with Alice until late that afternoon. During their outing, they behaved as if nothing had happened to them the night before. He took his cue from her, although he caught her looking at him a few times, and he was hard-pressed to keep from gazing at her.

When they returned from their long drive, they all separated to freshen up and take naps. Nick spent the time working in his room. He descended to the hotel lobby as soon as he could and looked about for Alice, hoping she might, too, want a word alone with him.

He stopped at the entrance of the veranda. Several guests were there and he'd almost turned back in disappointment when he saw her at the far end chatting with a couple. When she spotted him across the verandah she nodded and smiled. Encouraged, he walked over to the group. After a few pleasantries, they excused themselves from the couple.

When they were out of earshot, he turned to her. "Where's Austen?"

"He's still upstairs with Nanny Grove. I told her to put him to bed early this evening." She smiled at him. "He had a full day today. Thank you for planning such a lovely outing."

"You're welcome. It was nothing too extraordinary."

"You are good at organizing things."

He looked at her quizzically, not sure if she was complimenting him or not. He'd thought long and hard last night about how he should approach her. "I think we need to talk. Would you care to take a short walk before dinner?"

He waited, not realizing he was holding his breath

for her answer. She looked at him steadily. "Yes, I think we do."

He didn't know if her reply signaled good or ill for them, it was said so seriously. At least, it meant she hadn't dismissed his kiss.

This time, they walked along the boardwalk on the grassy sand dunes above the beach. The surf had continued rougher than in the preceding days and there were no bathers in the water nor many people on the sand.

They walked until they came to a small pavilion overlooking the ocean. Thankfully, it was deserted at the moment, most people having gone in to dress for dinner.

He motioned to the wooden bench set under the pavilion and took a seat beside her after she'd sat down.

Suddenly, all his neatly prepared speech deserted him. He cleared his throat. "I—"

"Wha—" she began.

They both stopped and then said, "I'm sorry—" at the same time.

"You first," she said quietly, clasping her hands on her lap like an obedient schoolgirl.

"I merely wanted to beg your pardon if I offended you last night. Was it presumptuous of me to—" he paused "—kiss you?"

He watched the color rise in her cheeks. Slowly, she raised her eyes and looked into his. Their deep blue pierced him anew and he wanted nothing more than to lean forward and kiss her again, this time showing none of the restraint he had last night. "No." The word was so low a whisper he would have lost it if it hadn't been so clearly apparent from the shape of her rosy lips.

Instead, he dared reach out and cover her hands with one of his. "I—that is—" Why was he acting so unsure of himself? He cleared his throat anew and began again. "I would like to court you, Alice."

The warmth grew in her eyes and then it slowly faded and she looked away from him at the ocean in front of them. "I thought about you last night, that is, about us. I didn't know what your intentions were."

He wanted to protest that his intentions were very clear but he remained silent sensing she needed to speak. He watched her profile and waited.

"I loved my husband and am not sure—"she bent her head and looked down at their hands "—if it's right to think of giving my affections to anyone else. Part of me feels as if I'm being disloyal to him."

He could see the words were difficult for her. They were no less difficult for him to receive. Would she ever love him the way he loved her? The irony was that he'd known her before ever Julian had met her.

He schooled his features to show nothing. "I don't want to compete with your late husband," he said, looking toward the ocean, whose whitecaps reflected his turbulent emotions. "I met you many, many years ago, and regret now that I didn't speak for you then."

"I never knew what our kiss had meant to you."

His hand reached out for hers again and he clasped it. "It meant the world to me. You were too young, and I left, thinking I would never have the right to pay my addresses to you, not if I remained in England. When I saw you upon my return, it was as if I'd been given another chance."

He squeezed her hands gently beneath his. "I would like to marry you, Alice."

She drew in her breath and he saw wonder in her eyes. Did it really come as a surprise to her? Before he could formulate any words, she tilted her chin the slightest degree upward and he found himself leaning down to her.

Once again, their lips met and he could think of nothing else.

She was the one who drew away first. "We mustn't here—in a public place like this…" Her breathing was rapid and she didn't quite meet his eyes.

"I'm sorry." He struggled to keep himself in check.

She moved a little apart from him and he felt a sense of loss.

He gave a deep sigh. "The Lord has allowed me to prosper and has given me the chance to come back and claim you. I don't ask you to know your mind now. All I ask is if you would permit me to call upon you when we return to London."

Slowly she nodded.

For now, it would have to be enough for him.

Chapter Fourteen

Alice felt sad to leave France. It had been a wonderful interlude, a time in which she wasn't required to think about anything back home. But she knew it couldn't last. Her work required her back in London. But she feared what a return to their normal lives would bring to the growing closeness between her and Nick when each returned to their work.

She was afraid to depend on Nick's attentiveness and thoughtfulness. What would he be like when he was pulled by the demands of his business? Would he even have time for her, much less a little boy, who'd grown dangerously fond of him?

As soon as she returned to her office, she put the final touches to the gala dinner for Nick, which was to be held that evening.

Even the lord mayor was going to be present. She smiled in satisfaction as she eyed the acceptance she'd just received in the post. It would be a grand event, a fitting event for Nick. No one deserved it more than he, who'd worked hard to achieve the success he was enjoying now.

She was looking over the menu in her office when she heard a throat clearing. She looked up to find her brother in the doorway.

"Hello, Geoffrey, what brings you here?" Her brother never came to the Housing Society office.

He walked into the office with barely a nod and took the chair opposite her desk. "I thought it the best place to find you this time of day."

She frowned at his grim tone. "What is it, Geoff? You sound as if you'd had some bad news."

The chair creaked under him as he leaned forward and removed his top hat and placed it on his lap. As usual he was impeccably dressed in a black frock coat and charcoal trousers. He fiddled with the brim of his hat.

"Are you still seeing that Tennent chap?"

She put down the pencil she'd been holding. "If you mean Nicholas Tennent, he is a friend of mine."

He frowned at her. "Is it true he showed up in Deauville at the same hotel you and Macey were at?"

"Yes." Who had told him? And why did she feel defensive as if she were still twenty-one?

He nodded at her as if he knew something she didn't. "You'd better have a care. Elizabeth Raleigh and her husband said they saw you there in his company quite a bit."

A British couple she'd seen one afternoon there. She shook her head at how quickly gossip traveled. "Mr. Tennent was very good company. He made himself very useful with Austen."

Geoffrey's lips thinned. "Careful he doesn't start looking at him as if he's his papa."

She looked down at her pencil, considering how she would answer. "Would that be such a bad thing?"

He made a choking sound. "I cannot believe you are even contemplating such a notion."

She looked at him steadily, her irritation changing to real anger. "Geoffrey, in case you've forgotten it, I am a full-grown woman who needn't consult with you about whom I am seeing."

"Except when it's an upstart scoundrel who is trying to muscle in on our family's firm."

"What are you saying?"

"He's bought out Steward."

She stared at him, the words making no sense. "Old Mr. Steward?" That was Father's principal partner, a silent partner who'd always left her father in full control of the day-to-day business of the company.

He nodded grimly. "Alistair was a trusting simpleton. Tennent seems to have charmed him at his club and convinced the doddering old fool to sell him his partnership. You know what this means?"

She didn't dare hazard a guess.

Geoff rubbed a hand across his chin. "He now owns fifty percent of our company, the firm our grandfather established and our father built up to what it is today."

She looked down at her desk, the papers she had been studying before her brother had walked in making no more sense to her. "I don't believe it. There must be some explanation."

Her brother gave a dry bark of a laugh. "Oh, Alice, don't be so naïve. There's an explanation all right. Tennent wants to get back at us for some slight that happened over fifteen years ago."

He jumped up and began to pace. "He'll stop at nothing until he destroys this family. Well, I won't have it!"

"What are you talking about?" Now, she was truly alarmed. Her normally stolid brother was acting positively choleric.

"Father sacked him. For what I don't know. Probably incompetence." He stopped in mid-stride and looked at her, thrusting his hat at her to drive home his point. "I spoke to Father's old secretary, not Simpson, but the man he hired to replace Tennent when he up and left Father."

She waited, dreading what her brother might say to destroy her newfound hopes for happiness.

"He says Father gave Tennent the boot without so much as a reference. It was right after that accident. He was in his rights to do so, since Tennent had only been with him a few weeks." Geoffrey shook his head in disgust. "It was then he took off for America. Now that he's made good, he probably wants to get back at Father."

Alice sat back in relief. "He already told me about Father. But he was almost thankful for it now. It was the reason he emigrated." She waved a hand. "My goodness, he's amassed a fortune. He doesn't need your company!"

Her brother wasn't listening to her. "It's clear Tennent has had it in for us since he has returned the wealthy American. He's out to prove something. He's got to be stopped or he'll destroy all our family has worked for for three generations—as well as your heart and reputation if you let him."

"You're wrong, Geoff."

Geoffrey pinioned her with a look. "This concerns you as much as it does me. This is Austen's future. Do you want some upstart secretary muscling his way in and stealing your son's inheritance?"

She gave an outraged laugh. "Nicholas would never do that!"

"So, it's *Nicholas* now? Gone as far as that, has it?"

She clamped her mouth shut. Seeing her brother's grim look, she relented enough to say, "Mr. Tennent wants to marry me."

"Hah! He not only wants to take over our firm, but he wants to have you, too! The filthy scoundrel. How dare he!"

Alice stood. "I won't have you saying such things about him!"

He leaned over the desk. "He doesn't care a whit for you! He just wants to humiliate us! He's out to prove a point!"

She put her hands to her ears, not wanting to hear any more.

"Don't you see, Alice? He just wants you in order to steal control of Father's firm."

"But you still have half the company. There's nothing he can do to buy you out!"

He leaned closer, his knuckles white atop the desk. "*You own ten percent in the company.* All he needs to do is marry you and *he'll control the firm.*"

"What are you saying?" she whispered. "Father disinherited me."

Geoff moved his head slowly from side to side like a pendulum, his gaze never leaving hers. "Not entirely.

Victor persuaded him to allow you ten percent. It was small enough not to make a deal of difference. Victor said we would merely invest your profits and keep them for Austen when he reached his majority. That's the only way Father would be satisfied to change his will."

She fell back in her chair, feeling numb. "Why was I never told this?"

"You can't let yourself be used like this!" Geoff jabbed a hand through his hair, his voice cracking with desperation. He'd never been so distraught, not even when she'd married Julian.

She stared at her brother. "Why didn't you tell me?"

"Because it was the only way Father would agree! You disobeyed him. Be thankful for Victor who championed you. Besides, the shares have made nothing this past year.

"All that's neither here nor there now. You've never lacked for anything. I've given you Father's house, you've a houseful of servants. What's of concern now is Tennent. He wants to ruin us, I tell you. He's bought up the company behind a front."

"What are you talking about?"

He gave a harsh laugh. "While he woos you, he's quietly bought the shares using another company, so none of us—least of all *you*—will know he's behind it."

It couldn't be. "There must be some explanation."

Geoffrey continued pacing. "Now all he needs is your ten percent, which he'll get as soon as he marries you. You haven't gone as far as agreeing, have you?" he asked, swiveling around to her.

She didn't bother answering, but continued trying to

sort through it. "B-but Nicholas wouldn't know about my shares. How could he know?"

"Oh, doesn't he?" he barked out a grim laugh. "He's made sure to find out everything about our firm."

Her world was cracking under her and she had no idea how it had come about. She leaned her head into a hand, trying to think clearly.

Geoffrey's voice grew quiet. "One of the board members came to tell me this morning. They're going to force me out as president and chairman of the board."

She drew in her breath. "How is that possible?"

"All he needs is full control and he'll demand my full resignation. I know it." He ran a hand through his hair, his eyes darting left and right.

"Why should he want to do that?"

He pressed his lips together, a sheen of perspiration covering the top of his lip. "Because he's a ruthless scoundrel. You've got to stop him."

"Me? What can I possibly do?"

"Don't let yourself be tricked by him. He can't think he can take us all over. He only wants you to solidify his hold on our business." He grabbed her hand. She'd never seen desperation in her brother's eyes. "You've got to help me. It'll mean my ruin otherwise." He looked away from her. "I've made some poor decisions.

Then his bloodshot eyes focused on her again, and his hand squeezed hers painfully. "Don't let him use you! He only wants to take you as the crowning achievement to his insatiable greed. Don't let yourself become his trophy! He cares nothing for you, only what your name represents. It's only his pride because Father thwarted his ambitions so long ago."

She broke away from her brother's hand. "Leave me, please leave me." Her voice cracked and she turned away from her brother.

She had to see Nick. That's all she knew after her brother left and the office grew quiet, broken only by the ticking of a clock on a shelf nearby. She didn't know how much time had passed as she sat there staring at her desk, unseeing.

Could Geoff's accusations be true? Was Nick only interested in getting back at her father through her? Had he pretended some attraction to her, was his kiss only pretense? Thinking back to it now, had what she took for expertise been in truth the carefully controlled performance of someone proceeding with his calculations, weighing everything as he did in business? Had he been playing a role, a role he may indeed have found distasteful?

She stood from her desk, unable to bear her thoughts.

But what need had Nick to stoop to feign an attraction? He was rich and powerful. He could have any woman he wanted. Why bother with her family?

She stood at the window looking through the film of curtain at the street beyond. Her thoughts went back to that summer she'd first met him. How infatuated she'd been.

All the fears of abandonment following his disappearance, of thinking herself unlovable, came to flood her now.

Oh, dear Lord, show me the way. Show me the truth. Is this man worthy of my love? she prayed.

She had to know. Like an automaton, she picked up

her gloves, hat and handbag, glancing down at her bare finger before donning her gloves. She'd removed her wedding band when she'd come back from Deauville.

Had she betrayed Julian's memory for someone so wholly opposed to his values? No, she wouldn't think it. It couldn't be.

She stumbled toward the omnibus stop by sheer instinct, her thoughts all consumed by Nicholas Tennent.

The omnibus was crowded with people and she squeezed onto the wooden bench between two women, a heavy-set one whose clothes reeked of sweat, and another who barely moved to make room for her. Alice held her lawn handkerchief to her nostrils, feeling sick as the omnibus began to rattle and sway over the cobblestones.

Bitterness and doubt crept into her thoughts, try as she might to suppress them, not least because of Nick's absence from Austen. Austen had asked for him every day. They'd seen little of Nicholas since their return from Deauville. He'd sent her a note the day after their arrival in London that he'd found several things pending at his office which would take him a few days to clear up. Had one of them been the takeover of her father's firm?

When she arrived at the number on Nick's business card, she glanced up in surprise at the imposing office building. Expecting a modest office within the building, she was further taken aback to discover the whole five-story building housed Tennent and Company.

She opened the polished wooden door, its brass plaque glowing. Inside, clerks bustled to and fro, others bent over their high desks, all looking important. It reminded her painfully of her father's firm. The few times she'd stepped across its threshold, she'd been confronted by the same hum of activity—of money being made, she'd always told herself. Now, it gave her a feeling of foreboding. Had she really stopped to think about what gave Nick's life meaning? All that she'd repudiated.

A young clerk cleared his throat beside her, and she jumped. "May I be of service, madam?"

"Yes. Yes, please. I should like to see Mr. Tennent." She handed him her card.

He glanced at it and gave her a slight bow. "Very well. Would you care to wait in a more private chamber?"

"No, thank you. I shall wait here." She clasped her hands over her handbag and edged against the wall.

"Very well, madam."

In a few minutes, he returned. "Mr. Tennent will see you, if you'd care to follow me."

He led her to the lift and held the door open for her. With a bang, he slid it shut and the brass cage began to rise with creaking sounds. She was calm enough by then to notice it went to the top floor. Up here, everything was hushed. The building featured more modern devices and more opulence than her father's. Oil paintings lined the corridors on the top floor and a thick Turkish carpet covered the anteroom floor. They stopped before a heavy mahogany door at the end of the corridor.

The clerk knocked and immediately entered. He stayed at the door and motioned her in. "Mrs. Lennox to see you, sir."

When Alice entered, Nick had already risen from the large desk and was advancing toward her, his hand held out. "Alice, how good to see you." He gave the clerk a curt nod. "Thank you, Jeffries, that will be all."

She heard the heavy door click behind her and felt at a loss as to what to say. The sight of Nick overwhelmed her. In the scant few days she hadn't seen him, she already missed him unbearably, and she realized in that moment she didn't want to feel this way about a man. The risks were too great.

He took her hand in his and she fought the impulse to draw back. But she detected a look of puzzlement in his features, and for a second she thought he would stoop down and kiss her. But he let go of her hand and stepped back.

"I was going to stop by Park Lane this evening to call on you." He ran a hand through his hair and half-turned away as if embarrassed. "I bought something for Austen."

"You needn't buy him things to assure his affection. He already adores you. Indeed, he has been asking for you every day since our return."

A frown formed at her words. "I'm sorry. I've been meaning every day to stop in at least for a few minutes, but it seems I've been tied to the office until late each night."

She looked down. "Yes, I understand." She'd grown up with such a father.

Suddenly, she didn't want to confront Nicholas. She wanted him to confide in her. She shouldn't have to be questioning him. He should be open and honest with her. There should be nothing hidden between them if they were to have a future together. She didn't realize the pleading look in her eyes as she looked at him silently, clasping her hands in front of her.

He took a step toward her. "What is it?"

She shook her head.

"You must have come by for a reason."

She gave a short laugh. "Do I need a reason?"

He touched her arm. "Of course you don't. But you seem, I don't know. Something's happened." He scanned her face. "Is it Austen?"

At the shake of her head, he continued. "Something with the dinner? It's still set for eight o'clock?"

The gala dinner. She'd forgotten all about it. What was she going to do about that?

His sharp tone penetrated her confused thoughts. "What's happened? Has there been a hitch?"

"No." She swallowed. Before he had to ask anything else, she said, "How is your business these days? You said you had much to do since your return."

"Yes." He gave a shrug and embarrassed laugh at that. "I've never taken a holiday before and didn't realize how much I'd find piled up at my return. Not that I wouldn't do it again. Not to worry, though, I'll have everything up to date in a few days and will have more time to spare."

She looked at him sadly. Would this be her future? Living with a man whose priorities were just like her father's? Without thinking, she found herself saying, "Geoffrey came to see me today." This was his chance to tell her.

He raised an eyebrow. "Is that unusual?"

She shrugged and approached his massive, oblong

desk, its ebony surface like a mirror. So much like her father's. "It is when he comes to my humble office."

"Maybe he missed you while you were away."

Was that cynicism in his tone? She glanced back at him. He hadn't moved and he reminded her of a silent statue, his features as if carved in stone. "Perhaps." She turned to study his desk once again. Lots of papers covered it but they were all neatly arranged. Were some of them concerning Shepard and Company? Now, Shepard & Tennent. "You seem to be very busy."

"Yes."

"Do you have much to do with my father's firm?"

He said nothing until she was finally forced to turn to him once again. She was struck by the intent way he was looking at her. "Why do you ask?"

She shrugged imperceptibly. "No reason, merely curious."

He walked around his desk to stand by his chair. "Shepard and Company and Tennent & Company are competitors, and in that sense, would have little direct involvement with each other."

"Yes, I see," she murmured, looking down at his papers again, feeling a disappointment so profound it almost wounded her.

She took a deep breath and looked up with a bright smile. "Well, I must be going. I have much to do and… and…you're busy." Her voice broke and she turned away quickly and hurried to the door.

Nick stared at Alice. What had happened? Before she had a chance to turn the door knob, he realized she was going to walk out without telling him.

"Wait!"

The word came out a brusque command. It succeeded in stilling her hand. In a few strides he was at her side before she had a chance to tighten her hand on the knob once again.

"What is it?" he asked, hardly daring to touch her sleeve.

She lifted stricken eyes to him. "Why didn't you tell me?"

What was she referring to? Was it because he had scarcely been to see her or Austen since their return? He wanted to make it up to her.

He searched his brain, but the only thing that came to him was his maneuver with her father's firm. She couldn't know about that. Could she? As the seconds ticked by, a sick suspicion spread in his gut. How had it been discovered?

"Tell you what?" he asked steadily.

She turned away from him as if she'd received a physical blow from him. He dropped his hand. "You know," she whispered.

The feeling in the pit of his stomach grew. "Does this have to do with your brother's business?"

The look in her eyes as she raised them to his gave him the answer he needed.

He shoved a hand through his hair, wondering how to explain. "Who told you?"

She gave a strangled laugh, turning away from him again. "*Who told me? Does it matter? Isn't it more important that I didn't hear it from you? When exactly were you planning to tell me?*"

He stared at her, finding it hard to believe—and yet,

all too easy to believe—that she was doubting him. "Sometime after we were married."

She stared at him open-mouthed then began shaking her head. "You were going to calmly put my brother out of business and tell me about it after we were married? You are a worse scoundrel than Geoffrey claims."

He gave a short, bitter laugh. "I should think he would know what it takes."

Her voice rose. "You go behind his back and plan to take over his firm and you have the temerity to call *him* a scoundrel?"

He stared at her, hardly believing she was so quick to judge him against her brother.

"You'll swallow him up with no thought to how it might affect me?" she whispered, eyeing him as if he were a monster.

He kept his voice deceptively soft. "Careful you don't draw the wrong conclusions."

"What other conclusion can I draw if I'm not given any?"

"You could trust me."

"A man who was treated badly by my father? A man who might be courting his daughter in order to gain full control of his business?"

Each word was like a slap in the face. He felt the accusation hit deep.

"Is that why you looked me up, Nicholas? Is that why you bothered to befriend Austen?" Her voice began to quaver. "You could have done anything to me, but why—why—" she wiped angrily at her eyes, her voice breaking "—why did you have to gain Austen's trust? It wasn't worthy of you!"

She turned back to the door. He planted his palm against it, not believing she would really leave him like this.

"Do you really think I would hurt you and your little boy?"

Her tear-filled eyes looked up into his, but she said nothing. "It's too late to cancel the gala, but I must tell you I shan't be present. I can't bring myself to honor someone who would stoop to dishonor my family in such an underhanded way."

He dropped his hand from the door, staring at her. Could she really doubt him to this degree? If that was the case, there was nothing left for him to say.

"Why, Nick, why?"

He stepped away from her. "I'm a ruthless businessman, remember?"

He watched her leave the office.

As the echo of the door faded, Nick continued staring at it, not believing the woman he'd waited for so many years had truly thought so little of him.

The image of her first husband, a saintly man, came to taunt him. She must have been measuring Nick against the curate all along, and finally found he couldn't measure up.

He felt his eyes begin to fill, and he stepped back, aghast to find himself crying—over a woman. He never cried, not since he'd been a lad of about four and seen how little time his poor mother had for sympathy for such things as scraped knees and cut fingers.

He swiped at his eyes angrily.

When he reached his desk, he stood staring down

at the papers lying there before sitting down. The evidence before him was irrefutable. Shepard and Company owned and had owned for years—behind the front of other firms—a number of housing blocks in the slums, of the kind Alice had pointed out to him, of inferior quality.

Complaints had been pouring into the city officials of sinking floors, flooding, leaking roofs—without much response from the government, since the tenants were people of little political or economic clout. But a few conscientious journalists had taken up the cause of the tenants and written about some of the worst complaints.

Nick sighed and rubbed the back of his neck. He hadn't yet decided how to break it to Alice. She'd caught him unprepared. He'd wanted to gather all the evidence before presenting it to her—and show her how he planned to rectify the faults of her family.

He sat down and slumped over his desk, all energy leaving him.

Since the day he'd seen Alice again, he'd allowed himself to believe their love might have survived over a decade, that there was a woman worthy of his trust, a woman like no other, who was willing to forsake all for their love.

She'd declared she'd been willing to forsake her family for him fifteen years ago.

But, now that her trust had been put to a test, she'd proven incapable of believing in his honor and integrity. Whatever she'd felt for him had not been strong enough to withstand her brother's poison.

He hadn't realized until this moment how much he'd wanted her trust. Did he want anything less of his future wife?

Alice spent the rest of the afternoon frantically seeking Macey. Now that she'd renounced her attendance at the dinner, she needed to inform someone. After all, she was the hostess.

When she finally found her at her small flat, Macey stared at her. "You're what?"

"I can't be at the dinner tonight. You'll have to do the honors for me."

"Tell me what this is about."

"I'd rather not." She turned away from her, unwilling to talk about Nicholas to anyone else yet, when she, herself, was still too hurt and confused.

Her friend sat down. "I'm sorry, my dear, but I will do nothing for you unless you tell me the real reason you can't be there tonight."

Alice finally sat down next to her with a long sigh. "I can't talk about it. Suffice it to say, I just found out something disquieting about Nicholas. It involves Father's firm."

Macey remained serious. "Who told you?"

"Geoffrey came to see me today."

"I see." Her friend was quiet a long time. Then she turned to her. "I don't know what it might be about. I know nothing of your family's firm. All I know is are you quite certain what he has told you about Nicholas Tennent is the truth?"

Alice searched her friend's eyes. "I don't know. But

he wouldn't lie about something so serious. I would soon know the truth. Besides, you didn't see him. He sounded desperate. I've never seen him in such a state."

"Have you talked to Mr. Tennent about it?"

Alice looked away. "I went to his office. I've just come from there. I had to know from him if there was any truth to it."

"Well?"

"He as good as admitted it! What am I to do?" She squeezed her eyes shut. "All he said was to trust him!"

"Maybe you ought to, my dear."

She turned to look at Macey. "But how can he ask that of me? I have Austen to think of, too. What if Nick is no different than Father was? How can I think about joining my life to his—to someone who stands for everything that I find so unworthy?"

Her friend covered her hands. "Only you can answer that. But be careful you don't misjudge Mr. Tennent. He seemed an honorable man to me."

"I don't know…" Alice rose. "I must think…"

Macey joined her. "Yes, think and pray. I'll be at the gala. I'll do anything you need me to do, but think long and hard before you leave him there. It would be a terrible humiliation for someone like him."

Nick sat at the head table, ignoring the buzz of voices around him and the clink of silverware on china. Miss Endicott sat beside him, in the place that had been reserved for Alice.

He eased his standing collar away from his neck with his finger, wondering how much longer before this cursed event would be finished. The meal was finally over and now the meeting would convene.

Miss Endicott patted his hand. "You're doing fine. Now, you'll just have to sit back and listen to a number of items being presented before we'll discuss the donation. Then after a few more speeches of appreciation and acknowledgement, I will present you the plaque and only then may you abscond." She said the last with a smile.

"All this for the privilege of having a donation accepted?"

She smiled sadly. "We Brits like to stand on ceremony. You must indulge us in this. You are the prodigal returned home—well, if not the prodigal, then the boy who made good."

"Where is Alice?"

His abrupt question gave her pause. "I don't know. She had a lot to think about."

He looked away, saying in an undertone, "Only one thing as far as I'm concerned."

"What is that?" she asked softly.

He turned back to her. "Would I do anything to hurt her?"

"Maybe you are asking a lot of someone who was abandoned by you once before."

He frowned at her. "I never willingly abandoned her."

"She might know that with her head, but her heart might still feel the pain of abandonment."

The words caused him much thought.

After that they spoke no more.

The speeches began, business colleagues speaking

about the needs of the growing city, others lauding him for his contribution to the business world. Finally, he was presented with his plaque.

It should have filled him with joy, but it left him cold. The one who would have made the evening truly meaningful for him was absent.

He would have long since left, but Miss Endicott had proven a true ally and he wouldn't dishonor her that way.

Afterward, people crowded around him, all vying for his attention. He answered as many questions as he could, smiled at people's expressions of gratitude until he felt his lips would crack.

"Excuse me, Mr. Tennent, would you answer a few questions for *The Daily News?*"

He braced himself for the journalist's questions. "Yes, of course."

"This is a sizeable endowment to one single charity. What made you select the Housing Society?"

"I was acquainted with Mrs. Lennox years ago and felt confident that any charity run by her would be a worthy one."

He continued asking Nick questions about his time in America and his decision to return to London. Nick answered each one in as general terms as possible, not disposed to have all his personal reasons in print for all to read.

"My invitation stated that Mrs. Lennox, as head of the Housing Society, would present the plaque to you herself. If she was the main reason you decided on this charity for your donation, may I enquire why she was not present this evening?"

The question only made him more aware than ever what others must be asking themselves about Alice's pointed absence.

"I don't know. You shall have to ask her. If you'll excuse me, I need to speak to some others." He turned away and made his way out of the room, ignoring any more requests for his attention.

Chapter Fifteen

Alice sat in her drawing room staring at the papers laid out on the table before her.

It was the day after the dinner. She'd heard nothing except for a brief note from Macey telling her everything had gone off without a hitch. She gave no other details.

Alice had lain awake most of the night by turns staring dry-eyed at the dark ceiling and tossing this way and that, wondering, worrying, fretting.

She hadn't had the energy or heart to go to the office this morning. It was almost too much to keep up a front before Austen at breakfast. It was with relief that she'd bid him goodbye as he went off to the park with Nanny Grove.

Then as she'd sat in the drawing room, her hands idle, her maid had brought in a large, thick envelope in the morning's post.

Not recognizing the writing on it, but seeing the name of Nick's firm on the return address, she quickly opened it.

Instead of any kind of letter, a thick sheaf of official looking documents fell out on her lap. Only a small white square of notepaper clipped to the top contained Nicholas's writing. She grabbed it up eagerly.

It only held one sentence:

I was saving these for your wedding gift. Seeing that is no longer a possibility, I am giving them to you now.

No closing, only the scrawl of his name: *Nicholas.*

Feeling a sharp jab of disappointment that there were no explanations, no apologies, nothing, she finally turned to examine the papers.

At first they made no sense. But her heart began to pound when she saw the fancy scroll of the name of Shepard and Steward, Ltd. across several.

Many of the pages seemed to be shares made out to her. She continued reading, growing more confused as she saw articles and documents about the London Building Society, among other building firms. Newspaper clippings she'd read herself detailed the problems and complaints with their substandard building practices. Further on she found numerous documents with the names of other companies. Little by little she began to decipher the information.

It listed all the companies that had invested in these building societies and described the amounts of their investments. It was like following a maze, so many companies seemed to be owned by others, making it difficult to track which company had invested in which building society.

Her head ached from reading so much fine print. But she didn't stop until she had succeeded in following the path of one, whose investment in the building societies was indubitably clear. Shepard and Steward, Limited.

The papers fell to her lap, as she stared before her.

What had her father been responsible for?

"Well, you see, I need to go away for a bit." Nicholas sat on the park bench facing the Round Pond at Kensington Gardens, his head bent toward Austen.

Alice held her breath, trying to catch his next words.

Austen swung his legs back and forth on the bench. "Where do you have to go?"

"Back to America. It's where I came from."

"Maybe I can come, too?"

Nicholas draped his arm across the back of the bench. "Maybe some day. But now you have your lessons, and your mother, and Moppet."

Before Austen could reply, Alice stepped forward. They both turned around.

Austen smiled brightly at her. "Hello, Mama."

"Hello, Austen. I'm glad you are still here." She'd taken a chance that perhaps she'd find Nicholas with him. She turned stricken eyes to him, afraid he'd get up and leave.

But he only watched her, his expression unreadable. Taking a deep breath, she walked around the iron bench to face them.

Austen's face turned serious. "Mama, Mr. Tennent has told me he has to go away. Why can't we come with him like he did with us to France?"

She moistened her lips, clutching her handbag in front of her. "I don't know. Perhaps he'll be very busy with his work."

Austen immediately turned to Nicholas. "Will you be very busy?"

She closed her eyes, too afraid of hearing his reply.

"I'll never be too busy for you."

She bit her lip, her eyes filling with tears at the reply. Trying to compose herself once again, she approached Austen and knelt down in front of him. "Austen, darling, Mama needs to talk to Mr. Tennent. I want you to go home with Nanny Grove now."

"But Mama, Mr. Tennent just came."

"I understand. But this is a serious talk."

"Are you going to say goodbye to him?"

She swallowed, finding it hard to speak. "I don't know... Perhaps—" she chanced a glance at Nicholas before looking away as quickly "—he can stop by and see you a bit later."

Nicholas's hand squeezed Austen's shoulder. "I'll do so, I promise."

Her son nodded his head to him then slid off the bench.

She stood and motioned for Miss Grove who sat knitting on another bench a bit farther away. "I'll see you in a little while, Austen." She leaned down and kissed his cheek.

He turned to Nicholas. "You'll come soon?"

Nicholas ruffled his hair and smiled. "Yes, very soon."

The two watched Austen walk away with his nanny.

Alice braced herself when Nicholas turned back to her. "I received the documents you sent me."

When he made no reply, she cleared her throat and looked down. "I came to ask for your forgiveness." She took another deep breath. "You see, before yesterday, I had no idea I owned a share of my father's company."

"Your brother didn't inform you?"

At his sharp tone she looked up and shook her head. "My brother and father never saw fit to involve me in the business." She gave a bitter laugh. "Especially once my father disinherited me." Moistening her lips she continued. "I was hit with a few too many surprises yesterday afternoon."

"I'm sorry I had to be among them." Nicholas shifted over on the bench. "Why don't you sit down?"

She complied, her knees feeling shaky.

He cleared his throat. "I began investigating your family's firm when I first returned. I admit I probably did it mostly out of curiosity. Your father was no longer around to give me the satisfaction of showing him I'd made good. The next best thing was to see how your father's firm had done over the years compared with my own." He paused. "I was also astounded to discover your father had disinherited you. I think this most of all prompted my investigation."

She watched his profile as he spoke. Her hand ached to reach out and touch his beloved face, to smooth his hair, but although he sat only a few inches from her, she felt he was miles away.

"What I found was that your brother had not only mismanaged your family's firm, but the types of investments were also unsound. The deeper I went, the more concerned I grew. Your brother is close to bankruptcy."

She shook her head. No wonder Geoffrey had been so frantic the day before.

He looked down at his loosely clasped hands. "I

didn't know how to tell you, perhaps that's why I kept silent. Your father's firm was responsible for some of the shoddy housing of the kind you were showing me that day.

"One of the companies responsible for investing in some of the building firms has another name, but your brother is the principal behind it, your father before him. They put up the money, hoping for a quick return on their investment."

She hadn't been wrong in her interpretation of the documents. "You should have told me."

His dark eyes gazed into hers and she wished with all her heart that she'd never distrusted him. "I didn't want to hurt you. I thought instead that I could put a stop to it by buying out your father's partner. When I discovered you also owned some shares, I saw my way clear to gaining control of the company, as well as shore it up before your brother ran it into the ground completely. It is, after all, your son's inheritance."

She shook her head sadly. "As Geoffrey pointed out to me."

"I was going to present you the shares I'd purchased on our wedding day—that is, if you'd ever agreed to marry me." His lips twisted. "I had no interest in running your company—as long as you discharged Geoffrey as president—and got rid of Victor as chief counsel. His advice has not aided your brother in making sound decisions."

"So, he, too, has been privy to Geoff's mismanagement?"

"Yes."

The silence stretched out before them. "I'm sorry,

Nicholas, for not trusting you." She looked down at her hands. "I was afraid to."

"Why?" he asked softly.

"I was afraid to feel what I had for you before."

"Was it because your father sent you away?"

She put a hand to her mouth, unable to stop the tears. "Because it hurt to love you. When Father dismissed you, I didn't understand that it would be for good. I kept expecting to see you, that somehow you'd come back—" Her words became incoherent.

"I'm sorry I left you the way I did that day, without a word. Believe me, it was not my intention."

She couldn't stop weeping. "I waited for word from you—some word, anything. My father said only that he had sent you away." She swallowed. "I cried and cried. I had nothing from you…and then I remembered that afternoon we went riding in Richmond Park—"

She dug frantically in her handbag. "After you left, I went back there and found these." She pulled out the two handkerchiefs they'd used that day. "You probably don't even remember, but you'd given me your handkerchief to dry my face. They were still there, lying on the rock where I'd spread them out to dry."

He took the two handkerchiefs from her. They were wrinkled but neatly folded in squares. His monogram was clearly visible in the corner of one. "Yes… I remember that day very well," he said softly, fingering his initials.

"It was all I had of you. Then Father sent me away in disgrace. It was so awful," she sobbed. "Being with those relatives was like being a prisoner. I never felt more alone in my life. I didn't understand being punished so cruelly just for loving you. Every day I expected you to come back, to contact me somehow. I dreamed of how you'd come back and rescue me…"

Somewhere in her incoherent speech, Nicholas had put his arm around her. He stroked her hair and murmured soothing words. "Don't fret yourself, Alice."

"I loved you so much… I would have gone anywhere with you—"

"Dear, sweet Alice, it wouldn't have been possible. I was penniless."

"I wouldn't have cared—"

She sniffled and Nicholas handed her her old handkerchief. She took it and blew her nose and wiped her eyes.

In a calmer voice, she continued. "For a long time I felt abandoned by everyone, even God. It wasn't until I met Julian a few years later that he helped me find solace. He showed me that the Lord loved me and hadn't abandoned me. Through His grace I was able to forgive Father—and you—for never coming back."

She sat up and looked at Nicholas. His dark eyes had softened. "I thought I was fully healed until I saw you again." She pressed her lips together, afraid she would begin to cry once more. "You showed me how fearful I still was. I was afraid of losing Austen, afraid of what you made me feel again…"

She clutched the handkerchief in her hand, ashamed of looking at him. "Can you ever forgive me for not trusting you?" she whispered.

He covered her hand with his own. "If you can forgive me for not trusting your feelings for me enough to confide in you."

"Oh, Nicholas, I was so afraid you would choose your business concerns over me."

He looked down, and for a moment she was worried she had offended him again. Then he said, "I love you and Austen more than any material thing I own. When my mother died, and I couldn't be here in time to say farewell, I realized how futile everything I'd striven for was without having someone to love."

She drew away enough to say, "I love you."

"I'll never replace Julian."

She placed her hand against his cheek wanting to erase the bleak look in his eyes. "You never will because you have no need to. You were in my heart first."

A smile began to warm the dark depths of his gaze. "Does this mean you will marry me?"

"If you'll have me, and Austen."

He nodded. "I love both of you and hope I can be the husband you want me to be, and the father Austen needs."

"Oh, Nicholas, will you promise to always tell me what is closest to your heart?"

He drew her toward him and she came willingly, at long last feeling she was in the right place. "I will trust you with my deepest dreams and fears," he whispered against her hair, "and never fear your love won't be strong enough to bear it."

She leaned toward him, her fingers tunneling his short hair, and he drew forward, his lips finding hers.

Long minutes later, she asked, "Are you still leaving for America?"

"Not immediately—unless you want to go. When I came back to England, I meant to come for good."

She smiled. "I'm glad you've come home, although it would be nice to see America."

"You shall."

Some time after, he murmured against her cheek, "I hope you'll get rid of Victor as your solicitor now."

"Of course."

"I'll take care of the matter if you wish."

She laughed against his chin. "That's all right. I've known him all my life. I'll do it."

"Only if I'm present," he growled, his lips nibbling her earlobe.

She smiled in gratitude and understanding. "Thank you. I hope I shall always have you around to face all unpleasantness."

"Your wish is my command," he chuckled.

"You are indeed a man most worthy."

Epilogue

September 1891

Nick breathed in the sharp tang of sea breeze and watched the view of the harbor coming in sight. Soon they'd be home again. Home.

He put his arm around Alice's shoulder and whispered in her ear, "Excited?"

She turned to him with a smile. "Yes. But it was worth crossing the Atlantic. I loved every minute of it."

"Especially the fact that we're not coming back empty-handed."

They both looked down at the bundle she held in her arms. "We're bringing home our own little Yankee," she said, her voice filled with tenderness.

"How's our little princess doing?" he asked softly, gazing down at their three-month-old daughter.

"Sleeping peacefully." Jean Anne Tennent, named for his mother, lay swathed in pink blankets, her shock of hair as dark as his. At that moment she stirred and stared up at them, her eyes as blue as Alice's. She yawned, her little bud of a mouth opening wide.

Nick felt a mixture of pride, deep humility and overwhelming love well up inside him, as it did each time he looked at the perfect little creature. He could still scarcely fathom this outcome of his and Alice's love.

When Alice had told him she was expecting, he'd gone past the hope of ever knowing the joys of fatherhood and was grateful just being able to share in Austen's upbringing. Alice had confided that after her first husband's death, she too had never thought to be blessed with more offspring.

Little Jeannie was truly a gift from God and they both thanked Him every day for her.

Austen's clear voice rang out, "Papa, look at all the ships!"

The name on the eight-year-old's lips still filled him with another sense of awe. Only a few weeks ago, the boy had taken him by surprise during their nightly bedtime story to ask permission to call him Papa.

"Of course you may…son," Nick had answered in a quiet tone, trying to mask the catch in his throat.

"Dear, be careful!" Alice's voice warned as she glanced at the boy, who leaned out far over the rail.

Nick reached for his daughter. "Here, let me take our Yankee while you grab our son before he falls overboard."

Alice chuckled as she relinquished her precious baby to her husband. She watched for a second as he cooed over his daughter. Alice never worried about Nick with either child anymore. He was an extraordinary father.

"Mama, look, we're getting closer!"

Alice moved to stand behind Austen and hold him by his suspenders. He'd grown a couple of inches in the last year.

His bond with Nick had only deepened over their year in America. When Alice had discovered her pregnancy, Nick had insisted they remain in San Francisco until the baby was old enough to travel. She hadn't let her confinement stop her activities, however. She'd seen and toured many benevolent societies and Nick had named her chairman of his entire charitable trust.

She took a deep breath, as they drew near the harbor. She was looking forward to their new life back in London and Richmond, and wherever the Lord would lead her with her beloved companion.

She turned to glance at her husband once again and caught his eyes. The warmth grew in them, as she returned the smile of the man whom the Lord had brought back to her life. The man who'd been her first—and last—love.

* * * * *

SPECIAL EXCERPT FROM

Love Inspired HISTORICAL

*Widowed father Boothe Powers needs a wife in order
to retain custody of his son. Emma Spencer was sure
to see the practicality of such an arrangement.
Emma's heart yearns for marriage and children.
But she has her own secret anguish...*

Read on for a sneak preview of
The Path to Her Heart *by Linda Ford*

"We don't even like each other. Why would you want to marry me?" At the untruthfulness of her words, heat left a spot on Emma's cheeks. She'd tried to tell herself otherwise, but she liked Boothe. Might even admit she'd grown slightly fond of him. Okay. Truth time. She might even be a little attracted to him. Had been since her first glimpse.

"I like you just fine."

"I'm a nurse. Have you forgotten?"

He hesitated. "Well, as nurses go, you seem to be a good one."

She snorted in a most unladylike fashion. "I'm thrilled to hear that."

"Surely we could work around that."

"I think not. Can you imagine how we'd disagree if I thought one of us or—" Her cheeks burned. She'd been about to say *one of our children*, but she couldn't say it aloud. "If I thought someone needed medical attention?"

"I'm desperate."

"Well, thanks. I guess." Just what she'd always dreamed of—the last pick of someone who was desperate.

"Wait. Listen to what I have to say." He pulled a battered envelope from his back pocket.

Nothing he said would change the fact they were as unsuited for each other as cat and mouse, yet she hesitated, wanting—hoping—for something to persuade her otherwise.

He waved her toward a pew and she cautiously took a seat. "This is a letter from a lawyer back in Lincoln informing me that my brother-in-law and his wife intend to adopt Jessie."

She gasped. "How can that be?"

He looked bleak. "I needed help after Alyse died and Vera offered. Only then she wanted to keep Jessie."

Emma pressed her palm to his shoulder. "Surely they don't have a chance?"

He slowly brought his gaze toward her. At the look of despair in his eyes, her throat pinched closed.

"I went to see the lawyer in town and he says the courts favor people who have money and their own home, but especially both a father and mother. My best chance is to get married."

She settled back, affronted to be no more than a means to an end, and yet, would her dreams and hopes never leave her alone? "And I was the only person you could think of?"

He shrugged. "You're fond of Jessie."

A burning mix of sympathy and annoyance shot through her. She withdrew her hand from his shoulder even though she ached to comfort him. She sat up straight, folded her hands together in her lap and forced the words from her mouth. "Yes, I'm fond of Jessie but I can't marry—not you or anyone."

Don't miss
The Parson's Christmas Gift & The Path to Her Heart
by Kerri Mountain and Linda Ford,
available December 2018.

www.LoveInspired.com

Looking for inspiration in tales
of hope, faith and heartfelt romance?

Check out **Love Inspired**® and
Love Inspired® **Suspense** books!

New books available every month!

LIGENRE2018R2

*With her family in danger of being separated,
could marriage to a newcomer in town
keep them together for the holidays?*

Read on for a sneak preview of
An Amish Wife for Christmas *by Patricia Davids,
available in November 2018 from Love Inspired!*

"I've got trouble, Clarabelle."

The cow didn't answer her. Bethany pitched a forkful of hay to the family's placid brown-and-white Guernsey. "The bishop has decided to send Ivan to Bird-in-Hand to live with Onkel Harvey. It's not right. It's not fair. I can't bear the idea of sending my little brother away. We belong together."

Clarabelle munched a mouthful of hay as she regarded Bethany with soulful deep brown eyes.

"Advice is what I need, Clarabelle. The bishop said Ivan could stay if I had a husband. Someone to discipline and guide the boy. Any idea where I can get a husband before Christmas?"

"I doubt your cow has the answers you seek, but if she does I have a few questions for her about my own problems," a man said.

Bethany spun around. A stranger stood in the open barn door. He wore a black Amish hat pulled low on his forehead and a dark blue woolen coat with the collar turned up against the cold.

The mirth sparkling in his eyes sent a flush of heat to her cheeks. How humiliating. To be caught talking to a cow about matrimonial prospects made her look ridiculous.

She struggled to hide her embarrassment. "It's rude to eavesdrop on a private conversation."

"I'm not sure talking to a cow qualifies as a private conversation, but I am sorry to intrude."

He didn't look sorry. He looked like he was struggling not to laugh at her.

"I'm Michael Shetler."

She considered not giving him her name. The less he knew to repeat the better.

"I am Bethany Martin," she admitted, hoping she wasn't making a mistake.

"Nice to meet you, Bethany. Once I've had a rest I'll step outside if you want to finish your private conversation." He winked. One corner of his mouth twitched, revealing a dimple in his cheek.

"I'm glad I could supply you with some amusement today."

"It's been a long time since I've had something to smile about."

Don't miss
An Amish Wife for Christmas *by Patricia Davids,*
available November 2018 wherever
Love Inspired® *books and ebooks are sold.*

www.LoveInspired.com

The final battle with the Red Rose Killer begins when he kidnaps Captain Justin Blackwood's teenage daughter.

Read on for a sneak preview of
Valiant Defender *by Shirlee McCoy,*
the exciting conclusion to the Military K-9 Unit miniseries,
available November 2018 from Love Inspired Suspense.

Canyon Air Force Base was silent. Houses shuttered, lights off. Streets quiet. Just the way it should be in the darkest hours of the morning. Captain Justin Blackwood didn't let the quiet make him complacent. Seven months ago, an enemy had infiltrated the base. Boyd Sullivan, aka the Red Rose Killer—a man who'd murdered five people in his hometown before he'd been caught—had escaped from prison and continued his crime spree, murdering several more people and wreaking havoc on the base.

"What are your thoughts, Captain?" Captain Gretchen Hill asked as he sped through the quiet community.

"I don't think we're going to find him at the house," he responded. "But when it comes to Boyd Sullivan, I believe in checking out every lead."

"The witness reported lights? She didn't actually see Boyd?"

"She didn't see him, but the family who lived in the house left for a new post two days ago. Lots of moving